William Russell

The privateer captain

William Russell

The privateer captain

ISBN/EAN: 9783337175573

Printed in Europe, USA, Canada, Australia, Japan

Cover: Foto ©Andreas Hilbeck / pixelio.de

More available books at **www.hansebooks.com**

THE PRIVATEER CAPTAIN.

CHAPTER I.

MORNING SHADOWS.

I AM about to transcribe an episode in my youthful experience, which, though comparatively brief, if measured by time only, has so impressed and shaped my life—now past its sixth decade—that it stands out in the light of memory as a towering mind-mark, to which all subsequent events appear subordinate, and to chiefly owe their form and colour, their shadows and their sunshine.

In that episode, Kirke Webbe, captain of the *Scout* privateer, was a prominent actor, and his character and history, as developed by the scenes in which I happened to be associated with him, possess, I think, an interest and value —especially now, when the "species" to which he belonged may be said to be extinct—apart from his influence upon my own individual fortunes. If, however, the ordinary sketches of his class which one meets with are to be deemed authentic portraitures, Captain Webbe, who was neither a vulgar ruffian nor a melodramatic hero, cannot be presented to the reader as an average specimen of the privateer. He boasted of having been a scholar of Christ's Hospital; was certainly well read in English literature; and his seamanship he acquired by six years' service in the royal navy as midshipman. Further than this, those of his deeds to which I am about in these pages to bear witness must speak for him; though, if proof of their verity be required, I can only refer to the internal evidence supplied

B

by the narrative itself: if that suffice not, I have no other to offer, as I do not choose to publish my own real name.

All that I positively knew of myself, of my antecedents and belongings up to the second week in February, 1814, may be shortly set forth. My name, we will say, was William Linwood. I was unquestionably a strapping fellow of my age—then a trifle over twenty years; and not absolutely frightful in features, or it could scarcely be an article of faith with me that Isle of Wight lasses, especially in and near Ryde, were, and doubtless still are, unless the presence of all-shadowing royalty has frozen the genial current of their souls, some of the sweetest-tempered damsels in creation. For the last ten or eleven of those twenty years, I had been domiciled at Oak Villa, near Ryde, on the road to Newport, with my grandmother, Mrs. Margaret Linwood, one of the oddest, worthiest, and most absolute of womankind. My earlier years had also been chiefly passed with Mrs. Linwood, though not in the Isle of Wight, whither she removed some twelve months previously to the departure of my father and mother for the United States of America, in 1804, a destination they never reached; the vessel in which they sailed having been captured in the Channel by a French letter of marque, and carried into the port of Havre de Grace, in or near which commercial capital of maritime Normandy my parents had since been detained as prisoners of war, on parole.

This was pretty nearly all of our family history that my inexorable grandame had decided, in her peremptory have-done-talking-of-it sort of way, should be confided to me till I attained my legal majority; or the advent of peace permitted my parents to continue their voyage to America, and me to join them there—a return to England not being, it would seem, contemplated as a possible eventuality.

Meagre as was this information upon matters of such paramount interest for a son, I should have been happier, less irritable, captious, when the subject was incidentally alluded to, had not certain fragmentary images or impressions looming through the mists of memory, suggested an affrighting solution; the more affrighting because vague, dark, undefined—of the mystery before which the kindest hands in the world had drawn, and persisted in keeping drawn, an impervious veil.

I remembered that, in the far-off time, I had been the petted favourite of a tall, portly gentleman, living in a fine house; that I had frequently ridden with him in a glittering carriage, drawn by prancing horses, and usually accompanied by my mother, whose pale, pensive face, and soft, low, tearful voice, seemed ever as vividly present to me as on the night I was awakened to receive her farewell blessing previous to her departure with my father for America. The tall, portly gentleman was, I knew, my mother's father, and for a time we were his only companions; but after a while, another lady and another child dwelt in the fine house, and rode in the glittering carriage with us; and I was finally carried off by Dame Linwood to her comparatively humble abode in South Wales, and never, that I could remember, had I seen the tall, portly gentleman again.

My mother came frequently to Llanberris, sometimes, not often, accompanied by her husband, whose image dwelt faintly in my memory. On one occasion, and the last time I saw him, he came alone. Evening was falling when he arrived, and I, then about six years old, was hurried to bed, but not so hastily as to prevent me noticing that he was strangely flurried, and that a few whispered words communicated his agitation to my grand-mamma. His face, too, was deathly pale, and, as I felt when he kissed me, cold as stone, like his hands.

Nancy Dow, my grandmother's confidential servant, looked as scared as they; and as she undressed, put me to bed, and kept guard over me, poured forth a torrent of talk, to drown, if possible, the sounds of weeping and lamentation, fitfully surging up from below.

She succeeded to a certain extent for a while; but ere yet—spite of her repeated entreaties that I would, like the good boy that I was, go to sleep—the slightest feeling of drowsiness had come over me, a loud, fierce knocking at the front door startled her into silence, as it did my relatives below, for the house was hush as death when the knocking ceased for a few moments, to be again and again renewed with increasing violence. Rude voices, too, made themselves heard from without, imperiously demanding admittance; and presently there was a crash of glass, as if the window had been broken through, followed by an explosion of discordant cries and exclamations. Nancy Dow flew down stairs, and I, not daring to get up, lay sobbing with terror, till the gradual subsidence of the incomprehensible tumult permitted slumber to weigh down my aching eyelids, and I sank into the dreamless sleep of childhood.

I was early awakened by poor Nancy, who had evidently not taken her clothes off, and whose very decided features were swollen by weeping into exaggerated unloveliness. She told me that my father and grandmamma were gone to London, and would not, perhaps, return for some little time; and I was emphatically cautioned not to speak of what had occurred the previous evening to the outdoor servants and helpers, when they came to their work—Mrs. Linwood managed, and successfully, a very large dairyfarm of her own—nor express surprise at my relative's absence.

The memories of children, however precocious, and mine was remarkably so, rarely take note of periods of time; and I could not say how long—reckoned by days and weeks—Mrs. Linwood, as I call her from habit—she having always greatly disliked to be " grandmothered "—remained absent; but measured by my pining inquietude, a long, long interval of dreary time elapsed before she returned. And then how changed, even to my childish appreciation! It seemed that a sudden, untimely frost had frozen over the genial current of her nature. True, it still flowed with as kindly and generous a warmth as ever beneath the cold, stern surface, but she had, as it were, placed a barrier of ice between herself and a world in which she had no longer faith or hope.

What could have been the nature of the calamity that had so suddenly darkened good Mrs. Linwood's clear noon of life?—for though a grandmother, she was considerably on the sunny side of fifty—was the question which, as the years grew on, and threw the light of their experience back on the scene enacted at Llanberris Farm on the evening of my father's last visit, incessantly pursued and harassed me.

I could not doubt that he had upon that occasion been subjected to legal arrest—for debt, mayhap! Strive as I might, it was impossible to hold to that precious suggestion. Many circumstances concurred to convince me that pecuniary difficulties had not been felt in our family. My father, who had never heen in business, was neither a gambler nor a spendthrift. Mr. Waller, the portly gentleman of my childhood, was very wealthy: and Mrs. Linwood herself had, I knew, for many years invested upon an average £800 annually: she would have grudged nothing to her only son. No; they were not the agents of a grasping creditor, that had broken into our peaceful Welsh home in unscrupulous pursuit of their quarry!

He must, then, have been seized by officers of criminal justice. Yet had Mrs. Linwood, when vehemently pressed by me to give some slight explanation of the occurrences of that memorable evening, declared that my father had never been arraigned for any offence whatever; and she was incapable of falsehood. Never *arraigned* for any offence! Those were her guarded words. The offence had perhaps been compromised—hushed up. Not a very serious one, then, or such a course would have heen impossible.

No serious offence! A rotten cable that to hold by. Dame Linwood's inexorable silence—the expatriation of both my parents—the careful avoidance of any allusion to Mr. Waller and his second wife, extinguished that hope as soon as it was formed.

An incident which occurred about six months previous to the hefore-mentioned second week in February, 1814, threw a ghastly light over the mystery.

It was my father's hirthday, and I was sitting with Mrs. Margaret Linwood in the miniature drawing-room of Oak Villa, of which the French windows opened upon our finely cultivated pleasure-garden, and heyond commanded a splendid view of the silvery Solent. It was a cloudless autumnal evening; and the faiut sea-hreeze, which barely sufficed to dilate the white sails of the numerous sailing-craft afloat upon the glancing waters, was subdued by the time it reached us, laden with the rich perfume of flowers, to a fragrant caressing sigh, in unison with the serene— and to us, ahsorbed by the painful thoughts suggested by that particular day of the year—solemn silence that reigned around. My venerahle relative, to whom those anniversaries were bitterly afflictive, seeming to tear open afresh the hidden wound that was slowly, hut surely eating her life away, was more than usually sad and thoughtful, and for the last half-hour or so, not a word had passed between us.

She was sitting with her back towards me, according to her wont, when unwilling that I should observe the emotions that swept over the tablet of her face, which was, however, clearly revealed to me in a tall mirror opposite; and swift tears, I saw, were trickling through her thin white fingers.

Gently I ventured to approach the subject ever, of late, uppermost in my thoughts.

"My grandfather, Waller, still resides, I presume, at the house in Cavendish Square?" said I, my gaze the while intently fixed upon the mirror. There was a slight start, and the partially concealing hand was half withdrawn from the face. The emotion was but momentary.

"Your grandfather, Waller, still resides at the house in Cavendish Square," was the quiet reply.

"With his second wife, Mrs. Waller, of course?"

"With Mrs. Waller, his second wife, of course. Captain Webbe met them, not long ago, in one of the parks."

"Strange, was it not, that, having a grown-up daughter of his own, Mr. Waller should have married again?"

"Not strange at all. He was not more than five or six and forty years of age; and Mrs. Hamblin was a widow, not far off, I should think, of thirty, though Time had dealt so gently with her, that she looked nothing like so old. A singularly beautiful woman," added Mrs. Linwood with a sigh, "and beautiful in mind as person. The marriage was in all respects an unexceptionable one."

"You once shewed me her portrait: the expression, it struck me, was a peculiar one—sweet, but very sad. That, however, might be only fancy."

"True—a boy's fancy."

"And the beautiful child, I so well remember, what —— Good Heaven, what have I said—done?"

Lightning seemed with my words to have smitten my venerable relative. A sharp cry of anguish escaped her, and her face, no longer masked by her hands, which tightly grasped her bosom, was convulsed with horror.

I leaped to my feet in terrible dismay; but before, in my confusion and affright, I could think of what should be done, or summon others to do it, strong-willed Mrs.

Linwood had, by a supreme effort, mastered her betraying outward self.

"Sit down!" she exclaimed with peremptory sternness. "It was a passing spasm—nothing more. I must consult Mr. Beale, for these attacks grow in frequency and violence of late. You may fetch me a glass of wine from the dining-room."

"You were speaking, William," said Mrs. Linwood, as she replaced the emptied glass upon the table, and with her face still carefully averted from me—"you were speaking, William, of—of Lucy Hamblin—Mrs. Waller's beautiful little girl. She died young—early in her fourth year."

"Ha!"

"Yes: the sweet child was—was drowned in the Thames, near Gravesend."

"Drowned! By accident?"

"There are various opinions; I have mine—a decided one, but, unsustained by legal evidence, worthless of course. And now, my dear boy, go and send Nancy to me: I do not feel quite well."

This, as I believed, partial unveiling of the terrible secret, rendered further suspense insupportable. My life was embittered, poisoned by it; and I passionately entreated to know the worst. Mrs. Linwood was deaf as iron, unyielding as adamant to my supplications; and I was still, at the beginning of 1814, moodily meditating the probable motives for her obduracy—chewing, as usual, the cud of dark and bitter fancies—when my listless glance was arrested by an advertisement in the *Hampshire Telegraph* newspaper, stating that Mr. Harrison of Portsmouth, the printer of that journal, had a complete file of the London *Times* from 1798 to 1802, to dispose of. Might I not, it instantly flashed across my mind—might I not find in the columns of that paper all that I longed to discover? I knew in what year, and at about what period in that year, my father's arrest had taken place. How was it that so obvious an expedient for ending the doubts and fears by which I was beset had not occurred to me before? At all events, it should not be neglected now; and an hour had not passed when I took boat at the old Ryde Pier for Portsmouth.

The bargain with Mr. Harrison was readily struck; and

the coarsely bound broadsheets having been conveyed to the Blue Posts Inn, I was speedily glancing through the leaves with feverish impatience. The file was, I found, far from perfect; many numbers were missing of the most promising dates; and I was half inclined—partly from despair, partly from *dread* of finding what I sought—to give up the search, when my eye lit upon the following paragraph:

"THE GRAVESEND TRAGEDY.—Mr. William Linwood, who has been so long in custody, charged with the murder, by drowning, of the child Lucy Hamblin, was yesterday set at liberty, with the consent of the law-officers of the crown, who have most reluctantly arrived at the conclusion, that in the absence of Mademoiselle Féron, who can nowhere be found or heard of, there is no legal evidence to warrant his detention. No moral doubt appears to be entertained by those who have investigated the circumstances, of Linwood's guilt; yet it is right to add, that the accused himself asserts his perfect innocence with an earnestness which, combined with his previous excellent character, might weigh considerably in his favour, but for the facts disclosed by Louise Féron during the tumult and agitation consequent upon the discovery of the dreadful crime—facts not the less morally conclusive that they were not declared, and have not since been confirmed upon oath. Mrs. Waller, the bereaved mother, is, we are rejoiced to hear, recovering from the effects of the attack of brain fever, which it was at one time feared would have resulted in confirmed insanity."

A vertigo seized me as I read; the dreadful lines swam, flashed as if written with fire, before my shrinking, blinded eyes. I had barely strength to close the terrible volume, stagger towards and ring the bell, and then dizzy, sick, —sick, as if unto death, I fell senseless on the floor.

Upon recovering consciousness, I found myself lying upon a couch near an open window, and sedulously ministered to by the landlady of the Blue Posts and one of her sympathising handmaidens. The vertigo and sickness had passed away, and, thanking them for their kindness, I asked to be left to myself—a request which, after I had given proof of the repossession of my faculties by swallowing the greatest part of a glass of spirits and water, was complied with.

Well, I had thoroughly succeeded in plucking out the heart of the mystery! I knew now, as well as Dame Linwood herself, that my father was adjudged by public opinion to be a cruel murderer! Accursed knowledge! compared with which the carking anxiety I had previously suffered was happiness—felicity! By public opinion so condemned! True; but assuredly, also—and the blessed thought flashed like sunlight upon my troubled soul—assuredly justly judging, clear-headed Mrs. Linwood did not believe him guilty! O no!—a thousand times no! And my own mother, the pure light of whose mild eyes sank so deep into my child's heart, that it still glowed there in undimmed, perennial brightness—she—I eagerly recalling to mind passages of her letters that I had been permitted to read—she, I knew, felt for her husband not love, compassion only, but respect, esteem, reverence.

Of what weight was rashly formed public opinion opposed to such testimonies? Not the slightest—of not a feather's weight; and, passing with boyish impetuosity from despair to exultation, I laughed, shouted, wept with the inexpressible joy springing from a devout, unshakable conviction of my persecuted, maligned father's innocence!

Innocence which it would be my duty, my high privilege to vindicate in the face of day before a misjudging world. I would hunt up the woman Féron—trace the atrocious calumny to its vile source! Success I could not doubt of, for I had faith in God and my own courage. But enough of these ebullitions of an undisciplined, puerile enthusiasm —an enthusiasm with which I was shocked to find Dame Linwood could not be persuaded to in the slightest degree participate. The discovery I had made through the newspaper pained, annoyed her, and she would add nothing to the information which I had, according to her, surreptitiously obtained. She knew nothing, could guess nothing of the whereabout of the Frenchwoman Louise Féron; and any stir in the unhappy business by a rash, inexperienced boy could, she was quite satisfied, lead to no useful result. Her son's vindication would, she nothing doubted, be brought about in God's own good time; and for that time she, I, all of us must humbly wait.

The worthy dame's obstinate fatalism, as I deemed it, made me terribly wroth; but all the indignation and eloquence in the world would have been utterly thrown away upon her, but for an occurrence which startled her into a belief that the good time she prayed and waited for might be near at hand. That occurrence, launching me into a sea of perils, the shadows whereof, ever so faintly cast before, would, for all my vapouring self-conceit, have given me serious pause, fell out thus oddly: it is not often that Fate knocks at one's door with so seemingly ludicrous a summons.

CHAPTER II.

THE SCOUT.

RYDE, in the Isle of Wight, though not in those days the gay and flourishing place it has since become, was, thanks to its natural advantages, a favourite resort of health and pleasure seekers; and one of its chief attractions to the latter class of tourists, was undoubtedly its commanding view of the maritime life and bustle going on in the great naval arsenal of Portsmouth, and the famous roadstead of Spithead, to which the Wight forms the natural breakwater. Very exciting to the unaccustomed mind of Cockney or other inland folk must have been the frequent spectacle of captured vessels brought in with the British jack flying above the tricolor, and anchored or moored amidst the cheers and cannon-fire of the victor-crews. And albeit, to find cause of triumph in the humiliation of another, "enemy" though he be, may not bear to be closely scanned by the light of the Gospel morality; yet how often have I seen reverently-pious eyes, seriously-pale, lengthened faces, gleam and glow with pride at such sights! At a yet later date, I am afraid, I have witnessed the same phenomena. Yet should I be the last to cast stones at others, since few could have felt fiercer joy than I did at such spectacles — my excuse being, that my parents were prisoners to the "enemy;" which spectacles, greatly to my unreasoning regret, became less and less frequent as the maritime might of Great Britain wrestled down the giant war, as far as the ocean was concerned, and so effectually blockaded or swept the seaboard of a hostile continent, that at the commencement of 1814, months had elapsed since a captured tricolor had graced Spithead; whilst the stars and stripes, with which we had fallen out about a couple of years before, yielded but a scanty harvest.

The news, consequently, that the *Scout* privateer, Captain Webbe, had brought in a fine Yankee bark, created quite a sensation amongst us islanders; and although it was Sunday morning, the second Sunday in February, I, instead of waiting to escort my grandame to church, hurried off to Ryde Pier, where I found a small mob of excited idlers like myself.

The prize had gone into Portsmouth harbour, but the *Scout* was still anchored at Spithead—a remarkably fine brig of her class, and admirably adapted by her long, low, sharply bowed hull, and tall raking masts, for a service in which speed was the prime requisite. She carried twelve guns of moderate calibre upon a flush deck, and had generally a complement of ninety men, maintained at a cost so onerous as to leave of late years, it was understood, a very trifling margin of profit to Captain Webbe and his owners, fortunate beyond all other "privateers" —or pirates, writ large, as some slanderers aver that he had invariably been.

Presently a blue-peter was run up at the *Scout's* fore— a warning, it was supposed, to the boat's crew that had come on shore about an hour previously, to hasten their return to the brig, whose anchor, I noticed, had already been hove short. The warning or signal did not appear to be much heeded by the men, several of whom were smoking and sauntering about in the immediate vicinity of the pier; and when, some quarter of an hour afterwards, I took my way Rydeward, I came, on turning a corner in the principal street, upon a number of the *Scout* seamen, amongst whom was Captain Webbe himself, whom I knew well, from his having several times called at Oak Villa, where he was always civilly, though coldly, received by Mrs. Linwood, who had known him previous to her domiciliation in the Wight.

The sailors, having just emerged from the Crown Tavern, were standing apart from Captain Webbe, who was earnestly conversing with a showily dressed middle-aged woman, whose piercing black eyes, sallow skin, and vivacious gesticulation sufficiently declared her nationality without the aid of a few French words I indistinctly caught. She had a servant with her, also a Frenchwoman, and seemed about to take leave of the commander of the *Scout*, when his always restless glance met mine, and, scarcely to be believed, though my own eyes saw it, a crimson glow, much resembling a blush, mantled his bronzed cheeks—a swiftly passing weakness!

"Ha, Master William Linwood!" he exclaimed, extending his hand with frank cordiality, "I am glad to see you looking so well. I intend paying Oak Villa a visit to-morrow. Mrs. Linwood is, I hope, in the enjoyment of her usual fine health."

I answered slightly, the lady's involuntary start and mounting colour having caught and fixed my attention. Recovering herself, she turned away with an assumed air of carelessness, and began chatting with her servant.

I passed on, and had not gone far, when, upon crossing the end of another street, I saw my grandame and her escort Nancy Dow coming onwards on their way to church. Not being in a devotional mood that morning, I accelerated my pace.

I had proceeded some distance, when the notion occurred to me, that as Mrs. Linwood would necessarily pass Webbe and his companions, if they still remained where I had left them, I should like to witness her rencontre with the fierce-eyed Frenchwoman. I turned back to realise that whim, but had not taken fifty steps, when I halted, struck with the absurdity of my purpose. As I paused irresolutely, a clamorous burst of voices broke the stillness of the Sabbath morning, and hurrying at the top of my speed in the direction of the tumult, I could presently distinguish my grandame's voice, crying "Help!—murder! Help!—murder!" reinforced by frantic yells of "Fire! fire!" from Nancy Dow.

I should explain that Nancy, in consequence of having narrowly escaped being burned to death just before we left Wales, in any pressing emergency invariably shouted

"Fire! fire!" As Dr. Johnson remarked of some clerical alarmists in his day, Nancy would to a certainty have cried "Fire" at the Deluge.

I could have no doubt, therefore, as to whence the furious outcries proceeded; but swiftly as I ran, I arrived too late. Mrs. Linwood having fainted, was lying senseless, when I came up, in Captain Webbe's supporting arms, and the only other person present, except a few curious lookers-on, was Nancy Dow. The sailors and Frenchwomen had vanished.

"What is the meaning of this strange scene, Captain Webbe?" I exclaimed, at the same time relieving him of his burden.

"What is the meaning of this strange scene?" echoed Webbe. "Ah! there, Master Linwood, you puzzle me. You can only learn that of your venerable relative; but the astounding *fact* is, that this impulsive, and, it would appear, most eccentric lady, no sooner caught sight of a person I was quietly conversing with, than she flew at her with perfectly feline ferocity, shouting the while, ' Murder! help! police!' and so on. But this is no place for talk: let me assist you to carry Mrs. Linwood into the tavern; we will speak further by and by."

Mr. Beale, who lived but a few doors off, was sent for, restoratives were administered, and my grandmother revived sufficiently to murmur: "Seize her—seize her, William: do not let her escape; she is—is"——

Desperately as she struggled for utterance—so desperately, that her face grew black with the effort—not another syllable could she enunciate: hysterical faintings, violent spasms followed; and Mr. Beale forbade me to remain in the room, my presence appearing to greatly excite her.

Thus circumstanced, I forthwith hurried away to seek out Webbe. A few minutes sufficed to reach the pier, whence I had the mortification of seeing the *Scout* under sail, and steering for the Channel, by the eastern passage, at a spanking rate, under courses, top-sails, and top-gallant-sails. An exclamation of surprise and anger escaped me, which elicited an unexpected response.

"You are mistaken," said a voice close to my ear. "That rascal Webbe has *not* hooked it with the Frenchwoman. Pray, don't trouble yourself to apologise : those ingenuous blushes are more than sufficient excuse. The Frenchwoman," added Webbe, "*is* on board the *Scout*, and if this breeze holds, may hope to reach Guernsey before nightfall."

"Who is the Frenchwoman? What is her name!" I demanded.

"'Madame de Bonneville, Modiste,' is painted in brilliant letters over her *magasin* in St. Malo's, Brittany."

"Ay, but her maiden name! Do you know that?"

"Yes; Louise Féron."

"Louise Féron! And you, perfectly cognizant, as I am sure you are, of the cause of Mrs. Linwood's excitement at meeting that woman, have connived at, aided her escape!"

"You appear, young gentleman, to strangely misunderstand your family's position relatively to Madame de Bonneville, formerly Louise Féron, who, I apprehend, can have no motive for wishing to 'escape' from Mrs. Linwood's surveillance. Suppose, however, we exchange this bleak pier for a cozy room at the hotel yonder, and there quietly talk over the many interesting topics suggested by this morning's encounter. I should have sought you to-morrow for substantially the same purpose, had that passage-of-arms not taken place. You will the more readily believe that," coolly added Captain Webbe, between the puffs of his cigar—"you will the more readily believe that when I inform you, that I had the honour and pleasure of supping with your excellent mother and her husband no longer ago than Monday evening last."

"You supped with my mother and father on Monday evening last!"

"Yes; positively so : at Numéro 12, Rue Bombardée—so named when rebuilt after its demolition by *les perfides Anglais* a few years since—Havre de Grace, *Département* of the Seine Inférieure. They are both well—that is to say, as well as under existing circumstances could be reasonably expected."

"This must be a sorry jest!" I angrily exclaimed; "or if not, permit me to ask what conceivable motive could have induced *Scout* Webbe to trust himself in a French garrison town, from which escape is proverbially next to impossible?"

"To which sagacious query 'Scout Webbe' can only reply by remarking, after the ancients, that the silliest child might ask the wisest man more questions in five minutes than he could answer in five hundred years—did wise men live so long, which, from regard for you, I could wish were the case. Gad! Linwood, what an explosive fellow you are! You cannot surely suppose I used the words 'silliest child' or 'wisest man' in a sense personal to you?"

"I do not care a button in what sense, or no sense, you used them! All I have to say is, that there are some topics upon which I do not bear jesting, and I will thank you to avoid them."

"That is quite right and spirited," rejoined Webbe, "though prompted by a misapprehension, as I certainly do not jest in saying I passed last Monday evening with your parents in Havre de Grace. This I undertake to prove to you, directly I have taken the chill off my stomach with a glass of hot, stiff grog."

We entered the hotel, were shewn into a private room; and Webbe, secretly enjoying, I was sure, the suspense in which he kept me, quite as much as the hot brandy and water he leisurely sipped—a stimulant which he politely regretted my immature palate prevented me from participating at that hour of the day—wrapped himself up in a real or simulated meditative reverie for some ten minutes, during which I had an opportunity of closely observing one of, in several respects, the most remarkable men of his day.

My impression of the man, as depicted in my note-book on the day after my first important interview with him, the general truth of which many now living will recognise, may be thus roughly rendered:

"Kirke Webbe, now approaching, I should say, to fifty years of age, is of medium height—say, five feet seven or eight—not stout, but broad shouldered and of sinewy frame, upon which years have as yet placed no appreciable weight. Of fair complexion originally, but now bronzed by sun and service, he is nearly bald; and what hair he has is of a light colour; as are his whiskers, except that in certain lights they seem to have a curious *green* tinge. There is a slight cast in his keen, restless gray eyes; and the strong lines about his mouth confirm and strengthen the predominant character of his physiognomy, which is that of a man possessed of a calm, courageous, indomitable *will*, neither debased by ferocity, nor accessible to the influences of a chivalric or disinterested purpose. In dress and speech, Captain Webbe affects the landsman and gentleman, and to a casual observer, would scarcely present a more vivid idea of a seaman than might a Royal Yacht Club captain of his own yacht."

As I have before remarked, the privateer captain had received a superior education; and his French accent, M. Laborde, an *émigré* of whom I learned that language, asserted to be perfect—that of a Frenchman born.

I was still engaged in the not over-satisfactory perusal of Mr. Webbe's physiognomical indices, when he, taking a carefully preserved note from his pocket-book, tossed it towards me, saying: "You have not seen that before, I think?"

It was a highly complimentary note from Mr. Secretary Croker, addressed to the captain of "the audacious and fortunate *Scout*," and expressed a polite regret that so much enterprise and valour had not found a more fitting arena for their display in the king's regular service.

Captain Webbe was, I knew, extremely proud of Mr. Wilson Croker's semi-official recognition of his services; which, if a forgery, as some asserted—an uncharitable hypothesis, but quite within the range of possibility—was, I may remark in passing, exceedingly well executed, both in the imitation of the secretary's handwriting, with which I happened to be acquainted, and the official seal.

I returned the precious document with a few civil words of course; Captain Webbe replaced it in his pocket-book, and drew therefrom a sealed letter.

"You doubted," said he, "that I passed last Monday evening with your captive relatives in Havre de Grace. This letter will remove that doubt. Do you recognise," added Webbe—"do you recognise the hand which traced this direction to Mr. William Linwood?"

"My mother's!" I exclaimed, starting up, and rudely snatching the letter. It was the first I had ever received from her; and with uncontrollable emotion, relieved by the scalding tears which fell upon the paper, I, after many efforts, read it to the end.

" MY BELOVED CHILD ! for child you are still to me, as
when, ten sad weary years ago, you were awakened to
receive your mother's yearning, last embrace. I cannot
as yet, my darling boy, realise you to be the fine tall youth
—tall as your suffering, persecuted father—described by
Captain Webbe; but the blessed time will come when,
strained in these clasping arms, my heart shall recognise
in the manlike son, the developed, matured promise of
the child of memory—yes, and that it will come speedily,
I have a lively hope and faith. It is now almost openly
said even here, that the power of the French emperor,
but a brief time since, so colossal, seemingly unassailable,
was irremediably shattered by the Russian campaign—
an afflictive yet merciful visitation of a just God, which
gives assurance that the woful days of captivity are
numbered. But alas, my son ! the restoration of peace to
Europe will not bring peace to your father's bruised and
fainting spirit; nor to mine, which is inseparable from his.
My pen runs on, dear boy, as if addressing one
acquainted with the nature of the burden beneath which
we have for so many years hopelessly languished. The
sad story will be related to you by Captain Webbe; and
you will, at the same time, hear from him that circumstances have recently come to his knowledge, through which,
with your aid, he may be enabled to restore your father to
society—to cheerful, healthy life ! God grant that it prove
so ! And whatever may be said of Webbe, he cannot be
accused of idle boasting. What the circumstances are, or
how *your* assistance, dear child, should be so absolutely
necessary to the success of his design, he declined to say,
and I feared to press him for his grounds of hope. He
assured me again and again that you would incur no
serious peril ; but what may such a fearless man esteem to
be serious peril ? I must break off, for Captain Webbe waits
only for this letter to be gone ; and but a brief delay in
the perilous position wherein, for the purpose of conferring
freely with us, he has placed himself, might compromise
his safety. With fear and trembling, now that this letter
will in a few minutes have passed from me beyond recall,
I commend you, my beloved, my only son, to an enterprise in which your mother can only aid you with her
blessing and her prayers.

EMILY LINWOOD."

c

I thrust the letter into my pocket, and, turning from the window, reseated myself at the table.

"Take a sup of brandy and water," said Captain Webbe, pushing his glass towards me; "it will do you good. Never care to hide your tears. I should have a poor opinion of the spirit of a youth whom such a letter, as I suppose that to be from a long-absent mother, did not affect to tears. You are quite resolved, I see, to go with me in this matter?"

"To the death!"

"Yes, I know, but we'll contrive, if possible, to cast anchor on this side of that mooring-ground: it is always, however, well to look the worst that *can* happen boldly in the face; it tends to prevent flurry when the worst presents itself, and steadiness of nerve is indispensable."

"The letter intimates that you will inform me of all the circumstances which led to, or may throw light upon, my father's unfortunate position."

"I am quite ready to do so, but you must say grace first."

"Say grace first! What do you mean?"

"Frankly this: If you are the lad of metal I have represented you to be, we are about to initiate a difficult enterprise, in which I, moved by various considerations—an old regard for your oppressed, broken-spirited father—a love of counterplot, if only for the excitement and mischief of the thing—and, to be quite candid, the promise by your mother of a substantial reward in the event of success—have determined to engage."

"I understand all that; and you but dally with my impatience."

"Steady—steady, my fine lad! It is never wise to spread too much sail, fair as the wind, and fine as the weather may be. That enterprise, I was about to say, to which any son who had a heart in his bosom would not hesitate to devote himself body and soul, will necessarily bring you acquainted with certain business secrets of mine, which I must have a solemn guarantee from you shall never, under any circumstances, be made known to my prejudice."

"What guarantee can I give?"

"That of your sacred word and honour."

"It is given already."

" You declare solemnly that, happen what will, you will never make known to my injury or prejudice any fact concerning me, or my transactions, which may by any chance become known to you."

" I do solemnly make that declaration—bind myself by that promise."

" As you shall answer to God at the last great day! "

" As I shall answer to God at the last great day!"

" Enough! Now, then, to business."

CHAPTER III.

AN AUTOBIOGRAPHY.

AFTER saying " Grace," as described in the last chapter, Captain Webbe suggested, that as it was a tough yarn he had to spin, it might be as well to ascertain previously how my grandame was doing, and so arrange that we might be secure from interruption. I agreed, and hastened to the Crown Tavern. Mrs. Linwood was, I found, considerably better, but still lamentably weak and nervous. A fly was at the door, in which, accompanied by Mr. Beale and Nancy Dow, she was about to be conveyed to Oak Villa. I placed my mother's letter in her pocket, and, having seen her safely off, rejoined my new friend at the Royal Hotel.

Captain Webbe had made preparation, during my brief absence, for a cozy as well as lengthened sitting. The fire had been replenished, and heaped up on the hobs; and a bundle of cigars, decanters filled with ruby and amber coloured wine—no doubt, for my especial delectation, as there was besides a plentiful supply of brandy and hot water—had been placed upon the table.

"Take a cigar," said Mr. Kirke Webbe, " if only to oblige me; it may prevent that quite sufficiently open countenance of yours from yawning insufferably, and moreover, shade, in some degree, its inquisitive brightness, which might else dazzle and confuse my ideas."

"I daresay, captain, you think that very clever—l don't. Nevertheless, I shall take a cigar—two or three, possibly, if you are especially tedious. And now, if you please, go ahead."

"Nay, I must first go back, and a long way, too—as far back as 1792—in the autumn of which year two gentlemen and bachelors, of about the same age—twenty-five, namely—who had never met before, made each other's acquaintance whilst shooting over the Lord Petre's well-stocked covers in the vicinage of the market-town of Romford, Essex. One of those gentlemen-bachelors was William Linwood, only son and heir to Robert Linwood, hide and skin merchant—who had departed this life in Leadenhall Street, London, about three years previously—and Margaret his wife, who, since her husband's death, had withdrawn to Wales, where she found exercise for her constitutional activity in the superintendence of a large dairy-farm, the profits whereof were to aid her son in achieving the high social position to which, in her fond opinion, his personal and mental gifts so well entitled him. I speak too rapidly, perhaps?"

"Not at all. Allow me, however, to remark, that your speech would be pleasanter if it were less sardonic—jibing; but that is, I fear, a confirmed habit, and one which you take perverse pains to cultivate."

"If that, Master Linwood, is your serious, well-considered opinion," drawled Captain Webbe through his nose, simultaneously with the ejection in the same way of two jets of smoke from a fresh cigar, "I must lose no time in endeavouring to mend my manners in that particular. To resume, nevertheless, a narrative to which a deeper interest attaches just now than to wisest words of babes and sucklings. The other youthful sportsman, I was going on to say, was Mr. Kirke Webbe, at that time, and in a social, pecuniary sense, an indefinite gentleman, whose parents had both died during his legal infancy, and whilst he was undergoing the preliminary ordeal of midshipmanship, consisting chiefly of mast-headings, on board his majesty's ship *Gladiator*. A worthy, most worthy couple," continued Webbe, with sudden seriousness, "who, from prudential motives, did not marry till late in life, after a courtship of twenty years, lived in perfect harmony and died within four days of each other, leaving to their idolised boy something over a thousand pounds, scraped together by ceaseless industry and inflexible self-denial—one life, one hope, one tomb!

"A striking proof, Master Linwood," resumed Webbe more briskly, after emptying his tumbler at a gulp—"a striking proof, I say, Master Linwood, that virtues, unlike certain diseases, are not always hereditary; unless, indeed, they are governed by the same law as transmitted insanity and gout, which are said to skip usually over one genera-tion, in order to fasten more certainly on the next. according to which hypothesis, my son should be a model youth."

"You have a son?"

"Truly, I have. Harry is a few months, I think, older than you, and about the same height and figure. But my good young friend, we are steering a very zigzag course with the story. Let us endeavour to keep a little closer to the wind. Kirke Webbe, I was telling you, having scrambled through the preliminary six years of midship-manship, would, there could be no doubt, have creditably passed for lieutenant—he would be a very sorry lubber that did not—when a difficulty occurred between him and Old Blueblazes, captain of the *Gladiator* "——

"Old Blueblazes!"

"His ship sobriquet, of course, derived from the flaming hue of his proboscis. A grim old salt was he, fit for nothing upon earth but fighting and drinking, in both of which accomplishments it is but doing him justice to say he was A 1. The difficulty with me fell out thus. But first please to understand, young sir," continued Webbe, "that I go over these matters with you, forasmuch that as it is certain some good-natured friend will inform you, if he has not done so already, that I was kicked out of the royal navy, it is well with reference to the copartnership we have entered into that you should be acquainted with the true version of the affair. The difficulty, I repeat, between Blueblazes and me fell out thus: the *Gladiator* lay at anchor in Plymouth Sound. The old fellow was, I sup-posed, in his cabin sleeping off the fumes of his after-dinner grog; the lieutenant of the watch, a moony sort of chap, was perched upon one of the guns about midships, reading a book, with his face towards the bows, when the devil, who so delights in finding work for idle boys and men, suggested to me and another promising youth to have just one quiet turn at leap-frog upon the sacred quarter-deck."

"A turn at leap-frog upon the quarter-deck!"

"Just that, my ingenuous young friend. I am not surprised that, landsman though you are, your hair stands on end at the bare mention of such an enormity. Mine did whenever I afterwards thought of it, gradually falling off in consequence, till I was left, as you see, nearly as bald as a coot.

"Well, I had my leap, and was making a back for my friend, when the captain suddenly seized me by the neck, and had I not clung to him like grim death, would, I verily believe, have pitched me into Plymouth Sound. Finding, however, that if I went over the side, he must follow, he dropped me on my feet, at the same time favouring me with a couple of tremendous cuffs in the ear, that set my brains spinning like a top. But for that, I could never have had the inconceivable audacity to up fist, and deal a post-captain a blow on the chest, which knocked him clean off his pins, and laid him sprawling upon the quarter-deck."

"*Are* you serious in saying that you knocked down the captain?"

"As sure as you sit there, I did—impossible, preternatural as it sounds. No great thing, either, to do in itself; one of the captain's legs being crippled with the gout, and the other a wooden one.

"Imagine, if you can, Master Linwood, the wild consternation, the hurricane-uproar that arose as it passed through the ship that that devil's cub, Kirke Webbe, had floored Old Blueblazes! Officers and men seemed to think the world had come to an end; and death, or worse punishment, was unanimously awarded to the sacrilegious culprit.

"Blueblazes himself, who at bottom was as placable and generous as he was bibulous and brave, was the least excited and angered of them all; and, though I was no favourite of the rough old salt, it was his cockswain that, in the dead of night, released me from confinement, led me past the sentry—who had suddenly become deaf as well as blind, the cramp in my legs causing me to stumble heavily when within a yard of him—lowered me from a port-hole into a shore-punt alongside, and cast off the painter with a curse—his own, and a purse—the captain's—containing ten guineas, which he flung after me.

"You now know, Mr. Linwood," resumed Captain Webbe, after another gulp of the fiery liquid, which had no more visible·effect upon him than water upon a duck's back—"you now know how it happened that the king's service and I parted company. I was then close upon twenty-one years of age: the day after attaining my legal majority, I obtained possession of the before-mentioned thousand pounds odd; and the next four years were passed in acquiring a knowledge of the ways of mankind, as displayed in London; an interesting study, which the limitation, rigidly adhered to, of my expenditure to two hundred pounds a year, greatly hampered, as you may suppose.

"Nevertheless, I may say without vanity that I had made progress by the autumn of 1792. Moreover, my thousand pounds odd having by that time diminished to two hundred, I bethought me that it would be prudent to delay no longer an endeavour to turn that knowledge to practical account; and it was more for the sake of being able to ask myself quietly a few important questions, than any love of sport, that I accepted leave to beat up the Lord Petre's Essex covers. There fate willed it that William Linwood and I should meet for the first time; be mutually pleased with each other, and swear eternal friendship; or rather, we should have done so, but for an untoward accident which befell us both."

"What accident?"

"Falling in love with the same damsel—the young and charming Emily Waller, sole daughter and heiress presumptive of Anthony Waller, Esq., of Cavendish Square, London, and then upon a visit at Hare Park, not far out of Romford.—Touch the bell, if you please; the fire is getting low."

"Pray go on: you tantalise one terribly."

"William Linwood and I fell into bondage instanter; he irredeemably—whilst I was a much less willing and tractable captive. In fact, between you and me, I doubt that I was really a captive at all. My fancy or imagination was no doubt considerably dazzled by the young lady's personal charms and graces; but much more, I am pretty confident, by the reflected lustre of her reputedly large fortune."

"I can easily believe that, Mr. Kirke Webbe."

"Which shews, Mr. William Linwood, junior, that you can appreciate character. Well, having then a very good opinion—which has really improved upon better acquaintance—of my worthy self, I saw no reason why I should not compete with Mr. Linwood for the favour of the amiable heiress presumptive; and thus it came to pass, as before intimated, that the flame of friendship received a damper.

"Very absurd that, you will say," presently continued Captain Webbe, "when I inform you that the lady did not condescend to honour either of us with the slightest notice, except by carefully avoiding the paths and places we usually frequented! I, for my part, bore the pangs of despised love with a noble equanimity; but poor Linwood, having fallen into a state of semi-distraction, finally hit upon the remarkable expedient of endeavouring to obtain access to Miss Waller's presence, by striking up an innocent flirtation with her *demoiselle de compagnie*, Mademoiselle de Féron."

"Louise Féron, the Frenchwoman we saw to day!"

"Louise Féron, the Frenchwoman whom your grandame so viciously assaulted a few hours since; but at the time I am speaking of, a handsome young person, calling herself Mademoiselle *de* Féron, and pretendedly the sole remaining scion of a recently extinguished and noble French house. She had been engaged to perfect Miss Waller in the French language, and her youthful mistress was much attached to her. Let me see—where was I?"

"Speaking of my father's flirtation with De Féron—or Féron."

"Right! To continue, then. How the unfortunate misapprehension on the demoiselle's part arose, I cannot say—her bad English and Linwood's worse French had no doubt much to do with it—but it is certain that she fully believed the young Englishman to be madly in love with her, and dying to make her his lawful wife."

" *Could* that be her serious conviction? "

" Her serious conviction! I should think it was, indeed; and a trifle over. I had abundant proof of that. Finding I had quite recovered from love-fever—a very mild attack, as I have said—Linwood gave me a letter one fine day for Miss Waller, which I undertook to place for delivery in Mademoiselle de Féron's hands. I met that volcanic individual in Hare Park, and fulfilled my commission. Fire leaped from her dark eyes at sight of the direction in Linwood's hand, and you should have seen the rage and hate that blazed in them as, having instantly torn open the letter, she devoured its contents. That done, she tore it to shreds, flinging the same at innocent me, and accompanying that demonstration by a shower of epithets and imprecations, which was quite decisive of her birth and status in French society.

" The next day but one, Miss Waller left Hare Park for London with her demoiselle de compagnie; and I lost sight of Mademoiselle de Féron for nearly three years, during which, Linwood, having managed to obtain a proper introduction to the family in Cavendish Square, had wooed, won, and married Emily Waller; and you, Master William, were passing with promise through the first of man's seven ages. Have you yet reached the *third*, may I ask? " added Captain Webbe with keen abruptness.

" The third! What the deuce do you mean? "

" That of the lover, to be sure—

With a woful ballad,
Made to his mistress's eyebrow.

" No; my time is not yet come."

" I am rejoiced to hear that," exclaimed Webbe; " it almost insures the success of our bold venture."

" The plague it does! As how, pray?

" Anon—anon, my dear fellow. I was saying," continued Webbe, " that three years elapsed before I again sighted Linwood after we left Essex. The same fate that had befallen him, had overtaken me. I also was a husband and a father. Mademoiselle Féron—she had modestly dropped the '*de*'—was still languishing in single blessedness—at least she said so then, and I believe she spoke the truth—and had lately re-entered your mamma's service as nurse, or nursery-governess, to your infant highness. What her motive could be for accepting a menial situation in your father's family, puzzled me. Poverty might be one compelling motive; but I wronged her grossly if some vague but abiding purpose of working mischief to the man by whom—to the woman for whom—she had been, in her own belief, scornfully slighted and wronged— was not another and more powerful one.

"A circumstance that occurred during my visit to South Audley Street, where your father then resided, confirmed that impression or belief; albeit it is, I admit, barely possible that I misinterpreted that incident or circumstance.

"You were suffering from hooping-cough, and a paroxysm of that distressing malady had left you exhausted, apparently dead, when I softly entered the drawing-room where Louise Féron was standing with her back towards me, and holding you in her arms. She did not hear my footfall, and her face and person, reflected in a lofty pier-glass, fronted me. I stopped suddenly short, shocked, though never a man of supersensitiveness, by the fiendish expression of the woman's countenance, immediately explained by her sudden, deadly grasp of the infant's mouth and nostrils with her disengaged right hand. The child's suspended breath would, I can scarcely doubt, have been for ever stilled but for the exclamation which betrayed my presence. Féron turned sharply round, confronted me with a face of flame; rallied, assumed as well as she could, an air of indifference, and left the apartment."

"You of course informed Mr. and Mrs. Linwood of what you had seen?"

"I did not; for several reasons. In the first place, I *might* have misjudged the woman's intention; and in the next, I felt quite sure she would not try it on a second time after a hint I quietly gave her, that the child's death, under any circumstances, should be followed by an investigation that would probably only terminate at the Old Bailey."

"You acted, Mr. Webbe, with unpardonable weakness, if not with "—— I checked with difficulty the words upon my tongue, and substituted for them—" Yes, with unpardonable weakness, as the catastrophe of your narrative, plainly foreshadowed by what I have already heard, too clearly proved."

"That which you have already heard does *not* fore-shadow the catastrophe of my narrative," retorted Webbe. "Clearly as you may be able to see through a millstone, it is hardly possible you can discern a catastrophe which has not yet occurred."

"You speak riddles; but go on."

"Could I have foreseen the lamentable consequences of interrupting Mademoiselle Féron's manipulation of the child's mouth and nostrils," continued Webbe with acrid humour, "I should have been strongly tempted to have turned noiselessly away, and left her to the quiet accom-plishment of her purpose."

"Upon my word, that is cool, Captain Webbe!"

"It would have been a blessing to all parties had I done so," said the privateer captain. "To you, who, dying in your innocence, would be at this moment an angel in heaven—a contingency which must now be booked as extremely doubtful at the best; to your father, who—the Féron's instinct of vengeance having been satiated—would not have had the best years of his life rendered miserable by an accusation which to this hour he has found it im possible to repel. But we are all poor short-sighted mortals; and, unconscious of the mischief I was doing, I, as before stated, saved your life."

"For which piece of mischief, many thanks, Captain Webbe. I drink your health."

"I, yours; hoping as I do so, that we may yet succeed in discovering a remedy for that unfortunate mistake of mine. But to make sail again. Anthony Waller, Esq., of Cavendish Square, finding himself lonely after his daughter's marriage—which he had never very cordially approved of, you must know—espoused a lovely young widow, and the mother of one only child, Lucy Hamblin, then in her third year, and really quite a miniature angel. Mr. Waller not only doted upon his handsome young wife —that, like reading and writing, comes by nature—but upon his little step-daughter; so that your nose, which, without flattery, it is difficult to believe can be the natural development of the unpromising little pug Mademoiselle Féron took such liberties with, was quite put out of joint.

" This vexed your mother, and, let the truth be told, mightily exasperated your father. There had been no pre-nuptial settlement; and it was feared that the lion's share of Mr. Waller's wealth would be diverted to his new wife and ' her intrusive brat '—a frequent colloquial amenity of my friend Linwood, duly reported in the proper quarter by the Féron, who, having managed to transfer her services to the Wallers, was now little Lucy's nursery-governess.

" Thus stood matters in Mr. and Mrs. Waller's seventh honey-moon—a mellifluous phase of the earth's satellite, which the observation that with extensive view surveys mankind from China to Peru, will have noticed to be of indefinite duration when the poor and pretty bride happens to be about half the age of the rich and senile bridegroom."

" Which was not the case in that particular instance, I beg to say."

" Very nearly the case, *I* should say; but we will not discuss that fact in natural history just now. The Wallers, I say, were residing, towards the close of their seventh honey-moon, at Clarence Lodge, near Gravesend. At that time, I was in personal communication with Mr. Waller, with the hope of inducing him to make one of a company for organising privateering enterprise upon a large scale. I did not succeed; but before I received a final ' No,' Linwood came down, unaccompanied by either his wife or son. That, however, though made a great deal of subsequently, was easily explained : your mother, as doubtless you are aware, having suffered much from ill-health during the first six or seven years of married life. I think she gave birth to four children, certainly three, who all died under a month old—a fatality which was the main reason that you remained in Wales with grandmamma. Be that, however, as it may, Linwood came alone, uninvited, and his reception was glum as winter. Nevertheless, he seemed to have made up his mind for a lengthened stay ; and, which certainly looked odd, seemed anxious to conciliate the favour of little Lucy Hamblin. Your mother explained to me the other day that he did so by her advice, she thinking that a better feeling might be thereby brought about between the families.

"The eighteenth of August—a date branded upon the memory of all of us—found William Linwood still a guest, and an unwelcome one, at Clarence Lodge. The day had been sultry, thunderous, and Mr. Waller and I, towards evening-fall, after a cool walk in the garden, were seated in the arbour, and enjoying some prime cigars.

"Mrs. Waller had been uneasy for some time on account of the prolonged absence of Louise Féron, who had taken the child out for a walk early in the afternoon; and when the day began to decline visibly, and no Féron, no Lucy appeared, Mr. Waller grew fidgety also. He had asked very often for Linwood, and was for the twentieth time remarking upon his non-appearance at the dinner-table, when we saw that gentleman enter the garden by the back-gate.

"His hair, we could not but remark, was wet and disordered, his face pale, his aspect generally flurried, ill at ease.

"Hollo, Linwood!" I exclaimed, as he was passing the arbour; "what is the matter? Have you seen a ghost?"

"Eh!—eh!—what?" he stammered; "a ghost—stuff! Has—has," he added—"has Louise Féron returned?"

"No," said Mr. Waller; "and—— By Heaven! here she comes by the same way that you entered, Mr. Linwood, and without the child!"

"Without the child!" echoed the woman, sweeping up. "Why, Mr. Linwood has brought home the child, has he not?"

"No—no!" exclaimed Linwood, in great agitation. "She left me on the sands, and rejoined you, did she not?"

"Rejoined me!" screamed Féron. "Why, I saw you with my own eyes take her into a boat, and sail out upon the river."

"No—no—no!" vehemently rejoined your father, "I meant to do so, but Lucy gave me the slip."

"Liar—assassin!" shouted the woman. "I *saw* the child with you—*alone* with you in the boat: you have drowned—murdered her! *A la garde!*" shrieked the seemingly frantic creature, as she rushed upon and grappled poor Linwood, who, in his bewilderment, had really made a movement as if about to run for it—"seize—bind the assassin! Help—help!"

" As for me," resumed Captain Webbe, after a consolatory drink—" as for me, I was knocked over—flabber-
gasted ; and it was hours before I could get my ideas into
any kind of order or ship-shape. And so confused now is my
recollection of the different versions given by Linwood
and Féron ; so mixed up are they in my mind with the
outrageous inventions and distortions of the newspapers,
that, if my life depended upon it, I could give you no intelligible digest of the conflicting statements. Enough to
say, that on the morrow, no doubt remained that Lucy
Hamblin had been drowned—her hat was cast ashore with
a mass of sea-weed—and public opinion gradually settled
down into a conviction that your father, for obvious purposes, had compassed the death of the child—a conviction
which his flight, in violation of his pledged word, seemed
to affirm beyond controversy. He was pursued and apprehended, as you are perhaps aware, at Llanberris farm.
Take a pull at the brandy and water, Master Linwood "——

" Go on, will you? Do you think I am made of
stone ?"

" There is little to add, except that Féron absconded,
leaving a note to the effect that she could not, would not,
upon reflection, appear as a witness against the husband
of the best friend she had ever known. Your father was
ultimately liberated without trial ; and after striving for
several years to bear up against almost universal obloquy,
took ship for America, and was captured in the Channel by
a French privateer. So ends the story."

" And with it the hope you have so wantonly kindled,
merely, it should seem, to trample it out ! What purpose
can be answered by the fast-and-loose game, which, as far
as words count, you seem to be playing ? "

" A great purpose will be answered by the game I propose to play, if you have the pluck and skill to perform
your part in it. I tell you again that the catastrophe
which will either acquit or finally condemn your father has
not yet come to pass. The last decisive act of the drama
has yet to be played ; and the curtain rose upon that last
decisive act, after an interval of nearly fifteen years, about
three months since only. Scene the first: Rue Dupetit
Thouars, St. Malo, Brittany. Enter from opposite sides, a

lady and gentleman, who, upon seeing each other, exclaim
at the same instant:

'Mademoiselle Féron!'

'Le Capitaine Webbe!'"

"Kirke Webbe, captain of the *Scout* privateer, met walking openly in the streets of St. Malo! Come, that is a
bold flight, even for a modern dramatist!"

"It is a positive fact that I was so met! And as to
walking openly in the streets of St. Malo, there is no wonderful daring in that: I was playing at rouge et noir, in
the Palais Royal, Paris, last Sunday three weeks. Just,
however, to bring back colour to those white cheeks, and
give you an appetite for the dinner I have ordered, and
which ought to have been served by this time, I will give
you a hint of some one else I met with in St. Malo—to
wit, a charming damsel of some seventeen years of age,
whom I propose that you shall marry."

"Let us have no untimely jesting, if you please."

"A charming damsel, whom it is part of my plan, and
may be essential to its success, that you should marry:
a most amiable damsel, who calls herself Clémence
Bonneville; but whose true name, if I am not the dullest
blockhead that ever breathed, is——Guess?"

"*Tut!* How should I be able to guess?"

"Whose true name is, I say, not Clémence Bonneville,
or De Bonneville, but—*Lucy Hamblin*—the child supposed
to have perished fourteen years ago in the Thames!"

CHAPTER IV

PLOTTING.

To speak, to think of dinner at such a moment was
revolting, insufferable! The callous animalism of the
privateer captain annoyed, disgusted me, and I flung out
of the house in a hot rage. The wind, I found, had increased to a gale—the ships at Spithead had sent down
their upper spars, in preparation for a dirty night; and so
piercing was the blast, that it took the wine-fire out of my

blood in a very short time, and I was enab
cool dispassionate view of Captain Webbe's
frank, confidential, straightforward communication,
result being to deepen, rather than efface, the feeling
mistrust with which I had listened to it.

I do not know that I could have given any very logical
or lucid reason for that mistrust; but I had, notwithstanding, a strong impression that he was seeking to
hoodwink, bamboozle me, and to carry out a purpose
widely different from the ostensible one. Yet, except that
he imagined it possible to palm off a daughter of Madame
de Bonneville for the lost Lucy Hamblin—an altogether
wild, insane project, of which it was really absurd to
suspect so cool-headed a man—I could not see what
sinister purpose he could have in view.

Then my mother, who had known him so many years,
confided in his good faith, if with some misgivings, and
commanded me to do the same. It was imperative, consequently, that I should not suffer myself to be discouraged
by shadowy dangers, having no existence, possibly, save
in my own imagination. Concluding, therefore, to place
heedful confidence, so to speak, in the privateer captain—
to follow his leading boldly, and with both eyes wide open
—I returned to the hotel.

Captain Webbe had finished his dinner, proclaimed by
his rosy gills and generally placid aspect to have been a
satisfactory one. I apologised for having so abruptly left
him.

"My dear boy, the loss was yours, not mine," replied
Mr. Webbe. "Besides, it is a common failing in the
morning of life, when the blandishments of passion take
the reason prisoner—— I forget the exact words of the
quotation, but the practical moral is, that inexperienced
youth is prone to attach a higher value to imaginary rap-
tures than to the sober reality of a southdown wether-
leg, done to a bubble—a weakness which the strong years
never fail to cure. A glass of wine with you, Master
Linwood."

"Willingly; and now, perhaps, you will have the goodness to sketch, and with as rapid a pencil as possible, the
action of the all-important, all-compensating last act you
speak of?"

" Certainly. Madame de Bonneville, *ci-devant* Louise Féron, exclaimed upon catching sight of me—she has about the sharpest pair of eyes I know of: ' Le Capitaine Webbe! Est-il possible!' Now, Captain Webbe, whether in French or English, is not a name to be ashamed of, but there is a time and place for all things—even for picking up stones, as I learned at school—and certainly the month of November, 1813, and the street Dupetit Thouars, St. Malo, were *not* the suitable time and place for so shrill a proclamation of that respectable name. Instantly, therefore, entreating silence and a word in private, I followed her into the *magasin*. A few minutes sufficed to establish mutually amicable relations ; and circumstances detaining me in St. Malo longer than I feared might prove beneficial to my health, we became mighty intimate."

" As a proof of that friendly intimacy," continued Captain Webbe with a grimace, as if half-a-dozen invisible surgeon-dentists were operating upon him at once, " I may mention that Madame de Bonneville, not having quite sufficient capital for her business, declared that she preferred being obliged for the trifle required—five thousand francs only—two hundred pounds sterling—to her old friend, Captain Webbe, than to her nearest and dearest relatives ! It was withal a mere bagatelle, as she said ; for which bagatelle, counted out in solid five-franc pieces, le Capitaine Webbe received in acknowledgment and acquittal : ' O that you are good! O that you are generous, my dear captain!' and a laugh," added Webbe with a savage snap of his teeth that would have taken a piece out of a pewter-pot—" a laugh which said as plainly as laugh could, ' You will take skinning more pleasantly, my dear friend, when you are more used to it!' "

Unquestionably genuine was the wrath which flashed from under the scowling brows of the privateer captain, and hissed in a concluding execration ! He could not, then, be plotting *with* the Frenchwoman !

" It was subsequent to the exaction of that pledge of amity that I first saw Clémence de Bonneville, and detected the imposture at a glance."

" Or imagined you did!"

" To the devil with imagined ! The pretended daughter has a clear fair skin, bright silken hair, sweet blue eyes

and a delicately moulded, sylph-like figure. De Bonneville's complexion is the colour of mahogany—her hair,
raven-jet, and coarse as horsetails ; her eyes, black as a
thunder-cloud; her person, large, bony, angular!   The
girl is an English girl—is the lost Lucy Hamblin.   That
conviction, fire would not burn out of me."

"I trust there are better proofs of that than contrasts
in features and complexion."

"There are abundance of proofs, and I rely upon you to
obtain them.   Now, don't fly out till you have heard all.
Clémence, as we may as well continue to call her, is, please
to understand, one of the simplest-hearted, most guileless
of maidens; and expressions which have escaped her,
when I have by a rare chance found her alone, satisfy me
that she has in some way discovered, if not the exact
secret of her birth, that she is not the daughter of Madame
de Bonneville, of whom she stands in terrible awe ; and
who, by the way, intends marrying her to one Jacques
Sicard, a relative of madame's, and a well-enough-to-do
master-bootmaker.

"That marriage," continued Webbe, finding I made no
remark, "still remains in madame's programme, which in
other respects has been lately entirely changed.   It was,
and not so very long ago, her intention, after Clémence
had become Madame Sicard—not before—to open negociations with Mrs. Waller, who, she is aware, cherishes the
memory of her lost child as tenderly as ever."

"Nothing more than proof of Clémence being that lost
child—unchallengeable, overwhelming proof, is required
for my father's effectual vindication."

"Quite true ; and the knowledge of that has, no doubt,
powerfully operated in finally determining Féron—she has
no legal right, I am positive, to the name of De Bonneville,
and Féron she shall be to me—in finally determining
Féron, I say, never to take a step that might lead to such
a result.   Cupidity might, however, have conquered hate ;
but a closer view of the possible consequences to herself
that might follow the avowal that Clémence was the child
alleged to have been drowned, has irrevocably decided her
never to make that avowal."

"Really, Captain Webbe, I can scarcely follow such a

labyrinthine maze of strange facts and stranger inferences. What frightful hazard would the woman incur by the restoration of Mrs. Waller's child?"

"The hazard of being sent to the galleys—that's all. Féron must have falsified the municipal register of baptism, to which offence the *code pénal* attaches that tremendous penalty. What surety would she have, now that peace is about to open France to the English, that Linwood, for example, might not set the law in motion against her? Then the woman has acquired a respectable position in St. Malo, and has a decided objection to losing caste, and much more beside, as she would do, were she to acknowledge that her pretended daughter is a child stolen from English parents. That she will never do: the question is decided."

"What, then, will she do—does she propose doing?"

"I will tell you in a few words. She has ascertained for herself that the Wallers are still wealthy, that Mr. Waller is extremely anxious that his daughter should return to England, and reside near him; that Mrs. Linwood is rich, and pines to embrace her son; that that son himself is consumed with an irrepressible longing to return to his native country—to slowly die there, as he in his morbid despondency of mind believes. Well, Louise Féron, if paid very—very handsomely for doing so, will continue to withhold the evidence that would, as she declares, convict your father; Mr. Waller can have his daughter to reside near him; Mrs. Linwood may again embrace her son: and that son may return to die slowly in his native country—favours to be enjoyed by Louise Féron's sufferance—and revocable, of course, at her pleasure!"

"And how is this woman-fiend to be encountered—baffled?"

"By the exercise of courage and cunning equal to her own," replied Webbe, throwing away his cigar, and continuing to speak with an energy and earnestness very unlike his usual sneering cynicism; but whether feigned or genuine, I was too little versed in the science of dissimulation to determine.

"The great point is," said Webbe, "to make sure that

my surmise—we will call it a surmise—relative to Clémence
is well founded — to ascertain beyond dispute that
she is indeed Lucy Hamblin."

"That will determine everything."

"Unquestionably; and fortunately the lost child has, I
am pretty sure, some indelible natural mark, which will
render its identity indisputable. Your grandmother will
tell you what that mark is—I do not wish to know it—
and when you have been furnished by me with an opportunity of applying that infallible test, and you are satisfied
that Lucy Hamblin is Lucy Hamblin, we shall be free to
take such steps as prudence, courageous prudence may
advise. If we are foiled, it will be your fault, not mine,
depend upon it."

"How will it be my fault?"

"Madame de Bon—— Louise Féron, I mean, intends
leaving St. Malo immediately after she can manage to get
there from Guernsey; and will be absent on business
affairs in Paris for at least three weeks. Clémence will be
left to the guardianship of Fanchette, a sort of half-ser-
vant, half-friend, and wholly corruptible, yet kindly, gossip-
ing old soul. Now, the *Scout* will be in the Thames at
the latest, I hope I may say, on Wednesday evening next;
you will embark in her for Jersey, whence you and I will
easily pass over to St. Malo."

"Pass over to St. Malo! Really, that is a very
startling proposition. Suppose, now, my companion and
guide, Captain Webbe, of the *Scout* privateer, should be
recognised by some person or persons, whom two hundred pounds sterling, counted out in solid five-franc pieces
would not bribe to silence—how then?"

"That danger must be risked — confronted. Your
mother expressed great confidence in her son's courage."

"I hope to justify that confidence; and it is surely no
proof of courage to shut one's eyes to danger! But go on
with your plan."

"Arrived at St. Malo, where, for various reasons, my
own stay will be brief, I shall introduce you to Clémence
and Fanchette with a flourish of trumpets that will insure
a gracious reception. Thenceforth all will depend upon
the use you make of your opportunities. To avoid the
possibility of being duped, which would not suit my **book**

any more than yours, I would simply ask Fanchette if she knows of any natural mark upon the young lady's person, and if she does, to describe it. Supposing, however, that I am mistaken, and that no such natural mark exists, there is another mode of at least achieving *our* purpose—the vindication of your father's character. There can, I think, be no question that Louise Féron, with a view to all probable and possible eventualities, took care to preserve some of the child's clothes or ornaments: a pearl necklace I remember hearing the little Lucy had on when she went out on the 18th of August with her traitorous governess; now, if you can manage by bribery, or by any other expedient, to obtain possession of any article we can prove belonged to the child, Louise Féron's hour will have struck, and I shall take care she knows that 'ce cher Capitaine Webbe, who will take skinning more pleasantly when he is more used to it,' set the hands, and swung the clapper! You will have means of direct communication with me," added Mr. Webbe; "and when matters are ripe, I will manage to bring you both safely to England."

"How is it, Captain Webbe," I suddenly exclaimed, "that you have not given your own son the chance of wooing and winning the guileless and susceptible Clémence? The value of the prize, in only a monetary sense, supposing her to be, provably, Lucy Hamblin, would have been great."

The privateer captain laughed out with gleeful good-humour.

"That, my shrewd young friend, was the game I *did* intend to play, and bitterly vexed was I at being thwarted in it. My precious soft-headed son had, I found, fallen extemporaneously in love with the pretty face of a penniless wench, one Maria Wilson, or Bilson, whom he had met with in Jersey; and it was quite useless to attempt, I found, stirring such a dish of skimmed-milk with so gallant a purpose! You will have an opportunity of making his acquaintance, as he will go with you as far as Jersey. We will now be going," added Captain Webbe, ringing the bell; "I shall be early to-morrow at Oak Villa: night brings counsel; and I will not doubt that I shall find you thoroughly resolved to engage in the task confided to your filial piety and courage. Good-bye."

I found my excellent relative quite recovered from the nervous shock occasioned by the unexpected apparition of Louise Féron. She had read my mother's letter, and she listened with flashing eyes and glowing cheeks to the recapitulation of my long conferences with Captain Webbe.

Her eager, minute cross-examination, if I may call it so, having at length obtained from me every word he uttered, every peculiar gesture or intonation I could recall to mind, she thus oracularly delivered herself:

" You must not hold back, William, from the venture, very hazardous and slightly promising as it may be. But I have no confidence in Webbe—and do you have none— or at least only so much as deeds, unequivocal deeds, will justify. I always suspected him of being a confederate of Louise Féron's—perhaps unjustly ; or they may have quarrelled. 1 have seen his son—a mild, limpid lad ; a masculine type, as far only as person goes, of his meek-minded mother, and the very opposite, consequently, of Kirke Webbe. Lucy Hamblin *had* an indelible natural mark, which will render the fraudulent substitution of another child impossible. But I don't know what it is ; and Mrs. Waller, whose mind has never quite recovered its once healthy tone, must not be excited by Webbe's strange story, till some proof of its authenticity has been furnished. Obtaining by book or crook a sight, and if a sight, possession of the pearl necklace, or some recognisable article of clothing, is a good idea ; keep your eye upon that. As to your engaging yourself in marriage, why, I dare say, William, the notion of marriage had never—but of course it had not at twenty—occurred to you before. The notion, I say, of such a thing, till the young woman is introduced to you by Mrs. Waller herself, as her undoubted daughter, is absurd, quite preposterous ; it throws an air of unreality over the whole thing. Still, I do not pronounce against the truth of Webbe's story, because it is in parts absurd, confused, improbable. All true, but incomplete narratives are necessarily so, from the absence of modifying facts and connecting-links. Fiction, on the contrary, is always coherent, plausible. Yes, my dear boy, you must act according to circumstances, with boldness and discretion ; above all, with discretion. I do not mean by discretion, timidity or hesitation. You must boldly grasp the nettle danger, it has been wisely said, if you would pluck therefrom the flower safety. True; but you must also be wary and circumspect in deciding upon the fitting time and mode of making that bold grasp. It is a heavy burden, a fearful responsibility to lay upon one so young, so inexperienced in the ways of men ; still, it must be. You have courage, zeal, a holy cause, and are not, I think, deficient, for your years, in common sense. I will see Webbe in the morning, and arrange that you shall have frequent communication with me. I shall also add considerably to the reward which your mother has answered for, in the event of success. Such a man can only be bound to our interest by golden fetters, of which there must be no stint."

After the foregoing fashion did my worthy grandame untiringly discourse or soliloquise, till, becoming aware that I was nodding indiscriminate assent to her dicta, she, with some petulance, exclaimed that it was time for boys to be in bed, and sharply ringing the bell, desired Nancy to bring Master William's chamber candlestick!

I was "Master William" with the venerable lady, I may here pause a moment to remark, when she, having passed her ninety-fourth year, fell calmly asleep in the arms of her already gray-haired grandson, on the evening of the 10th of July 1840, faintly ejaculating, whilst a seraphic smile played about her thin white lips: "The clock must be wrong, Master William, for, see, the dawn is breaking—bright—beautiful—divine! "

But more than a quarter of a century of life lay between her and that supreme hour when, on the Wednesday following her Sunday-morning encounter with Louise Féron, I left Oak Villa for London, taking with me her blessing, a well-filled purse, and several foolscap sheets of closely written counsel, adapted to all conceivable exigencies. Webbe had gone the day before to Portsmouth upon business connected with his American prize; but I should find him either at his private lodgings, High Holborn, or on board the *Scout*, which, from the direction of the wind since Monday morning, he had no doubt would reach the Thames before either he or I did.

I arrived in London on Thursday afternoon about five o'clock, and seeing by the shipping news in the papers that the *Scout* had brought up a little below Greenwich, I lost no time in getting on board. My arrival was hailed with great satisfaction by Captain Webbe, as the tide would soon be on the turn, and he was anxious the *Scout* should sail that evening. He was in the cabin taking a parting glass with his son, and chief officer, Mr. Robert Dowling.

"Pressing business matters, Mr. Linwood," said Captain Webbe, as he filled me a stiff tumbler, "prevent me, I am sorry to say, from accompanying you to Jersey. I shall, however, manage to meet you there before many days are past."

"That is, I suppose," remarked Dowling with something of a glum look and tone—"that is, I suppose, if the *Scout* don't happen to bring up in a French port instead of Jersey."

"Is there any fear of that?" I hastily exclaimed, glancing as I spoke at the pale, handsome face of young Webbe, upon which fear, if I did not misjudge him, was strongly marked.

"I don't know about 'fear,'" gruffly replied Dowling; "but the fact is"——

"Of course you don't know about 'fear,'" interrupted Captain Webbe; "nobody supposed you did. *Le Renard*, a French war-brig," added the captain, "whose commander is supposed to have a spite against us for balking him some time since of a valuable booty, sighted the *Scout*, it seems, as she came up Channel, and Dowling fancies she may overhaul us on our way to Jersey. Not at all likely; and if she attempts to do so, the *Scout* can shew a fine pair of heels——"

"Heels be——!" broke in Dowling. "Don't fancy, captain, that because you won't be on board, we shall"——

"*Chut—chut!* Clap a stopper upon that foolish gab—do," again interrupted Webbe. "Let's on deck," he added; "it's time I were on shore, and you off."

A shore-boat was alongside, into which Webbe presently jumped; the capstan was manned, and sent round with a stamp and go; the anchor was brought home, and in less than five minutes, I should suppose, after we left the cabin, the *Scout* was dropping down the river, helped with a light air from the northward.

By dawn the next day we here off Margate, and the wind freshening, the *Scout* made swift progress. The day was clear and bright—a wintry brightness—and it seemed that we were to have a pleasant, uneventful run. Whether from the effect of the sea-breeze, or the non-appearance of *Le Renard*, Harry Webbe's fine, if somewhat feminine features had assumed a rosier, healthier hue ; and his conversation shewed him to be a well-informed young man.

As the day declined, the sky became overcast; the wind rose and blew in fitful gusts, sometimes of great violence, though of brief duration; and I heard Dowling consult Withers, the officer next in authority, as to whether it might be advisable to bear up for Guernsey. It was, however, decided that the *Scout* should hold on her direct course, passing between the French coast and the islands of Alderney and Sercq. Cherbourg was passed; the race of Alderney was speedily run through; by the time evening closed in, we were beginning to slip past Sercq; and Mr. Dowling's apprehension of meeting with *Le Renard* was passing away, when the look-out on the foretop sung out: "Sail, ho ! "

"Where away?" queried Dowling, snatching up his glass, and hastening forward.

"Right ahead ! " was the reply; and sure enough a large gun-brig—six fierce teeth a side—hitherto concealed from us by Sercq—was standing directly across the *Scout's* course.

"*Le Renard!* by all that's lucky ! " exclaimed Dowling, as he closed his glass with a snap. "Turn all the hands up, Withers," he added, with stern promptness. "There's a hot supper, quite enough for every mother's son of them, just ready, so they had better look alive, or they'll not have time to ask a blessing before falling-to."

The tap of the drum, as in a man-of-war, beat to quarters, the men tumbled up the hatchways, and after one quite sufficient glance at the stranger, addressed themselves with a will to clear the *Scout* for action.

"Is a combat inevitable?" I asked, addressing Mr. Dowling.

"Why, no, young man," he replied; "we are not *obliged* to fight, though, as it happens, we can't run. We might knock under at once—haul down the jack flying at the fore, and be carried off comfortable and quiet as Quakers to Cherbourg. But the 'Scouts' not being Quakers, it's my candid opinion, since you ask me for it, that if you, in an hour or less from this, ain't gone to glory, or upon the road to it, you 'll be uncommon lucky; and besides that, will have something to talk of for the rest of your natural life. Luff!" he roared through his trumpet to the men at the wheel. "Bring her nose dead to windward. We must lie-to, or, by jingo, the dance will begin before our music is ready."

CHAPTER V.

A SEA FIGHT.

THE privateer was terribly overmatched in weight of metal and tonnage. The *Scout's* guns were twelve-pounders, those of *Le Renard*, eighteens, and the privateer's hull was but a walnut-shell in comparison with the solid fabric of the imperial war-brig. In fact, the *Scout* was neither built nor armed for such encounters, and had it been possible to do so, the officer in temporary command of her was bound by his instructions, as well as by privateer practice, to have avoided the combat, had it even been an equal one, distasteful to his own reckless impulses as flight might be. Escape *without* fighting was, however, it seemed to be tacitly agreed, out of the question; and *how* to fight with half a chance of winning, was the subject of a low-toned, lugubrious conference between Dowling and Withers, to which, as far as listening with bated breath went, Harry Webbe and I assisted.

Withers was anxiously sweeping the waters in all directions with his night-glass, in the hope of sighting a friendly cruiser, when Dowling came aft to concert with him the mode of combat.

"A king's cruiser would be a sight for sore eyes," said he, "just now—eh, Withers? But there's no such luck to be hoped for. The *Griffin* sprung her mizzen two or three days ago, and is at Portsmouth getting a new one; and the *Pelican* is cruising off St. Malo."

"I wish Webbe were here himself," remarked Withers. The superstitious reliance of the men upon his 'luck' is worth a score of hands."

"That's true enough; but wishing won't get him here. What, in your judgment and mine, is the best mode of tackling the Frenchman, is the pressing question."

"Infernally bad will be the very best mode we can hit upon; but the worst, certainly, would be attempting to play at cannon-balls with our ugly customer. He ought to smash us into chips, at that fun, in ten minutes or less."

"Right. There is but one chance—that of boarding— throwing all our fellows in a body upon his deck. That is plainly our game," added Dowling. "Veteran French seamen have been long since used up: *Le Renard's* crew must, therefore, be chiefly composed of young maritime conscripts, who, with anything like equal numbers, would have a poor chance in a hand-to-hand encounter with our fellows."

"And for that reason the French commander will hardly be such a fool as to give us an opportunity of boarding. That, however, is, I agree, our only chance; and now, as to particulars, if Le Moine is such a fool as to let us come within grappling distance of *Le Renard*."

These were quickly arranged. The *Scout's* guns were to be loaded to the muzzle with grape and canister; we were, if possible, to run alongside to leeward of the Frenchman, which would give the privateer's guns sufficient elevation to sweep the enemy's deck; and the men were to board in the smoke of the first and only broadside intended on our side to be fired. At Withers's suggestion, the seamen were to be told to arm themselves with any weapon they might prefer to the light cutlass—crowbars, handspikes, axes—anything deadly and weighty they could freely wield.

"And now to see all things got in readiness with our own eyes," added Dowling, and the two officers walked away.

The night, as I before intimated, had set in dark and stormy, the moon appearing only at brief intervals through a break in the clouds that swept swiftly across the sky, and I could not have distinctly seen Harry Webbe's face had he fronted me, which he carefully avoided doing. I was not, however, long in doubt as to the effect produced upon that sensitive organisation by the officers' conference. With as much swaggering, devil-may-care indifference as the flurried state of my own nerves permitted me to assume, I exclaimed as soon as the officers were out of hearing :

"I suppose, Mr. Harry Webbe, you will be favoured with a leading part in the tragi-comedy we have just heard outlined. I, unfortunately, am only a passenger; but your father's son will have, no doubt, the honour of heading the boarders!"

A low, inarticulate cry of shame and terror escaped the unfortunate young man, who, without further reply, hurried below. I followed, after a few moments' thought, and found Harry Webbe prone upon his face on the cabin locker-seats, sobbing convulsively. I closed and bolted the door, for I pitied the poor youth's anguish of mind, and a dim notion had, moreover, crossed mine that it might be politic, on my part, to win the regard of Captain Webbe's flexile, impressionable son.

"You have never been in action, I suppose?" said I.

"Never! O God!—never!"

"Ah, well, then, you will think nothing of it, I am told, after the first five minutes. Some of the greatest heroes that ever lived have confessed to feeling terribly nervous when first under fire; and I can well believe it," added William Linwood, with more truth than he meant his words should convey to his panic-stricken auditor, "for I myself feel deuced queer, I promise you. Suppose we try a taste of brandy," I continued, hitching down the keys of the spirit-locker. "Dutch courage must be better than none."

We both swallowed a bumper, with good effect as regarded myself, but poor Webbe continued to weep like the veriest girl, except that his tears now flowed silently.

"Come, come, my good fellow," I exclaimed, giving way in some degree to the feeling of contempt which extreme pusillanimity in a man always excites; "pluck up a heart, if it's ever such a tiny one. Depend upon it, we shall both live till we die, and not one moment longer, had no such devil's playthings as cannon-balls ever been invented."

This consolatory logic of mine appeared to revive him
more than the brandy; he ceased weeping, and looking
up in my face as steadily as the dull light of the lamp
swinging overhead permitted, he said with an approach to
firmness:

"It is not the vulgar dread of death which thus unmans
me, Linwood. I have lain for weeks within the shadow
of the tomb, expecting it every hour to close over me, as
calmly as a child resigns itself to sleep. No, no, it is not
the will, the mind, the soul which shrinks from the dire
conflict; it is physical nerve only that fails me. A horror
of bloodshed, of the flash of clashing swords, was congenital
with my being. My mother gave me birth, prematurely, on
board the *Wasp*, privateer, during her desperate action
with the French privateer, *La Flèche*. At one time during
that murderous fight, the enemy obtained temporary
possession of the deck, beat my father and his men below
to the cabin where my mother lay; and pistol-shots, the
clash of swords, the fierce oaths of men stabbing, slaying
each other, mingled with the woman's cry of travail—with
the wail of the new-born infant."

"Pray," said I, after a pause, for I felt somewhat mystified by the young man's glib eloquence—"pray, is my
friend Captain Webbe aware of the congenital cowardice—
I crave pardon—of the constitutional infirmity under
which his son labours?"

"Yes, I think so; but he, reasoning from himself,
believes that what a man *wills* to do, that he can do."

"Well, then it seems to me that, under the peculiar
circumstances, you should firmly tell Dowling you do not
mean to fight. This is not a king's ship, and he cannot
shoot you for congenital cow—— for constitutional infirmity, that is to say."

"I cannot, dare not, do as you advise," exclaimed Harry
Webbe with frenzied emotion, and quite heedless of, or
indifferent to, the sneer I could not suppress. "And this
not from any fear of incurring the contempt of my father
or of Dowling; for that I should care little—nothing: the
great, the terrible fear which haunts, dominates, distracts
me is—is "——

"What, in the name of wonder, besides pistol-shots and
sword-stabs? Speak out, man alive! We shall not have

many more minutes, you may depend, to waste in talk."

"I *love*, Mr. Linwood—to ecstasy—madness!"

"Oh, that's it: and loving to ecstasy—madness, you are naturally desirous of living over the honey-month, at the very least."

"Maria Wilson," continued the young man, "has but one fault, if fault it be—an enthusiastic admiration, namely, of what she imagines to be heroism—the heroism of homicide—of valiant human butchery: the phrase offends you; well, call it military heroism. She greatly admires my father, or, more correctly, my father's deeds, as reflected in the mirror of public opinion; and she has frequently expressed her regret that the probably speedy termination of the war will put it out of my power to gather laurels in the same field of sin and death."

"You are rich in fine words, Mr. Harry Webbe: nevertheless, proceed."

"No additional words, fine or otherwise, are required to describe my position," he sadly replied. "The time is come for gathering those bloody laurels, and I have no strength for the harvest: occasion calls, and I am not ready! Maria," he added, with a renewed burst of wild dismay—"imaginative, romantic, falsely judging, beautiful Maria, when she hears of this night's deeds, and my share therein, will hoot me from her presence."

"Zounds, then, why not try and muster up sufficient courage to make a show of fight! Such inexperienced youngsters as you and I will not be placed in front of the battle: it's not likely. O well, if the constitutional infirmity is *not* to be conquered, I hardly see what's to be done. Except indeed—except—— Yes, that might succeed; and if it did, would bring you off with flying colours—and a sound skin!"

"What might bring me off with flying colours, Mr. Linwood?" eagerly demanded young Webbe.

"Softly—softly; let me reflect a moment. It is evident by what is still going on overhead, that the ships are not near closing yet; so that we have plenty of time; and I must not forget that my tongue is apt at times to outrun discretion: let me consider."

I did consider: examined the brilliant idea that had

suddenly gleamed through my precious noddle, over and over again, and discovering no flaw, I presented it, hot and shining, to my anxiously expectant young friend.

Ah me! could I only have forseen the succession of dreadful scrapes it would get me into—that that mischievous Maria Wilson was, in fact——Never mind; or at least it's of no use of minding now—so I resume. This paragraph, the intelligent reader will observe, is a parenthesis.

" The problem to be solved is," I began, " to enable you to wrest bright honour from those ferocious *Renards,* without giving them a chance of conferring upon you a too immediate and unwished-for immortality. Well, I think, that can be managed."

" How—how can it be managed ? "

" Thus wise: common candour, however, bids me first distinctly apprise you, that if I succeed in rendering you this service, I shall expect a *quid pro quo.*"

" Of what kind—in what way ? "

" In this kind, in this way. I have a strong conviction, impression rather, that your good-will, your *active* good-will might be of signal service to me in the anxious business I am with your father engaged in."

" It might, it might; it *shall,*" he exclaimed, pressing my hand in both his as a pledge of amity and good faith.

" That is understood, then. Now to particulars. To begin with : I have an insuperable objection to a French prison, and, although I do not feel at all like a hero, I shall certainly do my best to keep out of one. That ' best' will not be a thunderbolt of war, you may be sure; and the less likely to be so, forasmuch that, as I before remarked, Dowling will never think of placing such youngsters as you and I in the front of the fight; the danger may not, therefore, be so very great after all. Now, I do not care a straw for my share of the ' glory' which the Scouts hope to achieve by the defeat of the Renards"——

" Well, well, but I do not under—— Ha! God!"

The sudden boom of a heavy gun arrested the poor fellow's speech, and shook him as with ague.

" The Frenchman's challenge ! " I exclaimed, with an effort to shew an unconcern I certainly did not feel. " He

has the first word, but is evidently a good way off yet.
Take another sip of cognac; and I don't care if I do the
same."

"Being a passenger," I resumed, "and not at all amen-
able to Dowling's authority, I may of course refuse to join
the comhatants."

"Certainly you may."

"And I certainly shall. Do you begin to take me? Are
we not both of about the same height and size? And if
we exchange clothes; if I don that heavy pea-jacket, with
its high up-turned collar; that fur-cap, and tie its large flap-
ears down over my cheeks, the deuce is in it, if, on such a
night as this, and amidst the smoke and bustle of battle,
any one will discover that William Linwood is on deck, and
Harry Webbe consequently the 'passenger' who has
turned in out of harm's way!"

"I comprehend. Well, will you do this?"

"Upon my honour, I will; and the more readily, to be
quite candid, that I do not see how I thereby increase my
personal risk, being, as I said, determined, in any case, to
do my little best to keep out of the French bilboes. The
struggle, as sketched by Dowling and Withers, will be
brief as fierce; and the moment it is over, or nearly so, I
slip down—you turn out—I turn in—and the thing is
done."

"Yes, if the French give our fellows a chance to board
—are beaten—and—and you are neither wounded—nor—
nor killed!"

"Don't mention it, there's a good fellow, unless you
wish to give me a congenital qualm. Ah! here comes
Dowling. Remember that your soul's in arms and eager
for the fray."

"Now, young gentlemen," exclaimed Dowling, "be
smart. The French won't decline the close hug we are
anxious for; and in ten minutes or less we shall be at
each other's throats. You have been splicing the main
brace, I see. Well, a glass or so does no harm; I will
take one myself. Now, then," he added, after tossing it
off, "where are your tools?"

"Tools! What tools?"

"Cutlass—pistols."

"Cutlass, pistols, indeed: not for me,

said I. "Being only a lodger, Mr. Dowling, I intend to turn in and try to sleep through this night's shindy."

"The devil you do! But you can't be serious."

"Can't I, though! You will find, sir, that I am perfectly serious. Besides, I object to fighting upon principle."

"Principle be——. I'd cut a better principle than you out of a frostbitten turnip! And what principle, may I ask, do you intend to steer by?" added Dowling, turning sharply towards Harry Webbe.

"I am prepared to do my duty," he replied, cool as a cucumber.

"Bravo! young man. I am delighted, perhaps a little surprised, to find you so plucky. The men, I must tell you, are not, I fear, so confident as they would be if your father were here. They have a superstitious faith in 'Lucky Webbe;' so, for this once, you must be 'Lucky Webbe,' and take his place, which will be in the front centre of the boarders—a little forward of the third gun from the bows. You will board, as you heard me explain to Withers, in the smoke of our own guns. About sixty rough dare-devils will leap with you upon the Frenchman's deck, and "——

"Go to Jericho with your sixty rough dare-devils!" interrupted I, in a real panic. "Why, confound it, Mr. Dowling, you can't mean that—that this young fellow—lad, as I may say—is to lead the forlorn-hope!"

"Have the goodness not to shove in your oar till it's asked for," angrily rejoined the officer. "Be on deck, Webbe," he added, "in five minutes at latest, or you may be too late to open the ball." With that he left us.

His announcement of the distinguished part in the imminent conflict assigned to Webbe junior almost knocked me over, and I had a mind to peremptorily retract the rash promise I had given. I was prevented doing so by shame—the compliment to my supposedly unshaken courage implied by Harry Webbe's alacrity in stripping, the instant Dowling's back was turned—mere acting, by the way, on the part of that humbug of the finest water—and more than all, by the reassuring conviction, that in the darkness of the night and confusion incident to such a struggle, the officer's abominable pro-

E

position—prompted, I could not help suspecting, by secret enmity to the absent skipper's son—of placing a comparative stripling in the van of the fight, could not be carried out.

In less than five minutes prescribed by Dowling, I was fully equipped for combat—loaded pistols in my belt; a straight cut-and-thrust sword naked in my hand: the disguise, as far as I could judge by the dim light of the cabin, complete; and I was taking a third thimbleful of cognac, when the officer's loud, fierce hail hurried me on deck.

"Plenty of time," said Dowling. "I was afraid that cowardly wretch, Linwood, might be pitching his 'principles' into you: place yourself somewhere about midships. Silence!" he shouted to the men; no jabbering till the guns have spoken. There is something else," he continued, "to which I require your attention. I am not going to prate to you about glory and Old England. Glory is a word, of which a million would not fill one hungry belly; and Old England can take very good care of itself. What really concerns you is, that in a quarter of an hour, or less, you will either have captured a ship worth ten thousand pounds at the very least; or have lost every mag and rag you possess, besides having the satisfaction to know you are on the way to a French prison. That's the right sort of growl, lads," added the officer. "It is quite clear, though I can't see your faces very plainly, that you understand the thing. I and the captain's son there will lead you, and we mean to win, I promise you. Now, make ready for work."

A second fierce, but, as it were, suppressed shout or "growl," followed Dowling's speech; then the men who had gone aft—hitching up their trousers, and each man tightening the grasp of his weapon, crowbar, handspike, tomahawk, cutlass, carpenter's adze or axe—took up their appointed stations; and silence, broken only by the whistling, howling wind, and the heave, swash, moan of the dark tumbling sea, pervaded the ship.

The situation, with its surroundings, was a trying, awful one to a young greenhorn who had never seen a shot fired or a blade drawn in anger. The night was darker than when we went below, and the huge mass of

bluff, precipitous Sercq, not more, apparently, than about
a mile to leeward deepened the gloom which the *Scout*
seemed to carry with her, as with only the jib and one
mizzen square-sail set, she forged slowly ahead to meet *Le
Renard*, which, similarly reduced in canvas, gradually
neared us. We could see that the Frenchman's deck was
crowded with men, and the gleaming port-fires gave warning that the deadly broadside which was to herald our
attempt to carry the war-brig by boarding, would be reciprocal.

Why Captain Le Moine did not avail himself of *Le
Renard's* superiority in weight of metal, and shot-resisting
solidity of construction, to cannonade the *Scout* till she
struck or was blown out of the water, was a puzzle at the
time, but subsequently explained by the French commander's anxiety to damage the celebrated *Scout* as little
as might me, and his confidence that *Le Renard's* boarders
would easily master the resistance of a mere privateer's
crew.

Ten minutes, perhaps, by the clock—two hours at least
counted by the beatings of my pulse—elapsed before the
vessels closed in the decisive death-struggle. At length,
the bowsprits of *Le Renard* and the *Scout* drew past each
other, a few feet only apart—another minute, and they
were directly abeam—had grappled: a sheet of blinding
flame flashed simultaneously with the roar of *Le Renard's*
guns, and the yelling shouts of her crew, echoed on our
side by the snapping of ropes, the rending of planks, and
the shrieks and curses of wounded and dying men!

"Steady! Englishmen—steady!" rose high above the
dreadful uproar, in Dowling's fiercely calm tones ringing
through his trumpet. "Remember to board in the smoke.
FIRE!"

Another glare of flame, not this time in *our* faces—another roar of cannon, accompanied, followed by ferocious
shouts, cries, curses, in the midst of which the Scouts
clambered over the bulwarks, and myself amongst them,
impelled by a kind of mechanical volition, leaped upon *Le
Renard's* deck.

The incidents of the next sixteen minutes, which 1 was
afterwards told the contest lasted, passed like a hideous
dream. It was a strife of raging demons, stabbing, smash-

ing, pistolling each other without method as without
mercy. The Frenchmen—youths chiefly—the latest haul
of the exhausted maritime conscription, fought with spirit,
but their comparatively slight frames and light swords
availed but poorly against the strong-limbed, stalwart,
privateers and their terrible weapons. Of course, I fought
fired, hacked, stabbed with the rest, yet the dreadful
struggle would have left only a confused, chaotic impression upon my memory, but for an incident towards its
close when the combatants had become thinned and the
sulphurous atmosphere had lightened somewhat.

At that moment, an eddy of the fight drove me against
Captain Le Moine, a gallant, white-haired, but still vigorous
veteran. He was fighting with the rage of despair, and
thrust at me with furious energy. I parried the stroke,
and would have avoided the combat; he was determined I should not, and pressed me fiercely whilst a sort
of ring of the Scouts—the victory being no longer doubtful
—gathered about us. Laborde had rendered me skilful
with the sword, but I parried the veteran's thrusts with
difficulty, the darkness obliging me to depend in a great
degree upon *feeling* his blade as it played round mine. All
at once, a crowding from behind drove me as it were upon
Captain Le Moine, who would not yield a step ; and made
a fierce pass at me. It was parried; and my recovered
point passed through the unfortunate officer's body. He
fell back dead as stone, and at that moment the moon for
the first time since I had left the cabin, looked through a
rift in the black clouds upon the pale face and white hairs
of the slain seaman, as if—for the accusing light was as
instantly withdrawn—to fix them indelibly upon my
memory.

And never, while memory endures, shall I forget the
Cain-like horror with which the dread sight filled me ; a
horror heightened, maddened by the exulting cheers of
the privateers for my *victory*. I broke wildly away, regained the *Scout's* cabin, and, flinging the accursed sword
upon the floor, heaped opprobrious abuse upon the
trembling wretch for whose sake I, in my unreasoning
fury, asserted I had defiled my soul with murder.

The violence of that paroxysm of passion presently
abated. I threw off my borrowed habiliments, and

hastened to hide myself—can the reader comprehend such a feeling?—in my cot-hammock. My reproaches, incoherent as they were, had nevertheless sufficed to sufficiently inform Harry Webbe how matters had gone, and he was quickly on deck with the crimsoned sword in his hand, coolly listening to the compliments of Dowling —Withers had been sped to his account—upon the hereditary pluck he had displayed, to which he and the surviving Scouts generally were pleased to say the capture of *Le Renard* was in a great measure attributable—an exaggeration prompted of course by the fact, that he was their captain's son.

CHAPTER VI.

THE BUBBLE REPUTATION.

REMORSE, or, more accurately, perhaps, the physical shock to a youthful slayer's unaccustomed nerves which red-handed homicide, however conventionally justifiable or meritorious, must always inflict, did not prevent me from falling into a sound sleep, that lasted till near twelve o'clock the next day, and might have continued longer but for a dreadfully discordant noise, which, when it had thoroughly awakened me, I made out to be a stave from the then very popular song celebrative of the capture of *La Pomone* by the *Arethusa :*

> On board, five hundred men did dance,
> The stoutest they could find in France,
> We with two hundred did advance
> On board of the Arethusa—
> The saucy Arethusa—

and so on, mentally applied, no doubt, to the previous night's business by the singer, a kind of steward's mate, who was putting the cabin to rights, and at the same time venting his exultation in that dismal manner.

"Hollo there!" I exclaimed; "leave off that row, will you?"

" Oh, is that you, sir?" replied the fellow. "The row, bless you, is over long ago, whilst you was a sweetly sleepin', sir. And the skipper as is, sir, Mr. Dowling, told me to be sure and give you his compliments when you woke, and say he was afeared you mout have taken rayther too much caudle afore turnin' in last night, seein' as how you slept so long."

"Tell Mr. Dowling, with *my* compliments, he is an impudent rascal, and that you are another."

"Thank ye kindly, sir. We are all that, as you say, and more besides, as you don't know on; but if it's the same to you, I'd rather you took the message and what follers, yourself."

Evidently I had fallen to a very low figure in *Scout* estimation; and as it did not seem likely I should gain much by a further interchange of compliments, I sprang out of the cot-hammock, and, changing the subject, asked where Mr. Harry Webbe might be.

"On deck, sir, now; but goin' ashore presently."

"Going on shore is he? And what shore, pray?"

"Jarscy, sir. The *Scout* has brought up in the roads till the tide serves to go into harbour."

"All right; and as you are going on deck, you can tell Mr. Webbe that I shall be with him in a brace of shakes."

I had escaped without a scar or scratch; and not only as regarded myself, but all things else, no sign or trace of the night's murderous hurly-burly was visible. The water was smooth as glass—so rapidly do the tides in the vicinity of the Channel Islands run down the wildest sea—a sun of spring was shining brightly through the cabin windows; and when I reached the deck, the aspect of "things in general" was so entirely the reverse of what it was a few hours previously, that I could almost have fancied I had been the dupe of a frightful dream.

The dead had been flung to the fishes, the wounded and prisoners were out of sight below, the deck had been swabbed and holy-stoned, damaged rigging set to rights, gay flags waved proudly overhead, and the victorious Scouts, dressed in their best, men as well as officers, were lounging about in high feather at their victory, and the substantial reward thereof to be derived from the sale of the splendid war-brig, with her guns, stores, &c., anchored a few fathoms off. Both vessels were lying at about the centre of St. Aubin's Bay, not far from Elizabeth Castle, a fort of some strength, connected with the mainland by a causeway dry at low-water, and at that time the only defence of St. Helier's port, Fort Regent having been only recently commenced. The island militia were exercising upon the sands of the bay, crowds of spectators thronged every point of vantage whence a view of the French man-of-war and her captor could be obtained, and, to cap the glorification of the exulting Scouts, the lieutenant-governor himself, accompanied by half-a-dozen officers in brilliant uniforms, came off in a boat to congratulate the conquerors, mere privateersmen though they were.

My appearance upon deck was nearly simultaneous with that of the major-general and suite. Mr. Dowling received his excellency with all imaginable deference, and after a few minutes' conversation, presented to him the "real hero" of the fight, "Mr. Harry Webbe, son of Captain Kirke Webbe, the genuine chip of the old block!"

Yes, and the handsome young charlatan accepted the major-general's compliments with a modest self-respecting dignity, enough to make one's hair stand on end at his consummate impudence. However, I choked off one of his prettily turned phrases by managing to catch his eye as it came trippingly from his tongue. He stopped suddenly, blushed brick-dust, and extended his hand with a sickly smile of friendly recognition.

Another of your brave youths?" said the general, with a condescending glance at my considerably savage self.

"O dear, no," replied Dowling. "Quite another sort of article. In fact," said he, "that young gentleman, Mr. William Linwood, is only a lodger upon principle when there's fighting to be done."

"Only a lodger upon principle," said the lieutenant-governor. "I do not comprehend the jest."

"I will explain it to your excellency," said Dowling; and proceeded to do so, much to the amusement of the general and his suite, as testified by the contemptuous smiles with which they honoured me, though I could not hear the *pro-tem.* skipper's words.

I was hot as flame, and should, I verily believe, have assaulted Dowling, had not Webbe caught me by the arm as I was about to march upon the mocking rascal, and begged me to favour him with a word or two below.

The young fellow's grasp and words checked the absurd impulse to which I was giving way; and a moment's reflection sufficing to shew me the folly of my anger, I answered:

"A dozen if you like—have with you."

"I hope," said he, as soon as we were alone, and he had secured the door—"I hope, Mr. Linwood, you do not repent of the magnanimity of your conduct in my behalf; you, that declared you did not esteem 'glory' at a straw's worth?"

"Magnanimity and glory be smothered in their own smoke! True, I volunteered, like a noodle that I was, to take your place with the boarders, little dreaming that I should thereby brand myself in the eyes of the world as an arrant coward? And then you come it so confoundedly strong before governors and generals, that—— In short, I find that I have made an enormous fool of myself—a discovery which, I need hardly say, is apt to preciously ryle a fellow's temper."

"Of what value would your chivalric generosity be to me, if I did *not* receive as of right the honour you have won?"

"Well, there is something in that, to be sure."

"The return you stipulated for shall be amply rendered. You are, I know, embarked in a nobler enterprise than ever cannon championed, or sword "——

"Bosh! humbug! You beat your father himself for fine phrases. Plainer words would more forcibly impress me:"

"Well, then, you are endeavouring to unravel and defeat a vile plot which touches not only *your* father's character, but his life."

"That is better. Yes."

"I have the power to greatly aid you in that enterprise; and if you remain faithful to your word in this 'glory' business, I *will* do so, *regardless of whomsoever I may offend.*"

"I accept that conditional promise, Mr. Harry Webbe, though I should have been better pleased if your eye, when making it, had more boldly met mine. That, how-

ever, may be congenital.—I have, however, very slight
confidence that such a white-livered fellow will keep faith
with me, now that his own turn is served," I added, but
not till Master Webbe had left the cabin.

I did not go on deck again till, the tide serving, the
Scout went into the harbour. *Le Renard,* in attempting to
do so, grounded between the pierheads, and had to be
lightened of her guns and stores before she could be
berthed. That night I slept, as did Webbe, at an inn or
hotel in the Royal Square, a locality which Copley's
painting of the death of Major Pierson must have made
familiar to many readers.

Harry Webbe left me soon after breakfast, for the confessed purpose of sunning his new, but far from " blushing "
honours in Miss Wilson's smiles. He had been gone some
three or four hours when a printed slip or proof of the
Gazette or *Chronique de Jersey*—I forget the exact title of
the only newspaper, I believe, then published in the
island—was sent up to Messieurs les Officiers du *Scout,*
with the editor's compliments, and a polite request that
the said messieurs would be pleased to correct any error
of fact that might have inadvertently slipped into the
flaming narrative, headed—"Combat Gloricux entre le
Scout, Lettre de Marque Anglaise, et *Le Renard,* Brick de
Guerre Français : Héroisme du Jeune Capitaine Anglais,
Henri Webbe."

Although not one of " Messieurs les Officiers du *Scout,*"
I took the liberty of running my eye over the proof, and
much amused was I at the editor's magniloquent exaggeration of the very modest facts, so far as I, *alias* Henri
Webbe, was concerned, till I came to the concluding paragraph—this :

"In signal contrast with the heroic conduct of M. Henri
Webbe, was the dastard behaviour of one William Linwood, who, excusing himself to M. Dowling, *second* of the
Scout, under the pleas, that he was only a passenger, and,
moreover, a coward upon principle *(un lâche par principe),*
when the action was about to commence, skulked off to
bed."

Pleasant reading, upon my word, I mentally ejaculated.
This precious paragraph—which will of course go the
round of the English papers—will give my relatives a de-

lightful notion of a fitness for a mission confided to **my**
courage ! Very true, unquestionably, that I had made a
stupendous ass of myself ; still, I must stop that game at
any hazard ; and I jumped up with the intention of
sallying forth to the printing-office, and thrashing the
publisher within an inch of his life. Fortunately, young
Webbe returned at the moment, in great elation of spirit
from his interview with the divine Maria. I shewed him
the offensive paragraph : he immediately volunteered to
prevent its publication, and went off at once for that
purpose. Whether or not he delivered the message I
charged him with—namely, that if the libel was published,
William Linwood would, upon principle, break every
bone in the editorial body, or what other persuasive he
had recourse to, I cannot say ; enough, that the paragraph
did not appear.

It greatly annoyed me, nevertheless, by shewing the
extent and working of the folly I had committed ; and a
haunting fear grew upon me that I should prove unequal
to the duty I had taken upon myself ; that I was too
volatile, glib, rash ! How could one who had been fooled
by a poor creature like Harry Webbe, hope to hold his
own with the astute conspirators I might have to cope
with ?

Then the non-arrival of Captain Webbe irritated me ;
and so especially did the growing coolness of his son. I
could scarcely obtain a minute's speech of the fellow, and
any hint of a wish to be introduced to Miss Wilson, sent
him off like a bullet from a gun. Did he, judging of me
by his own craven instincts, fear I should betray him to
her whose favour he had declared was his sole motive in
wishing to acquire, vicariously, a reputation for homicidal
heroism, to quote his own copper-gilt gibberish ? At all
events, see, converse with the young lady I would—dis-
please, anger, enrage him as my doing so might.

It was not difficult to gratify that whim. I obtained
her address of the waiter who posted his letters ; " Miss
Wilson, at Madame Dupré's, near the Third Tower."
Martello towers dot—one mile apart—the whole cir-
cumference of Jersey, and to the Third Tower was a
pleasant three-mile walk from St. Helier, on the road to
St. Aubin—a village near the further extremity of the **bay**

of that name. I could introduce myself as Webbe's friend; pretend that I expected to find him there—had called, in fact, by his invitation. He would never dare to challenge the deception.

So planned, so done. Watching an opportunity when Master Webbe was busily engaged on board the *Scout*, I hastened off in the direction of the Third Tower; and in something less than an hour, was quietly seated with Madame Dupré and Miss Wilson in the front parlour of the former's neat and pleasant domicile. My reception was a friendly one, and much abated the choler which raged in my breast against Harry Webbe, proving, as it did, that he must have spoken favourably of me to his charmer and her ancient companion, who, altogether unpractised in the conventional ways of what is understood by society, thought it the simplest thing in life that the acquaintance of their friend should introduce himself in the manner I had. Madame Dupré seemed to be a good-natured, lively, bustling body, notwithstanding her age, which could not be far short of seventy; uneducated, but speaking both French and English—the latter best—at least more intelligibly to me—the French of France, as taught me by Laborde, not enabling my unaccustomed ear to distinguish understandingly the French elements which no doubt exist in the island patois.

There was no need to inquire if such a skin-shrivelled, dumpy, bundle of a woman was a relative of the fair, elegant, beautiful Maria Wilson; a most fascinating person, though, as I soon discovered, of but ordinary attainments, and quite untaught in the accomplishments which are supposed essential to the perfect development of womanly grace and charm. No wonder that a fair, healthy complexion, luxuriant hair of a golden brown, blue eyes of unfathomable depth, a most delicate nose, sweet lovable lips, and a distracting figure, should have taken poor Webbe captive, or that he was jealous of permitting bachelor-eyes to look upon his precious treasure-trove.

It was not, however, the clear complexion, golden brown hair, blue eyes, delicate nose, lovable lips, and distracting figure, separately or combined, which, the instant I saw Maria Wilson, interested, fascinated me—an interest, fascination, distinct from love, or the drawing of that sentiment. I had been, young as I was, too frequently exposed to the influence of those charms—though never, perhaps, so harmoniously combined—to be in danger of sudden enslavement by such weapons. No; it was the peculiar *expression* of those deep blue eyes that enthralled me—the soul-shadow, as it were, which from one moment to another flitted over, and softened rather than dimmed the bright youthful face: a most peculiar sweetly-sad expression, which I was positive I had seen before, though where or when I vainly for hours, days, weeks, strove to recall, albeit as certain I had observed, *felt* it before, as of my own life !

An ethusiastic, romantic maiden too, as Harry Webbe had intimated: full to overflowing of that everlasting fight between the *Scout* and *Le Renard*, and could, or at least would talk of nothing else. I fancy the annoyance and vexation my countenance and manner must have expressed at hearing young Webbe's fabulous nothings so outrageously monstered, induced the gay-hearted girl—for gay-hearted she was, spite of the sunshine *broken* before spoken of—to prolong the entertainment for my especial behoof.

The ultimate effect was, however, widely different from what either of us contemplated. The avidity of the human heart for flattery, even in its best samples, is so subtle and eager, that it will detect and appropriate the intoxicating incense from the most apparently unpromising sources. Quite natural, therefore, that the young lady's fine reading of the narrative published in the Jersey paper, her vibrating voice and musical intonation giving to the bombastic rodomontade the sound of true eloquence, surprised, interested, flattered such a feather-headed youngster as I; that my imaginary plumes fluttered, dilated like a peacock's; for was it not really me—not Harry Webbe—she was glorifying so delightfully? Of course, I was quite conscious all the while that the repeated rallying by the young hero of the fainting Scouts, the cutting his way through Heaven knows how many Frenchmen, to get at that unfortunate Captain Le Moine, and end the desperate, doubtful contest by one stroke of his victorious sword was all bosh, humbug ! Still, what slight foundation there was for such a fantastic superstructure of lies, referred to me unquestionably : I felt, moreover, and an extraordinary elation of spirit accompanied the conviction, that the lady's regard was for the imaginary Webbe—not the real one—for me, in fact! So reconciled, consequently, did I become to Maria Wilson's warrior-enthusiasm, so swiftly did my impulsive temperament sympathise therewith, that, when suddenly passing from inflated puerility to lofty, masculine eloquence, she burst out with :

> Ye mariners of England
> Who guard our native seas,
> Whose flag has braved a thousand years
> The battle and the breeze ;
> Your glorious standard launch again,
> To match another foe—

I leaped at the last lines out of my chair, and with eyes filled with tears, fiercely flourished Madame Dupré's parlour-poker round my head, to that lady's wild alarm for her chimney glass and ornaments. So easily excitable is boyish enthusiasm by vanity, and a beautiful girl!

Madame Dupré repaid me for the fright with interest. "Pray, Mr. Linwood," said she, "do you know de name of de young man—what—my good—hid himself under de bed when de guns begun to fire?"

Was'nt I brought up with a round turn? Didn't my face burn like red-hot iron beneath Maria Wilson's searching, astonished look, called forth, no doubt, by my conscience-stricken aspect, as she must have interpreted it?

"I hear of him," continued the horrid old woman, "in St. Helier ; but not de name of de brave youth. Do you know it, sare?"

Before I could convert the choking rage in my throat to articulate sounds, there was a knock at the door.

"It is Harry!" exclaimed Maria Wilson, springing to the door and opening it. "Ha! you also, sir!" she added. "Do come in."

Not only young Harry, but *old* Harry was at the door ; Captain Kirke Webbe as well as his son! And what an astonished start—what a pallor of the young fellow's phiz —what a dark scowl upon the old one's, as they caught sight of me!

"You—you here, Linwood!" stammered Webbe the younger.

"How is this, sir?" ejaculated Webbe the elder, glancing fiercely at his son.

Only for a moment did Kirke Webbe's mask slip aside. "Why," he added, with a smile pretty nearly compelled to cordiality—"why need I ask? William Linwood must ever be a welcome guest with the friends of Harry Webbe?"

The two gentlemen then sat down, and Captain Webbe strove to bring about a natural, indifferent conversation. It could not be done: we were all dumbfounded—in some sort panic-stricken.

I, for one, by the discovery "that the penniless wench, Maria Wilson, or Bilson," Kirke Webbe had spoken of so contemptuously to me, was a young person well known to him, and evidently regarded with—what shall I say— affection, esteem? no, with respect, deference! Madame Dupré was also an old and intimate friend of his, there could be no doubt. What complicated knave's game was the man playing?

A question I had no time to pursue. Captain Webbe invited me to accompany him forthwith back to St. Helier; the arrangements he had made in the affair I knew of necessitating immediate action.

I acquiesced; bade adieu to the charming Maria, Madame Dupré, and Harry Webbe, and set forth with the captain of the *Scout*.

He was the first to break silence as we pushed on for St. Helier.

"You have acted nobly, Linwood," said he, "to my son, who has told me all. He knew it would be quite absurd to attempt to throw the dust in my eyes, which has, it seems, so completely blinded those who do not know him as well as I do. Well, it is a gift that makes him rich, and you none the poorer!"

"I am not so sure of that, Captain Webbe."

"*Tut, tut.* You will have abundant opportunities for establishing a reputation for courage, I promise you. The soft-hearted boy has set his soul upon espousing Maria Wilson "——

"Or Bilson," I interrupted.

"Ah, yes, I remember. Since, however, I saw you, I

have had a conversation with a relative of hers in London, which has altogether changed my opinion of the proposed match, and I feel obliged to you for enabling him to gain the lady's consent."

"Under a false pretence!"

"Yes; but that is nothing. He will make a kind husband; and the most romantic maidens, when transformed into practical wives, soon shake from their memories the sentimental cobwebs which enthralled their nonage. But you and I have more pressing matters to attend to. I leave you now by the First Tower, and Jersey *with* you, for St. Malo, if possible, if not, for Avranches or Granville, to-morrow evening."

"What is to prevent us from going direct to St. Malo?"

"Only His Britannic Majesty's sloop of war, *Pelican*, Captain Maples, which is, or was, cruising off that port. Here," added Webbe, "is my written address: 'Le Capitaine Verdun, chez M. Josse, Aubergiste, St. Catherine's Bay.' I shall expect you there to-morrow evening by five o'clock at latest."

I promised to be punctual; and we soon afterwards separated.

"Is Le Capitaine Verdun within?" I inquired, the next evening of a stout, well-dressed seaman, who was standing by the door of the public-house pointed out to me as that kept by Antoine Josse.

"Le voici—I am he," was the prompt reply.

"The deuce you are! Why, yes, that voice, and—— By Heaven, it *is* Webbe!"

The captain of the *Scout* laughed obstreperously. "Not an unskilful metamorphosis, eh?" he said. "This black wig, and dyeing my light whiskers of the same colour, make a strange difference in a man's appearance."

"That is true, indeed! This accounts, then, for the green tinge of your whiskers?"

"Yes, the colouring liquid leaves that tinge. Where are your things?"

I pointed to a laden porter at some distance off.

"All right. Tell him to bring them here. We are off in less than an hour."

"By what means," said I, upon rejoining Webbe, "do you propose getting to St. Malo? I can see the French coast plainly enough, but not the vessel that is to take us there."

"You soon shall. First, however, let me impress it upon your mind, that you are an American youth—a native, suppose we say, of Boston, United States. In that character, your atrocious French accent will cause no surprise. I—please never for one moment to forget—am Jules Renaudin, captain of the French corsair, *L'Espiègle*."

"What!" I exclaimed, "you, Captain Renaudin of *L'Espiègle?*"

"Just so; and if you take this glass, you will make out that gem of a cutter lying in the shadow of the French coast, in a line with those two sugar-loaf-shaped rocks. A boat you may also observe coming towards us, in obedience to the signal flying from my unsuspicious friend Josse's flagstaff."

I looked up to said flagstaff: two English jacks were flying, one on a blue, the other on a white ground.

"I was downright "mazed," as we used to say in the Wight, and for the first time a complete sense of the perilous nature of the adventure I was engaged in, of the desperate, lawless character of the man with whom I was associated, by whom I was to be guided through that adventure, flashed upon me!

It was too late, however, to retract—would be insanity to shew distrust, hesitation: the die was cast, and I must stand the hazard of the throw. The French boat reached the shore; our trifling luggage was thrown into it; Captain Jules Renaudin and I followed; and after a long, weary pull, we stood upon the deck of *L'Espiègle*, a cutter-rigged clipper, mounting four guns, and manned by as fierce a set of desperadoes, judging by their looks, as one would wish to set eyes upon; yet all, I saw in a moment, effectively curbed under the iron rule of Le Capitaine Renaudin!

The wind, though light, was fair for St. Malo; and *L'Espiègle* was quickly slipping through the water in that direction. "If this breeze last," remarked Captain Jules Renaudin to me, "we shall be in St. Malo by day-dawn, supposing always that the *Pelican* docs not snap us by the way."

CHAPTER VII.

AN UNEXPECTED GUEST.

WELL acquainted as I was with the French Language—my "atrocious accent" notwithstanding—I must confess to something of the same feeling, when I first set foot upon the deck of *L'Espiègle*, and heard Captain Renaudin give smartly executed orders in that tongue to his French crew, as the English seaman expressed when he declared that he could not for the life of him comprehend how the service could be carried on in a ship where they called the foremast a *mât d'avant*. I remarked upon the absurdity to Webbe.

"The feeling arises in part, I dare say," replied the privateer captain, "from the Englishman's instinctive belief that he is of legitimate right ruler of the seas, and, consequently, that it is a kind of impertinence for denizens on his domain to speak any other tongue than his."

"And to that instinctive belief, as you term it, must, I suppose, be also referred the surprise I have felt at noticing that the crew of *L'Espiègle* are, to all appearance, skilful and hardy sailors?"

"No doubt; since why a man born at Brest should not, other things being equal, prove as skilful and hardy as he who was born at Portsmouth, would puzzle one to explain. Other things, however, *not* being equal, as a rule, the seamen of France are not so hardy, so continuously hardy, as the British."

"Have the kindness to explain: I should like to have a reason for the faith that is in me."

"Willingly. If you or I were to take a heavy pick, shovel, and wheelbarrow, some fine hot day, and work with might and main in a stiff soil, at the foundation of a house, we should find it to be exhausting work, which only the most robust fellows could sustain with spirit for any length of time. Well, the rapid working of a frigate or liner's heavy guns in a close fight, where no particular aim need be taken, is harder, more exhausting labour than that ; and French, Italian, Austrian seamen are not, as races, physically equal to the work, *in* comparison with

F

Anglo-Saxon sailors. The fire of a French ship-of-war during the first ten minutes or quarter of an hour of a close rapid fight is frequently equal to that of a British ship-of-war: after that, although the foreigner's courage may be as untamed as ever, his muscles, as a general rule, begin to yield, his fire slackens, and the battle is lost. The same physiological fact governs in respect of stubborn holding out during long-continued stress of weather, or——Ha! I see her now. All right, so far."

To enable the reader to understand Captain Renaudin's abrupt break-off in his dissertation upon the comparative naval prowess of British and French seamen, it must be explained, that whilst he was delivering it, he had been anxiously peering through a night-glass at a distant speck upon the darkening horizon, which interested him much more than the topic he was carelessly discussing. A glint of moonlight had at last enabled him to decide that the said speck was *not* the *Pelican* sloop of war.

"The capture, not many months since, of the American brig-of-war, *Argus*, by that same *Pelican*," I remarked, after a while, "was a gallant exploit, was it not?"

"Well, yes; but the *Argus* was overmatched, though nothing like so hopelessly as the *Macedonian* in her action with the *United States*, which Yankees prance and crow so much about. Captain Carden was a brother-mid of mine, and I would have backed him with an equal force against all the Decaturs in creation. I might as well," added Webbe with unusual heat—"I might as well snatch up a belaying-pin, floor yonder little *mousse*, and then trumpet like a great elephant of my glorious victory! But enough of this. Had you not better, Mr. Linwood, go below? The air is chilly now, and will be many degrees colder before we again behold the sun."

"Do you remain on deck?"

"Ay, young man, till *L'Espiègle* is safely moored in French waters, or sunk five fathoms deep—which is considerably under the average, by the by, at any distance seaward off this coast—in those of the Channel. The rocks of Choisy, certainly, and the *Pelican*, possibly, lie in wait for us amidst the darkness ahead—two considerations that would 'murder sleep' as effectually as ever Macbeth did; the Capitaine Jules Renaudin's sleep, that is. Mr. William Linwood, of Boston, United States, may slumber as serenely as at Oak Villa—— Nay, never shake your raven locks at me! We shall weather Cape Danger, do not fear, threateningly as it may seem just now to loom upon us through the mirk night. Baptiste," he added in French, "conduct monsieur below, and see him properly accommodated."

Capitaine Jules Renaudin was right: the cold was becoming intense : and along the French shore a thick fog was rising, which would extinguish, so far as *L'Espiègle* was concerned, the dull lights that in those days doubtfully beaconed the vessel's sinuous course along a rockstrewn coast, which the fear of hostile cruisers compelled her to hug with perilous proximity. It was the rising fog, far more than the *Pelican*, that excited the fears of the commander of the French privateer ; and with good reason, I was seaman enough to understand, without the help of Baptiste's prolix verbal chart of the sands, shoals, rocks through which, in avoidance of that *maudit* corsair Anglais, *L'Espiègle* would have to feel her dubious way. There, however, being an equally dismal certainty that I could do nothing to help myself or the cutter, by remaining hungry and awake, I resigned myself to the excellent viands, wines, and liqueurs set before me by Baptiste, and with such tranquillising success, that when I turned in for the night, the fog, shoals, rocks, and Britannic majesty's cruiser had lost, for me, nearly all their terrors.

I had risen and dressed myself the next morning at a little after eight o'clock, as marked by my watch, albeit it seemed to be pretty nearly as dark as when I lay down in the hammock. We were, I found, becalmed in a dense fog, and had anchored to avoid being drifted upon a shoal or rock by the strong and seemingly capricious currents which prevail upon that rugged coast.

There was no danger, that I could imagine, to be apprehended, and yet a feeling of great uneasiness seemed to pervade the crew of *L'Espiègle;* the officers were conversing in low tones with each other, peering into the murky air seaward with their glasses, and from time to time anxiously consulting the countenance of Captain Renaudin, as if there would be read the earliest confirmation of their hopes or fears, whatever those hopes or fears related to. The captain himself was standing upon the starboard bulwarks, supporting himself by the rattlings, and looking forth seaward in one particular direction with unswerving earnestness.

He was, I saw, in no mood for answering idle questions, and I forbore to ask any; but I was afterwards informed that the *Pelican* had, it was known, sighted the *L'Espiègle* just before the fog reached and shrouded her. The wind immediately afterwards died completely away, so that there was no doubt the British cruiser was aware of the exact whereabout of *L'Espiègle*. I observed, moreover, that the men had pistols in their waist-belts, that arms of other kinds had been brought upon deck, and ranged conveniently at hand, and the two starboard guns cast loose and loaded.

"The fog, messieurs," exclaimed the captain, when I had been on deck some half-hour, perhaps—"the fog, messieurs, is, as you perceive, lightening fast; in a few minutes, it will have entirely cleared away, and if——Thunder of heaven! yonder they come! *Alerte!*" he shouted, jumping upon the deck; "be ready with the boarding-nets, and see that your arms are in working order. The wind, Bourdon," he added, addressing an officer, "will probably be here as soon, or sooner, than they; you had better, therefore, place at once two men in the bows with sharp axes, to cut away the cable at a sign from me."

The fog was indeed fast passing away; the sun, which in aspect like a red-hot cannon ball, had been dimly glaring through it, swiftly assumed his ordinary splendour, and with well-nigh the rapidity of a *coup de théâtre*, the dull, murky scene in which only ourselves and *L'Espèigle* had been visible, changed to a bright sky overhead, a clear blue sea around, with four large boats filled with seamen and marines—the red jackets and bayonets of the latter glancing brightly in the sunshine—pulling lustily towards us; but still, I judged, a good mile off; and in the yet much further distance, the British sloop-of-war, *Pelican!*

There being no further necessity for caution or concealment, the boats' crews gave a defiant cheer, and pulled with renewed vigour, in the hope of reaching us before the also rapidly approaching line of ruffled water, marking the progress of the breeze which they were, so to speak, bringing with them.

"Captain Renaudin," said I, speaking of course in English, which, fortunately, no one on board but us understood a word of—"Captain Renaudin, you will please to understand that I shall not fight against my own countrymen. You have led me into a terrible "——

"Bah! bah!" he interrupted, "we shall manage to do without your valiancy's help, I dare say. To tell you the truth," he added, in a calmer tone, whilst still intently watching the race, so to speak, between the boats and the breeze—"to tell you the truth, I would rather not myself; but self-preservation is the first law of nature. Have the men ready in the bows," he shouted, "to cut away when I lift my hand. Bourdon," he added, "place the best men by the sails, so that they draw without the waste of one precious moment; and take the wheel yourself. The guns I take charge of."

I leaned against the capstan in a state of indescribable agitation. The full magnitude, to myself and those dear to me, of the stake involved in the struggle about to take place, seemed for the first time to flash upon my startled senses. Should the boats—should the *Pelican's* launch, which greatly headed the others, reach us before *L'Espiègle* had got well under-way, there could be no hope, however brave the resistance offered, that the French privateer would get away before the remaining boats came up and rendered further resistance hopeless—useless. In case of capture, my own position would, to say the least, be a very unpleasant, if not dangerous one ; whilst as to Webbe, supposing him to be identified—and if sent to Portsmouth, he was sure to be identified—his doom would unquestionably be an hour's dangle at the yard arm; and with his life would pass away, I feared, all hope of accomplishing the purpose, to attain which, I had tempted these desperate hazards.

And those fearful issues would be substantially decided in ten minutes—in less, much less; the launch was now not two hundred yards distant, and the stout oars bent with the force of the rowers' efforts to reach us in time. Meanwhile, Webbe—fiercely pale, as it were—resolved, yet regretful ; for although he made no scruple of plundering his countrymen, he had a deep repugnance to firing upon, slaying them—had trailed one of the double-shotted guns— no grape or cannister had been used ; Webbe's aim being to smash the boat, if possible, not kill or wound the men —to bear upon the launch, but hesitated to discharge it till there was no other chance left him but to do so. Another motive might be, that it was, above all, necessary to make sure that the shot would *tell*.

Well, the launch was, I say, within two hundred yards of us when the first puff of the coming breeze fluttered the dangling sails, and *L'Espiègle* heeled slightly over to leeward.

" Cut away the cable! " shouted the captain, without for an instant taking his eye off the advancing boat. "Bourdon, be prompt, and, above all, calm ! "

The cable, severed by a few sharp strokes of the axe, flew through the hawse-hole ; the cutter's bows fell off; a second and more powerful puff of wind filled the sails; in another minute they would draw ; in four, or five, no boat could overhaul us. Would those precious minutes be vouchsafed?

I could hardly hope so. Excited, as it seemed, by the possible escape of the anticipated prize, the marines in the stern of the launch jumped up to fire; a movement that disturbed the equilibrium of the boat, and which I could hear the naval officer in command rebuke with a curse. Down dropped the jollies without firing, and in response to the sea-officer's stimulating appeal, the launch was made to fairly leap out of the water—so to speak—towards *L'Espiègle*.

A successful cannon-shot alone could save us. Webbe, seeing it to be so, fired. Almost simultaneous with the flash and roar of the gun, was his triumphant shout. The bow of the boat had been completely smashed, and many of her crew were splashing and sputtering about in the water ; only one, as we afterwards knew, being wounded, and that not dangerously.

A yell of delight arose from *L'Espiègle*, which drew forth a volley from the marines in the other boats—too distant to be effective. By that time, the French privateer was well under-way, and running with a fine breeze for Avranches. The depth of water, and intricacy of the navigation, forbade pursuit by the British cruiser ; and in less than two hours, *L'Espiègle* dropped anchor abreast of Mont St. Michel, of iron-cage celebrity. Quits, once more, for the fright !

Captain Jules Renaudin seemed to have a numerous acquaintance in Avranches; and this last exploit, which was nothing less, it soon appeared, than beating off a heavy British frigate with *L'Espiègle* of four guns, rendered him quite the lion of the ancient town. Avranches is built upon a hill at the mouth of the river Sée, and was formerly, I dare say, a place of importance. There was a curious old cathedral there, and other relics of bygone glories; but in 1814, the aspect of the town was drear and desolate in the extreme. The pulse of the national life of France did not beat high at that time; and in Avranches, as elsewhere, the emperor's reverses— the invasion by the allies of the "sacred soil"—were the sad themes of every conversation. Ay, and people were whispering with white lips and flashing eyes, that the insolent invaders were actually marching upon Paris!

Anything, therefore, however insignificant in itself, which tended to revive the preposterous prestige of French invincibility, and especially a success upon the sea, was hailed with an almost childish delight. So, Captain Jules Renaudin, and a judicious selection from the *équipage* of *L'Espiègle*, were invited to a banquet—" Monsieur le jeune Americain " having the honour to be included in the list of guests.

We were to have set out by diligence for St. Malo on the same day this patriotic festival was improvised, but Webbe determining, for reasons of his own, to accept the proffered honour, I had of course no choice but to acquiesce.

In sooth, I was rather pleased—young-man-like—I remember, with the idea of the entertainment, and especially of the ball which was to follow.

The preparations for the simple fête amused, interested me. It was to be held in a large granary, contiguous to *L'Hôtel Impérial*, which was cleared out for the occasion, decorated with evergreens and gay flags; and to be illumined, for that night only, by an enormous central chandelier, composed of three immense wooden hoops, slung one above another, and stuck full of tin candlesconces—the shabbiness of material being concealed by pink calico roses, variegated wreaths, rosettes, and so on. Four layers of loose boards, forming distinct tables, each the length of the granary, with deal forms on each side, would afford ample eating-room for the two hundred expected *convives;* and our preparations were complete, in time, and barely so. Our entertainers were not rich—by no means the *élite* of the place; but their good-will was of the heartiest; and the respectability, as well as legality of the banquet, was assured by the consent of M. le Maire to preside.

The days of omens, portents, had passed away, or I was too insignificant an individual to excite the intervention of the personages who are supposed to manage such things, for I certainly do not remember to have felt the slightest presentiment of what was impending over me. On the contrary, I was in unusual spirits, helped the men to tack on the candle-sconces, to rig the rope-machinery which held the enormous chandelier in trembling suspense over our heads, and the maidens to cut the roses, and twist the wreaths. In short, I made myself generally useful, and, I was even assured, agreeable, to the modest degree, of course, only which any one having the misfortune not to be born a Frenchman could hope to attain.

It seems now natural enough to think and write of the events of those days in a cheerful spirit. I live — have therefore survived the dangers which beset, encompassed me, and the darkest passages of my experience are illumined by remembrance of the signal mercies which preserved me through them. At the time, they were, Heaven knows, no subject for jest or mirth; and it, moreover, may be as well in this place, and once for all, to state, in order to keep well with the reader, that although I did not affect the solemn, grandissimo airs of "our hero" of romantic fables, nor stalk gloomily about amongst everyday people as if I was constantly before the lights in the principal part of a five-act tragedy, I nevertheless had ever before my eyes—ay, and there was ever beating at my heart and throbbing in my brain, a deep sense of the high filial trust confided to me, and an unswerving resolution to do or die in its fulfilment.

The banquet is prepared—served; the table is full. M. le Maire presides, supported on one side by Captain Jules Renaudin; on the other, by a gray-headed French officer *en retraite,* upon whose breast glitters the cross of the

Legion of Honour. I am seated amongst the common file at about the centre of the room, and all for a time goes merry as a marriage-bell—for a long time, to every one but myself, and it should seem a young man in the dress of a French naval *enseigne*, seated at the furthest side of the furthest table from, but directly opposite to me. His dark expressive countenance bears traces of recent suffering; but why on earth does he suddenly stop eating and gaze so fixedly at me! I have never seen him before, and shall not greatly care if I never do again. Bah! I will attend to my *poulet*, regardless of the fellow's persistent rudeness. I cannot, however, help glancing round just to—— Confound him; he is still sternly, fiercely glaring at me, Banquo-like, from amidst the busy, unnoticing guests! It is extremely annoying. Were it a young lady that appeared to be so suddenly taken with my handsome phiz, it would be another thing. Bah! I repeat to myself again; it is nothing to me; let him stare as much as he likes—I shall eat my dinner.

But I cannot eat my dinner; the fellow has filched away my appetite; and I am well pleased when the tables are cleared, the chandelier lit up, and the speeches begin—I shall the sooner be able to get away.

M. le Maire proposes Sa Majesté l'Empereur : received with enthusiasm of course. I sit down, after assisting to swell the applause, and almost leap again to my feet with uncontrollable surprise—panic rather! The naval enseigne has shifted his place—come near to me by one table, for a closer view, no doubt, and continues to stare fixedly at me with those dark gleaming eyes of his!

I am recalled to myself by M. le Maire, who, having proposed "the United States, and may the alliance of the French and American eagles be perpetual," requests their youthful and distinguished American guest to respond.

I rise for that purpose, amidst the acclamations of the company, and as I do so, a smile of exultant scorn, of deadly hate, kindles the pale face of my persecutor. Under such circumstances, and considering, moreover, that I do not care one straw for the two eagles, it is no wonder I blunder between them, make a very ridiculous figure of myself, and then drop down in my seat as hot, nervous, and uncomfortable as I have ever felt in my life.

"Captain Renaudin et l'équipage de *L'Espiègle*," is received with vociferous applause, and is replied to by Webbe in, I have no doubt, a most audacious speech, that I do not hear; at least it does not touch my mind, which is now fully pre-occupied by the naval enseigne, in whom I can no longer conceal from myself I confront a vengeful foe, whose spring at my throat will not be long delayed! I am right! Directly Renaudin sits down the young enseigne rises, and calmly claims M. le Maire's attention for a few words. It is granted instantly. " Silence pour Monsieur Auguste Le Moine!" exclaims this functionary, echoed by two hundred respectful voices—" Silence pour Monsieur Auguste Le Moine."

Silence for Monsieur Auguste Le Moine! The name strikes my ear like a knell; and I divine what is coming. I glance towards Captain Webbe, who, I see, has already left his place, and is pushing towards the centre of the apartment.

" Monsieur le Maire et Messieurs," begins the young enseigne, " the reverses that for a time have dimmed the glory of the French arms have to-night been spoken of with mournful freedom. You have heard of the coalition that has been formed for the humiliation of France; of the possible triumph of the multitudinous hosts whose presence already profanes our glorious, sacred soil. But, messieurs, permit me to remind you that it is not in the open field—the field of honour—our enemies gain their most fatal victories. (Bravo.) England, especially, perfidious England employs against us with more effect than she does her soldiers, or even her seaman—of whom I always wish to speak with the respect due to gallant men —England, I say, employs against us the more effective agencies of her gold—her manifold corruptions—her purchased traitors! (Bravos prolongés.) Yes, and to carry out her pitiless policy of corruption, she does not shrink from suborning to it, the courage, the audacity of her own bravest sons, whom she sends into our very midst in the character of friends—of *Americans*—to spy out where we are strong, and where we are weak; where her blows may be struck with least danger, with most advantage to herself! Of this world-known truth, messieurs, I will give you a new example—furnish you with a modern illustration. Listen!

"Many of you are aware that but a few days ago I was a prisoner of war to the English—that I have escaped from the island of Jersey by an almost miraculous chance. The fight, messieurs, wherein I was wounded and made captive, was that in which my uncle, Captain Le Moine, lost his life. With the chivalrous feeling that ever distinguished him, the commander of *Le Renard* disdained to avail himself of the means of facile victory which the superiority of his armament afforded, and risked all upon the chances of a hand-to-hand combat upon the deck—of a night-combat wherein skill is of slight avail against brute-strength. He has paid for that grave error with his life. Peace to his ashes; honour to his memory!"

"Peace to his ashes; honour to his memory!" echo numerous voices as the young enseigne pauses, overcome by emotion.

"I have but a few words more to say, messieurs. One of the most active of our foes during that terrible contest was a young man, the son, I have been told, of the captain of the English ship. My uncle attacked him, but his arm no longer possessed the vigour of his younger days, and after a few passes, the sword of the young Englishman terminated that precious life—a life devoted to the honour and glory of France! The night was dark," continues Auguste Le Moine, with gathering vehemence, "but at the moment my uncle fell, a gleam of moonlight shone upon the scene, and I clearly marked the features of his slayer. Shall I point him out to you!"

"Where? Who? Tell us!" shouted, screamed a hundred voices.

"Why, who but he who, in the guise of a friendly guest, has taken his seat at this banquet!—who but this pretended American, and really the English slayer of Captain Le Moine!"

A burst of incoherent rage echoed those words. I was seized by vengeful, merciless hands, and should, I doubt not, have been torn asunder, or trampled to death, when, just as all chance, all hope was gone, down came the enormous chandelier upon the heads of the raging crowd —knocking me and a score of others off our legs, and plunging the entire assembly in darkness and confusion.

I was lifted to my feet by the strong grasp of Captain

Webbe, and with the help of one of his sailors, hoisted out of the granary window.

" Off, and swiftly," he whispered, " to the *Lion d'Or;* I will soon be with you."

He had cut, in the very nick of time, the rope by which the chandelier was suspended, and with the help of his sailors, trampled out, as it by accident, the candles that remained alight after its fall.

CHAPTER VIII.

LE BOTTIER DE PARIS.

I HAD been rather stunned than terrified by the calculated malignity of Auguste Le Moine during its elaborate enunciation. The stupid, stereotyped abuse of England— that common staple of continental scribes and spouters effectually muzzled in respect of their own rulers—together with the absurd imputations upon myself, added a feeling of disdain to the astonishment which held me dumb; and even when seized by the rude hands of convivial guests, suddenly transformed by his artful appeal, and the wine they had swallowed into sanguinary ruffians, I did not realise to its full extent the perilous predicament in which I was placed : very likely, a partly unconscious, and, so to speak, instinctive reliance for effective succour from Webbe, gave me hope and courage. I had seen him leave his place by M. le Maire, and push towards the centre of the room, and although my fascinated gaze, fixed upon the naval enseigne, had not followed his movements, an impression of his near presence and active resolute solicitude must, I doubt not, have remained upon my mind. Webbe was one of those men that, in situations of sudden danger, assume an irresistible ascendency over others, less, perhaps, by their natural force of character and acquired coolness of demeanour, than by an always more or less empirical assumption of unswerving confidence in their own genius or fortune, backed by the reality or reputation of past successes. It was that aspect of imperturbable superiority that I had seen impose upon the crew of *L'Espiègle*, who had confidence in their commander, though none in themselves apart from him. It is not, therefore, surprising that it unconsciously influenced and sustained me during Auguste Le Moine's denunciation of the English spy, and slayer of *Le Renard's* unfortunate commander, and the brief, but terrible scene which followed.

Such a superstition could not for a moment support the calm scrutiny of reason; and during the hour or thereabout which elapsed between my breathless arrival at the Lion d'Or, and Captain Renaudin's appearance there, the folly of relying upon him to effectually shield me from the frightful penalty attached by the law of nations to the crime which, it would appear from young Le Moine's speech I had unwittingly committed, was painfully clear to my mind.

Webbe himself was excited—alarmed! He had succeeded in temporarily allaying the storm by solemnly asserting that Auguste Le Moine must have been misled by the casual view he obtained of my features during a passing gleam of moonlight; that I was really the American he, Renaudin, had represented me to be, or he had himself been grossly deceived.

" I have promised to produce you before justice," added Webbe, "should there be a necessity for doing so ; I, of course, remaining sole judge of that necessity—a mental reservation which will, it may be hoped, save you from walking in your own funeral procession, preparatory ⋅ to the unpleasantness of serving as target to a platoon of French tirailleurs."

" You talk jauntily, Mr. Webbe, of a catastrophe more imminent than you care to admit, and to which your counsel has conducted me."

" You do me gross injustice, young sir! Could I foresee the fight off Sercq—your bellicose Quixotism—the escape of Le Moine from Jersey—his presence at the banquet to-day, and recognition of the *Scout* hero amongst the guests? It is, at all events, idle to bandy reproaches or complaints. What is done, is done. The future, not the past, demands teasrnest and careful consideration. I fear we have not seen the last of Auguste Le Moine."

"My own fear! Strange, too, that he should recognise a face which no one but himself could have seen distinctly. It would almost seem to be the work of an avenging Nemesis."

"To Old Nick with Nemesis! There is nothing strange about it. Young Le Moine was wounded and lying upon the deck close by where his uncle fell; and his up-look would have a better view of your features than if he had been standing by your side. Moreover, you were recognised by more than one of the *Scout's* crew, who, from regard from me, they say, reinforced by a weightier consideration supplied by my son, agreed to keep the secret. They have done so, after a fashion, every man and boy belonging to the brig, being, I have no doubt, by this time in full posession of the fact—as a profound secret. Little, however, will Harry reck of that so long as he continues to shine a bright particular star in Maria Wilson's eyes. But this is foolish dallying with precious moments," added Webbe. "We have not, I repeat, seen the last of Auguste Le Moine, unless we can manage to throw him out of the hunt, and that, stanch blood-hound as he seems to be, will not, I think, be so difficult. *L'Espiègle* sails to-night at about twelve o'clock : she will creep round the French coast towards Havre de Grace, and you and I embark in her."

"Havre de Grace!" I exclaimed with emotion ; "then I shall soon see my mother—father."

"Not *soon*, Master Linwood. It is not impulsive, inconstant effort, but firm, patient endurance of the bloody spur, that will enable you to win the goal. When you embrace your mother, it must be with her husband's lost character, his renewed life in your hand. You should not wish it to be earlier."

"You touch the right chord with a skilful finger, Captain Webbe. What, then, do you mean by embarking for Havre de Grace ?"

"I mean that *L'Espiègle* will sail ostensibly for that port. You and I shall be put on shore to-night near Granville, whence we shall leave by diligence for St. Malo. Le Moine will be off at once, there can be no doubt, across country for Havre de Grace, where he will arrive much earlier than *L'Espiègle* possibly could, even supposing she did not, as she certainly will, put in at Cherbourg. By the time Le Moine has been able to ascertain, and act upon that fact, *L'Espiegle* will have again spread her white bosom to the gale ; whither to wing her flight, upon what particular errand bound, will depend upon the providence that shapes the ends of privateers—the chance, namely, of a good prize. Meanwhile, William Linwood, seizing Time by the only lock that swiftly speeding potentate is said to wear, will have seen sweet Clémence de Bonneville—ascertained beyond question that she is truly the lost child of Mrs. Waller—have reciprocated sympathies, confidences, sighs, wishes, hopes, vows with that most charming of damsels, and, aided by the bold privateer, have flown with her, and the blessings to you and yours, which make up her priceless dowry, to England, whence a bird of the air shall carry the tidings to the pining yet hopeful souls prisoned in France—hopeful because confident in the devotion of their son!"

"One word, Captain Webbe, if you please. You know that quince is a great improvement to apple-pie ; but that apple-pie *all* quince is "——

"A different thing altogether," interrupted Webbe, with a gay laugh. "True, true! The illustration is only less pertinent than venerable. In plain phrase, then, I believe that by the course I have indicated, we shall successfully dodge friend Le Moine till our little affair is concluded, adversely or happily, as fortune may determine ; and your suspicious interesting self is safely restored to Great Britain and your grandmother.—Ah, friend Cocquard!" he added quickly, "you bring a message for me."

"It is true, Monsieur le Capitaine," replied the landlord of the Lion d'Or ; and one that presses. "I am enjoined to say that Monsieur Le Moine, who made so deplorable a mistake at the banquet, has ridden off on horseback, to invoke the aid of the military commandant. Fortunately," added Cocquard, "the commandant's domicile is full two leagues distant from Avranches ; and Auguste Le Moine, it has been ascertained, did not finally determine upon seeking his intervention till about ten minutes since."

"Thank you, my friend. Two leagues! He will not do that in much less than an hour ; and should he find the commandant at home, another must elapse before they are here. Bah! it is nothing, after all. Plenty of time yet, friend Cocquard, to take a bottle of your best wine, and settle your little account, both of which you will please to favour us with immediately."

"With pleasure, Captain Renaudin."

"It will be touch and go," said Webbe, after the door had closed upon the complacent landlord: "I am used to this sort of thing; yet I could have wished that——

> Vi-ve le vin,
> Vi-ve ce ju divin,"

he added, breaking into the refrain of a drinking song, as Cocquard reappeared with the wine. "Do you know, friend Cocquard"—for whom he poured out a bumper—"do you know, friend Cocquard," continued the privateer captain, "that I consider it a bad compliment on the part of Enseigne Le Moine to doubt the word of a man who, as you know, Admiral Ducos testified, has deserved well of France."

"Parbleu, Monsieur le Capitaine—— Your health, messieurs. Parbleu, that it is a bad compliment! But what can one expect of a young giddy-brain without a sou except his pay! He is, besides, a Bonapartist *enragé*, which, between ourselves, will not, in a few weeks more or less, be a title of honour. I must, however, hasten to furnish monsieur with the little memorandum he has asked for."

"There is no instinct finer than that," laughingly exclaimed Webbe, "which prompts rats to quit a doomed ship. Bonaparte is done for, you may be sure! Seriously," he added, "there is no doubt whatever that that stupendous downcome cannot be long delayed. Well, the foundering of the empire will, I hope, afford me a plank of safety; to you, also, it may prove of service."

"For Heaven's sake, in what way?"

"Why, of course, by ridding you of Le Moine's persecution; if it should happen that he has not caught and settled you by court-martial before then! The "Restoration" will not shoot English spies, employed to act against the Usurper, as I find many persons are already beginning to call Napoleon, though as yet under their breath."

"Is it not folly, then, rather than wise resolution based upon mature counsel, to proceed to St. Malo, before that now imminent Restoration is an accomplished fact?"

"Clémence, meanwhile being married to Jaques Sicard, and all hope, consequently, of winning over that ingenuous damsel to our side, passed away for ever! I think I told you before that the nearness of the event which will open France to the English is a chief element in Louise Féron's calculation.—Ah, here is the little memorandum: good! Take another glass, friend Cocquard, whilst my young friend and I disburse the amount."

"Much obliged, messieurs," said friend Cocquard, as he gathered up the money, which, having pouched, he added: "If I might presume to advise Captain Jules Renaudin, I should say no time ought to be lost in gaining the shelter of *L'Espiègle*. Revenge, whether for real or fancied injuries, is swift of foot."

"Quite true, my friend. But revenge, take my word for it, will not be swift of foot enough this time, to put salt upon our tails. I expect Baptiste to call about this time," added Webbe; "the instant he does so, please send him to me."

Cocquard said he would, took affectionate leave of Captain Renaudin, and left the apartment.

"That is a deuced queer way for a landlord to take leave of a guest!" I remarked.

"Yes, especially to our insular notions. Cocquard, you must understand, has, like Monsieur le Maire, a share in *L'Espiègle*. We are therefore united in much stricter bonds than the embrace which so surprised you. Your portmanteau," continued Webbe, looking at his watch, "is, I know, in readiness. Swiftly the moments pass. It is now just upon half-past eleven, and Le Moine, accompanied, I have no doubt, by the commandant—that worthy soldier being anything but a friend of mine—must be now about upon his return. Baptiste will, however be here in a very few minutes."

"But why incur unnecessary risk by remaining here an instant longer?"

"I remain here so long, simply because I would not incur unnecessary risk. You do not, I hope, Linwood deem me such a fool as to court danger for the mere purpose of braving it! I wish to give time for the streets to clear of the excited banquet-guests and their friends, who, when I came in, were discussing the for and against of Le Moine's accusation, in numerous groups, and with a decided leaning, I could hear plainly enough, to believe him rather than me. Numbers give confidence; and spite of Captain Jules Renaudin's reputation for daring, and a general belief that the crew of *L'Espiègle* would back him in anything, they might, had we attempted to walk down the street towards the landing-place, even half an hour ago, have made an effort to arrest us—you, certainly. La Grande Rue," added Webbe, after an anxious look out of window, "is much clearer, but even now—— Ah, Baptiste, you are here at last, then!"

"To the exact moment, Captain Renaudin; it is precisely half-past eleven."

"It is very well. Are the boat's crew placed as I directed?"

"Yes; but if I might take the liberty of offering an opinion, it would be prudent to gain the landing-steps by the narrow street to which we may pass from the back of the Lion d'Or."

"Bah! Why, that is the way to the Corps de Garde!"

"Pardonnez. The way to the Corps de Garde is along La Grande Rue."

"That is your opinion, Baptiste; but on a moonlit night like this, I see further and more clearly than you do. Now, then, take the portmanteau Monsieur Cocquard will give you, and walk with it openly, deliberately, *le front levé*, down that same Grande Rue. We shall follow close behind."

"Linwood," said Webbe, "do as I do: take a cigar, and smoke it as we walk along. We must shew no sign of fear or hesitation: to do so would be as fatal as following Baptiste's advice, which would have insured our immediate arrest. A bold, confident front will be our best safeguard. In case of the worst, we must, with the aid of a score of my brave Espiègles, who have been carefully distributed to that end, fight our way to the boat as we best may. Come along!"

Courage begets courage, and I walked down the steep,

ill-paved street, and past groups of sullen, observant men —awaiting, it seemed, the return of Le Moine with the commandant—whose scowling visages were distinctly visible in the cold, bright moonlight, with more of real, as well as simulated coolness than I had hoped for. The assumption of easy, careless confidence by Webbe was consummate, as acting, and, it was plain, imposed much more upon the suspicious, menacing, but irresolute lookers-on, than his sailors, who, scattered here and there, picked each other up, as it were, as we passed along, and without apparent purpose, formed at last a respectable flank-guard.

Nevertheless, the bayonets of the Corps de Garde, past which lay our way, though we were on the opposite side of the street, disquieted, I could perceive, even Webbe, and, to my utter astonishment, he coolly crossed over, taking me with him, shook hands with the officer there, and having ascertained that he had no commands for Havre de Grace, bade him a friendly farewell, and we went on our way slowly, deliberately, as before.

For a while, that is to say, for I cannot deny that our pace was perceptibly accelerated as we neared the boat, and became conscious, without looking back, that the crowd was gathering thickly behind, and beginning to lash themselves into action by cries of *" Traitre !" " Espion!" " Chien d'Anglais !"* and the like holiday and lady terms.

The head of the narrow landing-steps being at last reached, Webbe faced abruptly about, confronting, and for a moment silencing the angry crowd, passing me at the same instant down the steps. The boat's crew quickly followed, then Webbe suddenly turned, and scarcely touching the steps, it seemed, sprang into the boat, which as instantly shoved off, amidst a roar of rage from the mob, who appeared to have, at one and the same moment, arrived at a conviction that it was their right and duty to arrest the supposed spy and traitor, and of the impossibility of doing so.

With what a tumultuous throb the checked, fluttering pulse renewed its beatings as the consciousness of safety rushed, as in a flood of glowing rapture, through every artery and vein ! That safety was absolute. The commandant, with 20,000 men, could not have stayed the progress of our boat towards *L'Espiègle*, and the fine breeze blowing would carry that vessel herself in less than half an hour beyond range of the best telescope in Avranches!

"That walk, Linwood," remarked Webbe, coming aft, and taking charge of the tiller, "was more trying to the nerves than a battle."

"Much more so, as far as my slight experience of battle goes. One fear troubled me," I added, "which you do not appear to have entertained. It was, that your French crew might not have been to be depended upon, in such a case, to act against Frenchmen."

"Fiddlestick! My gallant Espiègles are cosmopolites, whose *patrie* is the whole earth, with especial regard, however, to that portion thereof likely to furnish them with the most comfortable berths. An expansive idea, that, don't you think?"

"Expansive humbug, you mean!"

"No I don't. You may not have a soul above bunting, but those fellows have. Above consideration, I mean, of the mode in which blue, white, and red, or any other coloured bunting, may be arranged; whether diagonally, as in St. George's cross, or in three perpendicular strips, as in the tricolor. I have before observed, Linwood, that you are a person of limited geographical ideas."

"Stuff! Rubbish! At all events, you yourself must be a person of very limited geographical ideas, or you would not the other day have so long hesitated at firing upon St. George's ensign, as to place your own life in peril!"

"Weakness, my young friend—human weakness! He is a good divine, remarks the lady in the play, who follows his own teaching. Most extraordinarily good I should say, an example of the kind never having come under my observation. By the by, Linwood," added Webbe, "I will tell you, some of these days, when we have a leisure half-hour to ourselves, how it happened that I became Captain Jules Renaudin: you will find that, strictly speaking, I had no choice but to exchange for that name the one in which my godfathers and godmothers, simple souls! promised and vowed I should renounce the devil and all his works—— Peak oars! The boat has way enough!"

In two minutes, we were upon the deck of *L'Espiègle;*

and three hours afterwards, I, Captain Renaudin, and Baptiste had been landed upon the French coast above half a league eastward of Granville, and but a short distance from a cottage in which, when at home, Baptiste lived with his wife, a sharp, black-eyed Granvillaise.

Before leaving by diligence on the third day from our landing, I was metamorphosed into Jean Le Gros, a French youth, of Gravelines in the Pas de Calais, travelling with his uncle, Jacques Le Gros, also of Gravelines, upon affairs of business. Webbe, who had wonderful talent in such matters, pronounced the transformation to be complete; and positively, when I at last obtained a full view of myself, cased in a puce-red *redingote*, bright yellow pantaloons, and a blue-silk waistcoat, the general effect, aided by astoundingly manipulated hair, and two round gold earrings, which, after much persuasion, I had submitted to be bored for—the ensemble forming, it appeared, the gala dress, in those days, of young Pas de Calais—I was fit to choke with laughter—partly the laughter of mirth, partly of vexation!

" This is a charming dress to go a courting in," I snarled, addressing Webbe. "Very charming, upon my word!"

"O yes, it is indeed charming!" exclaimed Madame Baptiste, supposing, no doubt, that she echoed me. "Monsieur has now quite a distinguished air."

I thought the woman was poking fun at me; but no, she was serious as a judge. Her husband, evidently intending the highest compliment possible to human speech, declared I was completely *Françaisé;* and Webbe assured me I looked remarkably well.

I resigned myself; and Messieurs Jacques and Jean Le Gros reached by due course of diligence—about three miles an hour, exclusive of stoppages—the dingy, dirty city of St. Malo, and took up their quarters in the Hôtel de l'Empire.

Webbe, I must state in explanation, was, he informed me, known to but very few persons in St. Malo as Captain Renaudin, and those few, fast friends upon whose silence he could depend; and it being absolutely necessary to baffle young Le Moine, the last change of name and disguise was extemporised. I had feared there would be a difficulty with respect to passports; but they were found to be perfectly *en règle;* a seeming justification of Webbe's frequent remark that, as a police regulation, the passport-system was the greatest humbug ever devised. It is, however, possible that the confusion into which the public business had everywhere fallen, facilitated the procurement, by Baptiste, of the requisite papers.

Webbe left the hotel on the following morning, soon after breakfast, and did not return till near four in the afternoon. He was in high spirits. Madame de Bonne-ville had left home for Paris only two days previously, and on the morrow we twain were to dine, by special invitation, with the charming Clémence, and Fanchette.

"The game, or I err greatly, is in your own hands," said Webbe. "Clémence—Lucy, that is to say—already sees — thanks to certain hints of mine — the glories of a *milady* about to descend upon her. But the table-d'hôte dinner-bell has already rung twice. After we have dined, I shall have more to say and shew. Allons."

The privateer captain sat long at table, and drank freely—his custom always when there was no peril of seas or land to guard against; but at last we were alone; and after much rigmarole preface, designed to convince me of the loyalty of his motives, he drew from his pocket-book a much-worn printed bill, and was about to place it in my hands, when M. Jacques Sicard was announced; and without pausing an instant for permission, in bounced that gentleman, evidently in a high state of inflammation.

Rather a good-looking, intelligent young fellow, let me break off a moment to say, spite of his round bullet head and stout barrel-like body, inadequately supported by legs that were well enough of themselves, though not quite equal to the situation, a deficiency which I more than suspected had been artificially increased within the previous hour.

"I present myself, *sans façon,* messieurs," he began, "as it is my right to do, when coming to demand explanation, satisfaction, justice; which explanation, satisfaction, justice, you will refuse me at your peril!"

"What does the man mean?" I asked Webbe.

"I know no more than you. He appears to be tipsy, or "——

"Speak French, will you?" interrupted Sicard, striking

the table with his doubled fist. "Do you suppose a Frenchman, who has been educated in Paris, and lived there all his life till within the last three years, can understand that gibberish?"

"You are insolent, Jacques Sicard," remarked Webbe.

"No; it is you, Jacques Le Gros, that are insolent, in speaking before me in a *patois* I do not comprehend. It may be Bas-Breton for what I know or care: assuredly, it is not French."

"Well, what have you to say? Why are you here?"

"What have I to say? Why am I here?" explosively retorted Sicard. "O Dieu de la miséricorde, as if your own conscience, if you have one, does not tell you what I must have to say—why I am here! Well, then, I have to say you are a——— But I restrain myself; I resolved to do so when finally deciding to seek you here. Jacques Sicard, *mon garçon,* I said to myself, be moderate, be wise! Thou hast had provocation enough to exasperate a saint; nevertheless, be moderate, be wise. Thou art a tradesman, established three years, prospering and well respected; it is thy duty, therefore, to set an example to others. I shall do so; and therefore I do not say what you are, Monsieur Jacques Le Gros; but as to why I am here, I beg to say, I am here to obtain explanation, satisfaction, justice; and if not justice, vengeance—vengeance! Jacques Le Gros," he added, grinding his teeth and rolling his eyes, after a most formidable fashion.

Webbe laughed, mockingly, as few but he could. Jacques Sicard danced, gesticulated, screamed with rage.

"I am a Frenchman," he shrieked. "My heart, my blood, is French—French—French! Dou you understand?"

"Perfectly! You are a French boot and shoemaker!"

I interposed. The poor fellow seemed almost demented with passion, and I was anxious to hear what he had to say.

"Calm yourself, Monsieur Sicard," I said; neither my uncle nor myself wishes to insult, distress you."

"A la bonne heure!" said Sicard, subsiding into comparative moderation, and wiping his beady forehead, as he sat down. "That is polite, that is reasonable, and good French, moreover, though the accent is detestably provincial—guttural in the extreme."

"We are from near Calais; and as the English long held possession of that town, they may have left their accent behind as a souvenir," said Webbe.

"I have nothing to say to you," retorted Sicard; "I shall talk to your nephew only. This," continued the excited bootmaker, "is the case in a few words. Not many months ago, I was upon the best terms with my relatives, the De Bonnevilles. Madame de Bonneville had a sincere regard for me; and I—I—why should I not confess it?—I loved, adored her only child and daughter, la charmante Clémence, who "——

"Who in return," interrupted Webbe, "loved, adored le charmant Jacques Sicard, bottier de Paris."

"I shall not talk to you, old rogue!" replied Sicard with rekindling fury. "No, that is wrong; I withdraw 'old rogue;' but I shall only address your nephew. I have no pretension," he resumed, "to say Clémence loved me in return; but at least she permitted me to accompany her to church; sometimes, with madame's permission, to a walk on the ramparts when the bands were playing. In fine, I was well satisfied with the progress of the affair, till one fine day I find Monsieur Jacques Le Gros chatting to her in the magasin. Once or twice afterwards I witnessed the same thing, but it did not trouble me. I did not even ask the man's name. Why should it trouble me that Clémence sometimes conversed with an ugly old rogue? Ah, wrong again! I withdraw 'rogue,' but not old and ugly, which is exact, demonstrable. I repeat, it did not trouble me to find Clémence conversing more than once with an old, ugly—monsieur. Ha! I little knew what a venomous serpent was whispering at the ear of my Eve! I shall not withdraw that! It is exact, demonstrable! Clémence was no longer the same; the poor child's head was turned. She no longer discerns any merit in Jacques Sicard; and is ever dreaming of riches, grandeur, castles in Spain without number. Well, that malady of the brain yields slowly to time and the remonstrances of myself and Madame de Bonneville: Clémence recovers her charming spirits; again recognises the devotion of Jacques Sicard. Madame de Bonneville sets out for Paris, and I make an appointment to call on Clémence this very evening, and escort her and Fanchette to the theatre. I am happy,

joyous even. I dress myself with care—it may be admitted
with some taste—and I proceed to the Rue Dupetit
Thouars. Ha! I am spurned, derided! I hear from
Fanchette that that old, ugly rogue—that venomous serpent—— I withdraw nothing!" continued Sicard, springing to his feet again in a fresh access of rage, and empha-
sising with his fist upon the table—"not even rogue; that
that old rogue and serpent, whose name I hear for the
first time, has been there again! I understand, of course,
that I have been calumniated, supplanted! and I come
here for explanation!—satisfaction!—justice—vengeance!"

Bang, bang, bang! I thought he would have smashed
the table. Instead of that, the resounding blows brought
two waiters into the room.

"Have the goodness to turn this drunken rascal out of
our apartment" said Webbe.

"Drunk! drunk!—I—I," ejaculated the poor fellow,
vainly struggling in the throttling gripe of the waiters, "I
—I am Ja-a-cques Si—Sicard, a respect—respectable"——

"Bottier de Paris," suggested Webbe.

"And I—I will have sat—satisfaction! jus—justice"——

The door closed upon his struggles, and I thought we
were quit of him. Not so: escaping by a sudden effort
from his captors, he darted back, partially opened the door,
shewed us his flaming face, and shaking his clenched fist,
exclaimed: "And vengeance!—*scélérats!*—vengeance!"

He was re-seized, and this time effectually got rid of.

CHAPTER IX.

MADEMOISELLE CLEMENCE.

"MONSIEUR SICARD is an original," I remarked, as the
sounds of struggle and expostulation died away in the distance; "but he appears to be thoroughly in earnest. If,
moreover, he speaks sooth, your model maiden would
seem to be little better than a capricious flirt."

"Jacques Sicard is certainly in most profound earnest,"
said Webbe; "but being in both love and liquor, can

scarcely be expected to speak sooth, as you phrase it. Supposing, however, that he has by accident told the exact truth, it just amounts to this—that, coerced by Madame de Bonneville, of whom, as I have informed you, she stands in extreme awe, Clémence has been civil to the enamoured bootmaker."

"And that you have filled her young head with dreams of riches and grandeur, with visions of *châteaux en Espagne*, that have no better foundation than vague surmise, the evanishing whereof may, nevertheless, darken her future life."

"If you go on in that spooney, sentimental fashion, Linwood, I shall begin to think Sicard must have bitten you unawares. I have suggested no dream to Clémence that may not be realised, including the sublime one of becoming in the fulness of time Mrs. William Linwood—a magnificent possibility, which, by the by, I have never more than incidentally glanced at, when conversing with her. It is, besides, consoling to reflect that, failing that, which I can't believe she will, there are lesser heavens that may suffice for the modest felicity of Mrs. Waller's recovered daughter—of Anthony Waller's of Cavendish Square assured heiress."

"A few grains of common-sense would be an improvement to that heap of chaff, Mr. Webbe."

"That which you are pleased to call chaff *is* common-sense, my dear fellow, if somewhat chaffingly expressed. A more acceptable variety of the article to your taste may, however, be set forth in the printed handbill to which I was calling your attention when that boot-making buzzard broke in upon us. Mrs. Waller, you must understand, would persist, spite of all evidence to the contrary, in believing that her child might have been stolen, abducted, instead of drowned, and this was one of the advertisements issued to humour her fancy. I found it, by mere chance, the other day, amongst some old papers. It offers, you observe, five hundred pounds' reward for the recovery of the child, and contains a description of the little Lucy's person, and the dress and ornaments she wore on the day of her disappearance."

"This is indeed a valuable document," I exclaimed, after glancing over the handbill; "not on account of its description of the child's person—'fair complexion, blue eyes, light hair'—which would apply to thousands of children, but for the list of articles worn by the little girl, and which, as you suggest, may have been preserved by Louise Féron for an ulterior, if now abandoned purpose. 'A necklace composed of five rows of seed-pearls; attached thereto a gold Maltese cross, set with pearls, and having the letter L engraved on the back. Two-sleeve loops of seed-pearls; pale-blue silk frock—morocco shoes of the same colour'—— Ha! here also the indelible mark you have spoken of is alluded to—not described: 'The child has a natural mark difficult to discover if sought for, which will always be decisive of her identity, and may at any moment bring about the detection and punishment of the person or persons who, after this notice, shall conceal or assist in concealing and withholding the child from her parents.'"

"You informed me, Captain Webbe," I remarked, "that Louise Féron had charge of Mrs. Waller's child for several months : she must, therefore, one would suppose, be cognizant of this mysterious mark—a knowledge which, it occurs to me, would do away with any motive she would otherwise have had to preserve proofs of the child's identity—especially proofs which, traced to her possession, would fatally compromise herself."

"One would, as you say," replied Webbe, "suppose that Louise Féron must be cognizant of the said indelible mark; and yet, I am confident, from the covert inquiries she, to my knowledge, set on foot relative thereto, previous to her safer course of action being finally resolved upon, that she is as ignorant in the matter as you or I. I repeat that I am morally certain some, at least. of the articles enumerated in the handbill have been preserved, and may be obtained possession of by Clémence, with the connivance of Fanchette—a purchasable connivance, as I have before intimated, provided always that no harm shall possibly accrue therefrom to her darling Clémence."

"What harm could therefrom possibly accrue to her darling Clémence."

"Ruinous harm—harm without remedy would befall Clémence, should you refuse to carry out the honourable understanding, by means of which can alone be accomplished the great object we have both in view. And now, young man," continued Webbe, with assumed sternness, "let us, once for all, thoroughly comprehend each other. We are on the immediate threshold of an undertaking for the success of which I have ventured much, and resolutely. One false step now would be fatal, irremediable. We must walk, therefore, warily, as well as boldly; with a ·clear perception of the course to be taken, and whither that course will lead. I have apprised you that Clémence is under the absolute domination of her supposed mother : I mean, that Lucy Hamblin has been drilled, disciplined, into habitual fear of Louise Féron ; and nothing, be sure of it, but a sentiment stronger than that habitual fear will enable her, when the decisive moment comes, to do that which will give Louise Feron mortal offence. Clemence, you must be aware, cannot remain in St. Malo after placing in your hands the proofs of her supposed mother's crime, and of your father's innocence. If she did remain here, what do you suppose would follow the discovery of the poor girl's treachery, as Louise Feron would call it ? Simply the immediate disappearance of the so-called mother and daughter; and of what value, let me ask, would your dearly obtained proofs then be ? It would, of course, be said that your father had placed them in your hands ; and a very silly, transparent trick on his part the wise world would pronounce it to be. Yes, Clemence— no relative of yours, remember—must flee with you; but no assurance, however solemn, that she would be wel-comed with joy by a parent she has never seen—whom she does not remember, I mean, to have ever seen—will induce her to take that decisive, compromising step; of that be perfectly assured. The prospect before her would be too vague, too undefined, too shadowy. It would, how-ever, be quite another affair to elope with a betrothed lover, or as she, I have little doubt, will peremptorily in-sist, with a husband, and the ceremony can be quite as easily managed here as in Jersey. I have, as Jacques Sicard's ravings prove, successfully prepared the way for that consummation. Clemence—than whom a more charming, amiable girl, does not exist—knows who you are ; has heard the story, with variations, of your *Scout* Quixotism; knows and honours the motives that have prompted the noble temerity of your present enterprise; believes also that a portrait of her sweet self, missed by Madame de Bonneville soon after I left St. Malo's, and which I have unfortunately lost or mislaid, has in some degree influenced your adventurous "—

The entrance of a waiter interrupted Mr. Webbe. " A note," said the grizzled garçon, " for Monsieur Jacques Le Gros, from the Sieur Delisle, *courtier maritime*, whose messenger waits for the answer."

"Very well. Tell him he will not have to wait long."

The note appeared to both disconcert and excite Captain Webbe. A brief one—not more than a dozen lines, I could not help observing, as he threw it upon the table, with an affectation somewhat overdone, it seemed to me, of ill-humour.

" I cannot yet," he exclaimed, " wash my hands, as I hoped to do, of these rascally dodges. Pope was right : the devil, taught wisdom by his failure with the man of Uz, tempts now by enriching, instead of ruining men : by lying promises to enrich, more properly—judging from my own experience hitherto—fiend, like fairy money, having, I have found, an uncontrollable propensity to make unto itself wings and flee away. My return to Virtue must, it is evident, be postponed for a while ; and it *may* be that this positively the last infraction, on my part, of the laws of national morality, will enable one of the most interesting, in my poor judgment, of Virtue's vagrant sons to take something home with him that will considerably enhance the warmth of his welcome."

" All that is Greek to me, Mr. Webbe, except that it has the sound of a swaggering defence of something you are really very much ashamed of."

" A wiser man might have made a sillier guess," retorted Webbe. " I must forego the pleasure of your company for the remainder of the evening," he added, as he buttoned up his coat and put on his hat and gloves. " Delisle, the ship-broker, is anxious to introduce his friend Captain Renaudin to one Mr. Tyler, an American gentleman and shipowner, who is desirous of ascertaining the course of a richly laden bark, hailing from New Orleans, should steer in order to safely reach one of the French northern ports —Havre de Grace, if possible ; and it is said Delisle's opinion, which I freely endorse, that Captain Renaudin can insure the arrival of Mr. Tyler's ship at her destination with greater certainty than any other man he is acquainted with."

"Monsieur Delisle is, then, one of the few persons in St. Malo who knows you as Captain Renaudin, of *L'Espiègle*."

" Yes. *L'Espiègle* has never been at St. Malo, and Captain Renaudin only once before; when he came on a business visit to Monsieur Delisle, and chanced to run against, and find his disguise pierced through by the spit-fire eyes of that Jezebel, Louise Féron. Good-night. I shall see you early in the morning."

So saying, the privateer captain left me to the society of my own thoughts. I might have had pleasanter company. Whatever else appeared doubtful, it was abundantly manifest that I was a mere puppet in the hands of a reckless, unprincipled man, who, avowedly for his own interested purposes, had led me into dark and tangled paths whence there might be no issue, save through the portals of disgrace, of ruin, of death quite possibly! His insistance that I must, and forthwith, marry Lucy Hamblin—if Lucy Hamblin, Mademoiselle Clémence proved to be—at once perplexed and irritated me. What could be his motive for persisting in that outrageous proposition? The bare idea of marriage with a girl I had not seen, and who, it seemed, was so eager to unite herself with an utter stranger, revolted, disgusted me! Maria Wilson's romantic notion of the heroic qualities desirable in a husband, which to me, familiar with the seamy side of the heroism that had caught her fancy, appeared so extravagantly absurd, contrasted brilliantly with the sordid marrying motives of this much vaunted demoiselle Clémence. Attractive—handsome she might be—her eyes, hair, complexion required, I was told, the same adjectives to describe them as did Miss Wilson's; but the pure soul-light which diffused so inexpressibly pensive a charm over the countenance of the Jersey maiden, must, I was sure, be utterly wanting to the feature-comeliness of a damsel who could coquet with a conceited, vulgar snob; and, a supposedly favourable chance occurring, throw herself at the head of a wealthier swain, not at all covetous of, or flattered by

her preference! Perhaps, however, Webbe had misrepre-
sented her sentiments, as he did most things. I should
see and judge for myself before condemning her. That
were but equitable, more especially if she really was the
long-lost Lucy Hamblin. My doubts upon that all-important point had not been vanquished by Webbe's
hectoring assertion that such doubts were absurd,
ridiculous—very far, indeed, from being vanquished by
that bold talk. My grandame, Mrs. Margaret Linwood, a
shrewd observer, had suspected Webbe to have been all
along confederate with Louise Féron. If that conjecture
was well founded, the proofs indicated by the printed
handbill, which had turned up at so remarkably opportune
a moment, and alleged to be only obtainable by such
preposterous expedients, might be mere devices for im-
posing a supposititious daughter upon rich Mrs. Waller—
a wife, who certainly would not be supposititious, upon
William Linwood, the heir to at least his grandmother's
wealth!

The indelible natural mark—that ineffaceable clue which
was to guide us safely through any labyrinth of deceit
that cupidity and imposture could invent, I strongly suspected to be a myth. Mrs. Margaret Linwood, had, however, promised, that if she could, without danger of exciting
chimerical hopes in the shaken mind of Mrs. Waller, arrive
at a knowledge of what that mysterious mark might be,
she would forward me the important information without
delay, through Mrs. Webbe, under cover to that lady's husband, as arranged by the captain before he left the Wight.
Should she do so in time, and Mademoiselle Clemence
be thereby identified, beyond cavil, as Lucy Hamblin,
what insuperable difficulty could there be in persuading
the aspiring damsel to forsake a mean dwelling in the Rue
Dupetit Thouars, St. Malo—and the vile woman that had
stolen her—for a wealthy home in Cavendish Square,
London, and her own true, unforgetting, loving mother,
without encumbering herself with a hobble-de-hoy husband,
tricked off in bright yellow pants, puce-red redingote, blue
vest, round earrings, and hair à la Brutus. Hair à la Brutus,
by the way, was hair tortured to stand upward and outward, so as to form a rim for the hat to rest upon; and
nicely graduated downward to the nape of the neck. I

remember à la Brutus well; and the nervous shudder—as from a paroxysm of hydrophobia—which ran through me whenever I encountered my variegated image in the pellucid surface of the mirror. It was, at all events, impossible that the harlequin figure reflected there could excite an interest in the young lady's mind subversive of her future peace. I might be civil to the most susceptible of maidens without the remotest danger of acquiring an embarrassing hold of her affections. That was something—nay, it was much! Clemence would repudiate marriage as determinedly as myself——

At about this point of the maundering soliloquy, which might else have droned on till daylight, I discovered that the fire and decanter were both out; and forthwith crept, cold and comfortless, to bed.

I did not see Webbe till near noon on the following day. He came direct from Madame de Bonneville's, and invited me to immediately accompany him thither.

"The bootmaker's bristles," said Webbe, "have, I find, been smoothed down by Fanchette's assurance that Messieurs Le Gros will remain but a very short time in St. Malo, and that the refusal of Mademoiselle Clemence to accompany him to the theatre, was solely prompted by a suddenly recovering sense of the impropriety of accepting his escort to a place of public entertainment during Madame de Bonneville's absence from home. We are consequently safe from the shoemaker, which is as well, inasmuch, that albeit a goose's cackle saved the Roman Capitol, it might exert a less salutary action anent the safety of Captain Jules Renaudin, and aliases too numerous to mention. The feeling of decorum, intimated to Jacques Sicard, will also cause the ceremonious dinner, to which we were invited, to be dispensed with, and we shall drop in at the magasin for a gossip now and then, *par hasard*, as it were."

"That will be quite as well. Your pattern protégée is, it seems, apt at expedients."

"The desirableness of pacifying Jacques Sicard was my suggestion; the manner thereof, Fanchette's. But come; Mademoiselle Clemence awaits with natural impatience her introduction to the chivalrous knight who comes to rescue her from Madame de Bonneville and the bootmaker."

" Well, my ingenuous young friend," exclaimed Captain Webbe on the evening of the same day, as he drew his chair towards the roaring wood-fire before which I was seated. He had left me, I should explain, with Clemence and Fanchette, after a few formal words of introduction, and had been since engaged on business matters with his friend Delisle and the American shipowner. " Well, my ingenuous young friend, what think you now of my pattern protégée? I hardly need ask," he added. " There is a flush on William Linwood's cheek, a light in his eye, that are not, I dare wager large odds, caused by the fire-blaze, or by the wine he has drunk."

" Mademoiselle Clemence is a charming girl," I replied. " Honest, truthful too, or I strangely deceive myself."

" Whoever has looked upon her, or heard her speak," said Webbe, " must unhesitatingly endorse that eulogium. And her person—what is your opinion of that; of the characteristics of her person, I mean? English, Saxon, you cannot doubt?"

" I should altogether doubt it, were it not evident from a few words that escaped her, that she believes herself to be an English girl, and the daughter of Mrs. Waller. True, the young lady has blue eyes, a fair skin, brown hair; but, for all that, a more thoroughly French, or at least foreign, maiden I cannot imagine. An English girl of her age and class in society, introduced to a stranger under such peculiar, and, it must be admitted, embarrassing circumstances, would have been all bashfulness and blushes; whereas Clemence was impassive as a statue, comported herself with the most perfect propriety, and an *aplomb*, a *savoir-faire*, that in an English maiden would be effrontery, brazen-facedness—simply, I imagine, because in her case it would be assumed, and awkwardly, for an evident purpose."

" *Mauvaise honte*, which you call bashfulness, is not tolerated in any class of French society."

" So I comprehend. Her French education has, at all events, thoroughly Frenchified Lucy Hamblin, as I verily believe her to be, so deeply has the truthfulness of Mademoiselle Clemence impressed me. Fancy, now," I added " as I could not help fancying all the time our interview lasted, Maria Wilson in the same position as Clemence,

H

fancy the changing colour—the downcast, suffused eyes—
the tremulous speech of that genuine English girl, and "—
"Fudge about fancy and Maria Wilson!" interrupted
Webbe. "What just comparison can be instituted between
that namby-pamby wench and a girl of sense and spirit
like Clemence?"

"A very curious comparison, Mr. Webbe; or, more correctly, a strikingly illustrative contrast is suggested
by "——

"Fudge! Twaddle!" again broke in Webbe, with
marked asperity. "Let us, in the name of all saints, talk
of something more interesting than Maria Wilsons. You
Linwood," he added, with quick transition to a more *suave*
tone—"you, Linwood, have seen and conversed with Clemence. You admire—you believe in her! That is sufficient. The rest will come as surely as shadow follows
substance. When shall you see her again?

"To-morrow afternoon, when we shall exchange confidences. I am already '*mon ami*' with the frank-spoken,
and, I have no manner of doubt, frank-hearted damsel."

"Excellent! Still, be on your guard, Linwood: we
must have evidence clear as proof from holy writ that your
wife is the true Lucy Hamblin."

"Fudge about wife, say I, in humble imitation of Mr.
Webbe, who "——

"You will find marriage to be an indispensable element
of success," interrupted Webbe, with renewed asperity.
"In fact, it is only on that condition that I will render any
further aid in the business. Unscrupulous as I may be
in many respects, I will not have the ruin of that young
girl's character and peace of mind upon my conscience."

"Character! Conscience!" I mentally exclaimed.
"Strange words from the lips of Mr. Webbe; not mean-
ingless, however, I am quite sure. Significant, too,—
though of what I cannot as yet comprehend—must be the
privateer captain's querulous insistance upon marrying
me, out of hand, to Mademoiselle Clemence! I must
quietly, dissemblingly, await the solution of that riddle."

"Well, well," I said aloud, "your conscience will not, I
dare say, have to bear any very heavy load of my laying
on. And there is one thing, Mr. Webbe," I added with
vehemence, "which *I* will not bear for another hour of

daylight, and that is, these abominable Pas de Calais pantaloons. If hair à la Brutus, ear-rings, and a puce-red redingote are not sufficient disguise for an Englishman, Auguste Le Moine must do his best and worst, for draw on again these yellow inexpressibles, I will not, come what come may."

The captain's good-humour was restored at once; he laughed heartily, genially, and for the remainder of the evening, overflowed with jocund spirits. I silently scored myself a chalk, and had, I think, a right to do so.

The reader must not suppose, from my description of Mademoiselle Clémence, that she was a bold or forward maiden; on the contrary, she was a remarkably modest-mannered damsel; but it was the modesty of principle, of education, rather than that of nature or instinct, so to speak. In other words, she was a well-bred French girl; modest, but by no means bashful; self-possessed, not shy. Very pretty, too, was Mademoiselle Clémence; of most winning, graceful manners; and there was a caressing tenderness in her gentle, truthful voice, that was inexpressibly attractive. I was greatly taken with her, though not at all in the sense which Webbe supposed. In truth, much as I soon came to admire, esteem, ay, and to love Clémence, she was about the last person in the world I should have sought for a wife. I felt towards her as a brother would for an endearing, pure-hearted sister; and I often caught myself mentally comparing the calm, tranquil affection which so grew upon me for the gentle, confiding Clémence, with the passionate emotion that, circumstances favouring, would be inspired by such a person as Maria Wilson, to whom, oddly enough—as I had seen her but once—my thoughts, when engaged by such reflections, persistently reverted.

Clémence was alone, as she had promised to be, when I called according to appointment; and entering at once with the most perfect frankness upon the subject uppermost in both our minds, I was dismayed to find that the only proofs she could afford me of being the child of Madame Waller were a dim, fading recollection that she had once lived in a strange country, amongst strange people—some fragmentary hints, that had fallen from Madame de Bonneville, and Captain Webbe's confident

and confidential assertions, upon which Mademoiselle
Clémence placed implicit reliance.

Nothing, positively nothing more in the way of evidence,
could I elicit; and I was fast making up my mind that
Webbe had bamboozled himself as well as others, when it
occurred to me that it would be well to shew Clémence
the printed bill given me by the captain: I did so, and
doubt, uncertainty was at an end.

"O, mon Dieu!" exclaimed Clémence, who read English
very well, "I have seen these things, and lately too."

"How—when—where?"

"In the *armoire* up stairs, about a month since, when
mamma"—a very imperfect rendering of *maman*—"when
mamma was absent in the island of Guernsey."

"Tell me about it, dear Clémence—all about it, to the
minutest detail."

"It is very simple, mon ami. Mamma is, you know,
very strict, severe even, with me; and yet I love her!"
exclaimed Clémence, impulsively diverging from the all-
important topic; "and it will be a bitter grief for me if—
if—— Ah," she continued disjointedly, " I remember how
kind, loving she was when fever attacked m‸ ‸nd I should,
but for her, have died. It would be ungrateful of me,
then—nay, unnatural, even supposing she is not my own
real mother—if I did not love her—would it not?"

"Yes, yes. But pray, speak of your finding the articles
mentioned in this printed bill."

"Willingly, mon ami. When mamma was absent in
Guernsey, as I said, Fanchette asked me one day what
had become of my turquoise brooch—this which I now
wear. I said mamma had not given it to me when she
left; but Fanchette was certain she had seen me wear it
twice since then; and where, therefore, could it be? We
were both terribly frightened, for mamma attached a great
value to the brooch, and if it had been lost, would have
punished me severely. Well, we searched everywhere for the
brooch—vainly searched: it could not be found. Poor
Fanchette was greatly distressed, and tried to believe I
was right in thinking mamma had not given it to me when
she left St. Malo. Could we only be sure of that, our
minds would of course be at rest. But how make sure of
it? The armoire where mamma kept all her valuables was

locked; there was no key that would fit it, and we were in despair, for mamma was expected every day. Suddenly Fanchette rushed into my chamber one morning before I was up. She had found a key that would fit the armoire lock, and directly I was dressed, we would make a search and satisfy ourselves. We did so, carefully replacing each article as we found it. Presently, we came to a neatly folded and tied-up parcel, which I opened, and found therein not only the missing brooch, but a necklace made of rows of seed-pearls, with a gold pearl-set cross attached; other twisted rows of seed-pearls, which, no doubt, were the sleeve-loops mentioned here; a faded blue silk frock, shoes of the same colour, and a child's tiny underclothing. My heart swelled with emotion as I gazed," continued Clemence; "for it occurred to me that those were precious memorials of a sister who died young, and whom mamma often said, when she was angry, she had loved much better than she did me. But the brooch was found," she added, hastily brushing away her fast-falling tears, "and we, Fanchette and I, were happy."

" And those precious proofs are still, you say, locked up in an armoire of which Fanchette has a key?"

"O yes, I am quite sure of that. But how pale you look, and you tremble as with ague!"

"With joy, rapture, ecstasy, Clemence! Listen to me, dear girl, and you will comprehend why it is that this discovery, to which the finger of an overruling Providence guided you so agitates, bewilders, well nigh overpowers me."

Clemence listened whilst I told her all—told her of the mother's maddening agony at the loss of her only child, of my hapless father's persecution, with the correlative circumstances already known to the reader. The narrative, as it proceeded, cruelly agitated the gentle maiden, her head sank upon my shoulder, and she wept aloud in the fulness of her pity, her grief, her love, her indignation, as these passions of the soul ruled her by turns.

Fanchette had helped the weeping girl to her chamber, and returned to where I sat, when I bethought me of the indelible mark hinted at in the advertisement. Fanchette was in our interest—heavily bribed to be so; and although I did not like the woman, I could speak to her with perfect confidence.

"Clémence has no natural mark that I know of," said Fanchette in reply to my question.

"No mole or moles?"

"None— certainly none."

"No stain of blood—no malformation of limb—no peculiar scar?"

"Nothing of the kind that I am aware of; and I should know if any such existed."

"That is perplexing. You will tell Mademoiselle Clémence that I shall see her to-morrow," I added, as I rose to leave.

"I will, monsieur. Attendez," added the woman, as if with sudden recollection. "Yet no—that cannot be called a mark."

"What do you speak of?"

"Nothing, I fear, monsieur, of any importance, though I may as well mention it. Clémence, some years ago, was reduced to a skeleton by fever, from which it was for a long time thought she would never recover. She was attended by Dr. Poitevin, who, I heard one day tell Madame de Bonneville, that, by a curious freak of nature, her daughter Clémence had been born with one rib less on her right than on her left side. Surely that cannot be "——

"It *can* surely be," I interrupted with a burst—"it *must* be the natural mark spoken of. Hurrah! Do not forget to tell dear Clémence that I shall call early to-morrow. Adieu."

Singular coincidence of discovery and its confirmation! Webbe awaited my return to the Hôtel de l'Empire with a letter in his hand from Mrs. Margaret Linwood; hastily opening which, I read: "The indelible mark of Mrs. Waller's child I have ascertained to be, that, by a strange caprice of nature, it was born with one rib less on the right than on the left side!"

CHAPTER X.

LE PASSE-PARTOUT ET LE WASP.

NOTHING but the perfect guilelessness and candour of Clemence de Bonneville, associated in my illogical appreciation with the circumstances which appeared to place her claim to be the daughter of Mrs. Waller beyond controversy, could have rendered me disregardful of the surprising *aptness* of discoveries or revelations following each other in such dramatic sequence. The seed-pearl necklace and other of the stolen child's articles of dress, carefully concealed during fourteen years, had been found a few days previous to my arrival at St. Malo, in an armoire, of which Fanchette, suddenly overtaken by anxiety to find a brooch that had not been lost, possessed, or easily procured a key! Fanchette, Mr. Webbe's well-fee'd confederate, moreover, relates—attaching, however, in her ingenuous simplicity, no importance to the statement—that she had once heard a Dr. Poitevin mention the remarkable anatomical fact which, a letter from Mrs. Linwood placed in my hands ten minutes afterwards by the privateer captain, apprises me is the infallible test by which the most cunningly concocted attempt at fraudulent personation would be exposed and defeated! Not, by the way, in my hands, and under the actual circumstances, could that test prove so instantly decisive. Dr. Poitevin, I ascertained, had been dead some months; and it was out of the question that I should insist upon a young lady having her ribs scientifically counted for my especial satisfaction! I doubted that Clemence herself, being, if anything, the plumpest of us two, could do so with accuracy, for I certainly could not mine; and after many trials, was unable, for the life of me, to determine whether popular belief and Jeremy Taylor were correct or not, in insisting that, since Adam, every man was minus one, taken for the creation of his better-half, "from nearest his heart that he may love, from under his arm that he may protect her." Fanchette was, however, fully corroborated by Clemence, before whom, by way of proposing the question in as seemly a manner as possible, I placed Mrs.

Linwood's letter, with the passage I have quoted strongly underlined.

"Ah, it is very true!" exclaimed the sweet girl with a charming blush and smile, after glancing at the lines. "Dr. Poitevin declared so when I was ill of the fever."

"Dr. Poitevin declared so in your hearing, dear Clemence?"

"O yes!—or, stay; let me reflect a moment. Certainly," she presently added, "it seems to me that he must have done so; but it is a long time since, and having frequently heard Fanchette and maman mention the doctor's remark, I may, you know, have come to erroneously imagine that I heard it from his own lips."

"Be that as it may, I have not the slightest doubt, believe me, of the fact," was my reply. Nor had I; and it was that intimate conviction which rendered me contemptuously indifferent to the clumsily cunning artifices employed to confirm a truth, so manifest to my apprehension, that disbelief was impossible. Webbe had persuaded or terrified Louise Feron into restoring Lucy Hamblin to her mother, and he had adopted a deceptive, roundabout method of carrying their mutual purpose into effect, in order to enhance the value and consequent reward of his services—a reward which Feron was of course to share. To be sure, this hypothesis did not account for Webbe's unappeasable anxiety to have us married before leaving France; but he might be really afraid that Clemence—innocent as myself of all that underhand, behind-the-scenes work—would refuse to abandon her actual home except under the protection of a husband; in which case, Webbe would be under the disagreeable necessity of confessing that the difficulties and dangers attendant upon our enterprise were, primarily, of his own seeking. Subsequently, indeed, upon summoning to the session of calmer thought the mass of confused and contradictory statement with which my ears had been filled by Webbe, the fallacy of such reasoning appeared palpable enough; but at the time, the strong impression upon my mind must have been as stated—a dreamy of apprehension, which the ascertainment beyond doubt that proofs of the abduction by Louise Feron of the child my father was accused of having drowned, was really extant, within reach, if I blundered not, of my eager, trembling hand, may, by monopolising all my perceptive and reasoning faculties, have considerably aggravated.

To the same absorbing pre-occupation of mind must also, in fairness, be attributed another manifestation of perceptive obtuseness, the recollection of which, though the frosts of three-and-forty winters have since then chastened my pulse and cooled my blood, causes me even now, as I write, to glow and redden to my fingers' ends; and which, but that its omission would obscure my narrative, should certainly remain untold.

It will be readily believed that I deeply sympathised with the gentle-hearted Clemence, not only because of the grievous, irreparable wrong she had sustained by being stolen in her infancy from a loving parent and wealthy home, and subjected during twice seven years to comparative indigence and stern control; but with her deep sorrow at discovering that the woman whom she had loved as a mother was wholly unworthy of an affection, which she could not, as her tears testified whenever the subject was touched upon, subdue at will, or readily transfer to another.

Well, I expressed that natural sympathy with a warmth which it never once occurred to me would be almost certainly misconstrued, coming from a young man to a still younger maiden, who, concurrently with that young mau's appearance upon the scene, had discarded a former lover. The reader is already aware that I was mightily free with such expressions as "Dear Clemence"—that my tears mingled with those of the sobbing girl whose drooping head rested upon my shoulder. Other endearing, innocent familiarities recur to memory as I write; of which the legitimate interpretation and tendency was all unperceived by me during the first intoxication of spirit excited by the achieved success, as I supposed, of the momentous mission with which I was intrusted.

The only excuse I could make to myself when Webbe, affecting to look as fierce as a dragon whose golden fruit had been filched whilst he slumbered over his charge, called my attention to the obvious result of my thoughtless conduct, was that I could not, under any circum-

stances, have imagined the possibility of such a catastrophe. My previous intercourse with the better sex
afforded no warning of the peril I incurred of inadvertently awakening the susceptibilities of young and gentle
hearts. The damsels of the Wight must have been
strangely unimpressionable, seeing that, in the words of the
old song,

> I had kissed and had prattled with fifty fair maids,
> And changed them as often, d'ye see—

and the deuce of one of them had, to my knowledge,
cared a straw about the matter! There was, indeed, every
excuse for my inconsiderate behaviour, for, good Heaven!
who that saw me come shining forth in the trim previously
described, save that pale blue replaced bright yellow pants,
from the Hôtel de l'Empire upon those unfortunate visits,
could have believed that such a Guy might, by possibility,
agitate, except with laughter, the most sensitive of maiden's
hearts!

Yet, I could not deny the flattering impeachment. It
was only too true that the dear girl's charming spirits had
wholly forsaken her—that her appetite was gone—that
at the slightest hint of the peremptory necessity of flight
from St. Malo before Madame de Bonneville's return, her
complexion was one moment celestial rosy red, the next,
pale as the lily. Too true that her soft eyes were constantly
suffused with tears, and that, when speaking to me, her
voice was inexpressibly tender and caressive—her smile so
sad, so pitiful, that it would have touched the heart of a
tiger!

And this moral ruin was my unconscious work! So at
least declared Webbe, who had frequent private interviews
with her. The conflict between love and maidenly pride
was destroying her, and, unless I soothed that wounded
pride by feigning to reciprocate her love, I had discovered
Mrs. Waller's long-lost daughter only to consign her to an
untimely grave!

This was a delightful dilemma to find one's self suddenly
placed in; and how to act I knew not. I essayed what
effect a total change of demeanour on my part might have;
substituted, during two whole days, moroseness, gloom,

fretfulness, for the winning ways which must—it could be nothing else—have led captive her too yielding soul. Bah! The infatuated girl was more tearful, tender, caressive than ever.

Meanwhile, time pressed. Madame de Bonneville would soon return ; and Captain Webbe, who was getting perfectly ferocious, could not remain with safety to himself forty-eight hours longer in St. Malo ; whilst to every hint of flight, dear, susceptible Clemence replied by a burst of tears !

Now, what, in such a case, let me ask the candid reader, could I do ? A young fellow may live over twenty years unscathed by the tender passion, and yet not have a heart of adamant. Mine, at all events, though not pierceable by any power of Cupid, as I believed— having in that regard all my troubles, like a young bear, to come—was not insensible to the pleadings of gener- osity and compassion ; and after much woful cogitation, I made up my mind to capitulate—upon terms. As thus :

Having in the process spoiled about a quire of paper, I achieved a note, in which, after expressing the esteem and admiration I felt for the young lady, in terms sufficiently general to be literally true, but which Clemence would no doubt read and interpret by the fervid light of her own ardent feelings, I expressed a hope of being permitted to more formally declare how essential her favour was to my future happiness, when she, being restored to her true home, and having realised the vast change in social position that awaited her, I could do so without incurring the suspicion of attempting to surprise her into an acceptance of my suit before she had been able to appreciate that change of position, or take counsel of her parents.

This I thought very clever, inasmuch as it would leave her at liberty, after reaching London, to take a fancy to somebody else; and it would be odd indeed if she did not there meet with some one she would prefer to me ! Hitherto, she had practically the choice only of Jacques Sicard and myself, which could not, of course be doubtful; but Miss Hamblin, daughter and heiress of the Wallers of Cavendish Square, would have a wide circle of eligible admirers, in the blaze of whose adulation her slightly rooted liking for me would, I earnestly hoped, wither up and disappear.

I was myself the bearer of the note; and finding her at home, and disengaged, I placed it in the young lady's hands, with a whispered intimation that I would, with permission, see her again in the evening. She seemed to instinctively comprehend that I had brought her a declaration; and the dear, sensitive girl would, I feared, have fainted with the violence of an emotion that as often arises from sudden joy as grief. She, however, by a strong effort, mastered her feelings, and I took hasty leave.

This occurred at about one o'clock in the day; and as the dinner-hour was still three hours distant, and I felt extremely fidgety, ill at ease, dissatisfied with myself, I left the hotel for a stroll on the ramparts. The day was fine and mild, though we were but in the second week of March; and it being some imperial anniversary or other, soldiers were parading, and military bands playing there. Besides, I should be pretty sure to fall in with Webbe, whom I was particularly anxious to have a word with before he again saw Clemence, or, as I should say— Lucy.

Whom should I see upon the ramparts but Jacques Sicard, on duty as a lieutenant in the National Guard, and really a smart-looking officer! I should hardly have recognised him in such splendid guise, but for the glance he shot at me of dislike and disdain, fiercely expressive, moreover, of an inclination, restrained only by the bonds of military discipline, to then and there inflict exemplary chastisement upon the presumptuous rustic that had dared to thrust his insignificance between Mademoiselle de Bonneville and Monsieur Sicard, an established bottier, de Paris même! Poor fellow, thought I, if you knew but all!

I found Webbe with his old friend Delisle, and Mr. Tyler, his recent acquaintance, to whom I was introduced as "My nephew, Monsieur Jean Le Gros." Webbe was in a jocular mood; he had just taken a rise out of the American shipowner, anent some foolish vapouring by that gentleman relative to a Yankee frigate-victory over the Britishers. Few could do that with more causticity than

Webbe; and Mr. Tyler, one could see at a glance, was dreadfully ryled and wrathy. Nevertheless, he and the privateer captain exchanged an apparently hearty *business* hand grasp, and Webbe returned with me to the Hôtel de l'Empire.

I told him that I had made Clemence a formal offer, and that I was to see her again in the evening, but without entering into particulars. He was hugely delighted at the news. " Henceforth," he said " all will be plain sailing, and the necessity I am under of leaving St. Malo the day after to-morrow, can have no hurtful consequence."

" But zounds, young man," he exclaimed, " you are strangely down in the mouth for a valiant hero and successful lover! I suppose, however, that Shakspeare's remark—

Between the acting of a dreadful thing,
And the first motion, all the interim is
Like a phantasma, or a hideous dream—

applies as forcibly to marriage as to murder. We can't then, I think, do better than strive to solace the few hours we have yet to pass together, with brandy, cigars, and a fire; if a fire be obtainable at this hour of the day in a French hotel."

Brandy, cigars, and a fire were supplied, and Mr. Webbe favoured me with a programme of the arrangements that, in contemplation of my acquiescence before it was too late in the marital preliminary—failing which, nothing could be done—he had concerted with Fanchette. The essential points were, that the marriage was to be privately celebrated by a priest, spoken with or retained for that purpose; that on the evening of the bridal-day, I, the bride, and Fanchette, should set out by diligence for Granville, and on arriving there, lose not a moment in betaking ourselves to the dwelling of Baptiste, who had a lugger-boat in waiting to convey us to Jersey, where we should in all probability meet Captain Webbe himself.

Webbe's boisterous glee whilst running over these interesting details grated on my ear, like the exulting scoff of a victor. It was evident he knew that Clemence could not leave St. Malo except as my wife, and after that clever note of mine, a refusal to marry her would be absurd. These comfortable reflections did anything but raise my spirits, which Webbe perceiving, he proposed to redeem his promise of placing me in possession of the how and why he became Captain Jules Renaudin.

"That will do," I said; "go on."

"Of course, anything would *do* that promised to lighten the sadness which lengthens Romeo's hours,"——

"Pish! Pray, let me have your story, Mr. Webbe, without other frippery or garniture than is inseparably inwoven with the woof and warp of the story itself."

"You are a trifle waspish, my young friend. But that, taking into account the afflictive tortures of suspense you are now of course suffering—— Don't for Heaven's sake, jump up and jabber in that frantic fashion, Linwood. Really you are the most touchy popgun I ever handled. However, if a plain tale will put you down, be reseated at once, for here you have it without further preface.

"Once upon a time," proceeded Webbe, "I was a strictly orthodox privateer. I slew and pillaged upon the high seas only those whom the *London Gazette* proclaimed to be natural enemies, and the articles of war, and thanksgiving-for-victory sermons, enjoined all loyal subjects and Christian men to sink, burn, or otherwise destroy to the extent of their ability. Days of innocence and virtue, whither have ye fled! Shall I never again feel the sweet serenity of soul which attended upon the consciousness of knowing that the fellows I blew to kingdom come were natural enemies; that the cargoes I made prize of only ruined rascals that had the impiety to be born out of God-fearing, orthodox England"——

"Mr. Webbe, I am rather crabbed in temper just now, and mouthy attempts to confound legitimate, loyal war with piracy—your persiflage means that or nothing—will only increase that irritation. Either let me hear your "plain tale," or hold your peace: I am indifferent which, to be quite candid."

"Your politeness, I have before observed, Master Linwood, is, for your years, surprising. Nevertheless, as *I* happen just now to be in quite a heavenly frame of mind, I readily excuse an infirmity which, judging from your very bilious aspect, must be more offensive to its owner than to any one else. Seriously, though, I can't believe you have reason to be so nervously apprehensive that Clemence will have the cruelty to refuse—— There, there, don't jump out of the window or into the fire, and I'll steer as steadily as a flat broad-bottomed Dutchman.

"Once upon a time, then, as before explained, I was a strictly orthodox privateer; and for several years orthodoxy and a full purse kept, as is their natural wont, each other company. But all that's bright must fade; and slowly but surely the blockade of continental ports, constantly increasing in rigour and effectiveness, by the British cruisers, frightfully diminished the profits of that respectable line of business. Things, however, were not come by a long way to their present miserable pass ten years ago, or thereabout, when the baptism of fire and flood by which I became a child of France and a sharer in the glory of 'Les Victoires et Conquêtes des Français' took place. It was precisely at the time when Bonaparte, whose blazing star now seems so near its final setting, had assembled an immense army in the neighbourhood of Boulogne for the invasion of England. There is an old one-armed capitaine de corvette," continued Webbe, with out-laughing gaiety of heart, "living en retraite at Avranches, and who, by the by, was present at that blessed banquet, who has often explained to me how that little affair would, should, must, according to all scientific rules—but for one or two provoking illogical accidents—have come off. Had Villeneuve, he used to explain, persisted, in accordance with his bounden duty and positive instructions, in coaxing Nelson to continue seeking for him where he could not be found; and if Calder had not fallen in with and crippled a division of the French fleet, that fleet, favoured by a steady favourable breeze, would have safely convoyed the French Troops across the unguarded Channel to the shores of Albion, and landed them quietly there, in excellent condition. Those soldiers, as definitely arranged in the imperial programme, would, on the following day, have beaten, pulverised the English army; London would have been sacked, the House of Guelph and the British constitution abolished; England Scotland, Wales, and the town of Berwick-upon-Tweed parcelled out into departments, and the great emperor an the grand army have got safely back to France, whilst the British fleets were nowhere! A humbling lesson to the sublimity of intellect," added Mr. Webbe, "to reflect that one or two wretched accidents should have power to disconcert the most splendid conception of genius that has dazzled mankind since the days of that royal peer whose breeches cost him but a crown, which he held sixpence all too dear, and "——

"Confound your ceaseless chaff! It is irritating enough at all times, but especially so when the mind, torn, lacerated by conflicting doubts and fears, is"——

"Like sweet bells jangled, out of tune and harsh," interjected Webbe. "Just so. I remember that in the days of my youth, my own mind was in a similar condition, arising, in my case, from my being reduced for several weeks to a diet of weevily biscuits and foul cockroachy water, and not an over-supply of that——I've done—I've done. Stay where you are, and I'll run the remainder of the story off the reel without a hitch.

"Once upon a time, I resume—that time, as aforesaid— I was unsuccessfully dodging about in the *Wasp*, privateer a craft of about the same tonnage and armament as the *Scout*—off Ushant, till early one morning, it then blowing half a gale of wind, with every sign of more hands being clapped on to the bellows, when a large schooner hove in sight. We took her to be a French or Spanish merchant-man—a mistake, as we too late discovered. The schooner was, in fact, the privateer *Passe-partout*—a queer name, given her by her somewhat famous captain, Jules Renaudin —an unconscionable individual, who, not content with the exalted glory of being blown up with the *Orient*, of which he was a petty officer, at the Nile, had got himself appointed commander of the said *Passe-partout*, not so much with a view to commercial profit, as for the ungrateful purpose of having a shy at the nation that had given him such a hoist in life.

"You may depend upon it," continued Webbe, "that if I had known my customer, I should have given the *Passe-partout* a very wide berth. Gain, not glory, is the object of every privateer captain that understands his business.

Fighting is not our vocation, and should always be avoided, unless the prize is not only well worth the powder, but pretty sure to be won, at little cost. That was far from being the case with the *Passe-partout*, from which nothing but hard knocks was to be looked for. There was, however, no help for it, so at it we went ding-dong, and continued blazing away at each other for perhaps half an hour, when the *Passe-partout* caught fire—by what chance was never known—and ten minutes afterwards, blew up. There was so wild a sea running, that we could only pick up nine of the unfortunate Frenchmen, amongst whom was Captain Renaudin himself, dreadfully scorched and otherwise injured.

"Our own condition was a perilous one. The enemy's shot had told with terrible effect upon both the hull and spars of the *Wasp*. She made water fast; and during the following night, the gale having meanwhile increased to a hurricane, both the masts, which had been badly wounded, went by the board. We managed to rig up a jury-mast; the men worked bravely at the pumps; and by the middle of the third day after the fight, the *Wasp* had so far staggered—unguidedly staggered up Channel, that she was off Gris Nez, a point northward of Boulogne. By that time the pumps had become unserviceable; the jury-mast and a portion of the bulwarks had been swept away, and the raging sea made a clean breach over the struggling, straining ship, which no one but myself believed would float an hour longer. That was not my opinion, because I had noticed that for some time she had not sunk deeper in the water, whence I concluded that the leak was effectually choked by some substance, one of the sails probably, flung overboard for that purpose, having been sucked into the opening. No argument or persuasion could, however, persuade the men to remain; and as the *Wasp's* boats had sustained no material injury, the English crew, which, fortunately as it had turned out, were far short of the usual complement, took to them, happily without accident, though the operation was a very ticklish one, and pulled off, after vainly entreating me to accompany them, for the English coast. They were soon lost sight of; and next the French prisoners determined on trying their luck in a small boat, which had belonged to the unlucky *Passe-partout*

i

Renaudin was dying, and could not be removed. It was as well so, for the boat had not gone two hundred yards from the brig, when she capsized, and every man in her was swallowed up in the raging waters.

"The *Wasp*, though buried in the sea, still floated, and would no doubt continue to do so if she were not flung upon the shore, or bumped against one of the numerous rocks thereabout. During the night, Renaudin died; and when morning dawned, I was consequently the only living man man on board. The tempest had meanwhile greatly abated; and as the day grew stronger and clearer, I saw that the brig had drifted considerably southward, was then off Boulogne, and that numerous telescopes were directed towards her from that place. Renewed hope—I may say renewed assurance of life, once more pulsated vigorously in my veins, and I began casting about as to how I could best turn to account the fortunate deliverance which seemed to be at hand. I soon made up my mind, and the more speedily from seeing that boats were preparing to put off from Boulogne for the dismasted brig. I stripped Renaudin, bundled the body overboard, arrayed myself in his clothes, managed to fasten a tricolor to the mizzen-stump, and awaited my deliverance. It was not long delayed. The heroic Renaudin was safely conveyed on shore, and so sedulously ministered to, that on the following day he was able to favour his admiring auditors with the charming story published in *Les Victoires et Conquêtes*, under the head of Le Passe-partout et Le Wasp.'

"How he, Jules Renaudin, had engaged the British privateer off Ushant, in the *Passe-partout*, which, taking fire during the engagement, had left him and his gallant sailors no other chance of success other than that of taking to the boats and boarding the enemy. That was done; and victory, faithful to the glorious tricolor, crowned the audacious attempt. Then came the tempest; and Captain Renaudin related how it happened that the French and English crews persisting, spite of his commands and supplications, to quit the ship, had all miserably perished.

"This," said Webbe, "is a meagre outline of the precious flam which I, under stress of utter ruin and a French prison, extemporised, and, helped by my knowledge of poor

Renaudin's antecedents, derived from broken conversations with him since he had been on board the *Wasp*, nicely filled up and rounded off with many interesting details, to the great satisfaction of an applauding auditory. Renaudin was, I knew, personally unknown in Northern France, or I might hardly have risked so audacious a ruse. It succeeded, fortunately, to admiration. I was flattered, fêted, a handsome subscription was raised for me, and the hull and stores of the *Wasp*, which was cast on shore during the night, were sold for my benefit. Admiral Ducos, the French minister of marine, visited, warmly complimented me, and in frank compliance with a suggestion of some of my new friends, penned a certificate—I will shew it you some day —which sets forth that the bearer, Jules Renaudin, formerly one of the équipage of *L'Orient*, is a gallant seaman, who has deserved well of France and of all Frenchmen. I went in," added Webbe, " for the cross of the Legion of Honour; but Napoleon happening to be extremely busy just then with his own pet make-believe, mine missed that distinguished recognition, which was a pity. Still, I had done pretty well under the very awkward circumstances; and I have since, off and on, played in the honoured name of Renaudin a fairly successful, but deucedly delicate game, which I am not at all sorry is fast drawing towards a close. And now, my dear Linwood, we will, with your permission, adjourn to the table d'hôte—— Ah! you have no appetite! The idea of dinner even disgusts a sensitive organisation, over which the divine passion exercises just now despotic influence."

" Go to the devil!"

" All in good time. Meanwhile, may I ask the favour of being informed, as soon as you return from the charming, and, I *will* hope, not inexorably cruel Clemence, how —— Have a care, my dear fellow, homicide, even if effected with a decanter, is punishable in this country by the galleys! Good-bye. My compliments to dear Clemence."

CHAPTER XI.

THE SALIENT ANGLE.

It was less from lack of appetite, than as affording a respite from Webbe's blustering banter, that I declined accompanying him to the table d'hôte. I dined alone; not very heartily, to be sure; a depressing sense of helpless involvement prevented that. I was perplexed in the extreme, but it would be scarcely worth while to recite the moony meditations in which I remained plunged till evening had for some time set in, seeing that they resulted in the forlorn conviction that to boldly repudiate the absurd marriage urged by Webbe's overbearing insistance, and the tears and tenderness of Clémence, would not only break the heart of a gentle girl, whose only fault, within my knowledge, was loving too well and most unwisely, but might be in effect to pass sentence of death upon my father. My only hope, therefore, was in the girl's concurrence with the delaying suggestion embodied in my note, the answer to which it was full time I should seek.

Voices in loud altercation caused me to pause as I was passing forth, and I looked in for a moment at the guests assembled round the table d'hôte. There were several officers of the line and national guard there; amongst them the warlike bootmaker. The company appeared to be in a state of considerable excitement. Sicard was upon his legs, nearly opposite Webbe, declaiming with lively gesticulation upon Bonapartist and Bourbon politics in general, as well as I could make out, and with especial and malignant reference, it seemed, by the fixed direction of his flaming face and eyes, to M. Jacques Le Gros. The privateer captain, whose back was towards me, had, I supposed, presumed to differ in opinion from the shop-keeping warrior; but feeling quite satisfied that Webbe was able to hold his own against a regiment of wordy assailants, I went on my dismal way to the Rue Dupetit Thouars.

Truly a dismal way! A cold, driving rain was falling; and dirty, dingy St. Malo, darkly visible by the dull light of lanterns swung on ropes across the narrow streets, looked dirtier and dingier than ever. I had no umbrella, and as the distance was not very great, preferred hastening on to returning for one. It thus happened, that butting blindly ahead against the wind and rain with my hat pulled over my eyes, I missed the right turning; and after splashing along for more than the time that should have brought me near Madame de Bonneville's magasin, I found myself nowhere that I knew of, or could immediately ascertain, the streets being completely deserted. I made several starts in directions which I fancied should lead to the Rue Dupetit Thouars, without result, till I ran against an *autorité*, as he came sharply round a corner. The collision was violent, and a little irritated the gendarme.

"Sacre bleu!" he exclaimed; "who is this?" To which I replied by asking him how far off and where the Rue Dupetit Thouars might be.

"How far off? Where? At least a quarter of an hour off, if you walk fast. Go to the top of this alley; then turn to the right, traverse the *Place*, ascend the Rue St. Jean, and inquire again."

The cocked-hatted functionary, who was apparently bound upon pressing business, stayed no further parley. I went off, as directed, at the top of my speed, and was traversing the Place, when I was suddenly brought to a stand-still by a glimpse of two women as they rapidly crossed over at some distance from me, and disappeared up a narrow street. One of them, there could be no doubt, was Fanchette: the face of the other, as I for a moment caught it by the light of a lamp close to which she passed, seemed to be that of the fierce Frenchwoman I had once seen in the Isle of Wight—of Louise Féron, *alias* Madame de Bonneville!

So sure was I of this, that I impulsively called out and ran towards the women; with what intent, had I come up with them, would have puzzled me to say; when, having lost sight of the chase, and hot, steaming with excitement and exertion, I stopped to take breath and consider what I was to do, or had purposed doing. I didn't know at all. Probably a vague desire to cut in some way or other the Gordian-knot by which I was enmeshed and hampered, had caused the inconsiderate pursuit. As the reader already knows, I was ever rash and headlong. Should I meet and be recognised by Madame de Bonneville, our fine scheme would of course fall to pieces at once, not to speak or think of other correlative possibilities. And might not her inopportune return to St. Malo have the same result? Certainly it might, and it behoved me therefore to be trebly wary and circumspect; and first of all, to ascertain beyond doubt that I had not been mistaken—that Fanchette's woman-companion was really Louise Féron.

This step in mental demonstration was nearly *pari passu* with that, I having quickly resumed walking, which brought me to the corner of a street I knew, by the *épicier's* shop on the opposite side, to be the Rue Dupetit Thouars. Fanchette and Madame de Bonneville—if Madame de Bonneville it was that I had seen—did not, it instantly occurred to me, turn down, or, more properly, up that street. They had gone on in a straight direction. Most likely, then, fancy *had* fooled me. Besides, when one came to think of it seriously, was it likely that a person just arrived at home after a long, fatiguing journey by Diligence, would go owling about the town at such a time and in such weather? The notion was absurd. I might therefore venture, at all events, to call at the magasin, and end all misgivings upon the subject. I saw by the faint light cast into the dark street from the window, that it was still open, and in a few minutes, after peering in, and seeing only the two workwomen sewing away as usual at the further end, I opened the door and walked in.

" Is Madame de Bonneville within?" I asked.

" *Madame* de Bonneville!" was the reply in a tone of surprise. " *Mademoiselle*, no doubt, monsieur means," added the woman with a smile. " Yes."

" Madame is not then returned from Paris, as I thought she might have been?"

" No, monsieur. I do not think she is expected for several days."

I *had* been mistaken. There could be no longer question of it, and I passed on with a more assured step.

Clemence received me with a kind of gracious, pensive ceremony. She was alone, nicely dressed. and there was positive enchantment in her blushing smile, and the trembling tears which, as seen by the lamp-light, kindled her sweet blue eyes with a penetrating, softened lustre. "After all," thought I, as I raised the tips of her fingers to my lips and returned her low-toned, agitated greeting—"After all, since it is my destiny to be wedded in my own despite, Fate might have served me a scurvier trick—have mated me with a much less agreeable partner. I shall console myself after a while; never fear. Time will do more than reconcile me to a young and charming wife, whose disinterested devotedness would excite a grateful tenderness in the coldest, most obdurate of human hearts."

" You are wet, mon ami," said Clemence, without withdrawing her hand, which trembled very much, from mine. " Shall you not take cold? "

" O, dear, no, mademoiselle. Water to us amphibious islanders is a kind of second atmosphere."

The girl sighed, blushed, drooped her sad eyes, and re-seated herself upon the *canapé*. Evidently her thoughts were painfully preoccupied. Female instinct had, it was plain, detected the false pretence of my note, and she felt, sweet, sensitive child, that I did not love, though I might esteem, respect, even admire her. I would have given much to have been able to chase away that green and yellow melancholy by fervid words—*true* words I doubted not in a future though not present sense—that might deceive her into happiness. Just then, however, I could not, had my life depended upon doing so, I felt so down-in-the-mouth, so altogether damp, limpid, uncomfortable.

" I broke an embarrassing pause by asking if Fanchette was at home.

" No, mon ami : she wished to go out, rude as the night is; I also," added the maiden looking up and regarding me with a penetrating, puzzling look—" I also was desirous she should be away, in order that at this decisive epoch in our lives we might be secure from interruption."

"You reason with judgment, with delicacy, mademoiselle, under all circumstances," said I, hardly knowing in truth what I did say, so much had the young woman's peculiar look disconcerted me. I recognised in it a world of tenderness and purity; but, as it seemed to me, a compassionate tenderness, such as I, under the circumstances, had I been savage enough, might have expressed towards her.

Again a most embarassing silence, which I put an end to by plunging desperately *in media res.*

" You have read the note, mademoiselle, which I had the honour of placing in your hands to-day ? "

" O yes, many times over, and believe me, mon ami, with many bitter, bitter tears ! I am very young; entirely without experience of the world; still I feel, acutely feel the cruel grief which must ever wring the heart of one whose devotion is met with the chilling repulse of at best a sorrowing, sympathising compassion— a regretful pity, which "——

" Dear Clémence ! " I exclaimed, starting up, and taking her passive hand in both mine. " Be assured that "——

" Do not persist, mon ami," interrupted the sobbing girl. " Captain Webbe has been your faithful, eloquent interpreter. Me, with all his practised acuteness, he has not so well understood. It is true, however, that I agree with him in his appreciation of the manifold advantages that will be derived from our marriage. May I not, dear friend, cast aside at this supreme moment the affectations of girlhood, and speak out frankly, honestly, as all honest human souls should to each other? Yes, I fully appreciate the desirableness, the indispensability of this marriage : that it will not only insure justice, but temper that justice with mercy. I yield to that paramount consideration ; and to-morrow, since it must be so, I will pledge you my faith at the altar of God—a faith, mon ami, which you need not doubt will be kept as sacred as if our hearts beat perfectly in unison with each other. To-morrow be it then, monsieur ; and if "——

" Permettez, mademoiselle," I exclaimed, bewilderedly interrupting a proposal, equivalent, as interpreted by the young lady's look and tone of heroic self-sacrifice, to an offer on her part to be chopped into little bits at the command of cruel, imperious duty—" Permit me, mademoiselle, to say that I would not for the wealth of worlds take advantage of the peculiar, the extremely delicate circumstances in which you are now placed, and which cannot but influence a decision of lifelong consequences. It would be unpardonable to do so. Once restored to your true home—able to appreciate the vast change in your social position — within reach of maternal counsels, you will better"——

"Ah, my poor friend," interrupted Clémence with perplexing graciousness ; "Captain Webbe has revealed to me that generous nature ; shewn how fully capable you are of concealing, for my sake, the wound, which would nevertheless continue to bleed and fester inwardly. I may not selfishly accept that sacrifice. The brilliant future of which you speak, would not, if this moment realised, change or colour my sentiments in the faintest degree. It is true that, at first, I did not, as it were, feel the beatings of my own simple girl's heart amidst the throbbings of anticipative pride and exultation; and this is a remorse to me, since, had it not been so, the fancy excited by my portrait would not probably have grown to a passion which, be assured, though I will not pretend I can at present return, commands my liveliest sympathy, and will hereafter, I do not doubt—neither must you, dear friend—compel my warmest affections."

"Plait-il ?" said I, using a French idiom which it is impossible to precisely translate, but expressive, in this instance, of unbounded mystification and astonishment. "Plait-il ?"

Another explanatory word or two will be necessary before proceeding further with this confounding colloquy. I had risen, as previously stated, and taken the soft little hand of Mademoiselle Clémence in both mine. I continued so to hold it, and being a tall fellow benignly bending over a disconsolate damsel seated upon a French canapé or sofa, very low upon the feet, the musical low murmur, moreover, of the stream of eloquence with which I was favoured, obliging me to place my ear as close as politeness permitted to the sweet lips through which it welled, my upright legs and sharply inclined body formed two sides of an irregular square, of which the salient angle was towards the door leading from the magasin. The reader will now have realised my position *vis-à-vis* the amiable Clémence and the door opening into the shop, when uttering the interrogative exclamation of " Plait-il ? "

"True," resumed the damsel, in continuation rather than reply—" true, you have a right to be surprised that one so inferior in position and other social advantages,

should have forestalled you in the affections of one whom
a combination of romantic circumstances has invested,
in your partial eyes, with imaginary charms; but in
excuse, remember, dear William, how true, how devoted
he was to me when I was in reality but little better
than a poor *ouvrière*, with no prospect beyond——   Ha!
Ciel!"

Simultaneous, and mingling with the young lady's
abrupt exclamation, was a sudden rush of feet, furious
cries of "Scélérat!" "Coquin!" "Sacré Tonnerre!"
and the application of the toe of a boot to the seat of
my pale-blue pants—the before-mentioned salient angle
—so vigorously administered, as to pitch me into the
arms of the screaming girl in the most indecorous manner.

My comprehension of it all was as instantaneous as the
uproar and assault. I recognised by a flash of thought
that it was the "true," "devoted" Jacques Sicard who
had "forestalled" me in the affections, and kicked me
into the lap of a damsel, who, I had been gulled into
believing, was pining to death with unrequited love for
my precious, booby self. All this, I say, with the cor-
relatives, rushed in a moment with my flaming blood to
the tips of my ears and fingers, and I sprang round with
the rage and yell of a tiger.

The white wrath, under such circumstances, of an
athletic young man, must have had a somewhat terrifying
aspect; certainly it at once took the bounce out of Master
Sicard, who was, I saw, accompanied by a "National"
officer, with whom I had a slight speaking acquaintance.
The bootmaker leaped backwards with a cry of alarm, and
whipping out his sword, poked at, whilst he dodged me
round a table. I had no weapon, not even a stick, nothing
but my bare hands, with which I could not reach him;
no missile, but the brass lamp, was available, and seizing
that, I hurled it, after one whirl round my own head, with
all the strength that rage supplied, at Sicard's cranium.
The fellow turned away his face avoidingly, and the blow,
which must else have descended upon his brow or temple,
struck the back part of his skull, and he fell upon the
floor as if struck down by a pole-axe.

A torrent of blood gushed from the wound, and I
thought I had killed the unfortunate bootmaker. So did

Clémence, whose agonising grief as she clasped the insensible Jacques in her arms, and called upon all the saints in heaven to save him, was decisive of the hold he had obtained upon her heart; and although I had not felt, did not feel, the slightest love, in its conventional meaning, for the girl, I could at that moment have torn him to pieces—so fierce, so demon-like, under certain conditions, is outraged personal vanity.

"Monsieur cannot go away for the present," said my acquaintance, the officer of the national guard, mistaking a movement of irritability excited by the girl's wild ravings.

"I have no desire to go away," I replied. "The insolent fool, as you cannot but bear witness, brought the misfortune upon himself."

"I do not say the contrary," said the officer. "Still, monsieur, justice must take legal cognizance of the affair before you can be free to depart."

"That is but reasonable," I said; and seating myself, I moodily awaited the termination of the unfortunate business.

The shopwomen had run in with lights, lifted Sicard from the floor, placed him upon the canapé, and sent off immediately for a surgeon. The coming of that gentleman was not long delayed; and after carefully examining and probing the wound, he exclaimed:

"Reassure yourselves, my friends; the wound is nothing—that is to say, it is not in the least dangerous. Maître Sicard is only stunned, and will be well as ever tomorrow, I answer for it."

This was an immense relief to me—infinitely more so to Clémence, as her rapturous sobs abundantly testified. "Upon my word," thought I, "the favour that magnanimous damsel proposed conferring upon me to-morrow morning—her hand, whilst her heart was that blustering bootmaker's—was a highly flattering one. By—— But swearing is of no use. Yet that ever Mrs. Waller's daughter should be enamoured of a vulgar cordwainer! Still, what can be said? It is proverbial that misfortune brings strange bedfellows together."

"There is nothing, then, to detain me here any longer,' said I.

"Nothing whatever, monsieur, that I am aware of," replied the surgeon.

"Maître Sicard," observed the officer, who left the house with me, "is a really good fellow at bottom, but at the same time, it must be admitted, rash in temper, which has also been unusually tried this evening. He had already crossed swords with your relative, Monsieur Jacques Le Gros, before leaving the Hôtel de l'Empire."

"Indeed! Pray, how happened that?"

"They had a dispute at the table d'hôte, and Sicard, who had been drinking freely, insulted and challenged your uncle. Bah! It was over in a twinkling. Monsieur Le Gros, a *lapin*, as one can easily see, borrowed my sword, and that of poor Sicard was sent flying out of his hand the instant the blades touched each other. Your relative," added the officer, "has, it must be confessed, a tongue which stabs like a poniard, and I was not surprised at poor Sicard's rage at finding himself not only so easily disarmed, but mocked at over the market."

"He should bear himself more discreetly, if he would avoid such hazards."

"It is true. Cupid, at all events, favours him, if Mars does not. The sentiments of Mademoiselle Clemence towards him are no longer doubtful."

"Possibly. I think my road lies in this direction, does it not?"

"To the Hôtel de l'Empire?—Yes; but the distance is considerable, and I have thoughtlessly brought you out of your way."

"I do not mind that, now that the rain has ceased. Good-night, monsieur."

"Au plaisir, Monsieur Jean Le Gros."

I walked hastily on, but, absorbed in thought, missed the right direction for the second time that evening. Providentially so, a superstitious person would say, for again I caught sight of Fanchette with her strapping woman-companion—and—yes—my eyes did not deceive me, Captain Webbe had joined them! They crossed the street a considerable way ahead, and walked swiftly *from* me; I followed with eager yet cautious steps; it was, I felt forebodingly, to be a night of strange revelations.

Captain Webbe and his two associates stopped before

a respectable *cabaret*, and presently went in. I crossed to the opposite side for the purpose of reconnoit ring before attempting a closer approach. In a few minutes there was a light in one of the rooms on the first floor, into which the three new-comers, as I could see by their shadows on the blinds, were presently ushered. They took seats close to each other, and were about, I doubted not, to enter upon a conference, at which it was highly desirable I should make one, unseen by the speakers.

It might be managed, I thought; and crossing over, I entered the lower, or, as we should say, the bar-room of the cabaret, and called for a glass of liqueur.

"Can I speak privately with you for a minute?" said I, addressing the garçon, who brought an order for wine and oysters from the party in the first floor.

"Certainly, monsieur," replied the man readily, 'though with some surprise. "This way, if you please."

The negociation, marvellously quickened by the transfer of two Napoleons from my purse to that of the garçon's, resulted favourably, and I was placed without loss of time in a dark closet close to the part of the room where he proposed laying the supper; and the partition between being of thin wood-panelling, I could hear pretty distinctly for a time all that passed, subdued as was the tone in which Webbe and his companions conversed.

First, I discovered that Madame de Bonneville had been no further off than Dol all the while, there awaiting in ambush, as it were, the fruition of the plot concocted by her and the privateer captain, with the active connivance of Fanchette. The precise bearing or purpose of that plot was not so easily gathered from the scraps of discourse relating thereto. Madame's sudden arrival at St. Malo was, I also found, prompted by a misgiving as to Webbe's fidelity, of which she thought to more thoroughly assure herself by a personal interview before he went away.

"So many promising schemes," said Louise Feron, in English—Fanchette having, I supposed, been only partially admitted to the conspirators' confidence—"So many promising schemes for utilising the bold deed you and I carried through fifteen years ago, have been wrecked almost as soon as launched, that my anxiety—my suspicious anxicty, if you will—for the success of this last one, is quite ex-

cusable. It is full time, too, that the business should be
brought to a conclusion. The state of my affairs, and of
yours too, captain, demand its speedy settlement."

"That settlement—a marriage-settlement," replied
Webbe, "will, I repeat to you for the hundredth time,
come off before forty-eight hours have passed away."

"That is everything. If Clemence be once married to
young Linwood, I shall have taken hostages of fortune."

"No doubt of it : and Clemence will be a fortunate girl
too. Linwood, though easily led by the nose as asses are,
is a trump of a young fellow, as young fellows go."

"He will be rich—that is the main consideration. And,
dites-donc, Monsieur le Capitaine," added the woman in
French, "what is all that I read in the newspapers of
your son, who had slain one Le Moine, being detected
in the disguise of an American naval officer at a banquet
given at Avranches in honour of Captain Jules Renaudin."

"That is a droll story," said Webbe, which I will relate
to you after we have finished the oysters."

Their conversation during the consumption of the said
oysters referred to matters of no interest to me ; and supper done, they removed further off, so that I could only
hear what was said when their voices were unusually
raised. I knew by the frequent occurrence of the names
of Linwood, Le Moine, Harry, and, as I fancied more than
once, that of Maria Wilson, that Webbe was relating my
adventures, no doubt with his usual ad libitum variations.
The narrative greatly amused his auditors, and the *entente
cordiale* appeared to be re-established between the mutually
mistrustful confederates.

Webbe rose to go, and then madame, who intended
sleeping at the cabaret and returning to Dol on the following morning, said with absolute tone and emphasis :

"Remember, Captain Webbe, that I will not be juggled
with ; that you cannot play your own game out successfully without first *winning* mine. This marriage *first*, or,
by all that is sacred or infernal, I "——

"Madame, your suspicions are absurd, childish," interrupted Webbe. "Do you suppose I need to be reminded
that we are both embarked in the same boat, and must
float or founder together ? "

"Well, I merely remind you that I will not be fooled,
happen what may. And now, before you go, as to "——

᾽ did not catch the remainder of the sentence; and at the end of another ten minutes' low-toned dialogue, of which I could hear a confused murmur only, Webbe and Fanchette left the house: I did the same soon afterwards, reaching the Hôtel de l'Empire a few minutes before Webbe.

CHAPTER XII.

A CHANGE OF COSTUME.

PASSION had not entirely swamped the slight stock of common-sense I was possessed of; and restraining myself by a strong effort from forthwith denouncing Webbe's treacherous villainy to his face, I hurried off to bed, there to reflect quietly upon the course I ought to adopt. But quiet reflection was no more possible than sleep, till the wordless rage of mortified self-love, aggravated by the savage consciousness of what an egregious booby my own absurd conceit had helped to make me, had in some degree exhausted itself, partly, as I remember, by furiously punching the pillows, as imaginary substitutes for the privateer captain's head, and, but less frequently and fiercely, that of M. Sicard. "As easily led by the nose as asses are," was I! Why, ay, hitherto; but not *quite* so easily for the future, he shall find, now that I thoroughly know the gentleman who fancies he has got that prominent feature of mine so securely betwixt his finger and thumb. It strikes me very forcibly, noble captain, do you know, that, clever and cunning as you are, and close upon the winning-post as you and that Jezebel Féron believe yourselves to be, it will not be impossible to trip up the heels of both, for all that's come and gone yet. Very far from impossible; though assuredly whoever would successfully contend with such wily, practised devils, should maturely meditate his plan of battle.

I anxiously sought to do so. One considerable advantage that partially overheard conference certainly gave me: I now knew that Webbe and the woman Féron were not only confederate with each other in the abduction of Mrs.

Waller's child, but sworn accomplices in the sc*heme th*. was "to utilise" that atrocious deed. I was no longer *in* the dark, then, as to the sinister complicity of the privateer captain with the pretended mother of Clémence; and I comprehended that, whilst playing into each other's hands up to a certain point, they had individually a separate game to bring to a triumphant issue. "Remember, Webbe, that you cannot play your own game out successfully without first winning mine. This marriage *first*, or, by all that's sacred or infernal"——, quoth the woman, the unspoken threat evidently implying that she would at all hazards mar *his* particular project, should he prove false to her. Yes, but what could be the particular project contemplated by Webbe, to which my marriage with Clémence was the enforced, indispensable preliminary? There I was at sea again, without rudder or compass. The obtainment of the reward promised by my mother, and largely augmented as well as guaranteed by Mrs. Linwood! What else could it be? But how, on the other hand, would that marriage, simply because I should be tolerably rich, "utilise" her crime to the woman-conspirator's so complete satisfaction? She might, it was true, count safely enough that in that case the affection, mingled with fear, with which she inspired the stolen child, would stand between her and the legal vengeance of the Linwoods; but that, it was now apparent, she had boldly challenged by disclosing, through Webbe, the secret of her pretended daughter's birth. The realisation of the reward, which there could be no doubt she would share, was again the only rational solution I could arrive at; and tiring at length of a barren cogitation in which I only slipped from one untenable hypothesis to another, I bent my mind to the elaboration of a counter-plot, which, if carried out successfully, would effectually confound their knavish tricks, of whatever nature or design those tricks might be.

I must make a confidante of Clemence, to begin with. She would, of course, have already comprehended that, after her impassioned apostrophe, in my hearing, to the wounded bootmaker, marriage with me, were sh* still herself disposed to acquiesce in that dreadful martyrdom, was quite out of the question. Then Madame de Bonneville's conversation with Webbe would prove to her that that lady was on the verge of ruin, only to be averted by that impossible marriage, *or*, as I should put it, by her, Clemence's, flight with me to England, under the protection of some respectable female, whose services a handsome *douceur* would easily secure, taking with us the necklace, armlets, and other *pièces d'accusation;* I, on my part, solemnly pledging myself for Mrs. Waller and my father, that not only no legal prosecution of Madame de Bonneville should be instituted, but that half the reward, at least, promised to Webbe should be given to her upon the simple condition, that she made a formal declaration upon oath, of all the circumstances attending the carrying off the child Lucy Hamblin. I could further represent that if she, Clemence, should remain obstinately constant to the cordwainer, the Wallers might, possibly, be brought to acquiesce in her wishes; whereas it was plain that Madame de Bonneville would, for obvious reasons, remain inexorably adverse to such a connection. Finally, I resolved that, should all other inducements fail in determining Clemence to take wing at once from France, I would propose that she and Sicard should be forthwith united in the holy bonds of wedlock, and that he should accompany us to England: I would not, however, have recourse to that temptation except in the last resort, and after all less potent persuasives had been tried and failed. The rescue of my father's name from ignominy was the great end I was bound to keep in view; and if that could only be gained by forwarding a *mésalliance* between Lucy Hamblin and Jacques Sicard, the distasteful condition must e'en be complied with. Sicard bore a fair character. Mrs. Waller's daughter did not need to marry a rich husband, and the young people were strongly attached to each other: so that, positively, unless all novel-writers were arrant blockheads—a notion not to be entertained for a moment—I should be doing a highly meritorious act in assisting to legally unite two loving, ardent hearts, which must else be cruelly sundered—broken, perhaps, who knew! Still, in deference to an absurd social prejudice which I could not quite away with, the *bonne bouche* of the bootmaker should, I re-determined, be the last bait with which I would tempt the timid maiden to break the strong

K

fetters of habitual fear and subjection, and boldly seize
the fortunate opportunity, which missed, might never
again court her acceptance.

A good plot—an excellent plot; one that, unless I
blundered grossly, could hardly fail of success; and who
then would nave been led by the nose?—William Linwood
or the valiant captain who arranged the private marriage,
bridegroom personally unknown to the retained priest,
settled the scheme of flight, and kept Baptiste in readiness
to ferry over the happy pair to the British shore and
safety!

Really, for a while, I could scarcely credit my own
cleverness in devising so glorious a turning of the tables
—so delicious a hoist of the engineer with his own petard!
Modest misgivings as to the perfect soundness of my
calculations did not long disturb or keep me awake; and
after a comfortable snooze, I leaped out of bed in a
state of entire self-satisfaction, and with a confidence in
my own sagacity as cool and clear as the bright wintry
morning streaming in broad daylight through the chamber-
windows.

If Vanity, O paradise of fools, so frequently leads
otherwise sufficiently sensible men into thy dream-domain,
it not the less delights to plunge them, while they sleep,
into the real and fatalest quagmires which lurk beneath
thy cloud-like, illusive surface! As thus with me:

My haste in dressing was arrested by the discovery,
that the puce-red redingote and blue silk vest were
irretrievably ruined by large patches of lamp-oil. In
whirling the lamp round my head on the previous evening,
I had managed to plentifully besprinkle those garments
with the inodorous liquid, and to wear them again was impossible. I was consequently obliged to have recourse
to my original wardrobe; and as the pale-blue pants contrasted abominably with a decent English black coat, and
waistcoat, they also were exchanged for less gay integu-
ments. The transformation thus effected in my person-
ality mightily pleased me; and necessity having compelled me to so far cast off the piebald costume of the
I as de Calais, and as I was, besides, to leave France in a
day or two at furthest, it seemed to me that I might even
venture to complete the operation. I did so: discarded

the atrocious ear-rings, and not without considerable labour and expenditure of soap and water, dis-Brutusised my hair. The change was really marvellous : I was myself again; and having always piqued myself upon being a well-dressed young fellow, the thought flashed through me with a glow of exultation as I surveyed myself to as great an extent as possible in the diminutive dressing-glass, that Mademoiselle Clemence would now see to somewhat better advantage the individual, to accept whom as a husband had involved, on her part, so distressing a sacrifice. There was certainly no accounting for taste ; still, as between me and that bullet-headed bootmaker, there could, I flattered myself, be no——

Quick footsteps outside, and a sharp knocking at the chamber-door, suddenly challenged my attention to an announcement in the voice of the *femme de chambre* that "une jeune personne" below desired to see M. Jean Le Gros immediately.

"Une jeune personne," desirous of seing me immediately! Who, in wonder's name, could it be? Mademoiselle Clemence? Hastening to obey the surprising summons, I was met, upon emerging from the chamber, by a little scream from the femme de chambre, who started back, exclaiming : "My God, who is that?"

"Me, assuredly—Monsieur Jean Le Gros."

"My faith, it *is* the voice and droll accent, but"——

I was quickly out of hearing, but looking back as I turned down stairs, at the further end of the corridor, I saw the woman staring after me with wide-opened eyes and mouth—a pantomimic continuation, as it were, of her amazed, doubtful "but."

The "jeune personne" waiting in the hall was one of Madame de Bonneville's workwomen, and she too was apparently only convinced by the voice and droll accent that I was really the M. Jean Le Gros to whom she had brought a letter from Mademoiselle Clemence, with strict injunctions to deliver it into his own hands. At the moment she was doing so, and saying: "Monsieur Le Gros will then have the goodness to read it at once," a gentleman came out of one of the lower rooms, and was leaving the hotel, but turned sharply round, and looked keenly at the individual addressed by that name. It was Mr. Tyler the American. I had seen him but once, and that but for a few moments on the ramparts the day before, and as he, though with somewhat of a puzzled, mystified air, passed on his way without speaking, I concluded that he had not recognised me; and that, it vaguely occurred to me, was as well.

The note from Mademoiselle Clemence ran thus: " CHER AMI—I pray of you not to speak of yester-evening's sad occurrences to any one, especially not to Captain Webbe, till you have seen me. I begin to understand that we have both, to a certain extent, been the dupes of that man's cunning roguery. Please to send word by bearer—simply yes or no—if I may expect to see you at about eleven o'clock this forenoon. C."

"Say 'Yes' to Mademoiselle de Bonneville from me," said I.

"I shall do so," replied the woman. "Good-day, monsieur."

I had hardly regained my chamber, when the femme de chambre again tapped at the door, and opening it, I saw she was accompanied by one of the waiters.

"Monsieur, your uncle," said the woman, with a peculiarity of tone that jarred disagreeably upon my ear, "desires me to say that he waits breakfast for you."

"Very well. And pray, what message do you bring?" said I, somewhat fiercely addressing the waiter, who, whilst the woman was speaking, eyed me with insolent inquisition.

"None," he replied, turning carelessly upon his heel; "none at present, Monsieur *Le Gros*."

I was a good deal startled by the man's manner, instantly suggesting as it did, that with my usual propensity for running my heedless head against a post, I had done a very rash and foolish thing in resuming the precise dress I had worn at the Avranches banquet, and likely enough described in the newspaper paragraph Madame de Bonneville had spoken of. Webbe would know if I had thereby incurred any real danger, and I hastened to join him.

He was reading a newspaper when I entered the break-fast-room, and seemed to be struck with astonishment and dismay at my appearance.

"What, rash boy," he angrily exclaimed, "is the meaning of this fool's trick? Are you tired of your life?"

I explained why I could not wear the puce-coloured redingote and blue vest, but of course without mentioning *how* the accident occurred. The explanation or apology seemed to mollify Webbe's wrath, but not in the least to diminish his alarm.

"Read this," he exclaimed, handing me the newspaper.

I ran over the paragraph to which his finger pointed. It was a pompous version of the Avranches affair, copied from a Havre journal, and therefore supplied, it might be taken for granted, by Auguste Le Moine. My person and dress, to the very cross-barred satin waistcoat I had on, the fashion in which I wore my hair, as well as *l'accent guttural* of my French, were carefully described ; and I blushed with shame for the inexcusable folly I had committed in taking pains to realise to the most cursory observer the portrait drawn of the "infamous spy " by the newspaper. The article concluded by impressing upon all patriotic Frenchmen the duty of assisting to apprehend the said "infamous spy," and deliver him into the hands of justice.

"You can now appreciate the extent of your insane rashness," said Webbe, as the paper dropped from my hands. "Who has seen you in that dress?" he added with peremptory sternness.

"The garçon Edouard, the femme de chambre whose face is pitted with the small-pox, and one of Madame de Bonneville's workwomen, who brought me a note from Mademoiselle Clemence." I did not think it necessary to mention Mr. Tyler, my impression being that he had not recognised me.

A bitter oath broke from Webbe's ashy, quivering lips. It was plain that he thought the peril deadly, imminent, and of a kind which no courage or readiness of resource on his part might avail to turn aside or elude. Deadly, imminent peril to me only it at first appeared, not to himself.

"As if your position," he went on to say, "was not already, after the publication of this accursed paragraph in a St. Malo journal, sufficiently critical ! Come, how-

ever, what may, I am guiltless of your blood: you cannot but admit that. But it is madness to stand idly
babbling here. I must see that sly knave Edouard at
once. He was reading the newspaper when I came into
the room, and you may be arrested, walked off, and done
for, before the day is two hours older. Do not stir from
this till I return."

The privateer captain was soon back again, and appeared to be even more excited and perturbed than when
he left the room.

"It is as I feared," he said. "Edouard has identified
you, as he could hardly help doing, with the newspaper
portrait. A considerable bribe, coupled with an indirect
threat and promise, pointing to the future—he believing,
as the newspaper intimates, that you are a confidential agent
of the Bourbons, whose restoration is now only a question
of a few days or weeks, more or less—has perhaps secured
his and Marguerite's silence. *Perhaps*, I say; for there
was a knavish glimmer in the fellow's eyes when I placed
the rouleau of Napoleons in his hand, which forbids trust
in his purchased promises. Upon my soul, Linwood,"
added Webbe, "I cannot at all understand you. Ten
minutes ago, you were as alarmed as I am; and now your
cheek has regained its colour, and you listen to what I
say with the coolness of an iceberg. Is this a sign of calm
determination or of mere doltishness?"

"I am not going to be scared away from St. Malo, Mr.
Webbe, till the purpose that brought me here has been accomplished; of that be quite assured. And reflection tells me
it is preposterous to argue that I have made myself amen-
able as a spy to the sentence of a court-martial, able as I
am to prove the entirely pacific nature of the errand that
brought me to France."

"You talk of you know not what," rejoined Webbe,
with increasing heat. "Whether shooting you by sentence of a court-martial would be strictly legal or not, will
not weigh a scruple in the matter. The practical consideration is, that Schwartzenberg's irresistible march upon
Paris, and Wellington's triumphant progress in the south
of France, have so exasperated, maddened the French soldiery, that they would sacrifice a hecatomb of Englishmen upon much slighter evidence than that adduced by

young Le Moine against you. In this very paper there is
an account of the shooting of a French *émigré*, caught, poor
devil! at Rouen, and suspected only, the proofs being far from
conclusive, of being a secret agent of the Bourbons. The in-
flammable soil of France is on fire," continued Webbe,
"and had already become much too hot, I must tell you,
for the soles of *my* feet: I am therefore off at once; and
unless you are resolved to court destruction, you will follow my example. Of course, you and Mademoiselle Clemence," he added sharply, "have come to an understanding?"

"Mademoiselle Clemence and I *have* come to an understanding."

"What, then, do you mean by saying you will not be
scared out of St. Malo till the purpose that brought you
here has been accomplished?"

"Can I ask a young girl to take flight with me to
England at an hour's notice?"

"I should think so, when her consent has been obtained; the priest is ready at five minutes' notice to do
his office, and the life of her beloved *futur* is at stake. It
is your modest diffidence, Linwood," added Webbe, with
fast recovering calmness and good-humour, as he reseated
himself at the breakfast-table—"It is your modest
diffidence, Linwood, which suggests that difficulty. That
is an amiable quality of mind, I admit, but not without
its inconveniences, and, as I was remarking the other day
to my American friend, Mr. Tyler, especially so in regard
of his countrymen, of whom it is so prominent a charac-
teristic, causing them to so strictly respect the school-
copy maxim, of self-praise being no recommendation, as to,
possibly, hinder them from obtaining that paramount
position in the universal earth which they could, would,
should, might, or ought but for that to achieve."

"Richard's himself again!" said I; "his appetite for
breakfast and banter quite restored, I am glad to see. He
has been frightening himself and me with shadows."

"*Warning* shadows, my boy, of terrible realities, which
we must avoid or perish: still, having ascertained and
demonstrated the nature and bearings of the coming
danger, and the likeliest mode of avoiding it, there is not
the slightest use in whimpering about the matter; and a

hearty breakfast is, I assure you, a capital preparation for a day of peril and brave exertion. Let me help you to a slice of this excellent ham; and a cup of hot coffee, a fresh supply of which, if you will touch the *sonnette*, will, I daresay, be brought in by Master Edouard, whose equivocal phiz I should like to catch another and clearer glimpse of."

"Replenish the *cafetière*, Edouard," said Webbe, when that worthy answered the bell. "Whilst we have been idly discussing the awkward little affair you know of, our coffee has cooled to the temperature of the weather outside. And be sure to bring it yourself, *mon brave*, as I have another little word or two to read to you out of the same book that we opened together a few minutes ago."

"That fellow's grinning, sheepish face," resumed Webbe, when the door had closed after Edouard—"that fellow's grinning, sheepish face being interpreted, means that a struggle is going on in his brainpan between the honour-amongst-rogues principle of fairly earning the bribe he has pocketed, and an inclination to secure the favour, and, possibly, a few more Napoleons, of *Messieurs les Autorités*, by our betrayal. And if honour," added the privateer captain, drawing forth his gold watch, and transferring the long hand to his waistcoat-pocket—" and if honour is not strengthened, honour will, I plainly perceive, go to the wall—— Hush!"

" That will do, Edouard; we require nothing more, with the exception of a few last and most interesting words with you. Listen, *mon garçon*," continued Webbe: " I am about to place entire confidence in you; at the same time telling you frankly that it greatly annoys me to be obliged to do so."

"I can easily believe that, monsieur."

"To be sure you can. You must know, then, that my young friend here, being naturally desirous of living all the days of his life, deems it expedient to quit *la belle France* with as little delay as possible. To do so without incurring the risk of successful pursuit, he will require, or rather, as I shall accompany him, *we* shall require your assistance."

" My assistance, monsieur! "

"Your well-paid assistance, Edouard. I propose managing the affair in this way. Both of us have little matters to arrange, which will detain us till late in the evening, and we have settled to start at ten o'clock in a *chaise de poste*, which you will have ready, and have placed our luggage in, by that hour."

"But, messieurs, it is impossible! Such an act would "——

"Make you a richer man by fifty Napoleons," interrupted Webbe—"fifty gold Napoleons, mon brave, for a trifling service which *cannot* by possibility compromise you."

"Fifty Napoleons, monsieur, of course, means in addition to—to "——

"In addition to those you have already received?— Certainly. It is understood, then. You are sure of Marguerite?"

"Perfectly sure, monsieur."

"That will do, then. Stay; I have lost one of the hands of my watch; and as a correct knowledge of time will be essential just now, I will thank you to get a new one fitted, and if it can be done by the hour we propose leaving, have it cleaned."

"It shall be done, monsieur, without fail," replied Edouard, taking the watch. "It will be well, too, that no one should have an opportunity of reading this newspaper," he added, as he thrust the *Journal de St. Malo* into his pocket.

"A good thought, Edouard; and now bring us pens, ink, and paper."

"We shall lose the watch," said Webbe as soon as we were again alone, "as well as our portmanteaus and clothes. But nothing less would, I feared, satisfy him, upon reflection, that we should be here this evening at ten o'clock, to present him with fifty Napoleons."

"You do not then intend to do so?"

Webbe laughed out as merrily as if enjoying an excellent joke in the safe security of the\ *Scout's* cabin. "Once upon a time you know," said he presently, "there was a gentleman, that in pure kindness to his horse buttered his hay; and now I have so thickly buttered the promised provender of the greedy *ass* we have to deal

with, that the bare imagination of such a feast will seal
his lips till you, I trust, are far beyond the range of a
French firing party. Why, man alive, what are you
dreaming of? Once permitted to leave this hotel, we
should be simply mad to return! In one hour from this,
or less if possible, I shall have left St. Malo; in three, at
furthest, you, your wife, and Fanchette, will, I hope, be on
the road to Granville—— Ah! here is our friend Edouard
with pens, ink, paper, and sealing-wax. All right, Edouard;
you will not forget ten precisely, and—the fifty Napoleons."

The man grinned, bowed, and left the room, fully intending, I was sure, to fulfil his part in the bargain.

"And now, Linwood, my brave lad," said Webbe, "I
have to make a request which may carry an ominous
sound with it, but is in reality only a matter of common
precaution. I go overland to Cherbourg; thence probably,
if Auguste Le Moine is not in the way, to Havre de Grace.
You with your charming bride proceed to England, *via*
Jersey. Now, distressing as the possibility of being cut
down like the grass on one's wedding-day must be to the
sensitive mind of a youthful bridegroom, it is useless endeavouring to conceal from ourselves that you *may* be
overtaken and summarily shot; in which case you will
experience whatever consolation or the reverse may be
derived from the fact, that you brought the catastrophe
upon yourself. In justice to me, I therefore presume you
will not refuse to state that fact in a letter addressed to
your mother and intrusted to me, but not of course to be
delivered should you safely reach Jersey."

"I understand. If I lose my life, that is no reason, Captain Webbe thinks, that he should lose the reward he has
been promised. Give me a sheet of paper."

My pen scoured over the paper as I related Webbe's
confederacy from the first with Louise Féron, and I should
have poured forth all the bitter thoughts that were seething
in my brain, had it not suddenly struck me that the letter
might be a trick of wily Webbe's to make himself sure of
my secret thoughts and plans. He might open it directly
he left the hotel, and I should then be effectually baffled
as to the scheme which I still hoped to carry through. I
tore the betraying scrawl to shreds, and indited a letter
which, should he read, would but the more com-

pletely mislead the privateer captain as to my real thoughts and purposes; and having sealed, I handed it to him.

He had meanwhile written three letters, two of which he enclosed in a cover addressed to the seaman Baptiste; the other was for Fanchette.

"You will give to this to Baptiste," said Webbe; "it contains letters for persons in Jersey, and intelligible only to them, which he will deliver. This, as I shall not find it convenient to call at Madame de Bonneville's, you will place in the hands of Fanchette. It instructs her to go immediately after the celebration of the marriage—with respect to which there will be no difficulty or hinderance —to Monsieur Delisle, the *courtier-maritime*, who by that time will have provided a swift conveyance, in which you must all three take your departure from St. Malo without the loss of one precious moment. And now I am off; all my papers are fortunately in this coat-pocket, and I will not even go up stairs. You, however, must get the cloak I have seen you occasionally wear; and mind you keep the collar well up as you pass along the streets. Good-bye, my lad; keep your spirits up, and your weather-eye well open, and I shall stand godfather to your first boy yet. By the way, Linwood," added Webbe, pausing with the handle of the door in his hand, "a thought strikes me: the wreck of empires and the crush of crowns just now in progress—videlicet, the downfall of Bonaparte and restoration of the Bourbons, will at least have one important and beneficial result—that of recovering my watch and our portmanteaus when you revisit St. Malo with your wife. Good-bye, once more."

It then wanted about three quarters of an hour to eleven; upon the stroke of which I arrived at the magasin in the Rue Dupetit Thouars, and found Clemence anxiously expecting me. To her, I at once opened my whole heart; confided to her its hopes and fears, its wishes, apprehensions; and she, sweet, guileless maiden, with her head resting, after the old fashion, upon my shoulder, and sobbing with almost convulsive agitation, was hearkening, yieldingly as I thought, to my advice and entreaties, when the door was suddenly flung open, and Jacques Sicard, with his head bound up, and his face white as the paper upon which I am writing, presented himself.

"Monsieur Linwood," he hurriedly exclaimed, "you have been betrayed by a femme de chambre of the Hôtel de l'Empire, and gendarmes are already on your track!"

CHAPTER XIII.

MARIA WILSON.

MESSIEURS SICARD and Linwood, and Mademoiselle de Bonneville must, at that critical and exciting moment in their lives, have presented an interesting study to a painter of character—a somewhat puzzling one too ; for although the attitudes, no doubt very naturally struck, must have been chiefly expressive of astonishment and terror, other emotions could not but have revealed themselves upon three youthful visages, dull and blank as they might ordinarily be, confronting each other under such peculiar and delicate circumstances. Mademoiselle Clemence, in her abundance of commiserative sorrow, had, as before stated, reclined her sweet head upon my shoulder, and attracted by a correspondent of sympathy of soul, my arm had insensibly stolen, or was stealing, round the dear girl's waist. Now, this, tender proximity of a young man and maiden, though susceptible, as the reader knows, of a perfectly honourable explanation, was an awkward position to be surprised in by an irascible lover, who held, too, it seemed, my very life at his mercy. It will surprise no one, therefore, to be told that M. Sicard's sudden appearance and startling news flushed my countenance and that of Mademoiselle Clemence with confusion as well as fright ; that Sicard himself, after blurting out the announcement already given, stopped short in mutely questioning anger, his bloodless cheeks instantly rekindling with the fire of a still smouldering jealousy ; and that my first exclamation was a stammering expression of mingled apology and consternation. His addressing me by my real name must also have sensibly contributed to my bewilderment.

The young lady was of course the first to regain her self-possession.

"This is terrible!" she exclaimed; "but are you quite sure, Monsieur Sicard?"

"Mademoiselle de Bonneville," stiffly replied M. Sicard, "might do me the simple justice to believe that I would not trifle with the feelings of *any* person placed in such grave circumstances as those which surround Monsieur Linwood, much less one who has the honour of being, at the very least, Mademoiselle de Bonneville's very intimate and attached friend."

"Jacques, *dear* Jacques," said Clemence, placing her little hand upon his arm, and looking upon him with humid truthful eyes, "is the effusive confidence of yester evening so soon forgotten?"

M. Sicard's swelling dignity collapsed at once, "Pardon, chere Clemence," he hurriedly replied. "I am an ingrate, a fool — that is certain, demonstrable. Still, Monsieur Linwood will, I am sure, excuse a susceptibility which, though extreme, uncalled for, is, nevertheless legitimate"

"Mais mon Dieu!" interrupted Clemence with vivacity, "is this a time to talk of susceptibilities legitimate or the reverse! Do you not say that gendarmes are at this moment in pursuit of Monsieur Linwood?"

"That is true, mademoiselle, and not one moment must be lost. The agents of the public force," he added, "will not, fortunately, suspect *me* of assisting the escape from justice of Monsieur Linwood, otherwise Jean le Gros, otherwise"——

"Art thou *bavard*, Jacques!" again and angrily broke in Clemence. "Speak to us of what is to be *done*—of how Monsieur Linwood is to escape the danger to which he is exposed."

An earnest consultation then took place, to which I hearkened like one in a dream, gathering incidentally, however, therefrom, with hazy apprehension at the time, but made clear by subsequent explanation, that on the preceding evening Clemence had not only disclosed to Sicard the tender preference with which she—previously, in some degree, unknown to herself, perhaps—regarded him, but the secret of her English birth and parentage; the conflict of feeling and duty that knowledge had given rise to in her mind, and the difficult circumstances in which she

was consequently involved. The loving pair thereupon
took counsel together, finally agreeing that Captain Webbe,
alias Jacques Le Gros, was altogether unworthy of confidence or credit—some curt expressions of mine, elicited
by Sicard's attack upon me and Mademoiselle Clemence's
ebullient sympathy with my assailant, having caused the
young lady to doubt that I should, as the privateer captain
pretended, hang or drown myself for disappointed love of
her—that Maitre Sicard should see me, if he was well
enough the next day, frankly acknowledge the situation,
assure me that the flattering avowal of mademoiselle's
preference should remain without matrimonial result till
the *soumission respectueuse*, in the matter of said marriage,
enjoined by the French law, had been made to whichever
of the two ladies, Madame Waller or Madame de Bonneville,
might prove to be the disputed maiden's real mother; that
meanwhile he, Sicard, would render me all the aid in
his power to elucidate the sad mystery of which my
father had been the victim; and, above all, specially
charge himself to defeat any attempt by Madame de
Bonneville to withdraw Clemence beyond reach of legal
pursuit.

"Although a Frenchman to the ends of my finger-
nails," added M. Sicard, addressing me with immense
suavity, "I have no insurmountable prejudice with respect
to foreigners; and Mademoiselle Clemence, if proved
to be of English parentage, will be for me as charming, as
beloved "——

"Oh how tiresome thou art to prate in that way,
Jacques!" interrupted Clemence, "when every moment——
Grand Dieu, here are the gendarmes!"

Clemence made this discovery through a small glass-
window looking into the shop, she, like Sicard and myself,
being unseen by the terrible visitors. Sicard, with prompt
presence of mind, hurried me into a back room, and
quietly closing the door after him, rejoined Clemence,
with whom, after exchanging a sentence or two, he went
forward into the shop to confront, and, if possible, mislead
the gendarmes.

For me, I was dumb with passion—tossed in a whirlwind
of unutterable scorn of myself, in which dread of the
violent death with which I was menaced was for the time

engulfed—lost! Suddenly, as a gleam of lightning, the raging current of my thoughts was arrested: my frenzied glance lit upon an armoire in the room—*the* armoire, I was certain, from Clemence's description, containing the precious proofs, possession of which might yet atone for all my follies and shortcomings. It was locked ; Fanchette, who fortunately was from home, had, no doubt, charge of the key. No matter; the case was desperate; and whatever the consequence, get possession of those proofs I would. I shook the doors of the armoire with precipitate, mad fury —looked about for some effective instrument wherewith to break open or break in the strong oak framework, and espying a short iron bar that held the casement half-open, twisted it off, and forced the armoire lock, unavoidably tearing away, in doing so, part of the wood-work—found, after a nervous search, the precious parcel, and was contemplating the *details* of my prize with wild exultation, when Jacques Sicard reappeared.

"Thousand thunders!" he exclaimed. "What are you doing there ? "

I briefly explained, adding that with my life only would I part with evidences I had obtained by means which the actual circumstances perfectly justified.

"Speak low—speak lower, pray," said Sicard, softly fastening the room-door. "Messieurs les Gendarmes are still in the shop talking with Clemence : our assurance that you were not here apparently satisfied them : still a caprice may seize them to search the house, and—— Dam!" he added, brought up again as it were by the sight of the fractured door, and the parcel which I was depositing in my coat-pocket. "Dam! but this is grave! I appreciate your motives, Monsieur Linwood; but do you know that the French law punishes *vol avec effraction*—robbery by violence in a domicile—with the galleys for life ; and should that rogue Webbe's story prove, as I half suspect it will, to be *all* moonshine, I might myself, as consenting participator, be placed in a pretty predicament! It matters not," he added bravely; "I have promised Mademoiselle Clemence to see you safely through. I am a Frenchman—a man of honour, and my word is therefore sacred. Follow me, Monsieur Linwood. We can reach my house—the last place you will be suspected of hiding in—by the back of these premises."

"I take you to witness, Monsieur Sicard, that I have taken the articles you saw just now in my hand from an armoire belonging to Madame de Bonneville, *née* Louise Feron, without her knowledge or permission."

"That is positive—demonstrable; but, sacred thunder, come along, will you!"

"I should like to thank—to embrace dear Clemence once more; and assure her that"——

"Monsieur Linwood," sternly interrupted Sicard, "your head is turned, which, however, will not prevent its being struck off your shoulders, if you don't at once follow me. Come."

I need not further dwell upon the incidents of my escape from St. Malo, except to say that, thanks to the chivalrous *bottier*, I left it on the evening of the same day in the uniform, and furnished with the passport *visé* of one Adolphe Piron, a young officer domiciled with Sicard, and at that time confined to his chamber by illness. The general *débâcle* of all government that was taking place, rendered the plan easy of accomplishment; and, I dare say, had considerable influence in quieting the mind of M. Sicard anent the seriousness of the responsibility he was incurring, should his part in the affair be one day made known. He accompanied me boldly to the office of the Messageries Impériales, and bade me "Adieu—bon voyage," with a heartiness which, it struck me, was even more complimentary to Mademoiselle Clemence than to myself. The treachery of the *femme de chambre*, Marguerite, I have omitted to state, was caused by the double knavery of Edouard, who refused to share equitably with her in either the actual or prospective bribe he had accepted.

I reached Granville without molestation, except when halting to change horses at Dol, where a woman's face peering into the *coupé* of the diligence—which, with the shadow-startled conscience of one who sees in every bush an officer, I for a moment mistook for that of Madame de Bonneville—gave me a tremendous, though transient heartquake.

Baptiste and his lugger-boat were in readiness; and I reached St. Catherine's Bay, Jersey, and the *auberge* of M. Josse in safety, though the passage was a rough one, the equinoctial gales having just begun to set in with promise according to Baptiste's prediction, of something much fiercer to come.

We rested for a while in the sitting-room of the little public-house, and it was there I handed to Baptiste the letter-parcel intrusted to me by Captain Webbe. He removed the envelope, and read aloud the addresses. One letter was for Dowling, chief officer of the *Scout ;* the other for Madame Dupré.

"The chance," I remarked, "that those letters would reach their destination was at one time a very doubtful one."

"If these two letters had not reached their destination," said Baptiste with a smile, "others to the same effect would, rely upon it. That is to say," he added, "if they relate to matters of importance. Monsieur le Capitaine is much too wary a calculator to trust to only one mode of conveying his wishes or instructions."

"Do you think it prudent to deliver those letters yourself?" I asked.

"There is no danger," said Baptiste. "Jersey has no organised police ; and French—good French—being spoken by the better class, I shall, as heretofore, pass muster very well. It is not the first time," he added, "that I have brought letters for Madame Dupré and la jeune belle who resides with her."

"Monsieur le Capitaine is, then, an old acquaintance of those ladies?"

"That is very certain, monsieur," replied Baptiste, "and equally so that I must hasten to fulfil my commission."

We left the public-house, and walked together to the entrance of St. Helier, where we parted, and I proceeded to the hotel in the Royal Square which I had formerly patronised.

I was lifted into such a state of exaltation by the apparent certainty of speedily arriving in England with the priceless evidences of my father's innocence in my possession, there to take counsel of Mrs. Linwood and the Wallers as to what should be further and immediately done in the matter, that I scarcely heeded Baptiste's remark with reference to the long acquaintance and frequent correspondence of Webbe with Madame Dupré and her beautiful

L

ward; and had the mail-packet for Weymouth sailed early the next morning, as she was advertised to do, I should certainly have gone in her, and not consequently have seen Madame Dupré, Miss Wilson, or any of the *Scout* people, which famous corsair, by the way, had not, I was informed, left the harbour since she brought in her prize. It was not so ordered. The gale blowing dead ashore, and which, during the night, had increased to a hurricane, forbade the packet's attempting to leave the rock-environed island; and many days, even weeks might pass, I was informed, at that season of the year, before I had a chance of reaching England. It seemed that I was to be ever fortune's fool; but as fuming and fretting could do nothing towards short- ening the vexatious delay, I was fain to cheat the lagging time by seeking out, first the Scouts, and afterwards the ladies residing near the Third Tower.

I met Dowling on the North Pier; Baptiste was with him, and I noticed an angry flush as of baffled eagerness upon the officer's countenance, caused, I was not long in ascertaining, by his anxiety to go to sea without an hour's loss of time, and the impossibility of doing so in face of the tremendous weather. Dowling greeted me with rough cordiality, laughed a brief, scornful laugh at his own stupidity in having been for a moment duped into a belief in Harry Webbe's hereditary pluck; and finding how desirous I was of getting to England, offered me a passage in the *Scout*.

"The *Scout* will be the first vessel to leave the island," said he: "you may rely upon that; and I don't believe either that many hours will elapse before she gets away."

"You think this hurricane will soon abate, then?"

"No, I don't; and it may continue fierce enough to blow the horns off a bull, for anything I care, if it will but shift sufficiently to give us a chance of clearing Elizabeth Castle and Noirmont Point."

"The *Scout* sails direct for England?"

"The *Scout* sails for Portsmouth, and with sufficient directness to insure your arrival there before the mail- packet will in all probability have crept out of St. Helier's harbour."

I accepted Dowling's offer, and he undertook to have m

warned in sufficient time of the *Scout's* departure. " Harry Webbe," he remarked, "goes with us, but not the whole of the way. We shall drop him either at Guernsey or Alderney —at the latter island, if the weather will permit of it. Good-bye for the present."

We shook hands; and he, with Baptiste, went on his way towards the town.

I had a mind to go on board the *Scout*, but seeing that the privateer-brig was berthed at the further extremity of the South Pier, I swerved in purpose, and betook myself, with a kind of boding, bashful reluctance in the direction of the Third Tower.

So fierce was the tempest, that in addition to being wetted to the skin by the blinding spray, I could scarcely keep my feet along the unsheltered road which skirts the waters of St Aubin's Bay; and I more than once mentally balanced the delight—the dangerous delight, I almost feared—to be derived from the sight and conversation of Miss Wilson, with the more substantial, and certainly innocuous pleasures of a warm room and dry clothes; and I might perhaps have turned back, had I not have caught a glimpse of Madame Dupre's crinkled buff-coloured frontis-piece through the glass-window of a hired chaise, on its way to St. Helier. The old lady did not recognise, perhaps did not observe me; and tempted, spite of the suggestions of my better judgment, by the hope of a tête-à-tête interview with Maria Wilson, I strode manfully onward. That hope was realised. Miss Wilson was alone, and received me with winning grace and amenity. She was looking her very best, and certainly not the less so, to my mind, that the peculiar sweetly pensive expression which, as I have before remarked, shadowed from time to time the sunshine of her face, was still more strongly marked, or I fancied so, than when I had previously seen her.

I could not have believed it possible that the contact of her welcoming hand would have so agitated me; that the light of her smile would have so instantly fired my blood, chilled too, as it was by the piercing winter wind and drenching sea-spray. Mademoiselle Clemence had not, I remembered, produced, under nearly similar circumstances at all the same effect upon me; from which I concluded that my former interview with the Jersey maiden must, and

to a certain extent unknown to myself, have excited
a state of latent internal inflammation which required
but a spark from the same divine source to kindle into
flame.

Maria Wilson could not but observe my extreme emotion; and with the instinctive perception of girl-kind in
such cases, must, I suspected, have divined its cause; inasmuch that the bright smile was quickly absorbed by as
bright a blush, and the welcoming hand withdrawn with
confused haste, and necessarily some slight effort, from
mine.

By way of apology, I stammered out an inquiry for
Madame Dupré.

"Madame Dupré," said Miss Wilson, "is gone to St.
Helier to arrange some business matters previous to our
departure from the island."

"You are about to leave Jersey!" I exclaimed: "for
England, of course."

"No; for France. You are aware that we have received
a letter from Captain Webbe. He and Madame Broussard
—they are my guardians—insist that Madame Dupré and
myself shall embark with Baptiste for Granville; so that
directly the weather moderates, I shall leave Jersey—
probably for ever!"

The last words, spoken in a tone of sadnesss, and followed
by a sigh, added greatly to my excitement; my heart beat
wildly, and the jealous, cankering thought lurking there,
sprang rudely to my lips.

"Harry Webbe will not, however, accompany you.
He, I know, sails in the *Scout* for England *viâ* Alderney."

"You are mistaken, sir," was the reply. "Mr. Harry
Webbe will find means of reaching Cherbourg from Alderney. His father does not deem it prudent," she continued
loftily, 'that the gallant leader of the Scouts in their recent
victory should"——

This was too much, and I furiously broke in with: "The
devil fetch the Scouts and their gallant leader"——

"Sir! Mr. Linwood!" in her turn interrupted Miss
Wilson, and well-nigh as fiercely, as she rose from
her chair with indignant wonder, "have you lost your
senses?"

"Yes, I believe I have; at least I seem to be on the brink of losing them, so duped, self-duped, befooled have I been—— Pardon me," I added, yielding way, perforce, to the torrent of excited feeling which swept through me —"Pardon me: I am a foolish, wayward boy—rash as fire, but guiltless of intentional offence—especially towards you!"

My face was buried in my hands, but Maria Wilson's gentle toned reply—"I have nothing to pardon, Mr. Linwood; and if I had, the cruel disappointment which I cannot doubt to be the source of such painful emotion would amply excuse it"—caused me to hastily withdraw them, and stare bewilderedly in hers for its interpretation.

"Captain Webbe's letter," she went on to say, "intimates that he hoped you would be accompanied to Jersey by your newly wedded wife. That hope has not been fulfilled, and hence doubtless"——

"Say no more, Miss Wilson," I interrupted, "let me beg of you. I am, as I have said, a wayward, feather-headed boy, but even such a one may have a secret grief that will not bear probing. Let us talk of something else, of—of Captain Webbe, if you will. Do you expect to see him soon?"

"Very soon. He and Madame Broussard request us, as I told you, to join them in France before a week has passed."

"In order to the celebration," said I, with an effort—a poor one, I imagine—at Spartan firmness—"in order to the celebration—the immediate celebration of your marriage with Mr. Harry Webbe."

"Yes, it is so determined," replied the maiden with a blush, and I thought a faint, half-regretful sigh. "I speak unreservedly, Mr. Linwood, because I know you to be in the confidence of both Captain Webbe and his son."

"You have been informed, then, I presume, of my object in venturing to St. Malo?"

"Very imperfectly. Harry himself has but a confused notion that you went in search of a lost child; but perhaps the topic is a painful one."

I said it was not painful to speak upon the subject to her;

the reverse rather ; and I ran rapidly over the affair from beginning to end, so far at least as the end had been attained, rigorously omitting, of course, all mention of Webbe's complicity with Madame de Bonneville—the Auguste Le Moine and Jacques Sicard episodes—and everything, in short, that could be construed into a violation of the solemn pledge I had given, never to disclose anything prejudicial to Webbe, with which I might in the course of our adventure become acquainted.

Maria Wilson listened with an attention that, as the narrative proceeded, became breathless in its intensity ; and after I had finished, she remained for several minutes absorbed in what seemed to be a painful reverie.

The young girl shook off that mood of thought with some effort. "Strange," she murmured, as if speaking to herself as well as to me—" strange, that whilst you were speaking, it seemed as if several of the scenes you described were familiar to me ; that the misty veil, which obscures and distorts the earlier images of memory, was, as you spoke, partially, fitfully withdrawn ! Curious illusion, that, were I not certain of the contrary, would persuade me that the scene below Gravesend—that flat sandy shore and child playing there, the broad-winding river, the boat with its white glittering sails, ay, and the man and woman too— was a pictured experience, faded but not effaced from the tablet of memory, and brought out, as it were, by your description ! "

A wild idea flashed upon my mind. "You are not," I exclaimed, " a native of Jersey ? "

"No ; I was born in Madeira. My father was Captain Wilson, a retired naval officer of the East India Company's service. He died when I was in my fourth year ; and my mother, Marie Broussard, sister of my guardian, Adele Broussard, had preceded him to the tomb. I have been in Jersey about five years only. The earliest event," added Miss Wilson, " that dwells distinctly in my memory, is the wreck upon the Irish coast of the ship in which we sailed from Madeira. To the courage and resource of Captain Webbe, who commanded the ill-fated vessel, my aunt-nurse and myself were mainly indebted, I have always understood, for the preservation of our lives."

"May I ask if you have lately seen Madame Broussard ? "

"No; she has an unconquerable aversion to the sea. When I was *en pension* near Coutance, I saw her often. My aunt has been ever kind and good to me," added Miss Wilson; "and though a rigid Catholic herself, caused me, in compliance with my father's dying injunctions, to be educated in the Protestant faith, and the principles of a true English girl."

"Your kind frankness, Miss Wilson, has dissipated a fantastic idea which your previous remarks excited."

"That I, not the young lady in St. Malo, might be the lost child! Upon my word, I thought so! Reassure yourself, Mr. Linwood," added Maria Wilson with a gay laugh; "*your* fair *fiancée*, not Mr. Harry Webbe's, is the true Lucy Hamblin: there can be no doubt about that; and I sincerely hope that the course of true love, though it would appear for the present checked and turned awry, will soon run smooth again."

"Can you conjecture what motive Captain Webbe could have in telling me that you were till very lately unknown to him?"

"No motive whatever, except his love of mystification. Captain Webbe is, you know, an inveterate *farceur*—— Hush! here is Madame Dupré"

I stayed but a few minutes after the old lady's entrance; long enough, however, to hear that nothing but the frightful weather prevented the immediate embarkation of Madame Dupré and her fair charge, for France, under the guidance of Monsieur Baptiste.

Late in the evening, a message reached me from Dowling. The wind had veered sufficiently to enable the *Scout* to go out of harbour; the tide served, and I must be on board without delay. I complied with alacrity; and although it was still blowing guns, and the night was dark as Erebus, I intrusted myself without fear or hesitation to the well-round privateer-brig, and her hardy, skilful crew. A ticklish affair, nevertheless, was the getting away from the harbour and bay. Half-a-dozen touch-and-go tacks in that wild sea, and amidst hidden rocks, to get clear of Elizabeth Castle! Once, however, that Noirmont Point was weathered, the danger was held to be past, though the brig was buried in the sea, which swept her fore and aft; and Dowling, who had stationed himself by the wheel, came below for a few minutes.

"It must be urgent business that drove the *Scout* to sea on such a night as this," I remarked, whilst Dowling was taking an inside lining of strong brandy-grog.

"You are right: the urgent business of making money. A richly laden enemy's ship—I don't mind telling you, Mr. Linwood—is now, or will be early to-morrow, running up Channel in the direction of Havre de Grace ; which richly laden enemy's ship, I fully intend shall be a prize to the *Scout* before next sundown."

"An American ship, is it not ? "

"Guess again, Mr. Linwood, and you 'll guess wrong."

"Information concerning which has been furnished by Captain Webbe, in a letter delivered to you by Baptiste."

"Right again ! Duplicate information to that effect *has* been brought in a letter by Baptiste. You must be a wizard, Mr. Linwood."

"Have you been long associated with Captain Webbe, may I inquire, in these—h-e-m—these remarkable enter-prises."

"For more years than you have fingers and toes. Cap-tain Jules Reuaudin," added Dowling with a merry laugh, "I have not been so long acquainted with, though I shook hands with him within a few weeks of his first appearance in that character. He has no doubt told you all about that delicious trick. First-rate was it not ?

"He told me of his audacious personation of the deceased commander of the *Passe-partout.*"

"That was it. I was one of four out of the crew of the *Wasp* that took to the boats who escaped drowning. No other man but Webbe," said Dowling, "could have played such a game with success ; and between you and me, it has become much too risky of late years even for him. His 'luck' is really marvellous. Were it not for that, cool, wary, brave as he is, he would long since have had to walk the plank "——

"The pilot wishes to speak with you, sir," interrupted a seaman, half-opening the door. "We are off the Corbière."

Dowling hastened on deck, and I soon afterwards turned in. Harry Webbe, I should state, was on board, but had not shewn himself in the cabin—perhaps from an easily comprehensible repugnance to meeting me.

The wind had moderated by the morning ; but there was

still a tremendous sea on, and so dull and dark was the day, that when lifted to the crests of the giant waves, one could discern nothing distinctly that was more than three or four miles distant. That extent of furious sea was searched by vigilant eyes, from the tops as well the deck, in quest of the coveted prize, of which Dowling had been furnished with a pen-and-ink sketch, that would enable him to identify her at a glance. Two square-rigged vessels were sighted, running up Channel, almost under bare poles ; but the Yankee was nowhere to be seen, and a feeling of surly disappointment was fast spreading amongst both officers and crew of the *Scout*, when about 4 P.M., a large three-masted ship suddenly loomed through the thickening darkness, hardly half a league to leeward of the privateer brig. Dowling confidently pronounced her to be the *Colombia* of New Orleans; the course of the *Scout* was instantly changed, to meet and speak her, and a buzz of grinning exultation succeeded to the querulous murmuring of the corsair crew. The wind, I must here pause to remark, had not long before died away to a moderate puffy breeze ; ominously so, several of the old-salts were saying to each other, their judgment being apparently governed by the black cloud-mountains, so to speak, fast piling upon each other to windward, and spreading over the face of the sky.

The *Colombia* was a splendid vessel, of certainly over 700 tons burden; and as the *Scout* neared her, she hoisted English colours. That move was replied to by a shotted gun from the privateer, throwing a ball across her bows, which peremptory summons to parley was repeated in words, through Dowling's trumpet, as soon as the vessels came within hail of each other.

"What ship is that?" shouted Dowling.

"The *Caroline* of London, Captain Hollens, last from Jamaica," was the response: to which was added : "What are you?"

"His Majesty Kirke Webbe's privateer gun-brig *Scout*," returned Dowling. "Have the goodness to lie-to, and tell Captain Hollens to come on board with the *Caroline* of London's papers. And bear a hand, or we shall have to fetch him and them."

"You are mistaken after all," I remarked to Dowling, as I stood by him, and watched the lowering of one of the stranger's boats.

"I think not," he replied; "at all events, I shall take the liberty of sending the *Caroline* of London to Guernsey, upon suspicion. Mr. Harry Webbe," he continued, beckoning to that young gentleman, who had persisted in shyly avoiding me, "get ready to go on board with the prize-crew. Be smart," added Dowling, after an anxious glance to the windward.

Harry Webbe immediately dived below; two of the *Scout's* boats were dropped into the water, and one filled with armed men by the time the *Columbia* or *Caroline's* boat came alongside.

I could not, from where I stood, see the face of Captain Hollens as he came upon deck, and spoke with Dowling; but it struck me that I knew the voice—a peculiar one, and pitched in alt, as he replied to some sharp remark of the *Scout's* chief officer, followed, I could hear, by an invitation from that gentleman to accompany him below; a request which the captive captain had no choice but to comply with.

Mr. Harry Webbe quickly reappeared; and warned by the portentous aspect of the heavens, hurried into the boat first in readiness, and pulled off towards the prize. He and his boat's crew had just got safely on board when Dowling came on deck. That energetic officer was about to order the boat containing the remainder of the prize-crew to cast off, when at once broke the tempest in a hurricane-blast, that tore the *Scout's* sails to shreds: at nearly the same moment, the volleyed lightning shivered the foremast to splinters, and the shrieks of seamen struck down by that terrific agent, feebly mingled with the crash of a thunderburst, which shook every timber in the privateer's hull.

CHAPTER XIV.

THE LAST OF THE SCOUT.

A SELF-APPOINTED interpreter of God's ways towards man—a lofty vocation which, fortunately for its numerous professors, seems to require but very humble abilities for its successful exercise—would, I doubt not, have instantly discerned a special act of retributive Providence in the misfortune which overtook the *Scout* at the very moment of her nefarious triumph over the American ship. True, the avenging lightning did not reach Webbe —the concocter of the base treachery that had led to the seizure of the prize—had not even smitten down the willing instrument by whom that treachery had been, so far, successfully carried out; but those were minor circumstances which gentlemen that have mastered the mysteries of the moral universe could have had no difficulty in satisfactorily accounting for or explaining away. Happily for me, as I cannot, after all, help thinking, I have never had the slightest capacity for determining the counsel of God from atmospheric or any material or moral phenomena whatsoever : hence, though deeply impressed, awe-stricken by so terrible a manifestation of irresistible Power, my reliance on the justice of the Omnipotent was in nowise shaken, required no sophistical anodyne to soothe and strengthen it, when I saw and heard, as soon as eye and ear had recovered from the sudden glare of the red lightning, and deafening thunder-peal, that Dowling was standing erect, unscathed, daring, defiant as ever, whilst three poor sailors, whose limbs had been smashed by the falling yards of the splintered mast, were being carried groaning and shrieking below.

Nay, a feeling of admiration, of respect even, for the unquailing aspect and bearing of the chief officer of the *Scout* arose in my mind, and grew upon me to the exclusion, for the time, of all moral appreciation of the man. I recognised, with a kind of sympathetic exultation, an intelligent, courageous human will battling fearlessly with the brute elements—mind combating with matter. A sketch of the scene, blank and dull as it must be, drawn by me, compared with the fearful vividness of the reality, will excuse perhaps that sympathetic admiration.

Overhead, and everywhere around, the dull, leaden day had been extinguished, blotted out by sudden night and storm, save at one point where a rent in the piled blackness gave to view the red, angry sun, lingering for a moment upon the edge of the horizon, like a wrathful monarch— if the repetition of a fancy, vividly felt at the time, may be permitted—who, before he finally departs the hall of judgment, glares a last triumphant look at the sentenced victim, whose punishment he has delegated to inferior ministers. That last gleam of disdainful day, so to speak, quickly vanished, and the thick darkness was for many hours relieved only by incessant lightning flashes, and the white crests of the waves which, pursued by the continuous hiss and roar of the tornado, rushed, leaped in their furious speed over the comparatively lagging *Scout*, threatening every instant to whelm the partially disabled vessel in the raging waters, through which she hopelessly strained and laboured.

Hopelessly not only to a landsman's eyes, but to those of many of the scared Scouts. Not to Dowling's. *His* countenance, distinctly seen by the bright fire-flashes, was unblenched, his powerful voice, ringing through the ship in the pauses of the thunder, as cheery, nay, it struck me, cheerier than ever, and the faintest-hearted amongst us gradually gained confidence and courage from his example. He himself personally aided to carry out his calmly as rapidly given orders, in the prompt execution of which lay our safety. It was essential that the wreck of the foremast, with its top hamper of spars, sails, rigging, should be cut away and sent adrift with all possible dispatch; and Dowling was the first, with axe in hand, to leap at the work, as it were, and now labouring with might and main, now holding on to a rope or any other firmly fastened object, after shouting to his men to look out, whilst a sea swept the brig from stern to stem, shew how a brave man conjures danger by fearlessly confronting it. The bodies of two men, killed by the electric stroke that had shivered the mast, were dragged from under the superincumbent mass of wreck; Dowling, first carefully assuring himself that they were really dead, helped to throw them overboard at once, and lightly remarking that sudden death was sudden glory, resumed work, and inspirited others to do the same with unabated alacrity and cheer of spirit. At last the encumbering wreck was got rid of, and it was possible to commence setting up a jury fore-mast, without which no jib could be set—and *sans* jib, to steer the brig was impossible. The pumps were next rigged; the depth of water sounded; and it was only too plain that the *Scout* had sprung one or more dangerous leaks, rendering it imperative to lighten her at any sacrifice. This could only be speedily and effectively done by throwing the guns overboard; and Dowling, though with much reluctance, gave the order to do so. First two, then four guns were cast into the deep, with evident benefit in the way of easing the brig; but this was not sufficient. It was found necessary to sacrifice four more before the desired end was fully obtained, and the once formidable *Scout* was consequently reduced to an armament of two guns only.

Six or seven hours had been thus employed, and we were far into the night before the wind shewed any sign of abatement, though the electric storm had long passed away. Comparative safety having been so far attained, Dowling, who had twenty times during the last two hours crept out to the end of the bow-sprit, and gone up to the cross-trees of the mizzen, to ascertain the exact position of the ship, and whither she was driving, satisfied at last that there was no immediate danger of our running unawares, stem on, upon a rock or an island, went below, requesting me to follow him.

"You are an unlucky passenger, Linwood, to have on board," remarked Dowling, as we met in the cabin after refitting with dry clothes. "The first time we shipped you, a sharp fight: and now, a sharper squall! You are a regular Jonah! However, here's to your health, and better luck next time. I noticed," he added, pushing the case of Schiedam *schnapps* towards me, "that you and the American skipper were talking with each other whilst working at the pumps. You know him, it seems, and, consequently, that he is *not*, as he pretends, Captain Hollens of the good ship *Caroline* of London, last from Jamaica."

"I have nothing to say of the American gentleman; and no right to say it, if I had."

"And I have nothing to learn of him from you. I know as well as you do that he is a Mr. Tyler, owner and captain of the *Columbia*, hailing from New Orleans. It did not, however, strike me that you must, when in company with Webbe, have met him in St. Malo, or I should certainly not have offered you a passage to England, fully expecting as I did to pick up the said Tyler on the way. It was an error on my part, which, in certain quite possible circumstances, might lead to unpleasant results. Did he recognise you?"

"I think so; but he gave no intimation—in words—that he did."

"A Yankee, though not everybody except in his own opinion, is generally a cunning card. What *did* he say?"

"That the tempest which has burst upon us is a judgment of God."

"Upon himself then, as well as us, since, if we should be drowned, he will hardly live to be hanged! What I wish to know is if he said anything, in the way of boast, of the number of men on board the *Columbia*, and if they were armed? But of course he did not—" added Dowling: "A fool to ask such a question; though the apprehension of what answer might be given to it greatly disquiets me.'

"You are disquieted for the safety of Harry Webbe, and"——

"Disquieted for the devil as likely," roughly broke in Dowling. "Much truly am I concerned for that white-livered cur—Webbe's son though he be! How I could have been bamboozled by such a frothy young humbug in *Le Renard's* affair will be a puzzle to me as long as I live. I am disquieted, Linwood, for the safety of the prize consigned to the charge of Harry Webbe, and not more than half the complement of Scouts I intended to send on board."

"The second boat, then, did not reach the American ship?"

"No: the men, as you saw, were holding her off and on with boat-hooks when the squall struck us, and capsized her A great misfortune!"

"The sudden destruction of so many men is indeed a sad misfortune."

"No doubt; but it is not of that I am just now thinking: besides, a ticket for Davy Jones may at any moment be drawn from the seaman's lottery-bag. The misfortune I had and have in my mind is that the *Columbia*, whose crew, judging by her tonnage, cannot be much under forty men, has been taken possession of by only eighteen of our fellows—young Webbe counting for nothing, or worse."

"I have not seen the American ship since the hurricane burst upon us; have you?"

"Yes, more than once or twice. The last time, she was far away to windward, and seemed to be making tolerably fair weather of it. The *Columbia* should by this time," added Dowling, "have brought up in the Guernsey Roads, under the guns of Castle Cornet; *would* have done so were I on board in place of young Webbe. As it is, I'd take less than a thousand pounds for my share in her."

"About where, allow me to ask, may we ourselves be just now?"

"Getting back to Britain by the way we came from it, except that we are more closely hugging the French coast. If the gale had not slackened, we should be now driving through the Alderney race as if Old Nick was kicking us endwise. I must on deck again. You need not come," he added; "we shall manage to keep the *Scout* afloat without your taking another spell at the pumps."

Dowling had not been gone five minutes when Mr. Tyler entered the cabin. I offered him a change of apparel from my own wardrobe—a courtesy which he met by a glum refusal; though he accepted the mute tender of restorative schnapps. I was quite sure that he had recognised M. Jean Le Gros; but as he chose to be silent upon the subject, and no explanation was possible on my part without violating the oath Webbe had exacted from me, I gladly followed his example. We conversed with some effort—on his side, with an overdone show of politeness—for perhaps eight or ten minutes, and then Mr. Tyler retired to his sleeping-place. A naturally taciturn, but far from an ungentlemanly person, was Mr. Tyler; he seemed to be a fair specimen of the American skipper tribe, of whom I have since known hundreds at Liverpool, who, according to my experience, whilst distinguished for greater nervous energy than their British rivals, are nothing like so physically robust, nor, I think, so healthily developed, mentally. This opinion of mine, a wider experience might perhaps considerably modify; and be that as it may, I was favourably impressed by Mr. Tyler, and—saving the personal security of the English seamen on board the *Columbia*—I was heartily hopeful that his rich'y freighted ship might have been rescued from the ravenous sharks that had thought to make her their prey. And I could not help fancying that that same hope glittered vengefully in the sharp gray eyes of the American captain—very naturally so, if he knew the relative number of captors and captives on board the *Columbia* to really be as Dowling feared they were.

I was awake and up before daybreak; the uneasy working of the brig, the incessant jerk of the pumps, and frequent tacking during the night, which, as my cot-hammock happened to be lashed athwart-ship, caused me to be now head, now heels upwards and downwards, and the general bustle and trampling overhead, effectually preventing sound sleep, tired, worn out as I was when I turned in.

What the sailors called half a gale of wind was blowing when I went on deck, from the westward, and the *Scout*, I was informed, had been, during the previous three or four hours, in great danger of being embayed and driven on the French coast. Dowling and his skilful mariners had fortunately at length succeeded, spite of the half-crippled condition of the brig, in clawing her off, and she was then rounding the projecting headland known as Cape La Hogue, though at not more than half a league to seaward. Close to Cherbourg as we were, such near proximity to the French shores was doubly dangerous : but to bear up for Portsmouth, or even half a point nearer to the wind than we were sailing was, with our make-shift foremast—already severely strained and shaken—impossible. Still, if the wind continued to blow from the same quarter, and with no greater violence, we might hope to bring up in the Downs, if we were lucky, one day within a week.

We shewed no colours, either English or French: the former would have caused us to be pursued as "enemies ;" and the latter might have brought more "friends" to our assistance than would have been quite agreeable. Dowling's hope was, that before there was, sufficient light to make us clearly out, we should have gained such a distance from the French war-port, as, combined with the chance of meeting with a British cruiser, would indispose the light gun-craft, kept there in readiness for such purposes, to attempt seeking our nearer acquaintance.

n essential condition of that doubtfully hoped-for piece

of luck was that the dawn should be a dark, cloudy one and so, precisely speaking, it was; the coming day, as it slowly broke in the east, being as dull and gloomy as could be wished. Unfortunately, the light, as it stole on, shewed us that the weather was clearing rapidly to windward; and the yet stiff gale—or half a one in seamen's estimation—drove the breaking clouds before it with such velocity, that before the sun was half an hour high, it was shining in unveiled brightness over land and sea; and especially, as it seemed to us, lighting up for general inspection our crippled, creaking, labouring, laggard *Scout*.

By that time, we were nearly two leagues past Cherbourg, which was something, though not enough, as it soon proved. Dowling's anxious glance detected one—two—three gun-boats, impelled by sweeps and sails, leaving Cherbourg in pursuit, and it was quickly plain, even to my unpractised eye, that they were coming up with us hand over hand.

"If the *Scout* had not lost ten of her teeth," growled Dowling, "she would have made no bones of the little spitfires; and as it is, she may perhaps manage to crunch up one or two. She shall, at all events, have a snap at them.

As the privateer-brig could not luff, it seemed, without danger of carrying away her shaky jurymast, and it would hardly do to yaw with the Rochers de Calvados on her lee, Dowling gave orders to hew away sufficient space on each side of the helm to enable the *Scout's* two remaining guns to be used as stern-chasers. That was quickly done; the guns were loaded, run out, trained, and directly the pursuing gun-boats were thought to have come within range, fire was opened upon them. Without effect; the balls for some time fell short; and so small a mark did the French craft present, that the chance of striking them till they were very close indeed, seemed a desperate one. The *Scout*, on the other hand, could not well be missed, and we had not been more than ten minutes within reach of the boats' heavy guns, before she was hulled half-a-dozen times, and we had three men wounded and one killed. I remarked, however, that since the firing began, the venomous little spitfires, as Dowling rightly named them, had not gained upon us in speed.

" They know a trick worth two of that," said Dowling.
" 'Strike or sink,' is what they are saying to us in better
French than they often use ; and unless a cruiser heaves
in sight, and one never does when particularly wanted—or
our practice wonderfully improves—that will be about the
English of it before we are much older. Ha! by jingo,
Rawlings, that was a near shave ! Missed the centre boat
by a few inches only ! Try it again ; there's a good fellow.
D—— it, man, we must never say die till our toes are fairly
turned up to the daisies."

Rawlings did try again, and again, but, without success ;
and Dowling was once more about to essay what he himself
could do, when the last ball intended to be fired by the
mortified gunner struck the centre boat low down upon her
bow quarter. She filled instantly, and, weighed by her
heavy gun, disappeared before one could count twenty.
The other boats hastened to pick up their consort's crew,
we, the while, as may be supposed, cheering and firing with
wild delight. As soon as the half-drowned seamen had
been hauled out of the water—if, indeed, they were all
saved, which we had no means of knowing—a consultation
appeared to take place between the commanders of the two
boats, the result of which was, that, after favouring us
with a parting salute from their guns, they turned tail, and
made the best of their way back to Cherbourg, followed by
our full-throated cheers, and an asthmatic *Rule Britannia*,
extemporised by an amateur clarionet that happened to be
on board the always lucky *Scout*.

Not so fast with your "lucky" *Scout !* The attention of
the officers and crew had been so absorbed by the cannonade, that the pumps had been abandoned ; and when, in
reluctant obedience to Dowling's command, more than once
sternly iterated, the men returned to that disagreeable
duty, it was found that the pumps were choked. The next
minute a cry arose that the brig was foundering ! She *was,*
visibly so, it could not, after a brief, breathless examination,
be doubted, or denied !

" The brig has been hulled between wind and water, or
a butt has started," said Dowling. " Steady men ; let us
have no womanish panic, if you please. Clear and let fall
the boats, smartly and steadily. Place in each of them a
bag of biscuit and a barrel of water. There will be plenty

of room for all; and plenty of time too, if you go quietly to work, as seamen should. Now, then!"

"Look alive, Linwood," said Dowling, coming swiftly aft to where I stood with Mr. Tyler, who had been watching the progress of the fight—not its termination—with saturnine satisfaction; "Look alive, Linwood; the water is coming in like a sluice; and though I do not tell the men so, the *Scout* may take her final plunge at any one of the next ten minutes. There is a boat astern which we lowered during the night to pick up a lad that had fallen overboard. You can reach the painter through the cabin windows: draw her up close, and drop a keg of spirits, a jar of water, and some biscuits into her. I must remain here till the last; and if the men do not rush into the boats, all may be right—if they do, and I fear they will, all will assuredly be wrong. Cast off in that case, and I must jump overboard, and endeavour to reach you. Be quick and silent: present moments stand for future years."

This was said in a rapid under-tone. I needed no second bidding, and hurrying below, seized, first my St. Malo prize; and was turning to the spirit-locker, when I found that Mr. Tyler had followed, and was anticipating me in that particular.

"Pull the boat up close astern," said the American skipper. "The sailors will be less likely to notice her. I will attend to other matters."

I complied; and in less, I should think, than three minutes, we two were safely in the boat, into which we had conveyed sustenance for a week at least.

Those three minutes, more or less, had wrought a fearful aggravation of the position and prospects of the *Scout* and her crew. The brig was fast settling down by the head; and from the uproar upon deck, the tumult of shouts and curses, momently increasing in volume and fierceness, it was evident that Dowling, whose stern voice could still be heard above all the others, had lost his authority over the crew, who seemed to be struggling, fighting with each other for precedence in the boats, not one of which had—no doubt in consequence of that insane fight or struggle—touched the water!

"Suddenly, and simultaneously with a yet mightier

shout—this time of despair as well as rage—the *Scout's*
stern rose in the air—her bows sinking at the same
moment, as if she was about to take her final plunge.
With ready presence of mind, Mr. Tyler cut the painter
with a knife he held ready in his hand for that purpose, and
then seizing one of the oars, called upon me to ship the
other, and pull for dear life.

I pulled for dear life, and we were perhaps fifty yards
from the privateer-brig when that fearful shout of agony
and despair again arose, higher, wilder, than before; a
crowd of men rushed aft, madly beckoned and cursed us,
and then down, down went the doomed ship, with her
shrieking, howling freight of death; her mighty down-
draught drawing us towards her, spite of our frenzied
rowing, which happily, however, held us back till the sea-
sepulchre had closed over the privateer-brig, and the
breadth and buoyancy of our frail skiff sufficed to keep
us on the surface of the entombing waters!

" We were able to rescue seven only of the hapless crew,
amongst them Dowling, who had in some way sprained
or twisted his right ankle and foot, and was suffering
intense pain in consequence.

As for us, though the wind was high, and the sea rough,
we were tolerably safe, unless a change for the worse in
the weather should take place. Our boat was a stout one,
and we had enough to eat and drink for at least eight-and-
forty hours. To be sure, we had neither mast nor sail—
no means of propulsion whatever except two oars; but
as we had plenty of hands to take turn and turn about at
the rowing, we should be pretty sure of making the
Wight or some part of the English eastern coast, if we did
not fall in with a friendly sail, before those forty-eight
hours expired. To this effect, after the first horror excited by the catastrophe we had just witnessed had in
some degree subsided, we talked with and encouraged
each other. A sense—a selfish sense, no doubt, of good-
fortune, and present comparative security, aided to keep
our spirits up to a hopeful, almost cheerful point. Mr.
Tyler and I took the first spell at the oars, and pulled
away lustily, soon, however, finding that the force and
direction of the wind—probably also currents of which we
were ignorant—would prevent us from obtaining a greater

offing; and since better might not be, we were fain to
content ourselves with shaping the same course as the
Scout was sailing when attacked by the French gun-boats,
not one amongst us hinting, that I remember, at the desirableness of exchanging the dangers of such a voyage in
an open boat for the security of a French prison. Mr.
Tyler would, no doubt, have preferred making for the
nearest French harbour or practicable landing-place, but
he was wise enough to keep his wishes to himself.

Our progress was slow, much slower than we had anticipated. The boat was far too heavy for one pair of
oars; and when evening fell upon a day of great exertion,
Havre de Grace, which we had hoped to pass during daylight, was still considerably ahead on our starboard bow.
It was past midnight when we were abreast of that port,
and not more than a mile, if so much, to windward—
scarcely sufficient offing to enable us to clear Cape La
Heve, about a league further north, whose two lofty light-
houses had been our guiding-stars since the night set in.

The street-lamps or lanterns of Havre threw up dim lines
of light, which doubtfully indicated the number and direction of the principal streets; and it was with filled eyes
and a beating heart that I thought of two mournful dwellers
in one of those faintly traced thoroughfares—asleep, no
doubt, at that hour, and dreaming perhaps of their son,
and the fulfilment of the precious hope of late associated
with him—in my mother's mind at least; of their son who
was then so near to them, and they knew it not! It was
well they did not. Even to a sailor's imagination, as I
knew by the silence of my companions since night—moon-
less, starless night—had fallen, there was something appalling in being afloat upon the wide, dark, solitary sea in
a slight shallow boat which the eye could hardly distinguish from that sea, the only sounds meeting one's ear the
measured jerk of our own oars, the moaning swash of
waves, and the hoarse roar in the distance of the wrathful surf for ever spurned back in its ceaseless assaults upon
the unconquerable shore. How much more appalling, then,
would the vague, undefined imagination of such a scene be
to a woman's—to a mother's heart! Better, then, infinitely better, that they slept on unconscious of my actual
whereabout, and continued to dream of the great hope

which, I had never doubted, save during a few tumultuous
distracting moments, would, in God's good time, be fully
realised.

I crave pardon of the reader for this digression from the
direct current of my narrative. I do not, it will be con-
ceded, often offend in that way, which, perhaps, if I do not
linger upon it, will be my sufficient excuse. To resume,
then, we laboured through the night at the oars with less
and less success in the way of progress: the tide, which
about there flows like a torrent, was for several hours
dead against us, so that we could barely hold our own;
and at day-dawn we had but just passed the lofty headland of La Heve.

That lofty headland, as many readers know, is formed of
chalk-cliffs, and the sinuous shore at its base strewed with
jagged, fantastic rocks. This was once, it is said, the
favourite resort of Bernardin St. Pierre, the author of *Paul
and Virginia*, and a native of Havre de Grace, who there
studied the elemental phenomena which he, in after-life,
embodied in his description of the wreck of the *San Geran*.

I knew nothing of this at the time I am writing of; and
if I had, Bernardin St. Pierre would assuredly have found
no place in my thoughts, which were painfully pre-
occupied by two paramount facts — namely, the rapid
increase of the wind, and the existence of a current, which
helped the wind not only to drive us upon the shore, but
upon the most rocky part of the shore, whereon the surf
was leaping at a gigantic height, and with the sound of
thunder.

An accident capped the terrors of the situation. The
extra strength exerted by one of the seamen to keep the
boat at sea, had the effect of snapping the blade of his oar
short off, and we were at the mercy of the furious elements.

Dowling, who had scarcely spoken since we hauled him
into the boat, and who was still acutely suffering from the
injury to his foot, now interfered in his usual stern, decisive manner.

"Hand here the oar still left," he said: "place it in the
stern rowlock, and I will endeavour to beach the boat as
as favourably as may be, since nothing better can be done.
Remember, all of you to leap out, if you are not
thrown out of the boat, the instant it strikes the shore, and

then run swiftly ahead. Should the surf overtake you, fall down flat on your bellies, and cling to anything you can lay hold of—to the sand, by digging your fingers into it, if nothing better offers ; and so on, ditto repeated, till you find yourself high and dry. There are, I see, people, either fishermen or peasants, on the shore observing us. They will, no doubt, render what assistance they can, so that it's upon the cards that we may all yet live to be buried in an elm suit, with all the honours."

"And you," I exclaimed—"how, with that crippled limb, will you be able to manage ? "

" Like yourself—the best way I can, And now be silent, if you please, and prepare for a race with King Death."

The boat, urged by wind and sea, drove swiftly towards the shore, and was dexterously guided by Dowling to an opening between rocks, towards which we were directed by the gestures of the people on the shore. Ten or more fearful minutes passed, and then we were lifted and borne along upon the back of a terrific surf-wave, which receding, dropped the boat upon the shore with a force that smashed in its bottom, and threw us all out upon the pebbly sand. What immediately followed, I do not distinctly remember. I know that I ran landward the moment I regained my feet; that I was caught by the boiling flood, and smashed upon the sands; then followed a sense of suffocation, of despair, and, finally, spasms of excruciating pain, from which I recovered to find myself still on the rude shore, but beyond reach of the waves, and sedulously ministered to by a number of half-peasant, half-fisher French men and women, directed by a podgy, bustling little clerical gentleman, whom I afterwards knew to be the kind and good Father Meudon, parish priest of Monvilliers, a village not very far inland.

As soon as I had sufficiently regained consciousness, and felt the assurances of the good people about me that I had suffered no serious injury to oe true, my thoughts and inquiries reverted to my boat-companions. Two of them, I found, had been carried out to sea, and of course drowned. Dowling had been rescued with life, after incurring frightful injuries ; Mr. Tyler had escaped with even less of mishap than myself; and the four other sailors with not at all serious hurts and bruises.

We were all carried to farmhouses, the owners or habit-
ants of which if, according to our notions, poor in purse,
were abudantly rich in generous feeling. Mr. Tyler had
said he was an American, and the conclusion, which I did
not contradict, was, that we were all of the same nation,
though I am quite sure our treatment would not have been
one whit less kindly had our entertainers known from the
first that, except Mr. Tyler, we were all their "natural
enemies"—to quote an atrocious popular phrase of that
time and age.

It was all over with poor Dowling! He had been injured
internally to such a degree, that he could not possibly
survive more than a few hours—perhaps not one. This
was communicated to him as tenderly as possible through
me by the doctor whom Father Meudon had summoned in
great haste from Monvilliers.

The first officer of the *Scout* received the announcement
with a smile—brave, though feeble, " I would rather,"
he murmured, " have died in battle, than thus faint out of
life, as one may say : it, however, comes to the same thing
at last."

Father Meudon, with tears in his round, beady black
eyes, entreated me to explain to the moribund that he,
Father Meudon, prayed him to have heed, whilst there
was yet time, to the salvation of his immortal soul; only to
be assured, Father Meudon declared, through the instru-
mentality of the Holy Roman Catholic Church, into the
bosom of which he was ready and anxious to admit the
dying sinner even at the eleventh hour.

I translated what the kindly intending priest said; and
Dowling, with a slight glimmer about his eyes of the old
reckless privateer spirit, bade me tell the good little
gentleman that he would do more than that to oblige him,
only he must let him, Dowling, have some five minutes'
previous conversation with me.

Father Meudon was delighted with my paraphrase of
the dying seaman's reply, and after earnestly impressing
upon me the vital necessity of quickly despatching any
merely mundane business I might have to arrange with
his penitent, left the room.

" I must be quick and brief," said Dowling as the door
closed; " life, I require no doctor to tell me, is ebbing

fast. In the first place, Linwood, take this pocket-book.
I appoint you my executor. Will you undertake the
trust?"

"Most willingly."

"Thanks, thanks! The old couple—my father and
mother—live at Camberwell. You will find the address
amongst the papers. The money is of course for them.
Webbe, to whom I have ever done my duty, will, there is
no fear, do his by me. I think he will have to hand you
over about three hundred pounds, supposing the *Columbia*
to have slipped through our fingers. Let him state the
amount himself: if he cheats anybody, it will be himself,
not me. That also will be for the old couple. And if,"
said Dowling with a perceptible tremor of voice, "you
will see them, and say their son died as a British seaman
should, that would be kind."

I promised to see his parents; and the poor fellow,
having first swallowed a glass of wine—he was sinking
fast—proceeded:

"And now, having squared the yards as regards myself,
let me speak of something which, from certain words I
have heard drop, I believe concerns you, though how or
why I cannot understand. I allude to Maria Wilson,
who"——

"Ha!—— I beg pardon; go on, pray."

"What I have to say about her is shortly this: Somewhere about fourteen or fifteen years ago, the *Wasp* privateer took on board off Deal a Frenchwoman and a child.
Madame Broussard the woman called herself. I suspected
the child, which I do not think I saw during the voyage
out, to be Webbe's. That, however, was no business of
mine, and I may be wrong. Another sip of wine; and
don't, Linwood, glare at me so. My brain feels dull and
swimmy—give me the wine."

"It is in your hand. Let me hold it to your lips."

"Better, clearer, stronger now! We sailed to Madeira,
where we had often been before. One Wilson, a good
fellow, with odd ways about him, lived there. His brim-
stone of a wife—a Frenchwoman—died soon after giving
birth to a daughter, the Maria Wilson now in Jersey.
Well, Wilson himself had slipped his cable suddenly some
time before we arrived at Madeira, and had left a will

appointing Webbe his executor, and the guardian of his
child. The property was to be invested in the British
funds—only two hundred a year to be drawn out for the
daughter's maintenance and education till she reached her
seventeenth birthday, at which age she might marry, and
the accumulated money with interest was to be hers absolutely. Wilson, as I told you, was a queer stick——
This faintness again "——

Wine once more brought back light to the darkening
eyes—strength to the fluttering speech :

"We sailed for England with Madame Broussard and
two children, both, it was said, of about the same age,
and we got wrecked on the Galway coast. The vessel
was not the *Wasp*, mind you. Wilson's child," he faintly
proceeded after a pause, "will come into something like
twenty thousand pounds, and it would be a thousand
pities that that poor poltroon Harry Webbe should—
should "——

He stopped, and presently I could hear what is called
the rattle in his throat. I once more gave him wine; and
the expiring flame of life leaped up for a moment brightly
in the socket.

"It is no fault of mine, Webbe," he exclaimed, "that
the *Columbia* was recaptured! Bravo, Rawlings, a capital
shot! You 'll shave the Frenchmen's whiskers yet. Ha,
ha, ha! what a confounded splutter they make in the
water. Be ready, Englishmen, to board in the smoke.
FIRE!"

That was the last word audible to mortal ears Robert
Dowling uttered.

CHAPTER XV.

FATHER MEUDON.

YES, the last word audible to mortal ears uttered by Robert
Dowling, though the chafing spirit did not finally shuffle
off its mortal coil till some time afterwards. Father
Meudon, whom the loud tones of the privateer officer had

brought into the room, persisted in believing, or hoping in his large charity, that the indistinct mutterings of the moribund were spirit-petitions to the throne of mercy— that the expiring seaman recognised repentantly, in the crucifix held before his glazing eyes, the emblem and pledge of his soul's redemption from the second and eternal death; and so believing, Father Meudon recited the prayers and performed the ceremonies appointed by the Roman Catholic Church for dying penitents; that of absolution included—a vain mockery I thought at the time, though not, it may be, deemed so, the rebuking years have since suggested, by Him who blesses pure intentions.

Men bury their dead quickly out of their sight in France, and Dowling was laid in the narrow house scooped out for him in the sandy grave-ground attached to a rude chapel near the beach, dedicated to "Our Lady, Star of the Sea," on the evening of the day he died. My respect-ful acquiescence in the religious ceremonial prescribed by the priestly conscience concilitated the regard of Father Meudon; and his round, fat, good-humoured face shone with so benign an expression as we conversed together after the funeral, that it struck me I could not do a wiser thing, circumstanced as I was, than take him into my confidence. I did so, not unreservedly the reader will readily believe, but sufficiently to enable him to serve me if he willed to do so.

The worthy man listened with surprise and growing interest; and I was delighted to find that my being an Englishman increased instead of diminished his sympathi-sing friendliness. He had fled from Havre at the outbreak of the French revolution to England, and retained a lively sense of the kindly hospitality he had received there. He was pleased to add that, apart from their religion and lan-guage—the last of which he had not been able to thoroughly master twenty words of—there was in his candid judgment much in the institutions, customs, and character of the English people worthy of approval and esteem.

"It is fortunate for you, my young friend," said Father Meudon, helping himself to a powerful pinch from a *tabatière*, which was seldom out of his hand, "that I was not honoured with your confidence in the first instance, and I am going to tell you why. A commissary of police was here about an hour since, to ascertain the nationality, &c., of the foreign seamen reported to have been cast ashore; and being informed by me that they were all citizens of the United States of America, he, under the circumstances, accepted my assurance of that fact, which I could not, of course, have given had I known what I do now. This will give us time, which shall be wisely used if you, recognising that I am acquainted with the ground, and you are not, consent to be implicitly guided by my counsel."

"I shall most willingly, gratefully do so."

That is not perhaps so sure, seeing that, to begin with, I must forbid your attempting to proceed as yet to Numéro 12, Rue Bombardée, Havre. Pray, do not exclaim till you have heard my reasons. The first is, that if care, immediate care be not taken, you will fall seriously ill: there is incipient fever in your veins, brought on, no doubt, by the fatigue and anxiety you have undergone since the hurricane struck the corsair, though strong mental excitement bears you up for the moment."

"Surely, reverend sir," said I, "that is a consideration which should urge me to seek the asylum of my relatives' home without delay. The worst that can befall me is that I shall be a prisoner of war, or *détenu*—like my father—and, for a brief period only, the Empire being, it is everywhere said, on the eve of dissolution."

"Permit *me* to say, my young friend, that you argue from false, or, more correctly, from not well-established premises. It is doubtful, to say the least, that the *parole d'honneur* of a corsair officer would be deemed a sufficient security that he would not attempt to escape. True, you were a passenger, but that fact would have first to be established by judicial proof; whilst it cannot be denied that you escaped, in company with the commander and a portion of the crew, after a combat in which the famous *Scout* was sunk by French gun-boats. As to the dissolution of the Empire, that, I assure you, is by no means so imminent as its enemies would have the world believe. The imperial lion, though wounded and at bay, has still a terrible *patte*. News even has just arrived of a great battle near Montmirail, in which the Prussians were pulverised. No, Monsieur Linwood," continued Father Meudon, "we will not trust to such doubtful chances. That which must be done is this: You will presently, upon retiring to bed, take the composing draught, as directed by Monsieur le Médecin. Should dangerous symptoms have supervened when I visit you to-morrow morning, I shall at once proceed to Numéro 12, Rue Bombardée, and conduct hither madam your mother. If, on the contrary, I find you much better, I shall take counsel of a military friend of mine as to how you may be most advantageously constituted a prisoner of war, or détenu. I will now bid you adieu, as it is quite time you were in bed and asleep."

The door had scarcely closed upon Father Meudon when Mr. Tyler presented himself. His sallow skin was aglow, his keen, wary eyes aflame with exitement—with rageful excitement it appeared by the *furioso* tone in which he addressed me, and heaped abuse upon that treacherous varmint of an uncle of mine, whom, should he ever clap eyes upon again, he would annihilate, chaw up, in less than two twos!

So abrupt and violent an outbreak, after the strict reserve Mr. Tyler had imposed upon himself, surprised me not a little, till I perceived that it was rather an irrepressible burst of exultation than of anger which overflowed the American skipper's thin, cautious lips, with such astounding volubility.

" I can assure you, Mr. Tyler," said I, as soon as I could edge in a word, "that I am entirely guiltless of the treachery which you justly denounce, though my tongue is tied with respect to *how* I came to be associated with the individual you call my uncle, and threaten to 'chaw up'— an operation which, believe me, will require much tougher teeth than *you* possess. You have heard good news of the *Columbia* ?"

" You've hit the bull's-eye there, young fellow. A fisherman has brought word that an American three-masted ship that had been captured by the Britishers, and retaken by her own crew, came into Havre soon after daylight yesterday. That was smart work, I reckon; and just shews what a darned sight taller tune *Yankee Doodle* will soon be than your old, wheezy, worn-out *Rule Britannia !* "

" Yankee Doodle Dandy would not this time have

stuck a feather in his cap if the second boat had reached
the *Columbia*. However, I am very glad you have recovered
your ship."

"Well, I'm inclined to believe you are; and if not,
lying with an honest face must be a natural gift of
youthful Britishers. Let that be as it may, I ain't going
to hurt you after what we have passed through together.
So far from that, I wish you well, young man, and hope
that for the future you will keep better company than
I met you in. I ain't off to Havre to-night," added Mr.
Tyler, " as the barriers will be closed before I could get
there; but I shall be gone before you are up to-morrow—
so, good-bye."

Wearied in every bone and muscle of my body as I
was, a kind of confused, chaotic excitement forbade sleep ;
even the composing draught prescribed for me failed for
a while of its intended effect, and opening poor Dowling's
pocket-book, I glanced listlessly and dreamily over its
contents. There were Bank of England notes to over
one hundred pounds, several letters from the "old
couple," and one from Webbe dated about a week before
we left St. Malo. It enjoined Dowling to immediately
post a letter he would receive in the same parcel. Then
followed these words : "It is possible that Mr. Waller may
pay you a visit as soon as he hears that the *Scout* has
run into Portsmouth harbour. Should he do so, be sure
to speak very highly of my son. He will have read o'
the action off Sercq, copied from the Jersey into the
English papers; and as you value my friendship, as you
would render me an essential service, be careful that
no hint of the incorrectness of that statement shall reach
his ear. This, I ask of you, as a favour to myself, not to
Harry, who is, however, you must not forget, my son, and
something much better than that, though not a fire-eater
like you and me."

"Mr. Waller and Harry Webbe," I remember to
have drowsily murmured—"what, in the name of wonder, may be the meaning of that strange conjunction of names? And that cursed *Scout* action to be
for ever turning up in all sorts of places. Surely — but
no"——

Perception, physical and mental, grew duller—feebler.

The half-formed notion excited by the letter slipped from
my brain, the letter itself from my fingers, and falling,
dressed as I was, upon the bed, I was sound asleep almost
before I touched it.

It was mid-day when I awoke—fresh, vigorous, free from
fever and bodily ailment of every kind. There was no one
in the room; but glancing around, I saw a sealed letter
on a table by the bedside. It was addressed to M. Linwood, and, as I immediately conjectured, was written by
Father Meudon. It contained these kindly sentences:
" MY YOUNG FRIEND—We find you in a sound refreshing
sleep, and are careful not to disturb you. Your pulse is
regular, and Monsieur le Médecin is confident that you will
awaken in perfect health. *Dieu merci!* This being so, I
shall at once consult my military friend. He is a man in
authority at Havre, and I may not be able to see him till
the evening. As soon as I have done so, I shall call at
Numéro 12, Rue Bombardée, and gently prepare the good
people there for the joyful surprise which awaits them.
That is a duty which must not be neglected. There
cannot, I think, be much danger in your venturing to Havre
as soon as darkness begins to fall. The *retraite* is not
beaten before nine o'clock; and Pierre Bonjean, with whom
I shall speak presently, will be your guide. Take care to
be at the south door, in the Rue St. Jacques, of the church
of Notre Dame, not one minute later than eight o'clock,
and await my coming there, which will not be long delayed, you may be sure. Your friend, LE PERE MEUDON.
—*Nota Bene:* I have gathered up the notes and papers
that lay scattered on the bed and floor, restored them to
your pocket-book, and placed *that* under your pillow. You
are a sad *sans-soin*, I am afraid."

" A first-rate fellow is Père Meudon," exclaimed I,
springing off the bed; and having first bawled down stairs
to no purpose, and my appetite pressing, I hastened to
the kitchen, or, more correctly, the general sitting and
eating room below. There was nobody there, and the
doors were wide open, but *riz-au-lait* was simmering on
the hot ashes, and there was excellent bread and butter on
the table—ample materials for a hearty breakfast, which,
having despatched, I returned to my chamber, and bethought me of again looking at Webbe's letter to Dowling.

Curious! There was another letter, from Webbe to his chief officer, or rather a fragment of one, the sheet of paper having been partially burnt away, apparently by the falling of lighted tobacco upon it, which I had not seen the previous evening, though I could almost have sworn that I opened every paper in the pocket-book. This fragment of confidential correspondence was an important one, and at once demolished certain cobwebs which the paragraph in the other letter had begun to spin in my *gobe-mouche* imagination. The first part of the nearly half-destroyed missive had been seemingly filled with privateering business details, and the, to me, only interesting lines were these:

"You will be pleased to hear that we have identified Mrs. Waller's long-lost daughter beyond doubt or cavil. Even Linwood, one of the most suspicious young puppies I have ever met with, is satisfied upon that point. I am endeavouring to bring about his marriage with her under various false pretences; the true one, between ourselves, being, that I am confident his mother and her mother would be greatly pleased by such a result; and no wonder, since there could then be no doubt that the young couple would jointly inherit Mr. Anthony Waller's immense wealth; whilst I am equally sure that the gratitude of those ladies towards my worthy self for bringing it about quietly and without compromising them, would be counted out in many hundreds of golden guineas, and *you* know how welcome a haul of that kind would be just now. This, however, concerns you but remotely; and reverting to the financial difficulty with our Portsmouth agent"—and so on.

A gleam of light seemed to be thrown upon the dark riddle that had so long perplexed me by a communication not intended to meet my eye; and yet—shade of Œdipus!—how was that statement to be reconciled with——

"Ha, ha! Mossu Linvoude, there you are, awake and hearty!"

This abrupt greeting issued from the thick shock head, just visible above the sill of the chamber-door, of Pierre Bonjean, his body resting out of sight upon a step or rung of the nearly perpendicular ladder-stairs which communicated with the kitchen.

"I'm very well awake, thank you, Monsieur Bonjean, and quite hearty, which you will have no doubt of when you see what a breakfast I have put away. But tell me, my friend, is it a practice in this part of the world to leave the doors of your house open to all comers? Perhaps, however, you have not been long out."

"Every one of us since eight o'clock, and it is now past twelve. But there was no danger. I did not see Father Meudon arrive at the house," continued Pierre; "but he spoke to me after leaving it, and I shall be ready to accompany Mossu to Havre in the evening. I am also charged to say," added Bonjean, "that one Baptiste, who is now with your countrymen the sailors, wishes to see Mossu Linvoude."

"Baptiste!—Baptiste!" I exclaimed. "Surely it cannot be—— What is he?"

"A French seaman, it is certain, and belonging, he says, to the équipage of L'Espiègle, French corsair, now in the port of Havre. If Mossu," added Pierre, "does not wish to see this Baptiste, he need not do so."

"You mistake me, friend Bonjean. I am much astonished, but not at all displeased at hearing that Baptiste of L'Espiègle is here. Have the kindness to say I shall be glad to see him at once."

"I shall do so with pleasure. Good-day, Mossu Linvoude."

"Baptiste inquiring for me!" I went on to bewilderedly ejaculate—"Baptiste whom I left weatherbound in Jersey—Baptiste who—— Angels and ministers of grace defend us!—Captain Webbe himself!"

"Yes, Captain Webbe himself, in the body, and therefore neither a spirit of heaven nor goblin damned as yet; so you need not put the question. Well, what news? How did you escape from St. Malo, and where have you left your wife?"

"Clemence remains at St. Malo."

"I guessed so! Well, go on. But I know the rest already from the sailors yonder," pursued Webbe with rising passion. "The running-fight off Cherbourg, and the foundering of the brave old craft, I witnessed myself. There is a flaming account in the papers of the destruction of the English corsair Scout, mounting twelve cannons, by

N

two French gun-boats. D—n their gasconade, and their gun
boats too. The *Scout* gone, the *Columbia* retaken," he presently resumed with unabated fury—"the devil has
clapped me on both shoulders this time with a vengeance.
Dowling, too, is dead—nothing *but* songs of death. You
were with him, I hear. Well, what passed?"

"He appointed me his executor, chiefly that I might
transfer the money in his pocket-book, together with the
sum in which you are indebted to him, to his aged parents,
living at Camberwell."

"Which sum is not far under four hundred pounds. It
shall be paid, if, to do so, I am obliged to sell my shirt. A
brave, steadfast fellow was Dowling, true as steel, honest as
death. And he is gone! Well, there is an ebb as well as
flood tide in the affairs of men, which, once set in, soon
whirls the stoutest, richest-freighted bark to bottomless
perdition. It is now set in for me, for mine, and will
quickly, I fear, sweep us and our hopes to cureless ruin."

"That Captain Kirke Webbe should be so over-borne by
a few strokes of adverse fortune, is passing strange."

"It may so appear to you, Linwood; but you know not
all. Hearken, young man. You suspect me of double-
dealing towards yourself; and you have a right to suspect,
for the charge is partially true—partially only, and that
arising from circumstances which, if placed in their proper
light—as they shall be some day, if I live—would much
excuse, if not entirely justify that apparent double-dealing.
In the main, I have been true to you. I have been anxious
—absurdly so, perhaps—that you should marry Lucy
Hamblin. I know that the girl will inherit every penny
of Mr. Anthony Waller's wealth. The recovery of her
child has become a sort of mania with the mother, upon
whom her husband dotes as fondly—more so, if it be
possible, than he did fifteen years ago. Lucy Hamblin will
therefore, I repeat, be Mr. Waller's heiress, to the exclusion
of his grandson, should she even have married a chimney-
sweep. Of that rest assured; and let me again urge you
to re-consider the determination you have rashly formed, of
waiting till Mademoiselle Clemence is acknowledged by the
Wallers, before you make her bone of your bone, flesh of
your flesh. Intrust me with a note expressive of your
willingness, your desire to forthwith enter into the holy

ends of matrimony with one of the wealthiest and most amiable of maidens, and"——

" Your difficulties," I promptly interjected, "with Madame de Bonneville, *alias* Louise Feron, *alias* (this was drawing a bow at a venture) Madame Broussard, would be smoothed away."

That man would not have so much as winked at the sudden uncovering and discharge of a masked battery. He did not reply for about half a minute, and only in that half-minute's silence could I detect the faintest surprise or annoyance at the thunderbolt I had launched at his head.

" Well," said he, " that is a capital guess, if it be a guess Madame de Bonneville, *née* Louise Feron, *is* Madame Broussard. Ah, my dear fellow, you can little imagine what infernal complications that woman-fiend has involved me in. You shall, one day, and soon, if all goes well. Dowling, I daresay," added Webbe, " also hinted to you why I am so anxious that my son should espouse Maria Wilson."

" Yes, the young lady possesses somewhere about twenty thousand pounds in her own right."

"That is just it. I confess that I covet riches for my son as well as for myself. Your sublimer mind soars superior to such sordid considerations, or you would not reject the brilliant alliance which awaits your acceptance."

" Let me assure you, once for all, Captain Webbe, that my marriage now or hereafter with Lucy Hamblin—and mark me, I have not the slightest doubt that Mademoiselle Clemence is Lucy Hamblin—is absolutely out of the question—impossible, either now or hereafter."

" There is no more, then, to be said on the subject, though your senseless folly adds greatly to my embarrassments, and "——

Webbe paused abruptly, seemed to silently collect and marshal his thoughts and purposes, and then resumed more calmly:

" Within the next forty-eight hours, Linwood," said he, " I shall have either lost or won the game of life; and you can yet in some slight degree help me to win it. Here is a brief outline of my actual position: it will be obscure, unintelligible to you in parts, but minute explanations must stand over for a time. The *Columbia* was recaptured by her own crew after a sharp fight, and she is now in the port of Havre. My son prudently denied, when questioned, that he was Harry Webbe of Sercq-fight notoriety : and the *Scout* seamen will keep his secret. He is now as an officer at large on parole, free to go and come within certain bounds, but *gardé à vue*, as it is called. He cannot leave Havre. Now, Maria Wilson and Madame Dupre will arrive at Honfleur to-morrow ; that Jezebel, De Bonneville, the day after ; and if Harry does not wed the young lady before she arrives, his chance of doing so will have passed away for ever. Why, then, you may ask, do not Madame Dupre and Miss Wilson come on to Havre ? I will tell you : Tyler, the Yankee skipper, whom I met, and, indeed, almost ran against this morning, must, the sailors here tell me, have heard his name mentioned as the commander of the prize-crew on board the *Columbia*."

"No doubt of that ; and did he not recognise you this morning ? "

"Not he ; and it would have been rather strange if he had by a casual, passing glance. Don't you think so ? "

"Why, yes, divested as you now are of the Renaudin wig, the black dye washed out of your whiskers, and in other respects restored to your natural self. I do not think, besides, that Mr. Tyler, now that he has recovered his ship, will be disposed to act vindictively."

"You will cease to think so when I mention that Tyler's son was dangerously wounded in the fight on board the *Columbia*—nay, that it is feared he is hurt to death."

"That is indeed unfortunate—terrible !"

"I know Tyler well, brief as our acquaintance has been. Should his son die—and he *will* die—the American will move heaven and earth to be revenged upon his slayer—upon me—through my son. He cannot but have discovered by this time that Jacques Le Gros is Captain Kirke Webbe; and the accusation lodged with the Havre authorities by Auguste Le Moine against Webbe junior of the *Scout*—Le Moine being, fortunately for you, unhappily for Harry, away at Paris—will place in his hands a swift means of vengeance. Harry will be forthwith seized, lodged in prison, brought to a brief trial, and shot offhand possibly, in the present excited state of the soldiery."

"You surely are not going to propose that I shall pub-

licly avow myself to be the person denounced by Auguste
Le Moine at the Avranches banquet."

"No, no, I am not quite so unreasonable as that: besides,
Harry cannot part with his fictitious laurels, save in the
last extremity; and I must have expressed myself very ill,
if you do not understand that the mere incarceration of my
son would be fatal to his hope of marrying Maria Wilson.
Let me add, whilst I think of it, that you will incur no real
danger by visiting Havre. Before Auguste Le Moine
returns from Paris, if he returns at all, the imperial government will have been finally abolished."

"Father Meudon here is of a contrary opinion. He
speaks of a great victory gained over the Prussians by the
emperor."

"The fight at Montmirail? Pooh! Paris capitulated a
few hours after that battle was fought; and if Napoleon, instead of calmly recognising the utterness of his defeat, de-
termines to die with harness on his back, he will but slightly
defer the inevitable catastrophe. Havre, however, and I
dare say most of the garrison towns, will hold out for him
to the last; and, as I have before explained, it is this an-
archic state of things which constitutes our real danger. It
glanced across my mind to ask you," continued Webbe, "to
assure Tyler that Harry was not Kirke Webbe, the privateer
captain's son; but that device would not, I fear, hold water.
Save the boy I will, and if man may do it, get him out of
Havre this very night. One plan which I shall first essay
will require more money than I can for the moment
command, and I must request you to lend me all you can
spare."

"That, with Dowling's, which I can hereafter replace,
will scarcely amount to two hundred pounds."

"Which will more than suffice. Should bribery fail, or
I find it inexpedient or dangerous to try it on, another, and
upon the face of it, more desperate scheme must be attempted.
There are other matters," added Webbe, rising and putting
on his hat, "which I intended to talk over with you, but
time presses, and I must be gone. Farewell." He hurried
away, and ten minutes afterwards, he and the four rescued
Scout seamen were on their way to Havre de Grace.

Verily, a consummate actor was Webbe, I again and
again mentally ejaculate, after transcribing the foregoing

dialogue; for who could have imagined that, when talking
with such reckless, devil-may-care outspokenness—his rage,
and anxiety for his son, moreover, being perfectly real—he
was all the while playing a part, strengthening with wary
carelessness, as it were, the web of lies by which he had so
long blinded and bamboozled me! Yet so it was; and no
doubt it was that astonishing power of deception and fer-
tility of resource under all circumstances which constituted
his marvellous " luck," as it was popularly termed. I, at
least, in self-excuse, endeavour to believe so.

As usual, I was too restless and impatient to follow the
counsel given me, by waiting till evening-fall before
leaving for Havre ; and as Pierre Bonjean would, I found,
be away till close upon six o' clock, I e'en set off alone, about
two hours after Webbe left me."

It would be difficult to find in a country which the natives,
with quite pardonable partiality, mistakenly call " La Belle
France," a finer view than that commanded from the crest
of the *côte* which slopes down to the ancient Haven of
Grace, so named, says Mr. Murray, after a statue of the
Virgin of Grace—an altogether apocryphal derivation, by
the way. That southward slope of the côte or hill was,
even at the time I am speaking of, dotted with gay villa-like
residences—in a modest sense, no doubt, judged by British
villa notions—and I may mention, as an illustration of the
amenities of civilised warfare, if that be not a contradiction
in terms, that although fortified Havre itself was more than
once bombarded, the numerous dwellers on the exposed côte
were never once, I have been assured, molested or menaced
by hostile shot or shell. On the right, looking towards the
town, was the broad solitary sea, now tranquilly basking in
the slant rays of the westering sun, and not a sail, not a
boat to be seen thereon ; a vast solitariness which, together
with the tall masts of numerous vessels, sheltered, hiding
themselves, so to speak, in the splendid wet-docks *behind*
the town, struck my Britannic fancy as a tacit acknow-
ledgement on the part of the teeming French shore-popu-
lations that they had finally relinquished the domain of the
sea to their amphibious British foes. Over beyond Havre,
and directly across the mouth of the Seine, Honfleur—
Harry V., Shakspeare's Honfleur—glimmered in the paling
sunlight, which was, however, still sufficiently powerful to

shed a silver radiance over the winding river-street, to use
an expression of Napoleon's, which connects the cities of
Paris, Rouen, and Havre, and throw a mellowing splendour
over a vast and varied landscape waving in the leafy,
blossomed glory of the bursting spring.

Another time, I could have lingered for hours over so fair
a scene ; but more stirring emotions than beauties of land
or sea can arouse or still, were then tugging at my heart ·
and hastening onward through the suburb of Ingouville, 1
entered Havre and the Rue de Paris just as the clocks were
chiming the hour of five, without having, to my knowledge,
excited the slightest notice or remark.

The Rue St. Jacques leads out of the Rue de Paris near
the quay-end of the latter street, and I was soon at the door
of the church of Notre Dame. The silly self-excuse for my
morbid restlessness was, that Father Meudon might have
arrived there considerably more than two hours before his
time ; and more than willing to be deceived, I half persuaded myself that he was amongst a considerable number
of persons who, although no service was going on, were
kneeling on the stone flags with their faces towards the
illuminated altar. A closer look was decisive ; and soon
tiring of the silent solemnity of the place, I wandered forth,
and roaming vacantly about, presently found myself in a
large vegetable market in front of the Hôtel de Ville. The
busy, noisy scene fixed my attention for a while, and I was
listening with languid interest to a complimentary colloquy
between two *dames du marché*, which abundantly proved
that Billingsgate was not unrivalled in its peculiar line of
dramatic dialogue, when a familiar voice struck my ear,
and turning sharply round, I encountered Captain Webbe.
He was conversing eagerly with Bourdon, the lieutenant
of the *Espiègle*, and looking even paler and more excited
than when he parted with me a few hours previously.

" I wish to speak with you, Linwood," he hurriedly said,
" but I cannot spare a moment to do so. If you have time
and inclination," he added, " call upon me at La Belle
Poule, a cabaret on the quay, six doors from the Rue de
Paris. Adieu ! "

He strode on for a few paces, then suddenly turning back,
left his companion, came close to me, and said in English :
" My fear is realised. Tyler's son is dead. Good-bye."

This occurred at about half-past six o'clock, and as I soon sickened of the sights and smells of the ill-kept streets, I inquired my way to La Belle Poule, there to while away the hour and more which it still wanted of the time appointed by Father Meudon for our meeting.

The ground-floor room of La Belle Poule, a low cabaret much frequented by sailors, was nearly filled by that class of persons, most of whom I knew belonged to the *Espiègle*, though they did not wear the glazed hats upon which the name of the corsair cutter was painted. The guests, all more or less drunk, were exceedingly noisy, and Webbe, or Baptiste, as he called himself, was amongst the noisiest, and the especial favourite of the uproarious company. Young Webbe, pale as his shirt-collar, and suffering acutely from mental agitation, sat at a little distance from his father ; and close by him were three of the *Scout* seamen that had been cast ashore with me at La Heve. The fourth, I afterwards knew, had been placed in charge of a boat, which, the tide being at full, was waiting at the pier-steps beyond Francis I.'s Tower. The common Scouts, made prisoners on board the *Columbia*, were, it seemed, in actual durance. As far apart as could be, and looking on with make-believe indifference, were two gendarmes, the gentlemen, no doubt, by whom Harry Webbe was gardé à vue.

Webbe, who did not acknowledge me by word or look, was boiling over with patriotic enthusiasm. The victory at Montmirail, and the capitulation of Paris, purchased, he swore, by English guineas, afforded ample scope to his powers of glorification and abuse, which he lavishly availed himself of. The rascally English, who never accepted battle except they were three or four to one, came in for the lion's share of his copious vituperation, and evidently with savage reference to young Webbe and the *Scout* seamen, who, though pretending to pass themselves off as Americans belonging to the *Columbia*, he persisted were nothing but British brutes and cowards.

Now, as long as Webbe poured forth his voluminous wrath in French, the Scouts were naturally acquiescent, and even appeared to enjoy the seemingly drunken orator's eloquence, without, it was plain, comprehending a word of it; but when he began to interlard his abuse with explanatory

English, it was equally natural that he should quickly get
their backs up.

"Ha, ha!" roared Webbe, at the close of a flourishing
panegyric upon Napoleon, " pourquoi not vou sacré Goddems
—pourquoi not crier Vive l'Empereur ?   De grand empereur
that pouvait shoveler your misérable island into de sea ?—
eh, pourquoi not sacré Jean Boule Goddems ? "

"Go to blazes ! " grunted Skelton, as shrewd a fellow as
ever lived.

"Go to blaze, dites-vous ! " retorted Webbe.   "Ha, ha!
it is you one, two, three, quatre Goddems that shall go to
blaze ! Voulez-vous boxer, eh ? " he added, squaring up
and flourishing his fists in the faces of the Scouts.   "Voulez-
vous boxer one Français, vous one, two, trois—four sacré
Jean Boules.   Là, take dat for avoir say ' Go to blaze '—ha,
ha ! "

Suiting the action to the word, Webbe hit Skelton a really
tremendous facer.   Up sprang the English sailors, three or
four of the Espiègles pressing forward at the same moment
to sustain the assailant, and a general fight was improvised
in just no time.   Messieurs les Gendarmes. as in duty
bound, now interposed, and endeavoured to separate the
furious combatants;   an interference which was immediately
resented by both parties, who all with one accord turned
their fighting fury upon the unfortunate officers.   The din,
the row, the confusion was terrible—deafening,   I myself
got involved in the vortex, hustled and tripped up ;   and
when I recovered my feet, and the landlord relit one of the
extinguished candles, I perceived that myself and the two
gendarmes, who had not as yet picked themselves up, and
were bleeding profusely from nose and mouth, were the
sole remaining guests at La Belle Poule.

CHAPTER XVI.

MOTHER AND SON.

THE bodily hurts of the gendarmes were quickly relieved,
Cold water and a *petit verre* each sufficed to restore in that

respect; but the sacredness of authority, outraged in their persons, demanded a signal atonement; and having rehatted and generally readjusted themselves into official dignity, they sternly demanded the names of the ruffians by whom they had been assaulted. The landlord of La Belle Poule declared with ready volubility that he knew no more than did the pope of Rome who the infamous wretches were; and the officers, finding they were only wasting precious moments, sallied forth in quest of the individual who had been so audaciously withdrawn from their protective guardianship. Faithful to my heedless wont, I followed, and was not all surprised to see the hasting gendarmes come almost immediately to a stand-still, thoroughly at a loss which way to run, or what to do. The evening was pitch dark, the bleak quay deserted, except by the sabre-girt *douanier*, pacing slowly to and fro on his appointed beat; and he, when questioned, said he had not observed which way the men went, or indeed the men themselves, that had just before left La Belle Poule cabaret. The officers, finding themselves so exasperatingly nonplussed, might, in their eagerness to arrest somebody, I was beginning to be half afraid, pounce upon me, as a possible *particeps criminis* in the scandalous trick that had been played upon them, when, their eyes having become more accustomed to the darkness, their attention was attracted by a large cutter-rigged vessel which was being towed out of the harbour. It may be necessary to explain, that in those days, ere yet steam or the spacious *south* docks were, ships could only *sail* out of the port of Havre when the wind was easterly; and if it blew strongly from the westward, the towing row-boats were helped by carrying a hawser from the vessel to the north quay, at which a number of men tugged lustily, till the ship was well past the end of the south pier, which, being considerably shorter than that on the north side, enabled her to slant out to sea across the embouchure of the Seine. In the present case, the westerly breeze not being over-powerful, and no doubt, also, because it was expedient to attract as little notice as possible, boats only were employed on the departing vessel, which, consequently, made but comparatively slow way.

"What *bâtiment* is that leaving the port at this hour?' asked one of the gendarmes.

" The corsair *Espiègle*," replied the customs' officer.

" *L'Espiègle!—L'Espiègle!*" exclaimed the gendarme— " why, death of my life, now I think of it, the chief actor in the tumult, the infernal *bavard* who caused all the mischief, was the man we saw last evening in company with Bourdon, lieutenant of *L'Espiègle!*"

" That may be," remarked his comrade, "though I am not sure. But if so, what then ? "

" What then ! Why, *parbleu*, that it is then certain he is gone on board *L'Espiègle*, and will escape! For my part, at all events, and to make sure, I shall go to the commandant of the port, and get the chain raised at once."

A stout chain, I must inform the reader, was in those war-times drawn every evening across the entrance of the harbour directly after *la retraite* was beaten, in order to guard against a nocturnal visit from Messieurs les Anglais.

" Excuse me, messieurs," remarked the douanier, with an expressive shrug; " but to do that would, it seems to me, be a little absurd. Certainly, no boat has put off to *L'Espiègle* within the last ten minutes ; and, more than that, do you not see that your *confrères*, the gendarmes on duty, have not yet left her ? "

" That is true," growled the irritated official. " Ah, they are leaving the corsair this moment. We can question them."

The gendarmes whose duty it had been to see that no one left France in the privateer cutter whose papers were not *en règle*, landed at the steps nearly opposite the Rue de Paris, and assured their comrades that no one had been received on board *L'Espiègle* since she hauled out of the basin. A brief consultation ensued between the officers, of which the result was, that all four walked smartly off in the direction of the docks; whilst I, having still a full half-hour upon my hands, continued to watch with strong interest the progress of the cutter, which, after she was fairly quit of the gendarmes, the increased exertions of the rowers greatly accelerated. I felt sure that her unopposed departure was an essential condition of Webbe's success in effecting his son's escape from Havre, though how that could be, ignorant as I then was that a boat had been kept waiting at the Tower-steps for the young man and his rescuers, was not very clear.

Sail was got upon the privateer cutter as soon as a sufficient distance beyond the south pier had been gained ; she went off at a spanking rate, was speedily lost sight of in the thick darkness ; and I was turning away, when two guns, fired in quick succession, revealed momentarily her whereabout. Presently afterwards a large blue light shone over the waters, giving to view, clearly as in broad day, the cutter lying-to, and a four-oared boat crowded with men rapidly nearing her. I was no longer in doubt as to how the affair had been managed, nor that, thanks to Webbe's clever audacity, his son would on the morrow espouse Maria Wilson !

The philosophic platitudes with which I sought to soothe or stifle the sharp anguish which, with that thought, shot through me, failed miserably to do so till, when nearing the Rue de Paris, a man's face, distinctly visible in its spectre-whiteness, and stamped with the impress of a settled, stern despair, glanced across my sight. It was that of Mr. Tyler, who, accompanied by some half-a-dozen officers of justice, was hurrying past in blindly vengeful search of the son of the man who had, as he would say, compassed his own boy's death. Instinctively I shrank back into deeper shadow, and the avengers of blood passed on without observing me. Confronted with that giant grief, how insignificant seemed the passing smart of disappointed fancy—the fantastic sorrow excited by the memory-mirrored image of a girl I had spoken to but twice in my life, and of whom I knew nothing so certainly as that she felt for my interesting, moon-calf self, the profoundest indifference, if not contempt !

Still, comparatively slight, evanescent, unworthy of serious regard as might be the impressions photographed upon my facile imagination by the sunshine of a beautiful face, they did not wholly cease to shape and colour my thoughts till the first stroke of eight, booming from the tower of Notre Dame—" booming " was the word I should have used at the time, so deep and solemn an echo did it awaken in my beating heart—recalled me to my proper self, and the delightful consciousness that in a few minutes I should be locked in my mother's arms.

The slow strokes of the clock had not yet counted the hour, when I stood, panting for breath, at the church door. Father Meudon was not there, and I entered the church. A considerable number of silent men and women were still kneeling on the stone-floor, with clasped hands and contrite faces turned towards the illuminated altar ; but the good priest was not amongst them ; and some twenty minutes had elapsed when he entered the church, and recognised me by a glance and gesture which at the same time arrested my eager *abord*, and imposed silence till he too had knelt, crossed himself, and prayed silently, with clasped hands, before the glittering shrine. His devotions finished, the reverend father beckoned me forth.

" *Premièrement*, my young friend," said he, " I must apprise you that I have not seen your parents. They were out on a visit to some English friends, but would certainly return, the servant assured me, by eight o'clock. We will go there together, and I will precede you to their presence by two or three minutes only."

" Let us begone at once. Come."

" Willingly ; but not, if you please, quite so fast, and I may be able *chemin faisant* to acquaint you with the result of a less interesting, but still very important part of the mission I undertook in your behalf. The military friend I advised with," proceeded Father Meudon, " accompanied me, after hearing what I had to say, to Monsieur le Maire, who made no difficulty of handing me a ' permis de séjour' for William Linwood Junior, an English noncombatant, shipwrecked upon the coast of France. Here it is, and pray take care of it."

I thanked the worthy man, and no more was said till we were in La Rue Bombardée.

" This is Numero 12," said Father Meudon, stopping before a respectable house enough—one of the newly built ones—but certainly not such a residence as Mr. and Mrs. Linwood would have made choice of, had not all prisoners of war on parole been strictly relegated to certain specified localities.

The door was opened by a brisk-looking French servant, who, before M. Meudon could open his lips, exclaimed: "Monsieur et Madame Linwood are returned, reverend father, and will receive you at once."

I followed Father Meudon softly up stairs to the first floor, remaining behind at a sign from him, whilst he entered the front apartment. A mute entreaty on my part, aided by a suspicion of the truth, prevailed upon the servant-woman to leave the door open, and I saw that a lady and gentleman, habited in mourning, were seated at a table near the centre of the room. The podgy person of the priest was between the lady and me; and surely that care-worn, age-withered face—that bowed head, sprinkled with gray hairs, could not be my father's! The fevered throbbings of my brain, the fires that danced before my eyes, prevented me from hearing or seeing aught distinctly, but I presently heard a scream of joy, simultaneous with the upstarting of the lady, and the apparition directly before me of a face deep-graven on my heart of hearts.— "Mother! Dear Mother "—" My son! My beloved, darling boy!"

We were in the small hours of another day, and my father—overcome by the reaction caused by the seemingly unchallengeable refutation of the huge lie whose crushing weight had for so many years weighed upon his springs of life—had long since retired, before I had finished the narrative of my adventures since I left the Wight, so numerous were the interruptions of tears, laughter, kisses, praise. I told all; my pledge to Webbe, that I would disclose nothing to his prejudice that might come to my knowledge during those adventures, being no bar to that full disclosure, inasmuch that his secret was as safe with my mother as with me. Critical analysation of obscure and conflicting passages in that brief but crowded experience was tacitly adjourned to a future and calmer time; our hearts, brimming over with joy and gratulation, being all too full to entertain such topics. Strikingly akin to the faculty which clothes the palpable and the familiar with golden exhalations of the dawn, is the power of maternal affection to magnify the common-place doings of an only son into achievements of highest heroism; and positively, but for the humbling whispers of a self-knowledge which would not be wholly silenced, I should have been half persuaded, when my mother and I at last parted for the night, that I was a better kind of Bayard, wholly *sans peur et sans reproche*; my only fault, leaning to virtue's side, being an excess of dutifulness, generosity, and daring!

We did not again meet till late in the afternoon, and we could then talk over matters more quietly, soberly. So

fragile had my father's health become, so utterly incapable
was he of bearing strong excitement, that he could not
leave his chamber ; but my mother, I found, mainly agreed
with the inferences I had drawn from all I had seen and
heard during my companionship with Webbe. One thing
much surprised and gave me a high opinion of her penetra-
tion. She had discovered the secret of my preference for
Maria Wilson, although I had been especially careful to
afford no hint thereof, and had, in fact, slurred over what I
was obliged to say respecting her as quickly, slightingly as
possible. And gently, tenderly, with infinite gentleness and
tenderness, as if conscious as myself of the depth and
sensitiveness of the wound she probed, did she seek to
medicine the hurt by iterated assurances that love-griefs
caused by the chance sight of a pretty face were, could be
nothing more than mere surface-scratches—painful for a
time—such as a rose-brier might inflict ; and all as quickly
healed.

Finding I was not to be convinced by either argument or
illustration, she passed from that topic ; and we debated of
the course to be taken in order to the speedy recognition
and acknowledgment of Clemence de Bonneville as Lucy
Hamblin. The necklace, &c., could not, I found, be
identified by either my father or mother ; neither remembered to have seen the child wear them, though, of
course, there could be no doubt of the fact itself that they
were hers.

" So urgent do I deem the necessity," said my mother,
" of ending all doubt upon the subject before Louise Feron
can have time to devise some new and baffling iniquity,
that I wrote this morning, before you were up, to Mrs.
Waller, entreating her to come over with your grandfather
as soon as the French ports are open, which I cannot doubt
they will be in a few days at furthest, notwithstanding that
the Bonapartist authorities here affect to-day, as I have
heard, to disbelieve the reported capitulation of Paris. I
further urged upon Mrs. Waller," she added, "the paramount expediency of taking immediate, decisive steps
for putting an end to the girl's preposterous fancy for the
shoemaker."

" How will your letter be conveyed to England ? "

" By favour of Mr. Dillwyn, the United States consul at

this port, who has always been most obliging to us in that respect. Till lately, as you must be aware, my letters have been forwarded by him to New York, and thence *viâ* Canada to England; but now, in the actual state of affairs, he has means of direct communication with Great Britain. All," added my mother, he requires is, that he be permitted to take a copy of the letter or letters he forwards, in order that he may, if challenged upon the subject, be able to prove that he has not suffered himself to be made the channel of military or political information that might be used to the injury of France."

Later in the evening, when we happened to be speaking of the passing glance I had obtained of Mr. Tyler, just before the hour appointed for my assignation with Father Meudon, my mother asked me, with some abruptness, what manner of man the American captain might be. I described him; and upon mentioning that he had a hare-lip, she exclaimed:

"Then I saw him as I was leaving Mr. Dillwyn's office to-day. A commissary of police was with him, and so wild, so distraught an expression of face I have seldom seen. Poor man! his cross is indeed a heavy, afflictive one; and alas! the heavier, the more afflictive, that he rebels so fiercely against the burden that has been laid upon him."

"Was he going to Mr. Dillwyn's," I asked, "when you saw him?"

"Well, William, I did not notice; but it is very likely that he was, being an American himself, and a stranger here. Why do you ask?"

"It flashed upon me that—— But it is not likely Mr. Dillwyn would shew him your letter; or if he did, that you have inadvertently written anything that could put him on the track of Webbe or his son."

A flush of alarm tinged my mother's cheeks as she hastily said: "Certainly Mr. Dillwyn would not shew him my letter; and supposing he did, there was nothing in it that could possibly affect the Webbes—except, it may be— except—— Dear me, I fear I have committed a grave imprudence," she added with heightening colour.

"In what respect, dear mother?"

"Webbe's name does not once occur in the body of the

letter," she hurriedly replied. "That I am sure of; but in a postscript, there are, I think, these exact words: "The Jersey maiden is, I have little doubt, the wife, by this time, of Captain W.'s son. They were to be married at Honfleur, a town not very far from this, by water.'"

"That would, I fear, be sufficient hint for Tyler, should it meet his eye—a most unlikely thing, however, to happen. Besides, the ceremony which was to take place early to-day, once concluded, there will be no tarrying, you may depend upon it, so near Havre, and *L'Espiègle* has swift wings."

"I fervently hope no misfortune may overtake the young man, especially not through my fault or inadvertence: I should never forgive myself. But it is folly to worry ourselves in anticipation of a contingency that can never occur. Don't you think so?"

"Certainly I do," I replied; and we echoed each other again and again as to the extreme improbability of Mr. Tyler inquiring about the contents of a letter deposited with the American consul by a lady he had never before seen; or that, if he did inquire by some extraordinary chance—which chance *could* only arise from the circumstance that my mother was well known to the commissary of police, with him—that Mr. Dillwyn would gratify his curiosity; and we were still harping upon the subject when Father Meudon called to pay us a visit—a welcome one, turning, as it did, the current of our thoughts to politics, and such other mildly exciting generalities as make up the mundane gossip of reverend men. His confidence in the protracted duration of the Empire was, I found, much weakened; he thoroughly believed in the capitulation of Paris, and admitted that there were rumours, entitled to respect, of the actual or imminent abdication of the fallen emperor, either in favour of his son or absolutely.

"Let me, however, caution you," added Father Meudon, "that it is dangerous, when one is under the régime of *quasi* martial law, as we have for some time been, to talk above the breath of political events in a sense opposed to that entertained or promulgated by a general of division. Besides, direct communication with Paris is just now so difficult, and so much false news is flying about, that really one cannot be sure that Messieurs les Autorités may not prove to be in the right after all."

We agreed with the reverend gentleman that it would be highly imprudent—in foreigners, doubly so—to circulate or echo reports offensive to the ruling powers, and freely promised not to offend in that particular. He had not, as his silence upon the subject abundantly testified, heard of the riot at La Belle Poule—not, at all events, that the shipwrecked seamen, who, he had assured a commissary of police, were citizens of the United States of America, were amongst the chief actors therein. That was well; and the worthy father left us in quite buoyant spirits, excited by his reluctant admission of the proximate, if not actual downfall of the imperial throne, which would of course be the signal of immediate peace.

The reverend father's visit naturally brought up the memory of the kindnesses I had received at his hands, and I read aloud the note he had left for me by the bedside. Webbe's half-burnt letter to Dowling happened to be on the table, and as I placed it beside that of M. Meudon's, the exact resemblance to each other of the letters, in the texture and colour of the paper, nay, in the colour of the pale, weak ink, struck me as an odd coincidence, and I was about to call my mother's attention to it, when our vivacious servant-maid announced that " Monsieur Dillwyn, Consul pour les Etats Unis de l'Amerique," was below, and wished to speak with madame immediately. There came our fit again! However, it was necessary to see Mr. Dillwyn, and Annette being instructed to that effect, that tall, spare, high-mightiness of a gentleman presently made his appearance. He came to say that a brigadier of gendarmerie had called on him not very long after Mrs. Linwood had left his office, and requested to see the letter which, he was informed, that lady had intrusted to his, the American consul's, care. Mr. Dillwyn shewed the officer the copy which had been taken, and the brigadier of gendarmerie put it in his pocket, remarking that he could not himself read English, and walked away.

" The letter itself has been forwarded," said Mr. Dillwyn, " as I promised it should be, and there is certainly nothing in the copy now in possession of the authorities that can compromise you, Mrs. Linwood, or any one else, and 1 can hardly therefore comprehend the agitation which the announcement I have, upon consideration, thought it my duty to make, appears to excite. Indeed," added the consul, "I was for some time in two minds as to whether I need apprise you of an occurrence that can have no disagreeable result, and which I take to be a piece of hap-hazard official impertinence."

"Did Mr. Tyler of the *Columbia*," said I, "accompany the officer who took away the copy of Mrs. Linwood's letter?"

"No—certainly not: but, now you recall it to my mind, Mr. Tyler *did*, during the morning, one of the clerks informed me, inquire if Mrs. Linwood, the lady who had just before left the office, had not left a letter there? But what of that, since the letter in question referred solely to family matters?"

I said it would. be difficult, if not impossible to explain why Mrs. Linwood was so especially annoyed at finding that her private correspondence had been submitted to the inspection of the French police; and, finding that neither of us was disposed to be more communicative, Mr. Dillwyn forthwith took overpowering, high-mightiness leave.

Vain now to attempt concealing from ourselves that my mother's unfortunate postscript might have disastrous consequences in more than one direction; and, after long and painful cogitation, we were fain to console ourselves as we best could with the reflection, more or less well founded, that, as regarded evidence of complicity on our part with the escape of Harry Webbe, it would be impossible to prove that the words used applied either to him or his father; whilst, with respect to the young man's re-capture, time and distance were greatly in his favour. The brigadier's visit to the American consulate could not have taken place before twelve o'clock in the day, and before, therefore, the officers of justice could possibly reach Honfleur, Webbe, his son, and his son's spouse, might be hundreds of miles away. In addition to my mother's womanly concern for young Webbe, it was plain she was anxious for other reasons that his marriage with Maria Wilson should not be frustrated or delayed; and that she clung with an almost superstitious reliance to Captain Webbe's proverbial good-fortune, as a guarantee alike of the safety and the espousals of his son. On the morrow, I was to go forth, and as circumspectly as possible, ascertain the exact state of affairs, with the adoption of which resolution, our anxious council terminated.

Various matters kept me within till the day was far advanced, so that it was close upon two o'clock when I stepped on board the *Columbia*, which I found berthed in the southern and most considerable of the wet-docks behind, or inland of, the town of Havre. Mr. Tyler was not on board : he was gone, the chief-mate informed me, to attend the funeral of his son, which was to take place at three o'clock in the French Protestant Cemetery, at Ingouville. The mate, to whom I introduced myself simply as an English *détenu*, desirous of speaking with Mr. Tyler upon private business, was very civil ; and though I was obliged to frame my questions cautiously, I soon ascertained that the American captain had not left Havre since he entered it, and could not consequently have gone to Honfleur, if the police had.

" He'll never be the man he was again," observed the mate ; " and it ain't much wonder either, for his dead boy, the only one left out of nine or ten, was an uncommon promising lad, and the very apple of his father's eye."

" He was killed in fair fight, was he not ? " I ventured to remark.

"Cuss such a fair fight," rejoined the mate. "The *Columbia* was boarded by a set of rascally pirates in the pay of a tarnation scoundrel that had marked our course and timed us up Channel ! The cowardly young skunk that hooked it so clever the other night is the old sarpent's son ! "

I felt I was treading upon dangerous ground, and I came away, after eliciting that Harry Webbe had exhibited the white feather as unmistakably during the sharp fight on board the *Columbia*, as he did in the *Le Renard-Scout* affair off Sercq. I hugged myself ; it warmed the sickness at my heart to hear that. I was delighted to be able to look down with super-added, vengeful contempt upon the husband of Maria Wilson ! Verily, youthful male nature in love —unless mine was a singularly depraved specimen— is a very despicable human nature. I was delighted to know that the life-partner of a beautiful, amiable girl, whose happiness, if it contributed to mine, I would have given my heart's blood to insure, was a confirmed poltroon! O William Linwood the younger, I blush to record this fact of you, but an unquestionable fact it is for all that.

I thought I would go and see the funeral. I could accost Mr. Tyler after it had taken place, and gather from his demeanour, if not from his speech, whether he had any hope of speedily avenging himself upon Webbe or his son. I arrived at the little Calvinist chapel just before the funeral procession from the Hôtel de France, to which Mr. Tyler's son had been removed as soon as the *Columbia* came into Havre. It had been organised by the Pompes Funèbres rather in accordance with the father's purse and pride than with the mean chapel in which the body was received—the obscure burial-place which was to be its long, last home. A considerable number of respectable persons were in the chapel, amongst them the American consul; and the service, to those who understood the language, was impressively celebrated by a M. Ponsard, the French Calvinist divine. To my great surprise—though I hardly know why I should have felt surprise—Pope's familiar "Vital Spark" was sung in French by the choir. The concluding lines:

O Sépulture, où est ta victoire ?
O Mort, où est ton aiguillon ?

singularly impressed me, chiefly because of the father's fierce sobs mingling with and appearing to dispute, deny, and so disputing, denying, to enhance the effect and power of the swelling, soaring "Io triomphe"—the feeble murmur, it seemed, of earth-blinded, stammering unbelief, overborne, rebuked, silenced by a transcendent jubilate of Faith's tongues of fire!

I remained till all was done—till ashes had been rendered to ashes, dust to dust—and the Pompes Funèbres, the tedious part of their duty done, had gone off at a smart trot to their homes and stables. Mr. Tyler, impatiently shaking himself free of condolences, walked sharply towards the town, I following, at a distance for a while, and remarking, inquisitively, how firm, how determined his step became as he approached the quays. There was *hopeful* anticipation

in that firmly accelerated pace. I was sure of that before,
taking advantage of an obstruction of the thoroughfare by
the long-handled wheel-barrows then, and perhaps now, in
use at Havre, I slipped round, and met him face to face in
front of the custom-house, on Notre Dame quay. I was
about to speak, when he fiercely broke out with :

" I have nothing, and wish to have nothing to say to you,
young fellow. Look," he added, " here is the copy of your
mother's letter : take it ; it has, I hope, done its work—*my*
work ; and might in other hands have compromised you and
yours. Out of my way ! I am in haste !"

He could not prevent me following, and I did to the extremity of the north pier, where I witnessed the almost de-
moniacal cries of triumph with which he greeted the
approach of a small cutter-smack from Honfleur, at the
mast-head of which signals intelligible to him were flying.

Soon intelligible to me ! The tiny cutter ran as far up
the harbour as the flowing tide permitted, and immediately
landed her passengers, some half-dozen gendarmes, and with
them trembling, fettered, Harry Webbe. A literal howl of
ferocious exultation from Tyler met the unfortunate young
man as he stepped upon the quay, from which he shrunk
back affrighted as if struck at by a sword or axe. My own
enmity towards the craven captive vanished at once, and
with my usual insane thoughtlessness, I sprang forward to
interpose between him and his deadly foe. The gendarmes
thrust me roughly back, but the poor fellow had recognised
me and my purpose ; and his vain piteous cry for help
rang in my ears for hours afterwards.

Yes, and I had soon pressing need of help myself. As I
hurried along after the the gendarmes and their prisoner,
my steps were suddenly arrested by an enormous *affiche*,
recently posted, it seemed, by the crowd in front, from
which my own name stared at me in huge characters. Approaching nearer, I saw that it offered a reward of five hundred francs for the apprehension of a young Englishman of
the name of William Linwood, but calling himself Jean Le
Gros, who had committed a robbery in a dwelling-house at
St. Malo, and carried off, amongst other valuables, a seed-
pearl necklace, with a gold cross attached, having the initial
letter of Louise engraved on the back; pearl armlets, &c., &c.

" Tall, strongly framed, florid complexion, dark wavy

hair," read a voice over my shoulder, upon which a hand was at the same moment firmly placed. "Do you know, young man, I have a strong suspicion that you sat for that portrait."

"What is that you say?" I exclaimed, turning fiercely round.

"Nothing more, monsieur," replied the imperturbable gendarme, "than that I believe you to be the individual designated by the affiche, and that I, as a rigorous consequence, arrest you as the perpetrator of the robbery alleged to have taken place at St. Malo."

CHAPTER XVII.

JACQUES SICARD AGAIN.

WHEN the gendarme grasped me by the collar, I, William Linwood, must have changed my nature, had I not gratuitously aggravated the danger of my position by roughly shaking off the officer's hold, and forthwith knocking down the functionary, entirely unskilled in the noble art of self-defence as practised in the English prize-ring. The mad act received its immediate chastisement; and but for the resolute interposition of a *sergent de ville*, who fortunately came up at the moment, the patriotic mob, hotly indignant at seeing a French *autorité* floored by an Englishman, and a robber to boot, would very soon have left justice little or nothing to do in the way of punishing the audacious criminal. As it was, though I lost my "dark wavy hair" by handfuls, and was unmercifully cuffed, scratched, and pommelled, I had no bones broken; and assisted by two flanking gendarmes, each with an arm tightly locked in his, and guarded by four others in front and rear, I managed to walk along, defiantly erect, amidst the derisive *huées* of the crowd, towards the jail, and soon found myself safely deposited in the cell adjoining that which had just before received Harry Webbe.

The astounding suddenness of the surprise, the atrocious nature of the accusation launched against me, brought on, as soon as I was alone, a paroxysm of convulsive, rageful laughter; and I was still screaming and gesticulating like a caged maniac, when Father Meudon, who, chancing to be in the town, had heard of my mishap, entered the cell, accompanied by the civil and considerate sergent de ville. The officer, at M. Meudon's request, left us together, and the good father succeeded, with some difficulty, in subduing me to calmness and common sense.

The "robbery" imputation did not at all disturb him.

"That accusation," said he, "is, I can have no doubt, a mere flash in the pan; but there are, I hear, other charges against you, my imprudent young friend, which give me much uneasiness. It can be proved that you have travelled in France with false passports, and under two false names —those of Le Gros and Piron—which is a highly penal offence. You are also suspected of having actively abetted the escape of a prisoner of war on parole, and that, by the military code, is punishable by—death!"

"I assure you, with all solemnity, that I had no hand whatever, directly or indirectly, in the escape—the ultimately baffled escape—of Harry Webbe."

"I am rejoiced to hear it. Your rash young countryman will, I greatly fear, be made to expiate his offence by the last dread penalty."

"Great God!"

"And many hours, rely upon it, will not be suffered to pass before the irreversible sentence is passed and executed. Power to enforce their ruthless will is about to depart from the violent men who now hold military rule here; and what they purpose doing must be done speedily, if at all."

"Is their no hope, no chance of escape for the unfortunate young man?" I asked with emotion.

"*Hélas!* I fear, none whatever. His breach of parole, especially as he was actually *gardé à vue*, might have been, if not forgiven, mercifully judged, if one of your fellow *naufragés*, Mr. Tyler, had not denounced him to be the son of the notorious Webbe, captain of the *Scout* privateer. The nephew of Captain Le Moine, an officer deeply lamented here, not long since deposed before the authorities, that that son, after having with his own hand slain the commander of *Le Renard* in the action between that vessel and the *Scout*, had the audacity to enter France as a spy of the Bourbons, was detected and denounced at Avranches by himself, Auguste Le Moine; and only effected his escape by the careless or criminal connivance of Captain Jules Renaudin of *L'Espiègle*. That is the fatal charge which has kindled the fires of hate and vengeance in the breasts of his judges, and will wither up any inclination that might else prevail to deal mercifully with the unhappy youth. The imminent fate of your countryman affects you very painfully, I perceive," added M. Meudon.

" Very painfully, indeed. Does the young man admit that he is the person by whom Captain Le Moine was killed, and whom the nephew denounced at the Avranches banquet? "

" Denounced at the Avranches *banquet!*" echoed Father Meudon, with a piercing look; " I was not before aware that it was at a banquet in Avranches that Auguste Le Moine detected the Bourbons' spy! As to the accused's admission or non-admission," added the reverend father, " that he is the person inculpated, that will be of little consequence in face of Auguste Le Moine's sworn deposition, and the proof by Mr. Tyler of his identity."

" Proof, you mean, that he is Captain Webbe's son? "

" Precisely ; that will be quite sufficient to seal his doom, unless —unless," added M. Meudon, continuing to regard me with an anxious, searching look—"unless Captain Webbe's son can designate and *produce* some other person by whose hand he can prove Captain Le Moine fell, and whom young Le Moine afterwards confronted at the Avranches banquet! In that case—an impossible case, I must suppose—the real offender would unquestionably be substituted for Monsieur Webbe *fils*, both before the military tribunal and at the place of execution ; and that too, I repeat, before another day shall have fled into a past eternity."

" That stern, staring silence," resumed M. Meudon, after a few moments' pause, " thrills me with a fear—an undefined, shadowy fear, that you have not confided in me so unreservedly as for your own safety's sake I would fain believe you have. Well, I have no right to press you for that fuller confidence. Early to-morrow, I will see you again ; at present, I shall serve you best by going at

once to the Rue Bombardée. Adieu, young man; and
assure yourself that, under all circumstances—in any conceivable extremity, you may count upon my poor services
—upon the zealous exertion, in your behalf, of all the influence I possess with the authorities of Havre."

The sergent de ville let him out, and as the heavy door
closed sullenly behind them, shutting me back into the
dark silence, an inexpressible horror seized me. The reality
of the frightful peril I had exposed myself to, and which
I had never before quite believed in, confronted me in
terrible distinctness. Harry Webbe, there could be no
doubt, to save himself, would denounce me; and if he did
not, could I, dared I permit him to suffer in my stead?
Impossible! I was brave enough, as the reader knows—
that is, I could rush upon, grapple with, defy death in the
tumult of battle, in the conflict of elemental warfare, or in
the excitement of passion; but to sit there in solitary
gloom, fettered, powerless, though full of lusty life—to
await the deliberate approach of the King of Terrors,
whilst counting his stealthy, soundless steps by the hands
of the dial, whose tiny round measured the all of time
remaining between me and eternity, was beyond my
strength, and for a while I was overborne, prostrated by
fear, by a shuddering, nameless dread of the dark, fathom-
less gulf which, as M. Meudon talked, seemed to yawn
beneath my feet!

Not, however, for long did that trance of terror hold me
in thrall. Gradually my soul grew calmer, stronger, and
soon the current of my changeful thoughts was bent as
strongly in a hopeful direction. Might not, I argued—
might not Father Meudon have consciously or unconsciously exaggerated the danger? Unquestionably he might.
Then could I not, through him, warn young Webbe to
appeal to Auguste Le Moine himself to confirm his solemn
denial of being the person he, Le Moine, had denounced;
an appeal which could not with any decency be rejected,
and which, the *enseigne* being absent in Paris, would defer
the catastrophe till the power to murder either of us had
been taken from the Bonapartist authorities of Havre!
Again, there was no doubt that Captain Webbe was still
at large; and he, a man of boundless resource and daring,
would, we might be sure, leave no means untried to es.

tricate his son ; ay, and—a minor, but still important consideration with him—to extricate me from the fearful strait
to which his own unscrupulous machinations had conducted us !

The entrance of the head jailer and the sergent de ville
—the latter with a note in his hand—broke in upon my
sanguine dreaming, and flung me back into the sinister
reality of my actual position.

"An individual who says he is a friend of yours,"
said the sergent, "has requested to see you, and when
informed that he was too late for to-day, wrote and requested me to place this note in your hands, the answer to
which he awaits. You understand, monsieur," added the
officer, "that it is necessary we should see what your friend
has written?"

"That is only reasonable," I said, taking the note. "I
will first read it to you myself;" and tearing it open, I read
as follows :

"MON CHER MONSIEUR LINWOOD—I arrive from Honfleur to warn you of the abominable trick which that relative of mine, and for all that, true daughter of the devil,
Madame de Bonneville, was about to play you, and find
myself, from having been delayed, too late. Mademoiselle
Clemence, who discovered what was going on, and insisted
upon my coming, will be inconsolable. I pray you, therefore, to tell me what is the earliest hour to-morrow
at which I can see you, as mademoiselle, who is,
you know, somewhat *vive*, and extremely dislikes being
kept in suspense, will count the moments of my absence
from her with grave inquietude.—Votre serviteur, JACQUES
SICARD."

"Jacques Sicard, and from Honfleur !" exclaimed the
sergent de ville. "*Sacristie*, but that is droll enough! We
have a *mandat d'arrêt* from the deputy procureur-general
of Honfleur, brought by the officers who seized the other
young Englishman at that place, commanding us to search
out the said Maître Jacques Sicard, and lodge him safely
in the hands of justice."

"You have an arrest-warrant for Jacques Sicard !" I
exclaimed. "At whose instance, for the love of Heaven ;
and for what offence?"

"At the instance," replied the sergent, taking a paper

from his pocket, and glancing at it, " of Louise de Bonneville, *veuve*, *née* Féron; and for the crime of complicity in
the robbery which you, Monsieur Linwood, are charged
with. Had we known this before," he added with a laugh,
" we should not, *morbleu*, have refused the young man admittance here. But he is in the waiting-room, so there is
no harm done. *Allons, camarade.*"

The sergent and jailer hurried off, and I listened to
catch the first sound that might indicate Maître Sicard's
dawning   comprehension   of   the   pretty   predicament
he had quietly walked into. It was not long delayed.
First, an inarticulate scream of surprise and indignation,
followed evidently by an attempt to fly, easily defeated by
the prison guardians; then a swift crescendo succession
of yells, expostulations, threats, mingled with the gruff
deep bass maledictions of the officers, irritated by his
frenzied kicking and plunging; the uproar increasing in
violence and volume as it approached the door of my cell,
which arrived at, was flung open, and in staggered five or
or six gendarmes, bearing Sicard in an horizontal position
by the legs and shoulders; he the while striking out
viciously with his arms and heels, and calling wildly upon
saints and angels, and myself especially, the instant he
caught sight of me, to deliver him from the villains that
were strangling him.

" On m'assassine, Linwood! On m'assassine!" he
screamed as his bearers threw him roughly down upon one
of the beds in the cell. He could not, however, have been
much hurt, for he was upon his feet in a twinkling apos-
trophising his captors with foaming fury. " Hundred
thousand devils!" he shouted. " But this is infernal!—
impossible! It is the end of the world! Why, what, how,
sacred thunder, can this be, that I, Maître Jacques Sicard,
a respectable bourgeois of St. Malo, am outraged, massacred in this manner?"

"'Jacques Sicard,'" said the sergent de ville, reading
from a paper, "'*bottier par état*, domiciled at St. Malo,'
Here follows," continued the officer, "a description of
Maître Sicard's person, which it might not perhaps be
agreeable to that individual to hear read; we will therefore pass it. The mandat d'arrêt further declares "——
" What is that?—mandat d'arrêt!" interrupted Sicard,

whom a vague apprehension of the truth was fast subduing to submissiveness. "What is that, if you please, monsieur?" he added, wiping his streaming forehead.

"A mandat d'arrêt," resumed the sergent, "which sets forth that Jacques Sicard, bottier par état, domiciled at St. Malo, is charged by Louise de Bonneville "——

"How! what is that again. Why, sacred thunder, that person is my own near relative!"

"And 'une fille du diable,' nevertheless," said the officer, "if this note of yours is to be believed."

"That is correct; that is demonstrable. Still"——

"Maître Sicard," said the officer, "had better keep silence, if he can, till I have read the mandat d'arrêt—Is charged by Louise de Bonneville, veuve, née Féron, with complicity with one William Linwood, *alias* Le Gros, an Englishman, in robbing the said Louise de Bonneville, née Féron, of a seed-pearl necklace, to which a gold cross is attached with L, the initial letter of said Louise de Bonneville's baptismal name, engraved thereon"——

It was useless to read further: Sicard dropped down as if he was shot. "C'est la foudre," he groaned: "I am betrayed—annihilated—lost!"

He was at all events dumbfounded, and the other officials having retired, Monsieur le Sergent addressing me with great politeness, asked if I had any objection to Maître Sicard's remaining where he was for the night. To which I answered that I should esteem it a favour if he were permitted to do so.

"It is well, monsieur. This prison happens to be overcrowded just now; and as there are two beds here, permission to remain together may be accorded till further orders from superior authority. This is the more readily granted, I must tell you," pursued the officer, "forasmuch that Le Père Meudon, whom everybody esteems, not only engaged me to render you all the civilities in my power, but assured me that the charge of robbery would turn out to be an absurd, if not criminal blunder. I hope, notwithstanding the apparently criminating dismay of Maître Sicard, that it will prove so; and I have to add that any refreshments you may choose to order can be furnished from a restaurant close by, wine and *liqueurs* in moderation, inclusive."

I thanked him; and Maître Sicard, upon being asked what he would prefer for supper, having with indignant pantomime expressed his utter disgust at all things under the sun, I left the matter to the worthy sergent himself, stipulating only for some excellent brandy and cigars.

By that time, my naturally joyous, mercurial temperament had recovered, and something more, from the depression caused by Father Meudon's sepulchral croaking: the menacing shadows which had seemed to overhang the future—the immediate future—had vanished utterly; and I have never been, that I remember, in better cue for a jolly carouse, than on the night when I was a prisoner in a French jail, charged with felony, and in all likelihood to be dragged on the morrow before, and sentenced capitally by, a military tribunal, as a convicted spy! Who shall read me the riddle of that buoyant confidence under conditions so overwhelmingly adverse to such a state of mind! Is it that not only do sinister events cast shadows before, but that the silver lining of the threatening cloud also darts onward its avant-courier rays of light to cheer the gloom of the troubled soul, and rekindle in its darkened depths the lights of Hope and Faith! Possibly; but my own common-place interpretation in this particular instance is, that the exultation of spirit I experienced was owing to an unreasoning conviction, based upon previous lucky escapes, that something or other would turn up to shield me from apparently inevitable destruction—a conviction strengthened, sublimed by the secret assurance, simmering softly at my heart, and unblabbed of openly even to myself, that Maria Wilson was not yet at all events the wife of Harry Webbe.

I vainly strove to rouse Maître Sicard from his despondent state. He refused to be comforted. "My dear fellow," said I at last, "do you know that this sudden prostration is, under the circumstances, exceedingly absurd, you having been of course previously aware that I had been arrested upon the charge of robbing that unscrupulous fille du diable, as you have very properly named Madame de Bonneville.

" I know that!" savagely exclaimed Sicard. "Thousand thunders, if I *had* known it, I should not be here now— veritable, decided ass, as I have admittedly proved myself to be ! No, Monsieur Linwood, I was not even aware that Madame de Bonneville had discovered the abstraction from the armoire of a seed-pearl necklace, to which a gold cross is attached, with initial letter of said Louise's bap- tismal name engraved thereon, and which letter I was gobe-mouche enough to be persuaded *could* only stand for Lucy. Ah, mon Dieu!——— I tell you, Monsieur Linwood," he went on to say when sufficiently recovered, " that that traitress Fanchette helped me to mend the fractures of the armoire doors, in order that madame might suspect nothing ; and I, in acknowledgment, presented her with a first-rate pair of boots——— But what's the use of talking!"

" What trick was it then that Mademoiselle Clemence discovered that her reputed mother was about to play me ?"

" That she had formally accused you of travelling in France under a false name—that of Jean Le Gros, to be sure."

" Well, but my dear Sicard, Madame de Bonneville, bad. as she may be, will never proceed to extremities against you—her relative."

" But, sacred thunder, that is precisely what she will do ! You don't know that she has become a tigress—an unchained fury, resolved, *coûte qui coûte*, to be revenged upon you and me: upon you for not marrying Clemence; upon me for persisting, spite of madame's maledictions, that I *will* marry her, Naturally, I hoped that time would mollify her rage; but do you not see that she has passed the Rubicon, by publicly accusing me, her relative, as you say, of robbing her in conjunction with you ? Yes, and Fanchette can prove that by my own confession. I shall be sent to the galleys, that is quite clear, and her threat, only a few hours old, that she would effectually dispose of my insolent pretensions—insolent pretensions was the phrase—will be realised."

I persisted in asserting that he was really scaring himself with shadows; that Mr. and Madame Waller— who, I doubted not, would arrive in France before many days had passed—would prove beyond question that the articles I had taken were theirs, and had been stolen from them with their child many years since by Louise Férou; that "fille du diable" knowing this as well as I did, would consequently never venture, I urged, to appear before the tribunals in support of the accusation—and so on. This view of the case revived Sicard's spirits, and he was becoming himself again, when I, unawares, knocked him over once more.

"Tell me," said I, " what is the punishment awarded by the Code Pénal to travelling in France with false papers, or under a false name?"

"Two years of prison, with or without hard labour (*travaux forcés*), according to whether there are or are not extenuating circumstances. In your case," he added, with a tinge of *malice*, " hard labour will no doubt be awarded."

"That is pleasant hearing," said I. " Of course, then, you took especial care that Madame de Bonneville should not know it was you that furnished so-called Jean Le Gros with the passport of the sick lieutenant lodging at your house?"

Sicard sprang up bolt on end, as if impelled by a galvanic shock. "Hundred thousand thunders!" he screamed; "of course she knows it, and through that accursed Fanchette! Ah, there is no longer any chance. It is all over with me. I am finished—destroyed; that is certain —demonstrable!" and down he fell again in hopeless self-abandonment.

"Come—come," I remonstrated; " two years of prison is not, after all, the guillotine, nor one's lifetime. We shall survive it, never fear."

"And in the meantime my shop," he groaned—" and my three years' toiled-for connection, and my stock-in-trade left in charge of Dubarle—and Clemence—— Say no more; I am definitively done for—finished—massacred! And all, *sacre bleu*, in consequence of my good nature. Oh, it is desolating—lamentable!"

I ceased endeavouring to console him by words, and awaited what effect the *petit souper*—a very excellent one, brought in and nicely set out under the superintendence of the sergent de ville—might have in restoring his equanimity, which it was essential should be restored, if only that I might learn what had occurred at Hon-fleur.

The odour of the roast *poulet*, &c.; the glug-glug of the wine as I poured it out, had, as I anticipated, a vivifying effect. Sicard turned his face from the wall towards the table, sniffed approvingly; and finally re-marking, by way of apology, that if a man was sentenced to be hanged, it would be necessary to eat in the mean-time, got up, seated himself at the table, and when he was fairly at it, ate voraciously, though occasionally catching himself back, as it were, from the gratification of his appetite, to gaze around despairingly upon the gloomy cell, and exclaim : " But really this is desolating! —lamentable ! Nevertheless, one must always eat; that is certain—demonstrable ! "

The supper done, we were locked in for the night; and by the time he had consumed two or three glasses of strong brandy-punch, and as many cigars, Maître Sicard had, in a comparative sense, cast dull care behind him, and willingly consented to relate his experiences in connection with Madame de Bonneville, Clemence, and those sons of Satan, the Webbes, since I parted with him at the Messa-geries Impériales, St. Malo.

As the night was chilly, I proposed that we should get into and sit up in bed; in which position, with the aid of cigars, and brandy-and-water *ad libitum*, he could narrate and I listen in tranquillity and comfort. This was agreed to; we were quickly placed, and Sicard led off *con spirito*.

" I felt a lively satisfaction, Monsieur Linwood," he began, "in knowing you were definitively gone; in which state of mind my steps naturally took the direction of the Rue Dupetit Thouars, to impart and share that satisfac-tion with Mademoiselle Clemence. Ah ! with what kind-ness, with what graciousness did the dear girl receive me! —with what a charming solicitude did she listen to my account of the devices I had recourse to in effecting your escape ! Fanchette was there—not precisely at first, she was gone out to post a letter—but before long, and took —sly serpent as I now comprehend—as lively an interest as did her young mistress in what had,been done. Never have I passed two such delightful hours, never experienced

P

such effusion of soul, such exquisite *tendresse*——*Bref*.
I was happier than a king, and bade Clemence adieu in a
state of exalted felicity, after having assisted Fanchette
to mend the armoire with some carpenter's glue, which
would, she remarked, prevent the *pièces d'accusation* from
being missed till, at all events, your purpose in taking
them had been accomplished. My last words that
evening to Mademoiselle Clemence, who could not shake
off the nervous dread with which the thought of encoun-
tering Madame de Bonneville inspired her, were these:
" Fear nothing, *ma belle*. I promise thee once more, upon
the faith of a Frenchman and thy devoted lover, that I
will watch over and effectively protect thee from thy real
or pretended mother and my ·relative.' I have loyally
endeavoured to redeem that pledge," added Sicard, with a
groan—" and—here I am."

" Early the next morning," he resumed, " that detest-
able traitress Fanchette came to my shop for the boots I
had promised her. I fitted her splay-feet *à merveille*, and
she walked off *chaussée* as she had never been before.
Mademoiselle Clemence, she told me, had a slight nervous
headache, but would receive me in the evening. 'Bon!
all goes well,' I say to myself; 'and now I must turn my
attention to business, which, after all, must be minded,
whether one is in love or not.' There were arrears, as you
may suppose, to bring up; and it was eight o'clock in the
evening before I had finished and was suitably dressed for
a visit to my charming *fiancée*. At last I am ready, and
take my way to the Rue Dupetit Thouars. I arrive there,
find the magasin closed, and knock at the door; the blows
seeming at the same time to strike upon my heart. There
is no answer; I can see no light in the house, and I am
getting wild, distracted, when one of the workwomen
comes up, recognises and addresses me:

'Ah, Monsieur Sicard,' she says, 'the magasin has
been closed since before five o'clock. Madame de Bonneville returned in the morning; there was a terrible
scene—madame, with mademoiselle sobbing as if her heart
would break, quitted the house together, and have since,
I hear, left St. Malo by diligence, accompanied by Fanchette.'

" I am thunderstruck at hearing that," continued Sicard;

"my head turns round, and I am near falling on the *pavé*; but innate force of character sustains me, and I perceive that the time is come for redeeming my promise to Clemence, of, at all costs and hazards, watching over her safety. I hasten, therefore, to the Messageries. The diligence is gone long since, and in it, I am told, were Madame and Mademoiselle de Bonneville and servant. I can only follow in a hired vehicle; and as there is no alternative, I accept that expensive mode of travelling, order a voiture with two horses to be prepared; hurry to the sous-prefecture, get my passport *visé*; my *paquet* is soon made, and I am off in pursuit of the fugitives, leaving, of necessity, my business in charge of Alexis Dubarle, a good workman and *bon enfant* enough, but *bon vivant*—gourmand even, when he has the means. And now he will probably have command of the *caisse* of my establishment for two years to come. Oh! it is crushing—insupportable —infernal! Push the carafe a little further this way, if you please, Monsieur Linwood.

"Well," resumed Sicard, after a reviving draught of punch, "I follow the diligence in my two-horsed vehicle; but so many delays occur, that I lose instead of gaining upon the *fuyards*, and arrive at Honfleur full twelve hours later than they. Madame de Bonneville, Clemence, and Fanchette are, I discover, at the Toison D'Or. I—for economy, in presence of the eventualities before me, could not be disregarded—take lodgings at an auberge. The next morning, at about eleven o'clock, I present myself at the Toison D'Or, inquire for Madame de Bonneville, and am conducted to her apartment. Ah, my friend Linwood," exclaimed Sicard, "I find myself in presence of a tigress—of a tigress *enragé*, and a terrified lamb; for Clemence, whose eyes I notice are swollen with weeping, and who trembles with fear, is there also. Instantly I am assailed, overwhelmed with insults, maledictions, threats—imperious commands to immediately leave the hotel! Vainly I endeavour to bear up against that hurricane of rage, to obtain ever so brief a hearing. It is impossible; I am compelled to yield, and literally driven away by a merciless torrent of taunt, sarcasm, and abuse."

"You, of course, soon returned to the charge?"

"Not I, morbleu! I had not the courage ; besides, it
would have been useless. I determined, however, not
to leave Honfleur while my virago relative remained
there, and to watch sedulously for an opportunity of
seeing Clemence alone. Nothing, however, came of it;
and I was no further advanced till early in the morning
of yesterday. I had, with many others, been observing the departure of the corsair-cutter, *Espiègle*, which
had come into Honfleur during the night, and sailed
again with a light breeze just before dawn. When she had
disappeared round a projecting point of land, I walked
away to get my breakfast, but had not gone far, when a
commissionaire popped a note into my hand, addressed to
Monsieur Sicard, de St. Malo. I will give it you, in a
hundred times, to guess who the writer was!" added
Sicard with vivacity.

"I will guess it the first time—Captain Webbe, *alias*
Jacques Le Gros."

"You are right. The note stated that the writer was
in a position to place my affair with a certain young
demoiselle en bon train, and would do so if I would call
without delay at the Trois Rois de Cologne, and ask to see
Monsieur Baptiste. Of course I was only too happy to
accept the invitation, and, arrived at the Trois Rois, I was,
to begin with, introduced to his tall, handsome son. You
know what a tongue the old *gredin* has," continued Sicard,
"and will not therefore be surprised to hear that he explained most admirably everything in his previous conduct
that might, he said, have appeared strange or equivocal
to me ; and having so far cleared the ground, he presented
his plan of present battle.

"Madame de Bonneville," he said, "was determined to
discover through him where you, Linwood, were, in order
to bring about, *bon gré, mal gré*, the marriage which she
had at heart. "Linwood is at Havre at this moment,"
continued the Sieur Webbe, "and I do not doubt would be induced, notwithstanding all that has passed, to forthwith
espouse Mademoiselle Clemence, if Madame de Bonneville
could obtain speech of him, so potent are the influences
which she could bring to bear for that purpose. Now,
observe," he went on rapidly to say, "that I am here to
marry my son to a young English lady—her father at

least was an Englishman—of the name of Wilson, of which young lady Madame de Bonneville is guardian conjointly with myself, and she will effectually interfere to prevent the union of the attached young couple unless I first aid her to accomplish the marriage of Clemence with young Linwood. Fortunately, she does not yet know that I and my son have arrived here; for if she did, her jealous vigilance would be redoubled, and there would be no chance of a fortunate solution of our difficulties. Neither of us dare consequently shew out of this house; and what I require is an intelligent, trustworthy friend to be a medium of communication between us and Mademoiselle Wilson. If you will undertake the office, I pledge you my word of honour that an hour after my son's marriage, I will present myself with you before Madame de Bonneville, and defy her—you can easily understand under what menace—to withhold her consent to your union with so-called Clemence de Bonneville, and really Lucy Hamblin."

"There was an immence deal more to the same tune," drowsily continued Sicard, "which I am too sleepy to relate; but the end of it was, that I undertook the business—and a very awkward, delicate business it was ——I—I'll tell you why some day, and why Monsieur le Capitaine particularly chose—chose me to—to—— What was I saying? Oh, ah, yes! that after being crammed to the throat with instructions—cautions—promises—morbleu! wasn't he lavish of *them*—I carried notes and messages to and fro the Rue du Marché all the day long—— She was a charming jeune Anglaise—extremely charming, especially when dressed for the wedding, which—which was fixed to take place at seven in the evening—very charming, when she stood at the altar with le jeune Webbe—even Clemence—I thought—Clemence—Clem "——

"Wake up, and go on, will you?"

"Hein! what is it—what do you shake—shake "——

"Go on, I say, or I'll murder you!"

"To-morrow—to-morrow," he murmured, as his heavy head dropped helplessly upon the pillow.

"Were they married?—answer that," I shouted, "or by Heaven, I'll throttle you."

"Married—married—parbleu—I understand!—charming!—even Clemence "——

I might as well have shaken a log of wood; and I
jumped back into my own bed in a state of indescribable
agitation and dismay.

CHAPTER XVIII.

'TWIXT THE CUP AND THE LIP.

THE gloomy night-hours which, as they crept slowly
away, brought again into distinctness shadowy images
of terror that I had for a time cast behind me, did anything but weaken or allay the savage irritation which possessed me; and so insupportable did suspense at length
become, that long before the first rays of the gray cold
dawn looked in through the one, high-up, strongly barred
aperture by which light was grudgingly admitted into the '
cell, I once more sprang out of bed and shook the snoring
shoemaker till I got him partially awake. By dint of determined importunity, I elicited a confused, fragmentary
account of all that to his knowledge had passed at
Honfleur, with which I was the more content, that the
master-fear his half-told story had evoked, was, I clearly
ascertained, without foundation.

I am admonished by a glance at the crowded incidents
of the next four-and-twenty hours, and the rapidly narrowing space into which they must be compressed, to give the
remainder of Sicard's prolix, disjointed story in my own
words : I do so, at the same time helping out the halting
narrative with information subsequently obtained.

Captain Webbe was apprised by a note from Madame
Dupré, left for him at Les Trois Rois, mentioning that
Madame Broussard and daughter were already in Honfleur,
but, to the best of the writer's belief, were not aware that
Miss Wilson and herself had arrived. Madame Dupré had
also learned through a chattering servant at her lodgings
in the Rue du Marché, who was well acquainted with the
people at the Toison d'Or, that Madame Broussard, calling

herself Madame de Bonneville, had been followed from St.
Malo by a fiery-tempered young man, who had made quite
a scene at the hotel, and loudly accused the lady, in the
hearing of several persons, of being a confederate with the
" *scélérat* Webbe "—a phrase which he had twenty times
repeated. Madame Dupré added, that the wench's garrulous
gossip had given rise to vague feelings of alarm and distrust in Miss Wilson's mind, which, if not set at rest,
would, to say the least, cause the postponement of her
marriage with Mr. Harry Webbe.

A glimpse of Sicard as he passed the window of Les
Trois Rois, not only shewed Webbe the fiery-tempered
young man that had made a scene at the hotel, but suggested to his fertile ingenuity a ready means of dissipating
Maria Wilson's suspicions; a result which the impressionable, enthusiastic bootmaker, after being thoroughly
crammed with instructions, cautions, and promises, completely achieved. All essential preliminaries being
arranged soon after noon, it was finally settled that the
wedding should take place at the French Protestant chapel
at seven in the evening of that same day. The bride and
bridegroom being British subjects as well as Protestants,
the civil, which should have preceded the sacerdotal ceremony, and would have required certain formalities to be
previously complied with, was not deemed to be essential
by the officiating minister; and Webbe kept of course
whatever doubts he might have felt upon the subject to
himself. Madame Dupré and Miss Wilson would be perfectly satisfied with an ecclesiastical marriage, and should
the civil ceremony be thereafter found essential to its
validity, it could at any time be gone through with;
his son, meanwhile—the only important point—being *de
facto* the young lady's husband. Arrangements were made
for the immediate departure of the newly wedded pair :
and before sundown on the morrow they would, it was
expected, be safely landed, *L'Espiègle* aiding, in Jersey,
safe out of adverse fortune's reach.

Ten minutes previous to the appointed hour, Harry
Webbe and Jacques Sicard left Les Trois Rois, and
Madame Dupré and Maria Wilson their lodgings in the
Rue du Marché in close carriages, arriving at the Calvinist
chapel at nearly the same time. The minister was in at-

tendance; and the trembling bride, clinging to rather than leaning upon Madame Dupré for support, advanced with the bridegroom and Maître Sicard, who was to give the bride away, towards the altar.

Meanwhile, the carriage had no sooner driven off from Les Trois Rois, than Captain Webbe sallied forth in the direction of Le Toison d'Or, for the purpose of announcing his vexatiously delayed arrival to his good friend Madame de Bonneville, and especially to keep, in nautical phrase, that dangerous lady well in tow, till Mr. and Mrs. Harry Webbe had left Honfleur many leagues behind them.

The privateer captain's star was not that evening in the ascendant. Madame was out; mademoiselle confined to her chamber with nervous headache; and Fanchette herself in a state of semi-distraction. Her mistress was, she feared, in the custody of justice as a presumedly fraudulent bankrupt, a rigour which the sudden closing of the establishment at St. Malo, and her flight therefrom, would no doubt justify. To Webbe's impatient queries as to the grounds of her apprehensions, Fanchette replied that since about noon, madame had been in a state of wild excitement, going in and out as if crazed with rage or terror; that about an hour before Captain Webbe called, several gendarmes had come to the hotel, and demanded to speak with Madame de Bonneville, who, after a brief private parley, left the house with them, and had not since returned.

Webbe's explosive malediction indicated a truer interpretation of Madame de Bonneville's furious excitement, and her departure in company with the gendarmes, than Fanchette's. It had, in fact, come to her knowledge that Sicard had arranged with the French Protestant minister to celebrate the marriage of a youthful Englishman and woman, who, she doubted not, were young Webbe and Maria Wilson; although, so cleverly had Sicard managed, she was unable to discover the whereabout either of her ward or the captain's son. Thoroughly determined not to be foiled, she had at last, with much reluctance, placed herself in communication with the authorities of Honfleur; and the visit of the gendarmes, whom Mr. Tyler had caused to be despatched in hot haste from Havre was the consequence.

Without further acknowledgment of Fanchette's frank communication than the before-mentioned comprehensive execration of human kind in general, and Madame de Bonneville in particular, the privateer captain hurriedly left the hotel. Not a minute too soon either. The marriage-ceremony had been interrupted almost at the commencement, and Harry Webbe torn from his fainting bride by the rude hands of gendarmes, and marched off to prison; Madame de Bonneville remaining but a few minutes behind, to discharge a torrent of bitter reproaches at the insensible girl and Madame Dupre; which duty accomplished, she seized Sicard by the arm, and marched with him out of the chapel; greatly to that gentleman's mystification and astonishment, he hardly knowing whether he was taken into the custody or into the renewed good graces of his formidable relative.

Into her renewed good graces he had, after a few minutes, no manner of doubt, until an hour or more having elapsed, he found himself at his auberge lodgings, reckoning up recent occurrences, and by the brain-clearing illumination of a quiet pipe, perceived, to his extreme disgust, that although he had not been permitted a word with or a glimpse of Mademoiselle Clemence, he had been pumped dry of every particular known to him concerning Webbe, concerning me, William Linwood, and my whereabout, which the wily woman was desirous of ascertaining. That information determined her to prevent at all hazards my escape to England with the proofs of her crime in my possession. A *primâ facie* case to sustain an accusation of robbery was easily made out; and Jacques Sicard was recklessly included therein, when, on the morrow, the desperate woman heard that he had suddenly set out for Havre, after a stolen interview with Clemence. Active search, untiringly urged by the two officers who were maltreated in the mêlée at La Belle Poule, was made for M. Baptiste, but without the slightest gleam of success; and the gendarmes were fain to content themselves with the recapture of Webbe the younger.

The morning found me still anxiously, not to say despondently considering the chances of the future; a debate which was before long joined in, though not much enlightened by Maître Sicard. After breakfast, we adjourned to the quadrangle, which served for a common exercise-ground. Harry Webbe was not with the prisoners there, amongst whom we soon noticed a certain agitation of a hopefully expectant, if not positively exultant kind, presently explained to arise from a generally entertained conviction that the last hour of the empire had at length struck—a consummation which suggested a more or less well-founded hope that the restoration would signalise its advent to power by an act of clemency that would reach many of the inmates of that abode of crime and suffering. In proof of the correctness of the general belief, a large white flag, "*le pavillon sans tâche*," as legitimists loved to call it, which flew out from the summit of the tower of St. Thomas's Church at Ingouville, was pointed to.

"*Drapeau de Capucin!*" growled one of the jail officers —most of whom were old soldiers—as he passed us, and noticed the object we were gazing at, "may be welcomed by Capuchins; but the flag of France still waves over the ramparts and the Hôtel de Ville, and will continue to wave over them for a long time to come yet, traitors and cowards notwithstanding."

It is well known, I may be here permitted to remind the reader, that the soldiery of France refused to believe, even when disbelief seemed impossible, in the final defeat of the empire—a sad illustration of which feeling was the battle of Toulouse, fought by Marshal Soult after he had been formally, though not officially, apprised of his fallen master's abdication. General Véray, a Grand Cross of the Legion of Honour, and military commandant at Havre, was well known to be as stubbornly sceptical upon that point as the marshal, and sternly resolved, moreover, to guard the trust confided to him by Napoleon till *la force majeure* wrenched the sword of authority from his grasp. It thus happened, that whilst everybody in Havre, himself included, well knew that the French senate had solemnly proclaimed the new government, General Véray remained only the more fanatically resolved than ever to act as if Louis XVIII. was still a proscribed exile, and the soil of France unprofaned by the footstep of a single hostile soldier. It was this, I knew, which excited the fears of Father Meudon. Still, the passionate declaration of the prison official did not seem to me to confirm the good man's fears. The clergy of St. Thomas, I must have mentally argued, would not have hoisted the Bourbon banner unless perfectly assured of impunity ; and the blessed consequences to myself and mine of the change of dynasty, and all which that change involved, so lifted me, that I sprang forward with a joyous shout to greet poor Harry Webbe, who at that moment dismally emerged into the yard.

In such a state of nervous terror was he, that he staggered back with a faint cry of alarm, not immediately recognising me, or at least not my purpose in so boisterously accosting him. Recovering himself, he held out his cold shaking hand, and with a sickly smile returned my greeting. I told him of the great news, but it failed to excite a throb of hope in his fear-palsied heart ; and when, taking him aside, I explained to him, as Father Meudou had to me, that his breach of parole, would not, if he were brought to trial before the Bonapartist authorities, be visited upon him capitally, or even with severity, except to punish him for the death of Le Moine and his supposed subsequent entry into France as a Bourbon spy ; the falsity of which charge he could, if necessary demonstrate, without destroying or jeopardising me, by simply appealing to the testimony of Auguste Le Moine himself for its disproof — he turned sadly, impatiently away ; and I plainly saw that to trust in his firmness or manly feeling, in the trying ordeal to which he *might*, after all, be subjected, was in very truth to lean upon a broken reed.

All the more welcome, therefore, was the sight of that white flag, studded with golden *fleur de lis*, waving and glittering in the morning sunlight ; and I was half-unconsciously whistling the first bars of the old royalist air of *Vive Henri Quatre*, when I was politely invited by my friend the sergent de ville to return to my cell.

My mother awaited me there ; and her joyous aspect— joy-heightened by preceding grief and tears—confirmed my mounting spirits. The streets, she said, were full of gaily dressed folk, making holiday of the assured downfall of the imperial régime ; and. white cockades, it was said, were in the pockets of nine out of ten of the ficklo populace; though, from dread of General Véray and his exasperated soldiers, not as yet openly displayed.

"This at length accomplished revolution in French state-affairs," said my mother, "not only assures your safety, but that of Henry Webbe; which, as my indiscretion led to his recapture, I am most heartily glad of. It was only," she added, "in the first moments of bewildering surprise caused by the intelligence of your arrest that your father and I were disquieted by the accusation of robbery—a charge which of course you know from the prison authorities has been already formally withdrawn."

"Indeed, I know nothing of the kind."

There is no doubt, at all events, of the fact. We had it," said my mother, looking furtively around, and sinking her voice to a whisper, "from Captain Webbe himself, who called on us soon after it was light this morning."

"From Captain Webbe himself! You astonish me."

"You can't, my dear boy, be more astonished than we were to find that '*le bon campagnard*, Pierre Bonjean, from the neighbourhood of La Heve, called to inquire after the young monsieur whose life he had the honour to assist in saving," was ubiquitous, indomitable Kirke Webbe! Kind, excellent Father Meudon came in whilst we were talking together, and Webbe, with that instinctive sagacity which never misses a favourable chance, instantly avowed himself to be the notorious Captain Webbe, of the late *Scout* privateer; and having thus thrown himself upon the reverend father's honour, so improved his opportunity, that they left our house together, in furtherance of some plan to render Harry Webbe's deliverance doubly sure."

The sergent de ville entered to say that the ten minutes granted to madame, without the usual previous reference to superior authority, were expired, and that it was absolutely necessary she should go forthwith.

"Cannot my son leave this dreadful place with me?" she asked; "the charge upon which he was apprehended being, as you must be aware, formally withdrawn."

"It is true, madame," replied the officer, "that the charge of robbery has been withdrawn; but—but"——the man, I noticed, avoided my mother's eye—"but there are certain formalities to be observed which will at least *delay* monsieur's deliverance."

My mother's glance rested for a moment disquietedly upon the man's partly averted face, and then resolutely putting away, as it were, the vaguely uneasy feeling excited by his manner, she embraced me, and withdrew; remarking that Father Meudon would see me shortly, and by that time she hoped the formalities spoken of would have been complied with.

It was about half an hour afterwards when M. Meudon entered the cell, and startled me by his strange air and manner; and the more so, that he evidently strove to appear cheerful and unconcerned. It would not do. The expression of *bonhomie* habitual with him had vanished, and been replaced by the palely gleaming lustre which the soul, in presence of a great catastrophe or a mighty deed —the light of battle, for instance, seen on the charging soldier's face—seldom fails to impress upon the most common-place features. His greeting, too, was confused and awkward. Seating himself upon Sicard's bed, he first mechanically offered me his unopened *tabatière*, and immediately returned it to his pocket, without observing that I had no opportunity of helping myself to a pinch, if so inclined: next, as hastily drawing forth two letters, he gave me one, saying:

" It is sent to you by Le Capitaine Webbe. This is for his son. I will deliver it whilst you are reading your own; and return almost immediately."

This was Webbe's note:

" MY DEAR LINWOOD—' Finis coronat opus.' I think that was how we used to write it when I sported yellow stockings, and the o'erarching heavens shone, and dripped, at their sweet will, upon my hatless head: yes, Finis coronat opus, freely rendered by it 's the last deal and the last broadside which wins the rubber and the battle. Quite true; and it affords me much pleasure to inform you that the final, crowning stroke of our long tussle with the Féron has been the formal, explicit withdrawal of the charge of ' vol avec effraction ' preferred against you and the bootmaker; she having lodged in the greffier's office at Honfleur, a circumstantial declaration upon oath, that the articles she missed, and believed you to have stolen, have since been found: it would have been absurd, you will admit, for Captain Webbe and the Féron to have fought à l'outrance till, like the **Kilkenny** cats, they had mutually devoured each other ; and the final result is, that my son, whom the Restoration, and not one hour too soon, gives back to life and love—a *handsome* present you will acknowledge, if he be not exactly Achilles redivivus—will yet espouse Maria Wilson ; and Monsieur le Bottier de Paris même may, for any opposition on the part of Madame de Bonneville, raise Miss Lucy Hamblin to the diguity of Madame Sicard. Further, and to you the most interesting item of all, Madame de Bonneville, née Louise Féron, will make a frank circumstantial avowal of the fact and manner of the abduction of Mrs. Waller's child ; upon the reasonable condition of being guaranteed against a criminal prosecution. Thus then terminates with a flourish of trumpets our tragi-comedy, the green curtain ringing down upon— The Recovery of the Lost One ; A Wedding—two possibly ; and an uproarious tag, of ' Long life to Captain Webbe, and may he live till he dies an admiral ' —an aspiration which certainly beats the oriental compliment, ' May he live a thousand years,' into fits.''

" And I am quite sure, my dear Linwood, that you will not wantonly jeopardise so every way satisfactory a solution of the difficulties in which those dear to you have been so long involved, by any premature boyish boast of your *volunteered* part in an affair, the real hero of which, but for the fortunate Napoleon-catastrophe, would, there can be little question, have been despatched, before he was many hours older, with military honours, to paradise. Yours more sincerely than you believe, K. W.''

I had scarcely finished reading this curious epistle when Father Meudon reappeared, looking as painfully pre-occupied as before.

" This letter," said I, "from Le Capitaine Webbe is written in more hopeful characters than those which I imperfectly read upon that ominous brow of yours, Father Meudon."

" Since that letter was written," he replied, " I have met with Monsieur Tyler, and gathered from the outpourings of his unchristian rage that that *vieux tête de fer*, General Véray, is resolved to avenge the death of his friend, Le Moine, upon the young Englishman who broke his parole, should that deed of blood be the last exercise of his authority. I come," added Father Meudon, "from your mother whom the general's vindictive fury chiefly threatens, and I must not lose one precious moment in seeking to shield you from so cruel, so untimely a doom."

"Surely," I exclaimed bewilderedly—"surely the general, tête de fer as he may be, will not dare to display his Bonapartist feelings by a murder—for a murder it would be—in the face of a government that will hold him responsible for the atrocious deed?"

"Let us not, my young friend, deceive ourselves," said the reverend father. "The sentence which may doom both you and your young countryman in the next cell to a bloody death, would not be an illegal—at all events, not a grossly illegal one. More than that, the new government has vital need of the support of the military chieftains, who have won so much glory for France, so much renown and power for themselves; and you may be sure that much less legally justifiable deeds than the putting to death, by sentence of court-martial, of two Englishmen—one who had broken his military parole, the other a traitorous spy, it would be said—would not subject one of those celebrities to so much as a reprimand. General Véray has, be assured, no responsibility to fear. Still, do not be too much cast down. My military friend, Colonel Durand, has influence with the general; and I must invoke his good offices without further delay. Farewell. God bless you."

He left me stunned, struggling as it were to break through a horrible dream—hardly the less horrible that I felt it to be a dream—a fantasy as it concerned myself: the instinctive, unreasoning conviction of my own ultimate deliverance, before spoken of, not having been sensibly shaken by M. Meudon's revelation. Of Harry Webbe's doom, on the other hand, I felt an equally unreasoning presentiment—a doom which, it would be said, I had largely, my mother in a less degree, helped to bring upon him—and impelled by that strong unreasoning presentiment, I hastened—the cell-doors being left open during several hours of the day to afford the prisoners access to the yard—as soon as I had sufficiently rallied my faculties, to warn and advise with the unfortunate young man.

We had, I found, exchanged characters, or at least moods

of mind and temper.   He was now as cock-a-hoop as not long before downcast and despairing.   His father's letter, conveyed to him by M. Meudon, had wrought that change, confidently assuring him, as it did, that a brief interval only would elapse before he was liberated.

"Colonel Durand," said he, "who is well known for his 'legitimate' leanings, will, my father tells me, supersede General Véray in the command here before we are many hours older.   All shadow of peril will then have passed away, and I shall be free to immediately consummate the —the"——

He checked the ebullition of his jubilant thoughts, and looked away, as if half afraid that I should observe, perhaps resent, the triumphant, almost insolent radiancy which lit up his handsome countenance.

"Free to consummate what?" I sharply asked.

"To consummate a blessed purpose, Linwood"—he had sufficiently subdued himself to calmly reply — "the accomplishment of which I shall mainly owe to your chivalrous generosity—my marriage, namely, with Maria Wilson."

"Indeed!   There has, however, been already one slip between your lip and that cup, and there may be another."

"There is no fear, my dear Linwood.   To-morrow, or possibly to-day—who knows!—I shall be the happiest of men; thanks to you in a great degree.   Let me add, whilst I think of it," he went on to say, "that after calmly thinking over the suggestion you made this morning, as to the course of conduct I was bound for your sake to pursue, in the event of a court-martial taking place—of which there is now, thank God, no fear—I fully resolved, come what come may, never to divulge that Le Moine fell by your hand."

I was amazed, dumbfounded by the fellow's lying intrepidity of face and tongue, which he observing, and blushing to observe—he was not entirely depraved, it seemed—blurted out, that a man might have strong moral courage, however weak in merely physical nerve.

"Yes, strong moral, or *im*moral courage: I see that plainly enough."

The young humbug was but momently abashed, ¢

evidently quite aware of the pleasure he was affording me, said jauntily:

"So confident are we all that the once interrupted ceremony will be definitely celebrated before another day has flown, that the ladies, my father tells me, have already arrived in Havre."

"What ladies have arrived in Havre?"

"Madame de Bonneville and Mademoiselle Clemence, Madame Dupré and Miss Wilson. Immediately, therefore, this hateful jail-bondage is thrown off, I shall enter into that of wedlock, of which the fetters are Love's own sweet constraint."

"D—n such sugar-plum stuff! I am almost tempted to believe I am talking to a girl in sex as well as heart."

The only excuse I can offer for this unbecoming outburst is the fellow's ill-glozed, mocking taunts, which his mere words fail to convey an adequate idea of.

"Something I am not aware of must have occurred to vex you," resumed the simpering rascal, who was not at all put out or ruffled by my rudeness. "Ah, my dear Linwood, I only wish for your sake that a like happiness to that which awaits my acceptance"——

"Two ladies," interrupted one of the prison officers, throwing wide the door—"two ladies, with permission to see Monsieur Webbe, Englishman."

I leaped aside into a recess, and the next moment in glided the bright presence of Maria Wilson. Harry Webbe sprang forward with outstretched arms to meet her, and she refused not his impassioned embrace. How *could* she, I afterwards argued with myself, he being her almost husband, and in bonds; notwithstanding, however, which palliative consideration, I have ever since taken credit to myself for not having forthwith murdered the fellow with the heavy iron candlestick upon which my fingers were closed with homicidal force. Madame Dupré, who closely followed Miss Wilson, caught sight of me, and imagining I was a partner in Harry Webbe's cell-domicile, acknowledged me by a friendly nod, followed by a slight scream as I rushed past her into the corridor—thence to the quadrangle—anywhere to escape from those poniard-like caresses, vows, kisses, tears!

The Bourbon flag was still flying from the tower of St. Thomas's Church—a great fact, to which my attention was directed by one of the prisoners, who must have supposed I had not before observed it—a courtesy which I repaid by a coarse malediction upon flag and Bourbons both. Like Mr. Dickens's vivacious Fanny, I was just then violently wishing myself dead—a state of mind not at all conducive to political enthusiasm. After a dozen or two furious turns up and down the yard, I bethought me of Sicard, and not seeing him, made for our cell, passing the open door of Webbe's with hasty strides and averted glance, though it was impossible to altogether avoid hearing that the lovers were cooing and billing, laughing and weeping, all in a breath.

I was *de trop* again! Jacques Sicard and Mademoiselle Clemence were sighing, sobbing, and embracing each other under the gaunt sanction of a tall, large-boned, fierce-eyed Frenchwoman. Clemence jumped up, blushing and confused; and Maître Sicard, vainly striving to brace his voice up to a manly firmness, brokenly, huskily exclaimed: "Ex—excuse this weak—weakness, Monsieur Linwood: I—I am a Frenchman—you—you know to the ends of—of my nails; but some—somehow there is something in tears—the—the tears of a charming, amiable maiden, which—which melts the stoutest heart! That is positive, demonstrable!"

"You here!" I thundered, addressing the Frenchwoman, from whom I had not turned my eyes; "how dare you shew yourself here, Louise Féron?"

"How dare I shew myself here, Mr. William Linwood!" retorted the virago. "Well, I dare, that's all! Ay, and I shall dare much more than that, young man, if I find it useful or expedient to do so. Be advised by me—— Ah, mesdames, you are going!—our time must then be also expired. Come, Clémence!"

"Hélas!" spouted Harry Webbe, who had entered the cell with Madame Dupré and Miss Wilson——

> "Pleasures are like poppies spread,
> You seize the flower, its bloom is shed;
> Or like the snowfall in the river,
> A moment white—then melts for ever.
> Or"——

The measured tramp of armed men approaching along the stone corridor arrested his heroics, and took the colour out of his cheeks. " Halte ! " exclaimed a hectoring voice of command just without: the door was flung open, and at the entrance gleamed the bayonets of a company of grenadiers. The commanding officer stepped forward, bowed slightly to the ladies, and requested the sergent de ville and chief jailer, by whom he was accompanied, to point out his prisoners.

"They all three happen to be here," replied the sergent de ville. "'Harry Webbe, Englishman," he continued, reading from a paper, and placing his hand upon Webbe's arm, "capitally charged with breach of his parole; William Linwood, capitally charged with aiding the escape of said Harry Webbe, and further, with having travelled in France under the assumed names of Jean Le Gros and Louis Piron; Jacques Sicard, Frenchman, charged with having furnished said William Linwood with a false passport, and aiding his escape from justice.' You have them all three, Capitaine Lenoir."

"What is the meaning of this ! " exclaimed Madame de Bonneville. " What are you going to do with these young men, Monsieur le Capitaine ? "

"My duty, madame," replied the officer, " is to conduct them before a court-martial now sitting, by whose sentence they will be either shot or liberated within a couple of hours at furthest."

CHAPTER XIX.

A COURT-MARTIAL.

I MAY not deny that with the commanding officer's words a great fear fell upon me, although pride—Maria Wilson being present—enabled me to assume an air of defiance, which no doubt favourably contrasted with the demeanour of my fellow-prisoners. Jacques Sicard's suspended breath burst forth in a torrent of wordy, ignoble rage, bespattering his captors, the court-martial, and all others directly or indirectly concerned in the infamous conspiracy against him with volleys of unflattering epithets, till silenced by "*Taistoi, cochon!*" emphasised by a sharp blow on his mouth with the hilt of the officer's sword; whilst Harry Webbe, whose face had blanched to the hue of death, and whose knees smote each other at the bare appearance of the soldiers, presently gave unresisted way to the mortal terror which he had vainly struggled to master, and sinking down with a cry of horror at Captain Lenoir's feet, abjectly clasped them in the delirium of fear which deprived him of all self-respect and control.

"Get up, miserable coward!" exclaimed the officer, spurning the wretched suppliant with his booted foot.

My blood flamed at the humiliating sight, and casting off the hold of the soldier to whose more immediate custody I had been consigned, I darted forward, lifted young Webbe by main strength upon his feet, and retorted upon Lenoir with :

"It is you who in perfect safety insult a young man whom a—a sudden surprise has overcome for the moment, that are a miserable coward ! Courage, Webbe!" I added, vainly the while striving to make him stand upon his feet. "Courage !—a Frenchman's bark is a much grander thing than his bite at all times ; and so it will prove in this case. The bullets that will kill you and me are not cast yet, take my word for it."

Let not the reader suppose that this was a very daring act on my part. I must have felt, without reasoning upon it, that nothing I could say would in legal parlance damnify my actual position in the slightest degree. I was, besides, greatly irritated by Lenoir's brutal conduct towards Sicard as well as Harry Webbe; and then Maria Wilson, to say nothing of Clemence, was looking on.

Captain Lenoir stared at me with rather an expression of amused surprise than of 'anger. " You crow well for so young a cock," said he. "We shall presently see whether it is true or false fire that gives life to such bold words. As to this poor devil," he continued, "there must be, I think, some mistake, for he cannot surely be the young desperado, denounced by Monsieur Auguste Le Moine. If he were "——

"No—no—no; I am not he!" screamed the wretched

youth." It was not I that slew Captain Le Moine: I was below in the cabin, and took no part in the fight—no part whatever, I swear to you."

" Still your name is Webbe; and it was he that——

"No—no; it is a horrible misapprehension! "This is he," added the fear-frenzied young man, turning fiercely upon me—"this is he who on that dreadful night led the boarders of the *Scout*. Speak, Linwood: deny, if you can, or dare, that it was at your hand Captain Le Moine met his death; that it was you whom Auguste Le Moine denounced at Avranches "——His eye suddenly encountered Miss Wilson's, and instantly checked in his passionate appeal to me, he cast himself at her feet, and with sobbing agony exclaimed: "Ah, God! I am ruined—undone—lost!"

' On the contrary, you are, I think, saved," remarked the officer, "if what you say is true; and your *friend* does not, it seems, challenge its truth."

"It would be folly to do so, now that"——

" Enough! enough!" interrupted Lenoir. " You are not compelled to criminate yourself. It is a pity, besides, that a brave lad should perish to save the life of a wretched cur that—— But time presses. Fall in, if you please. And I advise you, Monsieur Webbe, to recover the use of your legs without delay. Quick—quick! It is only ladies, be pleased to remember, that are privileged to faint," he added with a glance at Maria Wilson, who had swooned in Madame Dupré's arms. " If *you* do, the remedy we shall use will be the sharp point of a bayonet liberally applied. Oh, you *can* walk, I see. Adieu, mesdames. March!"

Thus suddenly collapsed Mr. Harry Webbe's fighting reputation, destroyed by himself in the very insanity of terror, since a moment's cool reflection would have shewn him that if the military authorities of Havre were determined to be revenged upon Webbe, the privateer captain—and that, I felt, must be their chiefly actuating motive, as well as Mr. Tyler's—by the legal murder of his son, the violation of parole would be quite sufficient excuse for such a deed. I sincerely pitied the unfortunate young man, whose timidity was, there could be no doubt, constitutional, impressed upon his being by the circumstances attending his birth, and uncontrollable by any effort of his will; and now, should he escape the menaced doom by court-martial, the grace and ornament of life were gone for ever. Maria Wilson, he must have read as plainly as I did in her look and gesture of astonishment, indignation, contempt, as she freed the skirts of her dress from his trembling grasp, was irrevocably lost, and what more afflictive stroke than that could fate have in reserve for him!

And if lost to him, might she not be won by me in the bright future which, upborne by Love's light wings into the airy regions of romance, and loftily overlooking with youthful Hope's bold, creative eyes, the cloudy screen of present doubts and fears, was, I fancied, already flushing the horizon with rising, rosiest light! Assuredly I might win her; and that thought glowed within my heart, inflamed my blood with fire from heaven!

Some gleams of that transcendental illumination of mind must have been reflected upon my features, for Father Meudon, who entered the prison in a state of extreme agitation, whilst we were halted for a few minutes in the fore court-yard, was struck with astonishment by my aspect and bearing.

" How is this? " he exclaimed : " you look as if you were going to be crowned in the Capitol, instead of being dragged forth to suffer a violent, untimely death ! "

The strength and sincerity of the good priest's apprehensions rudely dissipated the volatile fancies which uplifted and sustained me in the region of dream-land, and I fell at once to the hard, common-place, matter-of-fact earth again.

" I cannot bring myself to believe, I have not been able to realise the possibility," said I, " that the members of the court-martial before which we are about to appear, will dare to carry out the ferocious purpose you impute to them."

" Dare! not dare! " echoed M. Meudon. " Have I not explained to you over and over again that there is no daring in the case; that the will of the general in command is the law during a state of siege, and Havre has been in a legal state of siege for several weeks past, though the military régime has not been rigorously enforced ? A few hours' delay," added the reverend father, " might have saved you; for there is now no doubt that the restored government will supersede General Véray; and that too, it is expected, by my friend Colonel Durand. Alas! the official mandate will arrive too late."

The reappearance of Captain Lenoir, who had been giving a written receipt for his prisoners, was the signal to proceed: the heavy, sullen gates were thrown open, and the next minute we were in the midst of a hooting, yelling mob, all of whom, whether Bourbonist or Bonapartist, were unanimously in favour of shooting or hanging the two English pirates, as they were pleased to designate Harry Webbe and me. The soldiers effectively protected us, however, from the physical assaults of the crowd, and their merely verbal attacks were easily borne. One paramount, well-established fact, Messieurs Mob were determined we should be fully impressed with—that our execution, namely, had been already settled to take place on the North Rampart, at four o'clock precisely, it then being about half-past one.

" The scoffs and curses of the canaille," said Father Meudon, who walked close beside me, "are fortunately much less formidable than offensive, and I am not without hope —a faint one, I grieve to say—that their brutal wishes may yet be balked."

" Is my mother," I asked, "cognizant of the gravity of my position ?"

" Not as yet. She believes you to be simply accused of the minor offence of making use of false papers. It will, however, be impossible to conceal long the dread truth from her, now that savage denunciations of the English spies and pirates are resounding on all sides. Le Capitaine Webbe," added Father Meudon, in a voice subdued to a whisper, " has, I hear, fled from Havre : there is no hope of aid, therefore, from that quarter. But what *could* he have done to help us had he remained ? Nothing, after all !"

The court-martial was to assemble in the Hotel de Ville; and as Father Meudon was speaking, we turned out of the Rue de Paris into the flower and vegetable market, where the crowd was so dense that it was with difficulty our escort hurtled slow way through it. Suddenly, there was such extreme pressure upon us that the line of march was broken in the rear of where I walked ; and the soldiers and prisoners were for a minute or two mixed up with the mob. I looked back, and saw a man wearing a blouse and a flapping broad-brimmed black straw-hat, which completely shadowed, and, except to a very near observer, concealed his features. He had viciously assaulted Harry Webbe, whose coat was nearly rent off his back in the struggle; and it was with difficulty the soldiers rescued their prisoner from the man's ferocious clutch. As I gazed, the broad, shadowing hat was slightly pushed aside, and I saw that the furious assailant was no other than Captain Kirke Webbe himself!

He had achieved his purpose of secretly thrusting a scrap of paper into his son's hand, which, when we had reached the Hall of Justice, Harry Webbe glanced at, and then passed to me. It contained these words: "Be bold—fearless; deny nothing—confess nothing: I will save you yet."

The caution had come too late with reference to the confession which Captain Webbe was chiefly anxious to prevent his son from making, and as for the promise to shield that son from the sentence of the court-martial, I could not, with all my superstitious faith in the privateer captain's genius for bold expedients and calculated daring, place the slightest dependence thereon. Force was hopelessly out of the question, and what could the subtlest cunning devise to arrest a doom which would be carried into effect immediately after it was pronounced? His father's positive assurance had, however, a vivifying influence upon Harry Webbe. A faint colour stole doubtfully back to his white cheeks, his drooping frame grew erect again, and his downcast eyes confronted the grim array which was presently before us with a trembling hope, a shrinking boldness as it were.

When we were marched into the Salle, two or three inferior officials only were present; but the public having been, after some demur, it seemed, admitted, the Salle was in a few minutes densely packed with excited spectators. Their impatience was not irritated by delay. Cries of "Silence!—silence!" by the huissiers, preceded the entrance of General Véray, Colonel Durand, and three officers of inferior rank, who took their places in stern silence at a baize-covered table, before which Harry Webbe, Jacques Sicard, and I had been ranged in line with a hedge of glittering bayonets immediately behind us.

General Véray was a fine, soldierly-looking, gray-haired

veteran; in the strong lines of whose war-and-age moulded features not a trace of human weakness or indecision could be seen. Colonel Durand's handsome face wore a kindly expression, strikingly in contrast with the iron sternness of the general's; and the other members of the court-martial did not interest me much, thoroughly aware as I was that the fiat of the majority is conclusive of the decision of such courts, so called. I shall pass briefly over the formalities observed at that mockery of a judicial trial. We, the prisoners, were sternly questioned, and made to convict ourselves either by positive admissions or by refusals to answer, which were held to be tantamount to admissions of guilt. Harry Webbe, whose frenzied fit of terror had returned upon him, could not, for example, deny that he had given his *parole d'honneur* not to leave Havre, and that he had violated that pledge by escaping to Honfleur, with the intention of passing over to Jersey—a fact which was wrung from Sicard. Colonel Durand ventured to suggest that the prisoner was *gardé à vue*, which greatly mitigated his offence; and that it was besides extremely probable that he had been coerced into breaking his parole by his father, the notorious Captain Webbe, who, it had been ascertained, was the Baptiste spoken of by the gendarmes as the originator of, and chief actor in the riot at the cabaret.

"That is certainly possible," remarked General Veray; "but that audacious corsair not being before us, we must deal with those that are. It was not, at all events," he added, with a look and voice of thunder, "Webbe, father, who, a few days after a combat with a vessel of the imperial navy, presented himself at Avranches, a garrison-town, in the character of a citizen of the United States of America."

Harry Webbe's wild denial of that part of the informal charge was confirmed by M. Auguste Le Moine himself, who I had understood was safe in Paris. He stepped forward, and assured the general-president that, if the prisoner who had broken his parole was Webbe the corsair-captain's son, he certainly was nôt the individual whom he, Le Moine, had detected and denounced at Avranches.

"That person is, however, before the tribunal: there is the young man," he added, pointing to me, "by whose hand my uncle fell, in perfectly honourable combat, I admit, and who, a few days afterwards—seduced, corrupted, no doubt, by the execrable English government—accepted the well-paid infamy, and will, I cannot doubt, receive from this tribunal the reward of a traitorous spy."

A grim assenting smile flitted over the general's cast-iron countenance, and an approving murmur ran through the vengeful auditory. All eyes were now turned from Harry Webbe upon me; and the president, honouring me with a stern, stony gaze, demanded if I admitted the facts stated by M. Le Moine.

"I admit, Monsieur le President, that I had the misfortune to deprive, in accordance with the usages of war, Captain Le Moine of his life; and that at a banquet at Avranches, I committed the folly of permitting it to appear that I was an American; but I deny, with all the indignation which so dishonouring a charge excites in the breast of an honest man, that I was in France for any hostile or unworthy purpose."

"You will not deny that you assumed various disguises in France, and passed under at least two different names. In St. Malo, you called yourself Jean Le Gros, and were confederate with Jacques Le Gros, pretendedly your uncle, and really the corsair Captain Webbe."

Mr. Tyler, whom I had not before noticed, rose in a tribune at the right-hand upper end of the hall, and begged to state that he did not believe I was in the slightest degree cognizant of Webbe senior's infamous schemes; and that he, Tyler, had seen me without any disguise in St. Malo—wearing, in fact, the very clothes I then had on.

"We are nevertheless informed," said the subaltern officer who acted as secretary, after translating what Mr. Tyler said—"we are nevertheless informed that William Linwood, whilst residing in St. Malo, was disguised as a French peasant of the proprietary class."

"That may be," said Mr. Tyler; "but I repeat that I saw him on the very day I left St. Malo in the dress he now wears."

"Although," persisted the secretary—"although you do not believe that the prisoner, William Linwood, was confederate with Jacques Le Gros, otherwise the corsair Captain Webbe, it is certain that he was on board the *Scout* when temporary possession was obtained of your ship, the *Columbia*. It is also well established," added the officer, addressing the

general-president, "that William Linwood was one of the
party at La Belle Poule cabaret, on the evening of the riot
and rescue of his now fellow-prisoner."

"Enough—more than enough!" exclaimed General
Veray. "The facts are too plain to require either comment
or interpretation. Who," he added, fiercely addressing me
—"who furnished you with the passport of Adolphe, Louis
Piron, by aid of which you for a time baffled justice?"

I did not answer, and Sicard was asked if he had not
furnished me with the said Adolphe, Louis Piron's passport.
The reluctant reply was a hesitating admission of the fact,
followed by a vehement denial that he either then or now
suspected or believed me to be a spy, or in any respect the
enemy of France.

There were but few more questions asked, and the court
were about to withdraw, not to deliberate upon our guilt and
doom, but to formalise their decrees, when Father Meudon
rose and requested that I might at least be allowed to give
my own version of the motives and purposes of my visit to
France. That very reasonable request was peremptorily refused. A statement which could not be verified, the general
replied, could not refute or modify well-established facts.

The members of the court-martial then retired, and a
buzz of animated conversation succeeded to the strict
silence which had been imposed upon the crowded auditory.
The conclusions that had been arrived at by nine-tenths of
the spectators were freely bandied about, generally accompanied by a jest or sneer—in a few instances only by an
expression of pity. It was decided that I, at all events,
would be shot at the breaking up of the court, and at the
open space near the North Barrier I heard a sous-officer say,
in reply to a question from an acquaintance. Opinions
seemed to be divided with respect to the fate of Harry
Webbe; and Sicard was quite forgotten in the eager discussion of the two Englishmen's chances of life and death.

Strange to say, neither the quite openly manifested determination of the members of the court-martial—Colonel
Durand excepted—to condemn me to death, the confident
opinions I heard expressed on all sides that my fate
was sealed, nor the cold, trembling pressure of Father
Meudon's hands enfolding mine, whilst tears streamed down
his pale face, brought home to me that the strong life

dancing in my veins was upon the verge of extinction. The day was bright and genial; the fresh breeze, admitted through the wide, open windows of the Hall, brought with it the odour of flowers, the merry voices of market-girls, the laughter of children, and in the distance, a military band was playing lively melodies. The common air was vocal with busy, lusty life, and refused, as it were, to entertain the idea of death—of black, dumb death, and especially of death by murderous violence! No question that this was a very illogical impression of mine; still, I felt it strongly, and it was not sensibly weakened till the door through which the court had passed was again flung wide upon its noiseless hinges, and the arbiters of fate stalked slowly to their places. The look of mournful compassion with which Colonel Durand regarded me, more startlingly impressed me than the stern visages of General Veray and his servile subordinates; and I suddenly awoke from a vain dream of security to find myself upon the edge of a precipice, at the bottom of which yawned a newly dug grave! My breath came thick and short; a dizziness seized me, and for a few moments I feared that I should disgrace my name and race by a degrading, and useless as degrading, exhibition of womanly weakness. By a great effort, I fortunately managed to keep up an appearance of unruffled, defiant composure, which powerfully excited the sympathy of Colonel Durand, and drew from General Veray a curt expression of regret that so brave a youth had rendered himself justly liable to a shameful death.

The reader will understand that all this while Harry Webbe was prostrated with abject terror; and I mention this the less reluctantly, that it throws into high relief—gives, in fact, the only moral value to the firmness he subsequently displayed, since what in him required an almost superhuman effort, would, to a son of ordinary nerve, have been a matter of course.

The command of the huissiers to keep silence was superfluous. The auditory held their breath that they might not lose a syllable of the tragedy of real life acted before their eyes.

Jacques Sicard, bourgeois and bottier of St. Malo, was convicted and condemned to one year's imprisonment. This was the first judgment pronounced; and although it excited the liveliest indignation on the convict's part, the spectators

seemed to be merely annoyed that it should have been permitted to delay the more exciting announcements for which
they impatiently listened.

" William Linwood," continued the military secretary as
soon as Sicard's indignant remonstrances had been silenced
—" William Linwood, a British subject, convicted of having
entered two garrison towns of France as a spy ; of being
confederate, whilst there, with the notorious English
corsair Webbe, and of having planned with him attacks
upon his imperial majesty's allies, the United States of
America ; convicted, moreover, of having conspired with
the said Webbe to enable his son, Harry Webbe, to violate
his *parole d'honneur*—is, by a plurality of voices, condemned
to be shot ; two hours' respite being allowed, that he may
avail himself, if so disposed, of the services of a minister of
religion."

A piercing, convulsive scream, which I too well recognised,
broke in upon the last phrases of the infamous sentence.
A sword passing through me would not have inflicted a
sharper pang, and I leant for support upon weeping Father
Meudon. " I will go to thy mother," he said, " but presently
return. Be comforted : thou art nearer Heaven than any
here—nearer than thy cruel judges will ever be."

" Harry Webbe, British subject," proceeded the unmoved
secretary, " convicted of having broken his parole, and of
being confederate with his father, Kirke Webbe, in piratical
attacks upon his imperial majesty's allies, the United States
of America, is condemned to be shot "——

" Mercy ! Mercy !" shrieked the poor fellow ; and he
continued to pour forth such a torrent of wild supplication
for pity, mercy—that it was some time before the general
could make himself heard and understood, to the effect that
the sentence of death would be remitted upon his, Harry
Webbe's acceptance and fulfilment of a precedent condition
to be named by the court.

" Anything—any condition, I will accept—fulfil," gasped
the prisoner.

" I believe that," said General Veray, " though that which
I am about to propose is one which, but that the public weal
requires it, I would not suggest, even to such a contemptible
caitiff as thou art. Listen : You are definitively doomed
to be shot, and that sentence will be carried out within, at

the latest, two hours from now, unless you are willing and able to ransom your life by—by—— Read the condition insisted upon, Lieutenant Rogier."

"The sentence of death passed upon Harry Webbe, a British subject," said Lieutenant Rogier, reading from a paper, "will be remitted, if the said prisoner can and will enable justice to lay hold of the corsair Captain Webbe, who is known to be either in Havre or the neighbourhood."

A cry of horror arose from the auditory as the atrocious proposal left the lips of the military secretary, and it was some minutes before silence could be restored. As for the son, he gazed aghast, speechless, upon his tempters with an expression which no words could interpret.

"Silence!" thundered General Veray, "or the hall shall be forthwith cleared. The proposal you have just heard," he continued, addressing Harry Webbe, "is dictated by a stern sense of public duty. The corsair-captain was the concocter of the traitorous conspiracies that have brought you, and what is much more to be regretted, the young man at your side, to the brink of an untimely grave. You are now offered a chance of avoiding that death. Which, then, do you choose—life or death?"

"You cannot mean this," gasped young Webbe; "you are men, not fiends in human form!"

"We are desirous of bringing a notorious malefactor to justice. You can aid us to do so; and by so doing, save your own life. What, once for all, do you say?"

"I cannot—dare not—will not"——

"Enough!" interrupted the general; "your blood be upon your own head. The court is adjourned. Captain Lenoir, remove your prisoners."

"One moment—hear me but for one moment!" screamed Harry Webbe.

"Do you accept the condition offered you?" sternly broke in the general. "Yes—or no?"

"No—no—a thousand times no!" shouted the young man with the courage and energy of despair; "I will die first."

"The answer does you honour, and seals your doom," said the general. "Let the prisoners be removed at once."

"I have a question to ask of Monsieur le Général," said Father Meudon, pressing forward to the front of the tribunal. "Does he pledge his word that if the corsair-captain, Kirke Webbe, is surrendered into the custody of this tribunal, the life of the prisoner, Harry Webbe, will be spared?"

"I pledge my word of honour to that effect. The corsair-captain once in our power, his son shall be immediately liberated."

"I accept that pledge," said a man, stepping briskly up. "I am Kirke Webbe, the privateer-captain!"

CHAPTER XX.

THE CATASTROPHE.

THE suddenness of Webbe's appearance, and the boldness of a self-announcement which was nothing less than sentence of immediate death passed upon himself, literally lifted the members of the court-martial to their feet, and a hush of astonishment, I might almost say of fear, inspired by a greatness of daring, in presence of which every man there felt himself morally dwarfed, pervaded the crowded hall. Certainly the calmest, least excited person there was the privateer captain himself: true, his face was paler than usual; but he was perfectly self-possessed, and the gleaming smile which played about his cold, stern eyes, and slightly curled lips, seemed the expression of a sovereign disdain, untinged by a shade of personal fear, of the men into whose vindictive hands he had surrendered himself. I say, "seemed" to be that expression, for could I have looked beneath the impenetrable iron mask acquired by many years' exposure to the hardening atmosphere of an ever-present mortal peril, I might possibly have seen a human heart, wildly palpitating before the immediate presence of the dread Shadow feared of all men, with whatever boldness faith, duty, pride, may enable them to confront it.

Still, not a momentary sign or hint of weakness could be discerned by the eager, vengeful eyes which searched Captain Kirke Webbe's aspect and bearing; and it occurred

to me for the hundredth time that, but for that unfortunate
game at leap-frog upon the quarter-deck of the *Gladiator*,
and his consequent dismissal from the British naval service, on the eve of a twenty years' war, he might have
won a peerage, and a monumental tomb in Westminster
Abbey.

General Véray presently reseated himself; motioned
his subordinates to their places ; the lieutenant-secretary
nibbed his pen with a business air, and the interrogatory
of the self-constituted prisoner forthwith began.

" You acknowledge yourself," said General Véray, " to
be Webbe, captain of an English corsair lately sunk by
French gun-boats off Cherbourg ? "

" I repeat that I am Kirke Webbe, late captain of the
Scout privateer, which foundered off Cherbourg a few days
since."

" And that you are the Jacques Le Gros whom the
commander of the *Columbia*, an American ship, met with
at St. Malo ? "

" It would be absurd to deny that in presence of the
gallant commander of the *Columbia* himself, who, to avenge
an injury done to him by a man, has endeavoured to hunt
to death a stripling, as innocent of offence towards him—
in a responsible sense—as yourself, Monsieur le Général.
That he has not succeeded in doing so," added Webbe,
" is solely due to the magnanimous offer of the court to
permit the boy to save his own life by the sacrifice of his
father's."

" You further admit," continued the general, " that you are
the commander of the French cutter, *L'Espiègle*, and, when
acting in that capacity, are known as Captain Jules Renaudin ? "

" Yes ; and who in that capacity, it has been established
by the unimpeachable evidence of the *Moniteur*, beat off,
with a slight vessel mounting only four guns, a British
frigate of forty cannons, after a running-fight of nearly an
hour's duration, in which the ascendency of French valour,
compensating for any odds, was, as ever, strikingly displayed.   That, messieurs, you will in candour admit to be
something *per contra*."

Old stagers in such scenes as the members of the court
were, the man's cool audacity took them completely aback,

and they mutely questioned each other with interchanged looks of indignant astonishment as to whether they could possibly have heard aright. The mob of spectators, on the other hand, greeted the privateer captain's jibing sarcasm with a buzz of satisfaction and approval. The French are no doubt an acute as well as brilliant people ; but for all that, he or she who could suggest a compliment to their genius or valour so outré, extravagant, that, if uttered without laughing, would not be taken by the mass of them *au sérieux*, must, according to my experience, have a great talent for invention. For myself, I was in doubt whether Webbe was comporting himself as such a man might when certain that nothing on his part could delay or accelerate the doom he had challenged, or whether he might not possibly have some expedient in reserve which would save him under all circumstances. My superstitious reliance on his fortune or " luck" could alone have suggested the latter hypothesis. Certain it was, however, that he had at all events perfectly succeeded in impressing the court with a thorough conviction of his reckless, devil-may-care sincerity.

" The prisoner's confession is ample warrant for his condemnation to death as a spy," said the general, looking round upon the members of the court, and gathering their, on this occasion, unanimous suffrages, given with a curt " Oui," or silent nod. " Record the judgment," he added, addressing the lieutenant-secretary.

" Stern and sharp," interposed Webbe, " as may be the practice of such courts as these, it permits the accused, I suppose, to speak a few words in defence or explanation, before definitive judgment is pronounced ? "

" Well, yes ; say on, but be brief."

" I have first to state most solemnly—and standing as I do upon the brink of a grave voluntarily dug with my own hands, my word ought not to be doubted—that the prisoner, William Linwood, is guiltless of the offences laid to his charge. He came to France, as Father Meudon will, if necessary, be able to clearly prove, for a perfectly legitimate, honest purpose"——

" That is true, messieurs ! " exclaimed M. Meudon ; " for an entirely innocent, laudable purpose."

" As to his assumption of the character and attire of an

R

American and French citizen, and passing by the name of Le Gros, all that was done by my direction and advice, and with no more thought on his part, that he thereby incurred the doom, than he had of lending himself to the work of a spy."

"I beg to reassert my thorough conviction," said Mr. Tyler, again rising from his seat, "that William Linwood is guiltless of participation in the crimes of the privateer Webbe."

General Véray, after briefly consulting his colleagues in an under-tone, said, addressing Webbe:

"We are disposed to place faith in your declaration as regards the prisoner Linwood, and the execution of the sentence passed against him will be respited, in order to a further investigation of his case. Have you anything to urge on your own behalf?" added the general with abated sternness—the courage and generosity of the self-immolated prisoner having somewhat won apparently upon the veteran's favour.

"Nothing that to-day would avail me!" replied Webbe; and for the first time I detected a flush and tone of anxiety—slight and swiftly passing, but distinctly discernible by me who knew him so well, and watched him with such breathless scrutiny. It resembled the irrepressible gleaming forth of the disquietude of a practised gambler, when about to turn the last decisive card upon which depends success or ruin.

"Nothing that would to-day avail me! The mighty emperor who raised France so high amongst the nations of the earth, has fallen: at this moment, the crownless monarch is being ignominiously driven forth into exile by kings who are indebted for their thrones to his generous forbearance; and who is there even amongst the veterans whose scarred brows the most directly reflect the glory which he has shed over all Frenchmen, that will now respect the wishes of one so contemned, powerless, cast down, when by so doing they must render themselves odious to the Bourbon whom foreign bayonets have placed upon a throne based upon a thousand victories, won for France by the great emperor? It would be folly to expect such self-sacrificing fidelity in these degenerate days; and I knew this morning, when I saw the white flag waving from the tower of St. Thomas's Church, that the time had passed when Napoleon's protection would have availed me. It may be as well, therefore, that an appeal certain to be fruitless should remain unspoken."

I should vainly attempt to describe the effect produced by this speech. Affected, bombastic as it may sound in English ears, nothing could have been more skilfully suited to the tribunal it was designed to influence. Even the miscellaneous crowd, who, if time-servers, worshippers of the rising sun of the Bourbons, were still Frenchmen, murmured hesitating, timid applause ; and General Veray, who had several times risen from his seat as if about to speak, and as often checked himself and sat down again, his keen, hard eyes flaming, softening the while, at the allusions to the past glory and present humiliation of the emperor, burst out, the instant Webbe had concluded, with :

" Perish the Bourbon flag and those who display it ! It does not wave over Havre yet; and whilst I command here, the emperor's authority shall be maintained intact, supreme as when his voice gave laws to Europe ! But hope not, crafty, audacious man, that assertion unvouched by clearest proof will save you. Your word is nothing ; but *prove* to me that you are under the especial protection of his imperial majesty, which could only be for some signal service rendered by you, an Englishman, to him or to France, and I will set you free, though the Bourbon and his allies were at the gates to forbid me doing so."

" The proof is easy, conclusive," said Webbe. " It was for a signal service rendered to General Bonaparte, and therefore to France, that I obtained the protection which, a few moments since, I had no hope would serve me in my present strait. It is true," he added, drawing forth a folded, carefully kept paper—" it is true I am an English · man ; but "——

" What paper is that ?" interrupted the general, with impatient vivacity.

" One written in a kind of hieroglyphic hand, which those who have once seen it never fail, I have been told, to instantly recognise. Monsieur le Général," added Webbe, " has no doubt, I perceive, upon *that* point."

" None—none whatever: it is the emperor's character,

and written when he was a young man : 'I commend to
the good offices of my friends and of all Frenchmen, the
bearer of this writing—a foreign seaman who has just
rendered me the greatest service that one man can owe to
another.—BONAPARTE, General of the Army of Egypt.'
How came *you* by this?" sternly proceeded General
Veray ; "and what was the great service spoken of?"

"It happened," said Webbe, in a voice which I strove
to persuade myself must be that of truth—so firm, clear,
sonorous did it ring through the hushed hall—"it happened
that I was in Malta when the French army, on its way to
Egypt, landed there and took possession of the celebrated
fortress of the Knights of St. John. One morning, when
the wind, having become favourable, the troops were re-
embarking"——

"Stop!" thundered General Veray—"stop till you have
heard me say that I was at Malta with the army, and distinctly remember all the circumstances, the minutest,
connected with the deed to which, I have now no doubt, this
paper refers. If you are 'the foreign seaman' mentioned,
you shall be instantly set at liberty; if, on the contrary,
I find you to be an impostor, and if you are one, cool,
astute, daring as you may be, detection is, be sure of it,
inevitable—you shall be as immediately shot. Go on,"
added the general, in a calmer, almost respectful tone,
after having keenly marked the effect, or, more correctly,
non-effect of his abrupt intimation and menace upon the
privateer captain—"go on; I begin to believe you—and
yet; but go on."

"One morning," resumed Webbe, "when the wind
having become favourable, the troops were re-embarking
under the personal supervision of the commander-in-chief,
a fanatical Maltese priest—a Spaniard, it was said, by
birth—suddenly rushed at the general, whose back was
towards him, with a naked poniard in his hand; and if
he had not ended that great life, he would most certainly
have inflicted a severe wound upon the Man of Destiny,
had not the 'foreign seaman,' who chanced to be on the
spot, perceived the danger in time to receive the assassin's
blow upon his own arm. Here is the cicatrice of the
wound inflicted by the poniard of the baffled priest," added
Webbe, turning up his right sleeve.

" Silence !" exclaimed the general, checking a movement of applause amongst the body of the audience. "All this may yet prove, so far as the prisoner is concerned, to be an audacious fable. Where," he added, continuing his interrogatory— 'where, on what spot did the occurrence take place?"

" On the esplanade overlooking the great harbour."

" Were any officers present with General Bonaparte at the time?"

" Not exactly present. Murat was sitting reading a newspaper upon one of the cannons a few yards off; and Kleber had just left the general-in-chief, who at the moment was observing the embarkation through a telescope."

" What became of the intentional assassin ? "

" He was shot within five minutes of his atrocious attempt by a party of the 2nd regiment of the line."

" How is it you remember so slight a circumstance as the number of the regiment ? "

" Because the 2nd of the line remained at Malta, and I several times afterwards saw and even drank with individuals of the firing-party."

" The affair must have caused a great sensation in Malta?"

" It caused no public sensation whatever, inasmuch as it was forbidden to speak of it, perhaps because a disposition to murder is thought to be epidemical. I know, at least, that one French soldier was punished for alluding openly to the matter."

" How was it that General Bonaparte did not, in return for such a service, recompense you in a more solid manner than by a recommendation to the 'bons offices' of Frenchmen, which might never have been of the slightest service to you?"

" I wished for no other recompense ; and besides that, General Bonaparte himself embarked within, I should say, a quarter of an hour of the occurrence."

" How is it that the document neither gives your name, nor states that you were an 'English' seaman ?"

" The omission not only of a name but of a date, as you will have observed, I can only account for by the general's hurry. As to the expression 'foreign seaman,' I so desig-

nated myself. It would have been as imprudent on my
part, at that time, in Malta, to afford a hint or suspicion
that I was Webbe, captain of the English privateer *Wasp*,
as to have made a similar avowal the other day at St.
Malo."

"How has it happened that you have never sought to
utilise this precious document during the many years it
has been in your possession?"

"My vocation as captain of an English privateer was
incompatible with a request to the emperor for any other
than a pecuniary reward; and I was too proud, and, I
may add, not sufficiently necessitous, to ask for alms, even
of a Napoleon, in recompense of what, after all, was but
an act of common humanity. It is, however," continued
Webbe, "not quite correct to say that I have made no use
of so precious a document, since, but for a secret reliance
that it might one day stand my puissant friend at a pinch,
I might not have ventured to play the hazardous game
which, but for the fortunate accident that it is General
Veray who commands at Havre, might this day have had
a fatal termination."

"And may have that termination yet," retorted the
general—"though, so much do I respect a man of nerve
and courage, that I heartily wish the contrary. I shall ask
you but another question," he continued, "and if you
answer that with the same readiness and precision as you
have all the previous ones, I can, and *will* doubt you no
longer."

The general paused before putting that last decisive
question, and my pulse beat wildly, my breath again came
thick and short, for I, for the second time, detected, or
thought I did, the faint flush of disquietude which I had
before observed. It had seemed to me during the last ten
minutes that I was the spectator of a duel fought with
flashing, fatal weapons, in which from one moment to another
a mortal stroke might be given and received. That dread moment was now I believed come, and my heart sank within me.

"Your look quails not," at length resumed the general,
"and your aspect seems to challenge and defy the menaced
question, which in itself is to me a more satisfactory
reply than you could make in words, for after all, one who
has shewn himself to be so intimately acquainted with the

Malta affair, will not find it a difficult one to answer.
Nevertheless, it shall be put. It is this: Where did General
Bonaparte write this document, and where did he procure
the paper and ink?"

"The paper and ink were supplied by an *invalide* who
had been partially crippled by an accident on board the
Guillaume Tell, I believe, and who was just then returning from the great harbour, where he had been to write
letters for such of his embarking comrades as could not
write themselves. The table used by General Bonaparte
was one end of a big drum."

"Enough. I am satisfied. You are free."

A burst of applause from the changeful crowd followed
the general's decision, which was, however, sternly rebuked
and silenced.

"By my authority, as the general commanding in Havre,"
said General Véray, "I revoke and annul the findings of
the court-martial upon all the accused, since it is mani-
festly impossible to pardon the chief offender and punish
his subordinates, and I order that they be forthwith set at
liberty. Record my decree in form," he added to the lieutenant-secretary, "and I will sign it at once."

"Captain Lenoir," said the general, after the formality
of signing had been gone through with, "you will escort
the acquitted prisoners to their homes. As for you, Monsieur le Capitaine Webbe," added the veteran with a grim
smile, "I advise you to quit France without delay. A
government may be installed here to-morrow from which
I shall not be able to protect you, and in whose eyes the
emperor's protection would be a crime, instead of, as
with me, an inviolable safeguard. The court is dis-
solved."

It was not long after three o'clock when I emerged from
that stifling hall into the free air : in but little more
than an hour I had, as it were, passed from life to
death ; and back from death to life! My brain swam
with the rush and conflict of emotions so acute and
violent, and, darting away in a kind of delirium from the
escorting soldiers, I pushed my way through the crowd
in I neither knew nor cared what direction, so that I
could obtain sufficient space to think, to breathe in.
That fevered tumult of the mind subsided, and I presently
found myself in La Rue Bombardée, whither I do not

now ask the reader to accompany me. There are incidents in the lives of us all before which, though an angel would smile as he looked thereon, it is imperative to draw a veil.

We dined late on that day; and I was sitting alone, as evening closed in, over the dessert, when Captain Webbe made his appearance. The torturing ordeal through which he had so lately passed, had not left a perceptible trace upon his buoyant, elastic spirits; and it was not long before I knew that his resolution to marry his son to Maria Wilson was as fixed and determined as ever. He said he should probably quit France in a few days for Jersey, though not for the reason suggested by General Véray, as he had nothing to fear from the Bourbon government, which, there was no longer any doubt, would be formally proclaimed in Havre on the morrow.

"Which formal proclamation," added Webbe, "would have taken place some hours too late for us, but for my success in bamboozling the illustrious General Véray to-day."

"That elaborate story was then a fabrication—the imperial voucher a forgery!"

"You have an unconquerable propensity, Master Linwood, to jump at extreme conclusions; the imperial voucher was perfectly genuine, and the story, with one slight variance, true throughout—the slight variance being, that the name of the foreign seaman was Hans Kliebig instead of Kirke Webbe."

"How on earth, then, came you in possession of the important document?"

"By a very natural sequence of causes. I was at Malta when the attempt was made upon Bonaparte's life, and Hans Kliebig was one of the crew of the *Wasp,* which was dodging about off and on in the vicinity of the island. Hans had the misfortune to be killed a few weeks afterwards in a brush with an armed French transport, and the paper in question fell into my hands. It was not, however, till General Bonaparte and Captain Webbe had respectively become emperor and Captain Jules Renaudin, that it occurred to me that such a testimonial might some day prove a trump-card in the very ticklish game to which I was inextricably

committed. And now as to matters of pressing moment. Madame de Bonneville has been arrested and lodged
in prison."

"Say you so? That is indeed a swift commending of
the poisoned chalice to her own lips."

"She is charged with having fled from her creditors,
and, as a consequence, with fraudulent bankruptcy. She
must, of course, be liberated by the immediate payment
of her creditors in full."

"Pray, who must of course liberate Louise Feron by
the immediate payment of her creditors in full?"

"I—you—your family; all of us who, from various
motives, are interested in not setting such a plotting, unscrupulous devil at defiance. In the note you received
from me in the early part of the day, I apprised you that
I had been compelled to compromise with her—— Ah,
the reverend Father Meudon, the very person I have been
wishing to see and speak with!"

"That wish has been reciprocal, Monsieur Webbe,"
replied M. Meudon, as he shook hands with me in silent
gratulation of my escape from that day's perils; "for I
was told you were about to fight a duel with Monsieur
Tyler, the American captain."

"It was fought an hour since," said Webbe. "At least,
I was twice fired at by Mr. Tyler, which was held by the
seconds to have afforded him complete satisfaction, as,
not being hit, it certainly did me. I hardly need say that
I did not return his fire. And now, my dear Linwood,"
he added, "I have to request, with leave of this reverend
gentleman, that you inform Mrs. Linwood that we, Father
Meudon and I, wish to speak with her for a few minutes
privately."

"Meaning that I may not be present?"

"That is my meaning. I am anxious to consult Mrs.
Linwood and Monsieur Meudon upon a matter chiefly
personal to myself, and for the present only them."

"Not having the slightest wish, Captain Webbe, to
force myself upon your confidence, I will at once convey
your message to Mrs. Linwood."

That private council of three lasted for perhaps an
hour, at the end of which, Webbe and M. Meudon left the
house together without seeing me, and my mother herself

not very long afterwards sent a message to say she was
about to retire to rest—my father had done so some time
before—and advised me, after a day of such painful excitement, to do the same.

I was in no humour to comply with such sensible
advice. This avoidance of me gave strength to the suspicion which had begun to dawn upon me, that the private
conference related to some scheme hatched in Webbe's
fertile brain for bringing about a reconcilement, and if a
reconcilement, the immediate marriage of his son with
Miss Wilson. My mother was, Webbe knew, strongly
desirous of promoting the match, lest, forsooth, her
precious son should throw himself away upon a mere
nobody, whom God had nevertheless gifted with rarest
personal and moral loveliness and grace. I was not so
clear with respect to Father Meudon's part in the plot,
unless, indeed, they were about to attempt carrying their
point by a *coup de main*, as it were, and celebrating the
marriage forthwith.

Absurd! impossible!—I must have lost my senses to
imagine such a thing. Equally absurd to fear, to suppose
that romantic, hero-admiring Maria Wilson could possibly
be induced to unite herself with the wretched craven that,
in her presence, had crawled in the dust before—been
spurned, in her sight, by the booted foot of an insolent
Frenchman, and resented it not. Never, never, never!

The eccentric *pas seul* which accompanied my arrival at
that delightful conviction, was arrested by a brisk rat-tat
at the street door, presently followed by a step ascending
the stairs, which I believed to be that of Father Meudon.
I was right—it was Father Meudon; his round face
and black eyes sparkling with radiant bonhomie, with
goodness enlivened by benevolent joy, and a few gleams,
perhaps, of gratified self-esteem.

" Ah, my young friend," he exclaimed, almost running
to, and then tightly embracing me, "allow me to again congratulate you! This is, indeed, a day of happiness. But
where is madame your mother?"

" In bed, long since."

" Madame is right, and you also ought to have been in
bed long since. So ought I, but never mind, I shall not
leave Havre to-night, so there is still time for me to sit
down and take just one glass of wine with you. You do

not know what that fierce, gentle, mean, generous Captain Webbe wished to consult Madame Linwood and me upon," added the exulting priest. "No, but I may tell you now, for the mission with which he intrusted me is accomplished, the object gained, completely, finally! Blessed are the peacemakers. Gloria!"

"What is accomplished completely, finally?"

"The reconcilement of two youthful lovers, whom a mis-understanding—no, not a misunderstanding, that is not true—whom, what shall I say?—a misfortune, yes, a mis-fortune, had estranged. Ah! the beauty, the grace, the ingenuous candour of that young girl! I give you my word," added M. Meudon, proffering me his snuff-box, "that never, to my recollection, have I seen a more charming person than Mademoiselle Marie Wilson. Do not be impatient, my young friend; that is no doubt a platitude to you who know Mademoiselle Wilson; but,"—

"But—but me no buts," I rudely interrupted. "If you have anything to tell me, tell it."

Father Meudon looked grave, almost offended for a moment, but his happy face, refusing to be wrinkled into that expression, relaxed immediately. "You are evidently suffering from febrile irritation," said he; "nevertheless I should like to make to you a participator in the pleasure I have this evening experienced."

"Proceed, Monsieur Meudon: I will listen in respectful silence."

"Well, this is what has occurred since I left you: Mon-sieur le Capitaine Webbe explained to madame your mother the estrangement that had taken place between the lovers, and its cause — before known both to you and me. Madame Linwood shewed the liveliest anxiety to remove that estrangement; and when Monsieur Webbe hinted that I, as an entirely disinterested person, could do so more effectually than any one he knew, madame entreated me to exert myself to the utmost to bring about so desirable a result. I consented, the more willingly that the young Webbe's heroic sacrifice of himself to-day, rather than be-tray his father, had given him, spite of previous prejudice, a high place in my esteem."

"The heroism of refusing to purchase shameful life by butchering his own father! Bah!"

" Not heroism in you, my young friend, nor in others physically and morally constituted like you, would there be heroism in such an act. You would do so as readily and instantly as you would interpose your person between your mother and the uplifted dagger of an assassin ; but the young Webbe is, you know, physically, morally, a— a "——

"A coward! out with it—a wretched coward! You will say nothing truer than that, reverend sir, if you talk for a week."

" Be it so ; and how much greater, sublimer, therefore, the effort which enabled him to triumph over that physical and moral weakness, that—— But the discussion, I perceive, irritates you, so I will just glance over the incidents of the last delightful hour, and take leave. I was to go, you understand, to the Hôtel de France, where Mademoiselle Wilson, Madame Dupré, and Mademoiselle de Bonneville, or Waller, are staying—not ostensibly as a reconciler of estranged lovers, but to speak with Captain Webbe, who would precede me there by a few minutes. Having in that manner introduced myself, it was arranged that Madame Dupré should refer to the doings at the Hôtel de Ville, and question me thereon—opportunity for me to dilate upon those agitating occurrences in a sense favourable to the young Webbe, who sat apart in an attitude of the profoundest dejection. I do not think I was ever so eloquent before," continued M. Meudon with swelling self-esteem; "and the result was that the way having been judiciously prepared by me, the proposition of reconcilement was made in a direct manner by Madame Dupré, and seconded, enforced by everybody. Such an appeal, judiciously prepared for as I stated, could not be permanently resisted; and at length Mademoiselle Wilson yielded reluctantly—yes, reluctantly, I must admit that—to our entreaties. With a modest grace which would have delighted you, as it did me, she rose from her chair, and gliding towards Webbe *fils*, who was fairly sobbing with excitement, said, in the sweetest voice in the world : ' Let the past be forgotten, Harry '——- Harry by the way," M Meudon interrupted himself to inquire, " is an endearing variation of Henry, is it not?' "

Repressing with difficulty a malediction upon both

Harry and Henry, I asked the priest if he had finished.

"You are ill, very ill," said he—"that is clear, and I will no longer detain you from needful rest, than to say that the reconcilement was perfect; and that to-morrow Marie Wilson and Harry Webbe will be married by Monsieur Ponsard, the Protestant minister at Ingouville—both bride and bridegroom being, unhappily for themselves, members of the heretical Anglican church. And now, my dear young friend, go to bed at once, and good-night."

I think I must have fainted after M. Meudon went away, for I had no recollection of the interval—more than an hour—which elapsed from the time he left till I crept to bed, not to sleep, but to toss about in feverish unrest till towards the morning, when I dozed off into dreamy broken slumber, during which the terrible events of the day oppressed my struggling faculties with shadowy, incongruous terrors. Suddenly light and calm took the place of darkness and tumult. I stood before an altar near a bride, Maria Wilson; but the next moment my grandame Linwood replaced her, and called upon "Master William" to come nearer. I vainly strove to do so; my limbs seemed to be manacled, till, with the fierceness of the struggle, I awoke.

Awoke to find my dream in part realised—that good Dame Linwood was bending over and calling upon Master William to arouse himself, in a voice broken with joyful, tenderest emotion. As soon as we could speak of anything but the joy of again seeing each other, I learned that immediately upon the receipt of my mother's letter, sent through Mr. Dillwyn, Mr. and Mrs. Waller hurried to Portsmouth, communicated with Mrs. Linwood, and hired a fast-sailing cutter, in which all three embarked for Havre, where they arrived shortly after the substitution of the white flag for the tricolor gave notice that the port of Havre was at last unsealed to the nations so long at enmity with France.

"It is late—nearly eleven o'clock," said Dame Linwood, "and Mrs. Waller is waiting with nervous impatience for you to rise and bring her recovered daughter to her arms. We have sent for Webbe, but he, his son, and the aspiring shoemaker who proposes to espouse Lucy Hamblin, are gone to some distance, it seems, to make arrangements for a marriage between Webbe's son and a Miss Wilson, which is to take place to-day."

I rose at once, and hastened down stairs to the tiny drawing-room. The first person I saw on entering it was my grandfather Waller, the tall, portly gentleman of my childhood. I did not recognise him, but he greeted me with affectionate cordiality, and turning round, presented me to his wife, Mrs. Waller.

Heavens and earth! Mrs. Waller was Maria Wilson herself, wanting only the bloom and freshness of youthful life; and ah! now I remembered where I had seen the sweetly pensive expression of face which had so struck me when I first beheld the Jersey maiden! Mrs. Waller's portrait to be sure, forgetful, senseless dolt that I had been, once shewed to me by Mrs. Linwood, wore that peculiar expression, as still did the beautiful original.

Instantly I seized the clue to the whole Webbe-Feron mystery. All was clear now; and simultaneous with that conviction, was the flashing thought that I might yet be in time to prevent the detested marriage with young Webbe. With a scarcely articulate cry, that I would bring Mrs. Waller her daughter, I dashed out of the room, down the stairs, into the street, hailing a passing empty *fiacre*, and was swiftly driven off to the Hôtel de France. Maria Wilson and Clemence, both dressed as brides, were there alone, Madame Dupre herself being temporarily absent. I said they must both come with me at once upon a matter of life and death. They yielded mechanically, as it were, to the fiery impulse communicated to them, and in less than ten minutes the fiacre set us all three down at No. 12, Rue Bombardéc. The street door opened—I seized Maria Wilson's hand—we ascended the stairs, closely followed by Clemence; and dragging the terrified girl as it were towards Mrs. Waller, I exclaimed: "Your daughter, madam, your lost child!" I heard the cry and sob of maternal recognition, and then the room, the figures swam around me, and I knew nothing more till some half-hour afterwards, when having, by the help of vinegar, burnt feathers, and other stimulants, regained consciousness, I learned that the drama had at last been finally played out. Webbe, who returned to the Hôtel de France a few minutes after we had left it, at once hurried to the Rue Bombardée with the desperate hope of being yet in time to prevent Miss Wilson from seeing my mother: the Wallers arrival he had not heard of. In presence of the scene which there awaited him, he saw that further deception would be useless, absurd, impolitic, and he at once acknowledged that Maria Wilson was the long-lost Lucy Hamblin; Clemence, the true Maria Wilson!

I have little to add, and that little must be very briefly set down. Webbe's version of his and Louise Féron's substitution of one child for another was, that till about three years before negociations were opened with my mother, they were really not aware that there existed an indelible mark which would render the scheme of passing off the niece of Madame de Bonneville—who was really the sister of Captain Wilson's wife by the same mother, though not by the same father, and had in her younger days as often gone by the name of Broussard as Féron— for the true heiress, impossible. They believed the assertion in the hand-bill to be a mere ruse, intended to frighten the abductors into restoring the child. That discovery made, a compact was ultimately entered into by which Madame de Bonneville consented that young Webbe should marry the true heiress upon condition that she, Madame de Bonneville, received the twenty thousand pounds odd belonging to her niece, who was to be compensated for her loss of fortune by marriage with rich —according to French ideas, rich William Linwood, my noble self. There is nothing else of importance, I think, which the narrative itself does not sufficiently explain; and now as to the results that followed the elucidation of the plot, and the defeat of the plotters, in which those readers who insist upon what is called poetical justice — a myth, I fear, which has no tribunal in this unpoetical, work-a-day world—will find themselves disappointed.

In the first place, abundant care was taken that my father's vindication before the world should be full, complete, unchallengeable. It was so; and he lived to a good old age in happiness and honour.

No one was disposed to deal harshly—I ought perhaps to say justly—with Captain Kirke Webbe; and about three weeks subsequent to the final frustration of his marriage project, he sailed with his wife and son, and something like three thousand pounds in his pocket, for the Cape de Verd Islands — the reward promised by my mother and grandmother having been paid to him. He departed in high spirits, and I must be excused for saying I could have better spared a better man.

Maria Wilson, alias Clemence de Bonneville, espoused honest Jacques Sicard, and the happy pair finally domiciled themselves in a handsome villa upon the Havre *côte*. Madame de Bonneville was supported by her niece in undeserved competence, which she did not, however, live long to enjoy. She was drowned about six months after her niece's marriage, while crossing in an open boat from Havre to Honfleur.

Light flows upon the paper as I write down the last paragraph which I shall pen—light and warmth—a pale, cold reflex of the soul-sunshine which has shed a glory over my noon of life, and now gilds the evening of my days: This, copied from the London *Times :* "Married at St. James's Church, William Linwood, Esq., grandson of Anthony Waller, Esq., of Cavendish Square, to Lucy Hamblin, daughter of Mrs. Waller by a former marriage."

Vale, vale.